THE SHIFT

ELUDING DESTINY

BOOK NINE

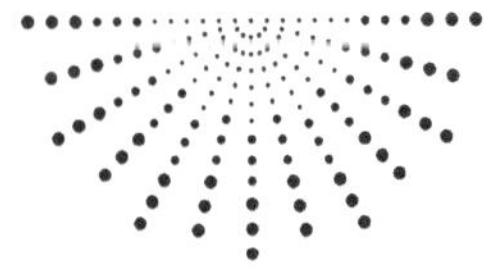

CHARLIE NOTTINGHAM

LIQUID MIND PUBLISHING

THE ELUDING DESTINEY SERIES

Eluding Destiny

The Horrors That Created Us

Aftershocks

The Precipice

Land of Light

The Quiet Army

Sacred Sins

Flash Back

The Shift

Lost to Time

Gods Among Us

The Cover Up

Blank Slate

Sign up for Charlie's newsletter and receive a free copy of the Eluding Destiny prequel, Blood Bar:

https://liquidmind.media/eluding-destiny-prequel/

CONTENT WARNING

This book contains detailed sex, drug abuse, addiction, captivity, adult language and situations, mentions of rape and suicide, extensive gore, violence, torture, and detailed homicide.
It is intended only for mature audiences.
Reader discretion is advised.

CHAPTER ONE

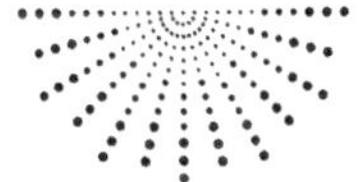

JANUARY 1, 2024 - LAILA

My heart slammed against my ribcage as it rose and fell fast with the heavy breaths panting in and out of my lungs. I held a ball of bright violet fire in one hand and my daughter against my hip in the other.

I couldn't believe it. No one in their right mind could.

It wasn't possible. I was the queen of impossible but this... It couldn't be real. It couldn't be. Doppelgängers aren't a thing, not even in our world. There cannot be two of the same people existing in the same place, or two different places, for that matter, at the same time.

And yet, here I stood before myself.

I blinked a few times, hoping I'd wake up in my bed. Hoping it was all a nightmare. Not my typical post-trauma terrors, I'll admit, but I'd rather it have been a dream than reality.

If the past twelve hours had been a terrible manifestation of my own mind, the world still had a chance. We'd still have time. We wouldn't be standing at the edge of the apocalypse.

"Laila, put the fire down," Mary said. "You need to relax—"

"You need to shut the fuck up," I snapped.

"Ouch," the woman in the rocking chair said.

I looked between the two them. "What the fuck is going on here?"

"I told you what's going on." The woman's gaze was nonchalant, yet serious. "I'm you."

"You aren't me, I'm me." I shook my head quickly. "I'm me, and this... This isn't real. This isn't happening."

"C'mon, quit with the dramatics." She rolled her eyes, sat forward, and exhaled. "You don't have to act all big with me. I know you. I *am* you. Older, smarter. But I am, Laila. I'm you."

My breaths drew closer together, and my head shook.

Not possible. This is not possible.

"Throw it at me." She gestured to the flames in my hand. "Go ahead, Lai. Throw it at me and see that it does nothing. I'll have to borrow some clothes then."

We stood in Milly's bedroom. If I threw it, I'd run the risk of catching that four-hundred-dollar rocker on fire. Had she been a threat, I would have done it without a second thought. But she was sitting there with a calm demeanor, waiting for me to settle down so we could talk. And although I was one to throw punches and stomp my feet, I couldn't bring myself to do it. Some part of me knew she wasn't lying.

She sighed and raised her palm. Bright licks of purple flames ascended through the air. I felt the wind pick up and watched as the fire turned to a ball of swirling water.

"How is this possible?" I asked. "This isn't—it can't be possible."

"The tree of life has a number of attributes." She closed her hand to a fist around the water. "It's not just about immortality, not in this life. It's tied up with time."

"What the fuck does that mean?" I asked. "You—you're a time traveler?"

"Thanks to Lux's careful genome mapping that led Mary and Dad to have us in the first place," she said. "Look, this is going to be a long and complicated conversation. Put your fire out. Tell Celena and Hannah to take Micah up to the main house. I'll put on a pot of coffee, and the five of us will talk."

"The five—wait, why would I let Micah leave?" I asked. "Is something going to—"

"Might confuse him a little bit if he sees two of his mommies sitting down for a cup of joe, don't ya think?" She arched a brow.

I swallowed hard but kept the fire in my palm. "Who's the five of us?"

"Me, you, my Jeremy, your Jeremy, and Mary," she said.

Granted, I was incredibly flustered. I had no clue what was going on. But one thing was made incredibly clear.

Mary had been lying to us about something huge. Evidently for quite some time.

My throat swelled as I looked between the two of them. "You know her?"

Mary turned her gaze toward the ground. "Yes. Yes, I have for a while now."

"And you kept this from me?"

"I told her she had to," Laila said. "But we'll get there. For now—"

"Why the fuck should I believe any of this?" I squeezed Milly tighter, eyes darting between them. "Clearly, you're a fucking liar. And you—you're—I don't even know you."

"Yes, you do. Twenty-four years ago, I was you. I was standing exactly where you are right now. And I remember how that felt. I remember the fear, and the uncertainty, and the shock you're feeling. But you know what else I remember?" Her green eyes cascaded between mine. "I remember thinking about all of the signs. The messages, the mystery CIA that showed up here and tortured my prisoner, the strange woman on that viral video. And I didn't want to believe it either because learning something like this isn't easy to accept. But we both know some part of you believes me. Some part of you even trusts me."

Well, when she put it like that.

Yeah. Some part of me did. I didn't understand it. But she wasn't giving off any vibe that suggested I should be scared. She didn't hurt my daughter a moment before. And, well, if this were real, if it were true, then a lot of things I hadn't been able to understand were starting to line up.

I pulled Milly tighter to my hip. "You keep saying that. Twenty-four years ago. What do you mean?"

She rubbed a hand against her mouth. "In twelve days, once you see what's about to happen to our planet, once I teach you what you need to learn about the tree of life, you're going to go back. To the year 2000."

Even if that were possible, could I do that? How could I leave all of these people behind? I'd built an army. I had thousands of people counting on me. I couldn't leave them all behind. "What?"

"I told you. This is going to be a long, complicated conversation. Your head's going to hurt. And—"

"I can't just run away from this; this is our war—"

"You're not running away. You're collecting extra time," Mary said. "Time that you need. You're not ready to fight this, Laila. She is."

You have time.

That's the message the CIA gave us. That's what Lux had said too. That's what that woman on that video last year said.

My gaze kept bouncing over the two of them. I felt my heart hammering away in my chest, trying to grasp what was happening. But the more that I thought, the angrier I became.

If she'd been around for the last twenty-four years, where the hell had she been? Why hadn't she helped us? If my son was her son, how in the fuck did she let that man take me hostage and steal him from us?

"You've been around all this time, and you just let all of this horrible shit happen to us?" I snapped. "You knew I'd be kidnapped, you knew where Chris was, you knew where my baby—your baby— was and you just—"

A sudden ache slammed across my cheek. The other me, the older me, ran her fingers over her knuckles. "Damn it. Mary, get the others back to the main house. Laila, meet me outside."

She disappeared.

I felt an ache in my hand then too, and another in my gut. Jeremy.

"Laila," Mary began.

"Don't," I said. "Just don't."

I teleported to the back patio.

CHAPTER TWO

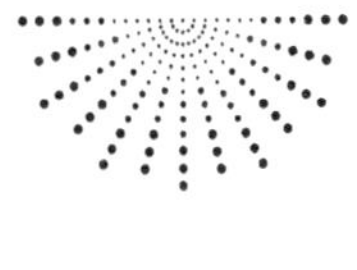

JEREMY

He had to be a shapeshifter. Maybe a Demon. Or, or an Angel. We knew we weren't on good terms with them, especially after the one Laila killed last night. But how could he be here? He wasn't wearing a necklace. The barrier spell kept anyone who wasn't tied to it or wearing a gem encrypted with our DNA out.

But if he was a shapeshifter, or a Demon, or an Angel, how was he here?

And why didn't my energy affect him?

Unless he's telling the truth.

I stood there in disbelief, staring blankly as I watched the blue energy dissolve into his skin.

He appeared in front of me. His fist raised and thrust into my cheek. As the pain soared through my jaw, I teleported behind him and put an arm around his neck. But just as I teleported out of the perimeter to the muddy, snow covered outskirts of our property, he teleported in front of me once again, gripping my shoulders and sending us back to where we'd been a moment before on the edge of the house.

"Listen to me, Jeremy," he said, hands tightly clamped to my shoulder blades. "Listen to me—"

"Who are you?" I exclaimed with wide eyes.

"I just told you who I am." His gaze shifted between mine. "I'm you, Jeremy. An older you, but I'm—"

I teleported a foot back and bludgeoned my fist to the side of his face. The pain swelled up my arm as he spit blood to the sidewalk. He disappeared. I looked around because I knew this trick. I'd done it a thousand times. He'd reappear before I even had enough time to realize he was back and—

Boom, a fist to my gut.

I doubled over; wind knocked out of me. He grasped my shoulders and lifted my gaze back to his. "Stop being a little shit and fucking listen to me. Just listen."

"How are you—"

"Jeremy." I heard Laila's voice rounding the corner from the fence. "Jeremy, stop."

"Get the kids and—" I began.

But I stopped dead in my tracks.

She stood beside the fence in a white blouse, pair of jeans, and a full face of makeup. She'd been a wreck last night. Not that I blamed her, but I expected her to still be in her pajamas with her hair in a messy bun. And I would have just assumed she was doing her typical, 'everything's fine, I'm going to fake it 'til I make it' persona.

But another Laila appeared beside her. My Laila. Wearing one of my T-shirts, a pair of bleach-stained sweatpants, and holding our two-year old against her hip.

She teleported to me and held her hand over my bloody lip, casting white light into the split skin. I barely felt the pain as I looked between her and the... well, the other her.

I grabbed ahold of her hip, pulling her away as the other me appeared beside the other Laila.

My gaze slid between the three of them. "What the fuck is going on?"

"Well, if you hadn't tried to kill me, you'd know," the man said.

I looked at Laila, then at Milly, checking over her for any signs of pain or trauma. But she was fine. Her eyes were wide, her hands were trembling, but she was fine.

"I don't know," Laila whispered with a fast shake of her head. "I don't know."

"Like I said," the woman beside the gate said. "Let's put on a pot of coffee and talk."

CHAPTER THREE

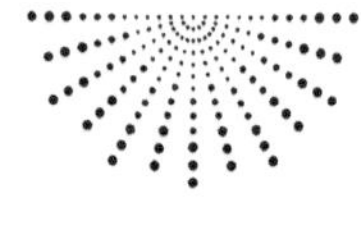

LAILA

Mary managed to get everyone else back to the main house before we stumbled into the kitchen, incredibly confused and disoriented. I stood by the patio door, watching the woman who looked exactly like me walk through my kitchen. She smiled as she ran her fingertips over the butcher block counter tops. Her gaze shifted to the picture of Micah with Chris on the fridge. The only picture we had of him before age three.

Jeremy stood beside me, hand tight at my waist. "Where's Micah?"

"Back at the house with everyone else," I whispered, watching the other Jeremy carefully. His eyes moved over the house, lips pulling into a smile. A slow breath loosened his shoulders.

"Feels good to be home again, doesn't it?" He smiled at the woman who stood by the fridge.

She huffed and turned to meet his gaze. She struggled a smile to her lips. "Told you these counters would stand the test of time."

"Technically, they're only three years old," he said. "We'll have to replace them in a few years."

A half smile tugged at her lips. "We'll see."

Jeremy cleared his throat beside me. "Alright, I thought we were going to talk."

She turned to him and smiled. "Sorry. We've missed this place."

"Only got to live here for a few years before we had to leave," the older Jeremy said.

"Now we get to live here during the apocalypse." She frowned. "Yay."

"What the fuck do you mean?" I asked with a look between them. "What the fuck is going on?"

The older Jeremy sat at the dining table. Laila, or older me, I guess, followed. "Come on and sit down. We have a lot to go over."

"Yeah, no shit," Jeremy said.

"Well, let's get to it then." He gestured to the other side of the table. It was so surreal. Their voices were identical. If my eyes were closed, I wouldn't know who was who. "Come on. Sit down."

I started to the table, unable to take my eyes off of the two of them as I lowered myself on the wooden chair. They did make a beautiful couple. *We* made a beautiful couple. It was strange to see us together in the flesh. Of course, I'd seen us together in photos a thousand times. But they moved like two melodies in perfect synch. It was like two puzzle pieces snapped together to form a perfect picture.

They weren't much different than me and my Jeremy. She looked just like me, aside from the fact that her hair was shorter, cropped just below her shoulders. And him... Well, he wasn't much different either. But in the same instance, he was.

His hair was far shorter, long on the top and shaved on the sides in a trendy fade. Black still, with a few hues of gray. It was cute. Really cute actually. But it was hard for me to believe that Jeremy would ever willingly cut his hair that short. And his shoulders and arms were broader, stronger. Still sleek, not bulky, but significantly more toned than I'd ever seen him. He must have worked out a lot in the past twenty-four years. My Jeremy wasn't exactly scrawny, but next to him, he definitely looked skinny.

"So obviously we know the two of you," she said. "But let's make this a little less complicated. You can call me Lila. That's the name you'll take on soon, Laila."

"And I go by Nick." The man looked at Jeremy and smiled. "Nix is a little out there, ya know? Nick's close. You'll answer to it quicker than you think."

Jeremy looked between them and shook his head. "How is this... I- I don't understand."

Nick took a deep breath and rubbed his short beard. "Look, I know this is crazy. I remember sitting where you're sitting right now. I remember not trusting me. Or him, I guess. But this isn't a bad dream. You aren't going to wake up. This is real."

"But how?" Jeremy asked. "How am I sitting across from myself right now?"

"Time travel's complicated," Lila said. "The four of us, and the others, I guess, are all a part of a time loop paradox. But technically, two. Both a predestination paradox that Lux created and a causal loop that I created. Today is the ending of our causal loop and the start of yours."

Prior to Peterson, I didn't know all that much about time travel. But I'd done some reading.

A causal time loop means that a sequence of events is the cause of another event. Otherwise meaning that it has no start or end. It's a circle. When we would go back in time, that would be the start in our eyes, but considering in twenty-four years that we would send our younger selves to do the same, it simply cycled back around.

Predestined timelines are exactly what it sounds like. A force outside of the scenario decides what will and will not occur within it. Some things can change, minute details, but ultimately, it comes back to the same outcome.

Like when Mary killed Moe. She did it because she was trying to keep me from being kidnapped. But by trying to prevent it, she caused it when I met Ray. Because it would happen no matter what.

"But the predestination paradox has been long going," Nick said. "You could say it started when Lux killed us in the Elder's Hall, or you could say it began when he set our parents up to create us."

Jeremy looked to Mary in the corner of the room. "This is what you meant. When you said you can't elude destiny."

"I thought that I could prevent what the past five years have done to the two of you," she said. "I thought I could keep you from being taken and Micah from being kidnapped. But some things have to happen."

"We tried," Nick said, turning his gaze from Jeremy to me. "I thought I could keep that from happening too. I know that's what you're thinking, Laila, 'why did we let this happen to you?' And we tried, as I'm sure you will try. But believe me when I say that outcome was a hell of a lot worse than this one."

From seeing what happened to Moe, I understood that. But I still made me bubble with rage, and my stomach hurt with annoyance. I never cared what happened to me. But my baby didn't deserve it.

I clenched my jaw as I looked from him to her. "You let me get kidnapped, fine. But how the fuck do you justify what happened to Micah? Him being kidnapped, the scars he'll live with for the rest of his life, if you knew when we'd find him, you could have stopped it. You could have—"

"We fucking tried." Lila's tone sharpened. "Peterson was working with Lux. He's seen every outcome. And he shifts the timeline to keep things in order."

"What the hell does that mean?" My expression surely looked as pissed as hers.

"You found Micah in 2022 in California," Nick said. "In our life, we found Micah in England in June 2023. In your life, you were held captive in Canada."

"In ours, I was in Ohio," Lila said. "That second compound in Brazil? Ours was in Australia."

"Predestination," Nick said. "We *tried*. We tried like hell to help you two, we really did. But Lux knows every outcome. He kept shifting things to keep us from figuring it out. That's why Peterson was moving so much at the end there. We were onto them too. And he knew. They both did."

"We did what we could. And we fought like hell, like you two will. But that's the thing about predestined time loops." She bit her lower lip. "Some events may change. Details shift, but the end comes out the same every time. The sacrifice happens. We got a little bit of peace, and then we go back in time to prepare."

My jaw tightened, and I leaned back in my seat.

It did make sense. I had a thin grasp on time travel, but I did understand. That didn't mean I had to be happy about it.

Jeremy gazed between them. "What else did you change then?"

"Not as much as we would have liked," Lila said.

"More people survived nine´eleven in this world than ours," Nick said. "There were two planes that hit the Twin Towers in our life. The one that hit the Pentagon killed everyone inside. We kept that from happening, but we couldn't stop it all."

"The pandemic that hit four years ago?" Lila said. "In our world, almost a hundred and fifty million people died. We were still fighting it at this time in our lives."

"Really fucked up the plans for what happens next," Nick muttered. "That was one of our top priorities this time around. Get it under control in less than a year so we kept as many people safe as possible."

Celena and I had been on top of the virus news when it started. And yes, we questioned how a vaccine was developed so quickly and how the authorities were able to get it under control in less than half a year.

But *we* were responsible for that?

"Wait," I paused, blinking for a moment. "Wait, what do you mean?"

"We're the reason that vaccine came out only days after the coronavirus was declared a pandemic," Nick said. He squinted slightly. "Well, not actually *us*. We don't know shit about epidemiology. But we got the information to someone that did."

"We've been working with a lot of important people for a long time. We were doing everything we could for everyone we could," Lila said. "Connor and Naomi, they were on your case for a reason."

It was so much to take in at once. My brain was throbbing, and my vision was a little fuzzy. I was trying to absorb what they were saying, but I was so confused.

Although, it all made sense too. It made *perfect* sense. They were par animarum. They were gods. They'd gotten their information from two other par animarum.

But if they knew Connor and Naomi before we did, how many other did they know? All of them?

I rubbed my temples. "My head's spinning."

"That's okay." Nick smiled. "It's a lot to take in."

"So we...we went back in time," Jeremy murmured. "Or we *go* back in time. That's what you're saying."

Lila said, "That's what we're saying."

"When?"

"Twelve days," Nick said.

"But why?" Jeremy asked.

Lila huffed. "You really have to ask?"

In fairness, I didn't, aside from the fact that she'd told me upstairs.

Micah and Milly. Us. We weren't ready to fight the apocalypse, not really. Even Papy had said something at a Chambers Meeting about needing Micah to fight this.

"The first being our kids." Nick looked to Milly in my arms with a smile. It slowly fell. "So they don't have to grow up in an apocalypse. So they're old enough to help us fight it."

"Another being so you guys can see what's about to happen," Lila said. "So you know *how* to fight it."

"And to find the others," Nick said. "You know about ten now, right? Hannah and Kai, Wyatt and Celena, you two, Connor and Naomi, and Asher and Avery."

"So they are," I murmured. "Asher and Avery, they're par animarum too."

Jeremy had called that one.

"Yeah, but their beginning lies in the past too. But you'll see that one day."

Their beginning lies in the past. That's how they knew us. Not because they knew Laila Callidy and Jeremy Skoulda, but because they knew Lila and Nick Salesky.

"It was you," Jeremy whispered. "You two were in the car that day.

You were the ones that came to question Peterson with Naomi and Connor."

"Introduced them, actually," Nick said. "But yeah."

No shit.

I'd been so worried about strangers coming to torture him, but they weren't strangers at all. They were us.

Naomi had threatened to keep our kids from us though. I huffed.

She was bluffing. They probably told her that was the only way we'd budge and let them come. Which was true. And smart.

That also explained Adam's response. Saying that he trusted whoever they were. That he *knew* them. Because he did. They were his brother and sister in-law.

"That was us," Lila said. "We didn't have much time to interrogate the bastard in our life. We only had six months before our end came. We needed some intel."

"It wasn't just you though, was it?" Jeremy asked. "Someone else was with you."

Nick laughed and looked at Milly. "A few someone elses."

I turned down to her and then back up at him. "Milly?"

"And Micah," Lila said. "And a few others."

Sure, later, I'd wonder more about why she wanted to be there. But for now, all I could think about was that little two-year-old.

I thought hard for a moment. "If we go back to 2000, that'd make Micah..."

"Twenty-nine this June," Lila said. "And Milly will be twenty-seven."

I looked around. "Are they here too?"

"Well, not at the moment. But you'll meet them." She smiled. "They'll help us send you back."

CHAPTER FOUR

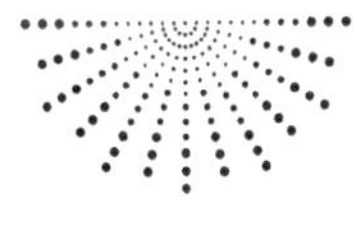

JEREMY

"Who is 'you?'" I asked with a look between them. "Because I'm not leaving my brothers and sisters to fight this—"

"Them too," Nick said. "Don't worry. You're not going back alone."

"Twelve others will go back with you, not including the kids," Lila said. "But there is a catch."

"There always is," Laila grumbled.

"Humans can't survive the shift," Nick said, gazing at the photos on the wall.

"Wait," Laila whispered. "Wait, are you saying I have to leave Jenna behind?"

"No," Lila said. "But she will have to leave her humanity behind."

Leave her humanity behind.

The only way I knew to do that was...

Shit. Someone would have to turn her.

"And you'll be pretty shocked at who chooses to stay." Lila turned to Laila, forcing a sad smile. She glanced at Rachel's purse on the end of the table.

No.

Jesus fucking Christ.

How happy I'd been for my kids to have their grandma. And she was gonna be gone all of their lives.

My stomach hurt. My head was throbbing, my hands were sweating, my legs felt like jello. Fuck, I hated our lives.

I could practically see Laila's heart shattering. "You told me to spend more time with Mom. This... this is why."

She was quiet for a moment. She cleared her throat. "There's a lot more we have to go over now. We can be depressed later. We'll have to go soon."

So they were just popping into our lives, dumping all this information on us, and disappearing?

"Where to?" I asked.

"We have to announce how we're going to save the planet," Nick said. "To the people who'll listen, anyway."

"What does that mean?" Laila asked.

Lila swept hair from her face. "The Fae Realm."

"In two days, we're going to open thousands of portals around the globe," Nick said.

"When we do, we're going to send as many people there that will go," Lila said. "It'll be safe there. Only the Fae and Elvan people can open breaches to that world."

Huh. Our original plan. We'd always said that if shit hit the fan, that's what we'd do. Pack our shit, open a portal, jump through it with some jewels, and disappear into the Realm of Light. Once we'd learned who we used to be, we decided that wasn't fair. We couldn't save ourselves and leave the souls that we'd brought to this earth to rot.

Sure was ironic though.

I supposed that's how Avery and Asher fit into the picture. Surely we were taking the survivors to the place where another pair of gods like us could protect them.

"We'll move as many humans there as possible," Nick continued. "Then we'll stay here and fight for our land."

"There's no reasoning with Wormwood," Lila muttered. "They... They have a plan, and they intend to follow it. So this is ours."

"You've been in contact with them?" I asked.

Her jaw tightened. "We had a conversation. And they made their intentions pretty clear. They want what the Conclave agreed to give them when we got this planet. They don't give a shit that we have nowhere to take the people. They just want their souls."

The Conclave, those were the leaders of Matriaza before we came to earth. At least, that was my understanding of it. I didn't know for sure; that's just what I assumed from context clues.

"And their land," Nick said. "They aren't very happy about the condition the planet's in. They think the damage would be irreversible if they wait any longer to take it back."

To some extent, I supposed that was true. Humans were running this planet into nothingness. All the leading scientists said so too.

But that didn't make it any easier to grasp.

It was here. It was really happening. We'd had some peace for a while, but that was gone now. The world was about to fucking end. And we were gonna watch it happen.

I stared at my cup of coffee on the table. "When?"

"When are they coming?" Lila asked.

"Well, yeah, that too. But when did you have a conversation with them?"

"When you broke the seventh seal," Nick said.

"And about two weeks," Lila answered. "Hopefully, we'll have most of the population to the Fae Realm by then."

I nearly laughed. Did they really believe that all of earth's population would be willing to do that? Shit, during the pandemic, we couldn't even get people to stay in their houses. Granted, I was one of them. But I had shit to do. There was a Werewolf that needed killed. Either way, that wasn't going to happen.

I huffed. "And you expect the entire population of Earth to just jump into some spinning hole in the ground?"

"And what about the people that don't?" Laila looked between them. "You're just going to let them die?"

Lila sucked her teeth. "We're going to try to *not* let them die."

"But as much as I hate to admit it, Peterson was right about some things," Nick muttered, head shaking a bit. "We can't save everyone. It's an inevitable fact of war."

It felt like a thousand daggers to the chest. My throat practically collapsed in on itself. I'd known for years that this day was coming, but it hit so much differently now. Maybe it wouldn't have if I didn't see the older version of myself and my wife on the other end of that table.

Lila looked pretty okay. But so did Laila in times of crisis. Nick though, he tried to fight it, but I could see his heart breaking behind his eyes. It wasn't his expression. There was no pull in his brows, no downward curve of his lip. He'd clearly adopted Laila's ability to pretend everything was okay over the last twenty-four years. But I knew those eyes.

Shit was about to be worse than it'd ever been. And we couldn't save them.

"The videos," Laila whispered. "The ones that were leaked last night. Did you do that?"

"Why the hell would we do that?" Lila asked.

"Then who the hell did?"

"Wish we knew," Nick muttered. "Maybe Peterson had it on some type of timer? Maybe he set someone else to do it? Maybe it was Lux? I have no idea. But we didn't want that out there any more than you did."

"Did it happen in your life?" Laila asked.

"Long before today." Lila nodded. "I thought it was to wreak havoc before. To strike fear into the human race about our kind, about the two of us. And that it did. We didn't leave this property until the end started in our time. They wanted me dead. The people, I mean. But... I don't know. Maybe it was just Lux's way of hurting us one more time. Thought it'd be different this time, you know? It didn't happen when it happened before so I thought it wouldn't this time around. But I don't know. Maybe there's a reason behind it. But we came back from January 12, 2024. We don't know what happens after that day."

Laila said something else, but I wasn't paying much attention anymore. Those videos sucked, but if the world were about to end, they didn't matter.

I kept looking at my two-year-old in Laila's arms and thinking about how if this were real, if this weren't some bad dream, she'd be in the same position we were in twenty-four years from now. My little girl was going to have to deal with the reality of knowing that we—her parents and her big brother—were responsible for the end of the world.

We were responsible for the end of the world.

You can't save everyone.

How the fuck was I supposed to accept that?

How was I supposed to watch the world burn?

My head was pounding, and my thoughts were chasing each other.

It'd been a long while since I wanted an escape as much as I did in that moment. But I did. For the first time in a number of years, all that I wanted to do was jam a needle in my vein and forget. I didn't want this to be real, but if it was, I had no idea how I'd handle it sober.

Then Milly reached her arms out for me, and the craving dissipated. It didn't disappear, but it dissipated.

She was how. Micah was how. Laila was how. They'd have to be. They were the only things that made it worth it.

We were doing this for them. We'd have to leave our lives behind. But we were doing it for them, so that they could live for a while before their world burned around them.

I lifted Milly from Laila's lap to mine.

"Jeremy," Laila said.

"Huh?" I turned up to meet her gaze.

"Did you hear that?"

I shook my head.

"Turn the news on this evening," Nick said. "Any channel will be fine. But we're going to make the announcement."

I gave a nod.

"Stay in the perimeter unless we say otherwise," Lila said. "You can talk to others in the supernatural community and fill them in. Or you can take some time to let this sink in. But either way, just try to come to grips with everything we've told you. We'll be back tomorrow."

I swallowed.

Nick's sad gaze moved over me. "You'll be immortal soon, but you aren't yet. So stay here and stay safe."

CHAPTER FIVE

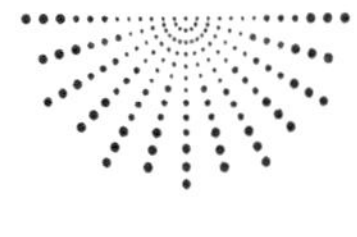

LAILA

I didn't know what to think. I didn't know what I was supposed to feel or how I was supposed to react. Regardless, I wasn't feeling much of anything. I was in shock.

I met myself. I met another version of my husband. And I just found out my mother knew about all of it. She tried to keep it from happening and caused us more pain than if she would have just left shitty enough alone.

Jeremy hadn't said a word since they left. He just kept staring at Milly and me. I thought I was taking it poorly, but I wasn't sure if he was taking it in at all. He was like a zombie. But I knew what he was thinking because I knew that look. I'd thought that it was just the way he looked when he was sad the last time, but in hindsight, I'd put it together. He wanted to get high.

Not that I blamed him. I wanted to get shit faced. But we couldn't. There was too much riding on us. There was too much at risk. And our kids needed us. Whether he realized it or not, I needed him just as much.

After a few silent moments, I asked if he wanted to go up to the main house and get Micah. He gave a quick nod and pulled on his tennis shoes.

We loaded into the forester and started up the icy gravel path. Not a word was spoken as we bounced in and out of the potholes. I wasn't sure what there was to say. Their words were still slowly absorbing into our psyche.

It was happening. It was really happening. We had two weeks before Wormwood touched down and wiped out the human population.

I'd known the end was coming for three and a half years. Ultimately, I knew all roads would lead there. But I prayed we were wrong. I prayed that life would go on as it always had. I supposed I should've known better than to pray.

There were upsides. We had our babies, and we had each other. But every blessing comes with a curse. Although that was a metaphor in most cases, it was true in a literal sense for us.

I went to unbuckle Milly from her car seat, but Jeremy beat me to it. She giggled up at him, saying something about how she liked his hair that way. And he smiled. That pained look almost left his eyes. Not entirely, but almost. And when it did, ease settled through my shoulders. If she and Micah were how he'd keep from relapsing, I'd be happy with that.

But from the looks on Lila and Nick's faces, I knew this was going to get a lot worse. Things were about to get bad. We'd be there to see it go down. And I just wasn't sure that our kids would be enough to keep his head above water. I prayed they would, but I recognized how addiction worked.

As I pushed open the mahogany door to the main house, Tink came barreling toward me in an eruption of barks. I leaned down to pet her with a smile. Then another thought dawned on me.

Would we have to leave our fur-baby behind? That'd break my heart, and it'd *destroy* Micah.

"Mommy." Micah grinned as he ran into the foyer. "Mommy, where was you?"

I smiled, pulling my shoes off. "Just had to talk with some friends."

He looked at Jeremy behind me and turned his head to the side. "What's wrong, Daddy?"

Jeremy forced a smile. "Everything's okay, buddy. Come here."

Micah took a few reluctant steps forward. Jeremy lowered himself to the ground and put an arm around his waist, pulling him close into his chest. His eyes closed against Micah's long black hair, holding Milly against him with the other.

Leah stood in the doorway to the kitchen, concerned eyes moving between mine. *Is everything okay?*

I slowly shook my head.

She took in a slow, deep breath.

"Twelve others," Leah whispered. "Does that include the two of you?"

"I don't think so." I gazed over Micah, Milly, and Luka in the sunroom. "They said the kids don't count either."

"So who gets to go then?" Jenna asked.

My heart fell as our eyes met. They said she'd have to leave her humanity in this time. I'd heard what they said, and I knew what they meant. But I didn't know how to verbalize it.

"Lai." Adam moved his arm around her shoulders, scared eyes heavy on mine.

"Humans can't survive the shift," I murmured. "So any humans that want to come…"

Jenna's breath caught.

"How do you even know these people were telling the truth?" Brody said. "This-this could be a trick. Or-or—"

"It wasn't," Jeremy whispered with a shake of his head. "It's us. *They're* us."

"Okay, let's say that's so," Wyatt said. "Who goes?"

I looked around the room at all of my loved ones. My sisters, my brothers, my mom, my friends. I wished it could be everyone. But I saw Lila's face. Mom wouldn't.

"Who wants to?" Jeremy asked.

Mom lowered herself to the stool at the kitchen island. She gazed at the granite countertop. "I don't want to become a werewolf."

My stomach sunk, and my eyes closed. I pulled in a deep breath.

"Well, I'm going," Leah said. "All that I have here is my family. And if you're all going back, I'm gonna be beside you."

"Can I..." Max murmured. "Can I come? I'll get bit, I will. I just— you guys are the only family I have left."

I thought back to the night his mother died. The night that I told her I'd keep her son safe. It was her dying wish, and I made a promise. We weren't leaving him behind. If the roles were reversed, I knew he'd take me.

Celena looked at me with dopey blue eyes. "Can my mom and dad?"

I turned away, blinking at the water that burned my eyes. I didn't want to tell her no. But older people don't always survive the change. And even if they did, they'd be taking up two spots. With her and Wyatt, that made four.

Kai and Hannah were a given. As were Adam and Jenna. Leah, obviously. Max. Brody. Wyatt and Celena. Same with Chris. That brought us to ten, and I'd made Moriah a promise when this began that I'd have her back. Eleven.

"Will they take on the change?" Jeremy asked.

"I doubt it."

"Then no," Jeremy said.

"I will," Jenna murmured, lifting her head in a quick nod. "I-I I'm not leaving my baby. If Luka's going, I'm going."

"We will too," Hannah said. "We will, right, Kai?"

His gaze was locked with the countertop. "Aye. Aye, we'll go."

"I don't have shit to lose," Chris muttered. "I'm coming."

Brody looked at Gwen, squeezing her hand. "No. No, I'm not leaving."

That wasn't going to go over well. No matter how much he argued with his siblings, I knew the Skouldas. They were all coming, or none of them were coming. And the majority ruled. His ass was coming.

"Well, you can't stay here." Leah scoffed. "I'm not leaving my little brother—"

"I'm a grown man, Leah," he snapped.

"Brody," Gwen whispered. "Love—"

"No." He shook his head. "No, I'm not leaving you here."

Her eyes moved between his. "Let's go talk in private."

"There's nothing to talk about." Brody shook his head again. "I'm not leaving—"

"C'mon." She stood and took his hand.

He clamped his teeth together. His jaw was tight, his shaking hand clutched to a fist. It was taking everything he had not to cry. But he reluctantly stood and followed her up the steps.

Damn it. Poor Brody. He'd wanted a relationship for so long. He finally found a girl that he loved with his whole heart. But she wasn't going to come, and she loved him enough to make him do it. After all, she was already immortal. She'd make certain he took his opportunity to become so too, with or without him.

I turned to Wyatt and Celena. "What about you two?"

He looked down at her. I knew he wanted to say yes. But she had a mom and dad still. All he had was his half-brother, and they weren't too fond of each other. Wherever Celena went, he'd follow.

"I—I don't know. I don't know, give me a minute," Celena said.

"That's what, eight then?" Leah asked.

I looked over Mom at the kitchen counter. "Yeah, if you count Brody."

"We're counting Brody," Jeremy said. "If I have to pull him in by his hair, we're counting Brody."

As I'd thought.

"So four spots left," Leah muttered.

"Who else should we bring?" Hannah asked.

It wasn't eight, it was eleven. I knew that. Celena would come, as would Wyatt, and Moriah. That left one. And there were two people left that I could think of. One, I would happily do without. But the second wouldn't count anyway. She was still a child.

"Lydia," I murmured. "I love that little girl. She's-she's too young to handle this. And twenty-four years from now, she'd be a valuable attribute to all of this. She's a healer and she can grow plants and shit. She's young. She won't count either."

"We should call Ray then," Leah said.

"More like call him back." Jeremy sat his phone on the table. "He's been calling all night."

"What about Moriah?" Hannah met my gaze. "That was the deal you made her, right? When she helped us find Micah and Chris, the deal was when the end comes, you guys help her."

Not that I was particularly thrilled about it either. But loyalty is loyalty. And if we were going to another time, we'd need a Witch. She'd complete our circle of abilities. Helena had always been our on-call Witch, but Moriah was a more powerful one to have in our corner.

"Yeah, that was the deal," I said.

"Well, Ray won't send Lydia without him," Adam muttered. "So Ray and Moriah take us up to ten."

"Leaves two spaces." I looked at Mom. "Mom, you could—"

"Baby." She sent me a sad smile. "I'm human. I plan to stay that way."

"But—"

"I'll be here." She smiled. "I won't even have the chance to miss you."

"But we'll miss you." Jenna made a face. "We need you. Our babies need their grandma—"

"And they'll have me," she said. "In 2024. And besides, those last two spots are Celena and Wyatt's."

Celena looked up with watery eyes. "I haven't decided yet."

"You know you're going back," Mom said. "You may not want to leave your parents, but coming from a parent's perspective, I know what they'll say. They're going to want you to go back and be safe for as long as you can."

She may not have been psychic, but she may as well have read my mind.

"Okay, then Ray can stay," I said. "And you can come—"

"Laila." Mom shook her head. "That little girl already lost her mother. Because of you. You can't take her from her dad too."

She wasn't wrong. In fact, she was incredibly right. But that didn't make it any easier.

I tightened my jaw to keep it from trembling. The knot forming in my throat got thicker. "I don't want to leave you, Mom."

She smiled and blinked tears away. "I don't want to leave you either. But I'm not going to take someone's spot who needs it more than I do."

"Well, maybe we can take thirteen then," I said. "Maybe—maybe we can make two trips, and I can come back for you."

"I'm not becoming a Werewolf, Laila." Her sad green eyes shifted between mine. "No, baby."

CHAPTER SIX

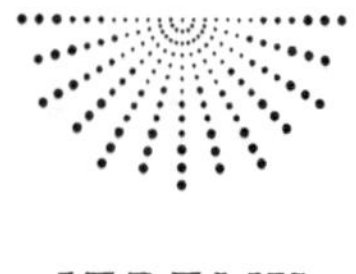

JEREMY

I breathed in a long drag off of the joint between my lips. The bitter wind burned my cheeks, but the hot smoke warmed my chest. Micah, Milly, and Luka frolicked through the yard, dropping to the ground and making snow angels.

Typically, I waited until they were asleep to smoke if I did at all. It'd been a long time since I smoked in the daytime. But it was better than the needle I wanted so badly.

I just needed to breathe for a minute. Weed usually helped me do that. But it wasn't helping today. The only thing that did make me feel remotely okay was looking at them.

They were going to be okay. They didn't even know what was going on. They'd be fine. They had to be, right? Nick and Lila, they said we were going to meet our kids. That meant they were okay.

They'd be okay.

They did look happy.

A day ago, so did I. But in less than twenty-four hours, my life shattered around me. That's always how these things went. I was at the edge of my happily ever after, and then life came and slapped me in the fucking face.

In a month, I'd be living an entirely different life. I wouldn't have the home I busted my ass to build with my bare hands. I wouldn't have the diner that brought me so much pride. I wouldn't even have my name.

Nick. I wasn't a Nick; I was a Jeremy. And Laila was Laila. Lila's closer to Laila than Nick is to Jeremy, but it still wasn't the same.

Soon, nothing would be the same.

I liked stability. It kept me level. It kept me from falling off the wagon. But this wasn't close to stable. This meant that my life, the life I fucking loved, the life I'd fought and killed to build, was going to disappear. My identity would recede. Everything that made me me was going to be gone.

"Hey," Brody said as he stepped out the back door.

I glanced at him and took another hit. "Hey."

"How're you doing?" He leaned against the snowy railing beside me.

I took in a slow breath and let out a quiet laugh. "I don't know. What about you? What happened with Gwen?"

His blue eyes turned to the ground, reaching for the joint. I passed it to him, and he took a hit. "I think she broke up with me. Then we fucked so I'm a little confused but... I don't know."

I noticed the redness in his eyes, and my stomach sunk. "I'm sorry, man."

He nodded and took another hit. "She said she had to set me free. Something about how our destinies don't line up. She's meant to be here, and I'm meant to be there. Whatever the fuck that means."

"I'm sorry, man," I murmured.

I didn't know what else to say. Breakups are always hard. But a breakup on top of all this? That'd have to be damn near impossible.

"Yeah. Me too. Thanks, though." He turned to the kids in the yard. "They're grown now then, aren't they?"

"Micah's my age. Milly's a year older than you," I said. "Said we'd meet them. I guess they're going to help send us back."

"That's gonna be fucking weird," he muttered. "Especially with how much they look like you guys."

I huffed. "Yeah, it's all pretty fucking weird."

"Story of our lives," he muttered. "So Rachel. She's not coming?"

"Her and Laila are in there crying. Jenna's kind of a mess too."

"Wyatt and Celena are gonna bite her, huh?" he asked.

"Yeah. Next week," I said.

"And Max too?"

I nodded.

Silence set in for a moment. It was fair to say that neither of us had any idea what to say or what came next. What was there to say? Our lives were shitshows? They always had been, what else was new? It was just a slightly bigger shitshow than usual.

"Laila said they were the same age as you guys." Brody gave a puzzled look. "How do you think that worked?"

No fucking clue. My best guess was the tree of life thing we'd heard so much about over the last couple years.

"I don't know. Guess we'll find out soon. They said they'd be back tomorrow." I looked at Milly as she smashed a ball of snow on her brother's head.

How was I gonna do this to them? How was I just going to uproot their lives? Sure, kids are adaptable. But holy shit, what the fuck were we going to do? Where would we live? How were we going to pay the bills?

It hit me. This was why they told us to cash everything out. This was why they told us to get old bills. Because anything past the year 2000 could be looked at as counterfeit. I wondered if they were the ones who came to Papy in that dream and told him to give us a million dollars.

This was also why they'd had us form a stockpile. Why they told us to get composting toilets, and chickens, and water filtration systems. Not for us to use, but for them.

After a moment, Brody flapped his lips in a trill. "Guess I better cash out what's left of my trust fund."

I glanced his way. "How much do you have left?"

"Fifteen grand, I think." He massaged a temple. "Enough to get me started, I guess. But not really enough to start over."

"Maybe our best bet would be to combine our finances when we get there," I said. "We'll need a place to live. A big piece of land for the wolves. Especially now that there's gonna be five of them."

He chewed his cheek. "Housing market was pretty shitty back then. We aren't going to find anything as nice as what we have here."

Well, obviously I knew we weren't going to find a piece of land with two giant houses on it. We'd probably end up under the same roof again. But at least we'd *have* a roof.

"Me and Laila have almost a million in the safe. Plus the kid's trust funds." I rubbed a hand down my beard. "Leah's got a nest egg too. Adam has a little something, and Chris has got around a hundred in the bank. We'll find something."

"You and Lai will need some money to start a new business though."

A deep breath. "Yeah. Guess so."

"Hey," Laila said at the back door.

I turned and forced a smile. "Hey, you."

"Ray and Lydia are packing a bag," she said. "And I called Moriah back. Adam's going to go grab them all after dinner."

I drew in another hit off the joint and offered it to her. She took a few steps forward, took it from my hand, and breathed in a long drag.

"Anything on the news yet?" I asked.

"A lot of reports on the videos that got leaked. 'Is it a hoax? Experts say no.'" She rolled her eyes. "But no. Nothing from them yet."

"We cooking back at the house?"

"No, Leah is. I figured we'd stay here until we see the news report. Otherwise, we'll end up back here to bullshit about it."

I tucked an arm around her waist and pulled her into me. "Probably true."

"I'm gonna go start packing a bag. Let me know if anything comes up," Brody said.

"Will do," Laila said.

As he went inside, she leaned forward and rested her head against my chest. "Ya know what sucks?"

"Our lives?"

She laughed and drew another drag off the joint. "We're going to have to go back to smoking shitty shwag weed."

I chuckled and kissed her hair. Usually, it was me making the jokes in times like these. But this time, she'd be the one to keep us on our feet.

CHAPTER SEVEN

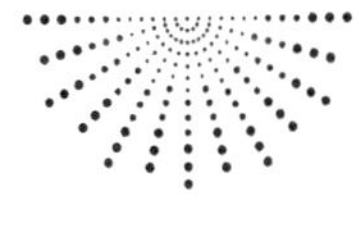

LAILA

"Mommy, can I have some cake?" Micah asked.

"Sure. For snack later." I unhooked Milly's bib and laid it on the back of the highchair.

"But—"

"No, you already had cake for dessert. You can wait. Now go play with your cousin in the living room." I set Milly on the ground.

"I can't stay in here with you?" he asked.

"We have grown up stuff to talk about," Jeremy said. "But we'll have cake and hot chocolate before we get your bath. Alright?"

"Alright," he grumbled. "Come on, Milly. We have *kid* stuff to talk about."

I laughed. The two of them joined hands and giggled their way to the front room. "I bet they're best friends now."

Jeremy licked his lips and nodded.

"Watch them hate each other." Leah laughed. "Hey, do you think I can meet them too?"

"Well, if they're helping us travel back in time, I'm sure we'll all meet them," Hannah said. "God, I bet Milly's gorgeous. She has like, your face on my body."

Sounded like a backhanded compliment, but that's just how we communicated around here. And all it took was someone with eyes to know what she meant. All bodies are beautiful, but Hannah's was hotter than mine. It just was. She had a big ass, pretty boobs, and a tiny waist. I had none of the above.

"The best of both worlds." I grinned.

She shoved my shoulder with a laugh. Jeremy's unblinking eyes stared at his cup of coffee on the table. And I knew that face. His head was spinning. This was hard for all of us to process, but he took it the hardest. I lowered myself beside him and slid a hand down his upper arm.

He turned to me. "What?"

"Are you okay?"

"Yeah, just tired. I didn't sleep last night."

I twined my fingers through his and lifted his knuckles to my lips.

"I wonder if I'll get to meet grown Luka." Adam smiled from the island. "I wonder what he looks like, you know? He looks so much like Jen now, I'm curious if he still does."

"I don't know, I guess we'll see," Jenna said.

"I wonder if you guys have any other grown kids we'll get to meet," Celena said. "It'd be cool, wouldn't it? Like, what if you learn the names, and then you decide to change it when they're actually—"

"Can we just stop?" Jeremy said with a look her way.

She glared at him. "What crawled up your ass and died?"

Uh-oh.

He licked his teeth. "You guys are all acting like this is normal. Or okay, or something we should be happy about, and it's not. It's fucking not. Yeah, we're getting away from this, but the rest of the world isn't. People are about to die. Hundreds or thousands or maybe even millions of people are about to die and you're all laughing and carrying on like everything's fine. Everything isn't fine. This is the god damned apocalypse. Nothing about this is fine. Meeting your future self and your future wife and your grown children isn't fine. This isn't natural. This isn't how it's supposed to work. This is a fucking shitshow, and you all need to take it seriously."

The room grew so quiet that the only sound was the distant *Paw Patrol* theme song.

Not that I disagreed with him. I knew this was bad. But we all got through shit differently. Dark humor and ignorance worked for most of us. Typically, he was the king of it.

Celena's gaze narrowed. "I get that this sucks, but you aren't losing shit, dude. You get to bring your whole family. Your kids are going to be just fine, and so is your wife and your brothers and sisters. I have to leave my mom and dad here. So believe me, Jeremy, I'm well fucking aware of the fact that a lot of people are going to die. But at least the people who matter most to you are going to be immortal in a couple weeks. My mom though? My dad? They won't. They aren't going to be invincible; they *could* die. So don't talk to me like I don't understand because I do. But I can't stop this from happening any more than you can. So yeah, I'm going to smile. I'm going to laugh. Because what the fuck else am I going to do? Mope and hate my life? I've played that bit. So have you. And we both know it gets old pretty quick."

He stood. I touched his hand, but he pulled it away.

"Baby—" I began.

But he was gone. Just vanished.

I took in a slow breath, closed my eyes, and shook my head.

"I'm sorry, Lai, but that was uncalled for—"

"No, I know," I muttered. "Don't apologize. You're right."

"But he wasn't wrong," Max muttered from his seat on the maid steps. "The world's about to be a battlefield."

"Yeah, but that isn't our fault," Celena said.

It wasn't, not really, but Jeremy didn't see it that way. To him, this was our fault. Mine, his, hers, Wyatt's, Hannah's, Kai's, Naomi's, Connor's, Asher's, and Avery's. We were gods. We came to this world to cultivate the souls on this planet.

Now, tons of them were about to die.

In his eyes, we were supposed to protect them. And we were about to fail miserably.

"He's just not taking it well," I muttered.

"And we haven't even gotten to the bad parts yet," Brody said.

"Watch him, Lai," Adam said. "When he gets like this—"

"I know." I rubbed my forehead. "I know."

He was gonna relapse. I wanted to believe that he wouldn't. I wanted to believe he'd be okay. But I knew him. When things were at their worst, that's what he did. He got high.

I didn't know how I'd handle it. Things were different now. We had two kids. We had been planning to have another, although I supposed that plan was out the window now. Either way. I couldn't just tell him to get out and get clean. It wasn't that easy. My babies needed their daddy.

"We should check the news," Wyatt said.

"I just did," Brody said. "Nothing yet."

I placed my chin in my palm.

He could have gone back to the house. Or maybe to the local pharmacy. No, he wouldn't do that. Not right now, not yet. Not when the entire world just saw a video of him bringing me back from the dead.

Fuck.

It's funny how life works. Less than a day before, I was sipping champagne and talking about how good the past year had been. Then 2024 hit and our lives went to shit.

But Celena was right. Moping wouldn't solve anything. We had to stay as happy as we could be. We had to look for the good in this. Even if it was fucked up. Because we had no other choice.

CHAPTER EIGHT

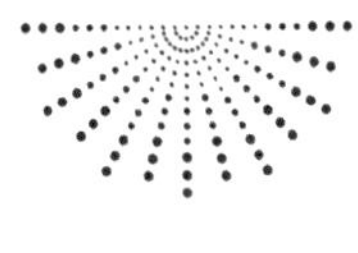

JEREMY

I stood on the balcony overlooking the snow-covered trees in the distance. My phone buzzed in my pocket, but I ignored it. I needed to cool off.

It wasn't Celena's fault. But damn it, I just couldn't take it anymore.

I wasn't happy that I was about to meet my grown children. I didn't want that. I wanted to watch them grow up; I didn't want a snapshot of who they'd be in twenty-four years.

That isn't how parenthood is supposed to work. I was supposed to get old and gray, watching my face wrinkle in the mirror over the years as I took them to soccer games and bowling tournaments. I was supposed to see the age spots appear on my arms as I watched them grow into who they were going to be.

I wasn't ready to see my little man and my baby girl as adults. I just wasn't.

No part of me was ready for any of this. I wanted to go back in time. I wanted to relive 2023 over and over again because it was the best year of my life.

Actually, I take that back. I wanted to go back to that day in the Elder's Hall five thousand years ago. I wanted to slice Lux's throat before he had the chance to stab my wife in the chest. Before he killed my children and the other twenty-two of us.

I wanted to rewrite the story from the beginning.

But that wasn't an option. Or maybe it was. But if it were, Nick and Lila would have done that by now and none of my current life would have ever happened at all.

Damn it. It wasn't fair. None of this shit was fair, or right, or just. It was all bullshit. Our entire lives were fucking bullshit.

"I thought I heard something out here," Mary said at the balcony door.

I glanced at her and then looked back to the evening lit trees.

She leaned against the banister beside me. "How are you doing with all of this?"

I huffed. "It doesn't really matter, does it? We are where we are, it is what it is, and we have to do what we have to do."

She lifted her shoulder. "I suppose." Silence as I stared out into the trees. "So Laila's pretty mad at me, huh?"

"I don't know. We haven't really talked about anything," I said.

"And you?" Her gaze shifted to mine. "Are you mad at me?"

"No. I'm just... I don't know. Just wish everything was different."

"Mm," she murmured. "I think we all do."

Silence crept in for a long moment. I stared out over the field a while longer. I wanted to take in that balcony for as long as I could. It was my favorite part about the house. I didn't want to leave it, but if I had to, I wanted this memory to hold onto.

The cool white against the naked trees. The glow of the town behind them. The glistening snow that fell from the clouds above. The bright moon against the dark blue sky.

It looked so normal. So homey, so comfortable. What would it look like by the time we left?

Mary cleared her throat. "A few days from now, we won't see each other again for a very long time. Well, I suppose I'll see you. But you won't see me."

"Yeah. I guess."

"Before you go, I... I know I've said this before. And I don't know if I'll ever stop saying it. But I... I'm still very sorry for what I did to you."

I fought the internal sigh that echoed within me. That shit didn't matter to me right now. All that mattered was what was right in front of me. Doing what I could to help people in the coming days.

So I just said, "I know."

"And I understand if you still hate me for it. I'd hate me for it too. I doubt you'll ever be able to forgive me for it, but I really want you to know how sorry I am."

I looked at her and frowned. "I get it, Mary. You were trying to save your daughter. Trying to save the world, I guess. I'd do a lot worse to keep my kids safe. I get it."

"I still wish I hadn't," she murmured. "Funny, isn't it? That I wasn't exiled for having Ally do what she did, but for asking too many questions. For trying to figure out why they were stockpiling doomsday weapons."

"They don't like that," I muttered. "Asking questions, I mean."

"Guess they inherited that attribute from our father," she murmured.

I laughed. "Guess they did." I thought for a moment. I'd always known he was her dad, but I supposed I'd never asked much else. "Did you ever meet him?"

"No. That's well above my pay grade."

"How's that work then?" I asked. "Who raised you?"

"My sisters. Other Angels," she said. "The same ones who took my grace and kicked me to Hell."

Sounded about right. Self-righteous, holier than thou, cock sucking motherfuckers. Whatever Daddy said, they'd do. He'd say jump and they'd say how high.

Fuckers. I didn't want my kids to be like that. I wanted them to question me. I wanted them to have their own minds. I wanted them to be good people. I wasn't always one of those. Questioning me was how they'd gauge if they were.

"Bastards," I muttered.

She chuckled. "I suppose."

"Bet it was weird for you. All of this. Helping Annie raise me, then me falling in love with your daughter," I said. "When I brought Laila home to meet the family, that must have been strange."

Mary smiled and turned her gaze to the ground. "It was. Very strange. But a blessing all the same. I always wanted to meet her. I watched over her from a distance, but to actually meet her, to share a meal and hear her speak about her life. How much she loved it, how happy she was. That... It was a wonderful day for me."

"Yeah, me too." I smiled, thinking back to that night. "Did you keep an eye on all of your kids? Or just Lai?"

"Some more than others," she said. "Celena was interesting to watch. Seeing her was like clicking over to a family channel after watching a horror movie. I suppose she had her horror moments too, but she was rather light. Strong, but soft. Smart. She thinks about everything she does before she does it. I never had to worry about her much; she keeps herself well-guarded. And Kai... Well, I didn't get to see him often. Getting to the Fae Realm isn't easy for us. And when we do arrive, there is no welcome wagon. I'm sure you saw that."

I huffed. "Oh yeah. They hate you guys."

"For good reason," she said. "But Laila... I don't know, I bonded to her in a way I didn't with most of my children."

"Why's that?"

She smiled. "When those two were born, something changed in me. Kai came first. And he was gentle, even then. He latched and fed easier than any child I ever nursed. But then Laila came and" —she laughed— "that little girl floored me. She burned me, you know."

Sounded like my wife. She always had been a force to be reckoned with.

"Doesn't surprise me." I smiled.

Mary was smiling too, eyes in the distance. "I lifted her to my chest, and she burned the clothes to my skin. But then, I think she felt it. And she healed me. As if she was apologizing." Her smile widened, eyes glassy "She opened her eyes and looked at me. *Really* looked at me. And she smiled. I know they say infants don't do that, but Laila did." Her smile slowly fell. "I wanted to keep her, actually. I wanted to send

Kai with Luka and keep my fiery, smiling little girl. But they told me I couldn't. They told me I had to give her to Luka and Rachel. I see why now. I know she had to live a human life to love this world the way she does. She... she belonged here. And I probably would have messed her up. I'm not built to be a mother. I'm not like her, or you, for that matter. I'm not kind enough to be a good parent. I wish I were, but Rachel is Laila's mother. A good one, the kind she deserved to have. She wouldn't be the Laila we know and love if I hadn't given her to them."

Well, I agreed to some extent. I'd always loved Rachel. She was a wonderful woman. A wonderful grandmother to my children, a perfect mother to my wife, and the best mother in-law I could have asked for.

But Mary wasn't all bad either. Strict, but nice too. She'd bandaged my scraped knees as a child—after scolding me for climbing trees and riding bikes without tying my shoes first, of course. But she wasn't bad. Not until that shit with Ally, anyway.

I looked over her pained gaze and frowned. "You weren't a bad parent, Mary."

She laughed. "Thank you for saying that. But we both know it isn't true."

"I wouldn't be the man I am if it wasn't for you." I smiled. "You weren't as good as Annie, I'll admit that. But you were consistent. You taught us discipline. You weren't always kind, but when you were, it made us appreciate it more. I'm softer with my kids than you were with us, but you showed me how to set rules. And I'll always be grateful for that."

She smiled at me for a moment. She turned her gaze downward as it fell. "Well, thank you. But I'll never be able to call myself a good parent, Jeremy. Not because I gave my kin away, I can justify that. But because of what I did to you. When I offered Ally that exchange... I know that you understand now, but I don't. I see you and Laila, what you've done to protect your children, and I wish I would have done things like that to keep you safe too." Her head shook a bit. "I don't know how I went through with it. Even if you can, I can't justify it now. I'll always hate myself for that."

A slow sigh.

I hated what she'd done. But like she'd said, I'd done far worse for my kids. And I'd do it again.

"You thought it wouldn't hurt me. And honestly, it doesn't. I don't have nightmares that haunt me from that night. It didn't give me PTSD like when it happened to Lai. The only thing that does hurt is that you're the one that set it up." Her sad gaze shifted back to the ground. "But I do forgive you."

She looked up, hazel irises twinkling with the tears. "You don't have to say that. I—"

"No, I do," I said. "I forgive you, Mary. I did a while ago. And hey, I'm sorry I didn't want you at the wedding. I just...I didn't know then what I know now. I was angry still. And jealous, honestly, that you put me through that to protect her when I looked at you as more of a parent than she did. But I do, I forgive you. I can't forget what you did. But holding onto anger and resentment like that doesn't help either of us. I had to forgive you to move on. And I have."

Her lips pulled into a sad smile. "Thank you, Jeremy."

I returned her smile and turned back to the field. But I'd been doing some thinking. A lot of loose ends were starting to tie up. That comment she'd made last Christmas when we'd asked if she'd been with her other family, she laughed because she had. Clearly, she'd been a big part of their lives.

"So my kids," I said. "The grown versions. You've met them?"

She lowered herself to the patio chair. "I have."

"What are... what are they like?" I asked.

A quiet laugh escaped her. "Amazing. Smart, smart as whips. Well, Micah and Milly anyway. The others are a bit naïve still."

My stomach spun.

We brought more kids into this world knowing what would happen to it? No. No, that was wrong. That wasn't fair to do to them. I loved my kids more than anything, but if I knew Micah and Milly would have to live through this before Laila got pregnant, maybe I'd have worn a condom.

"So there are. Others, I mean."

"There are."

I licked my lips. "I won't meet them, will I?"

"Not until they're born, no."

A touch of relief softened my shoulders. That was good. I didn't want to. Because I didn't want to have them anymore. Wiping them from the timeline hurt my heart a little, but it'd be better for everyone in the long run.

If I met them though, I wouldn't be able to disassociate that way. I'd fall in love. I'd make sure I busted in Laila at just the right time so they could be born and grow into the people I met. That's all it would take for me to change my mind.

"Micah though," I murmured. "Is he okay? Knowing who he is, knowing *what* he is in all of this. Is he...is he alright?"

She smiled. "He is. He's a wonderful person, really. Perhaps the best I've ever met, which is saying a lot because I'm very old."

A sense of peace washed over me when I heard that. All I'd ever wanted was to raise my child to be a good person, and I guessed I had. Or would, rather.

"He doesn't... He isn't angry that we...that we lost him? That they sacrificed him?"

"No, I don't know if that boy is capable of anger. He's a very gentle creature. He's always smiling. Always. And it's contagious, his joy. He wants to help everyone and everything."

I smiled. Sounded like my little man. "Still a vegetarian then?"

"Vegan, actually." She laughed. "Loves animals. He has Laila's passion in that way. He's not fiery about the things he cares about, but he is passionate. But he has this calm rationality to his viewpoints. He isn't the type to scream in your face about what you're doing wrong. He's the type to softly explain, making you see every side of his argument and leaving you forgetting how you felt about it in the first place. He's yet to get me to stop eating meat though."

I laughed for a moment. Then my smile fell. "And Milly?"

She laughed again. "A pistol, that girl. But kind, too. She reminds me of Laila, but not quite. I suppose she reminds me of who Laila was early on. When you two were just kids in love? That fury to her?" I smiled as she went on. "She struggled for a while. After learning the whole picture, who we all are in the story. But, well, eventually she realized what we all have. That many facts of our reality cannot be avoided."

I l turned my gaze downward. "Are they... are they happy?"

"As happy as they can be with all things considered," she said. "But you'll see soon enough."

"I'm not looking forward to that part."

"What part is that?"

"Meeting them." I raked greasy hair from my face. "Seeing them all grown up. This isn't...this just isn't how these things are supposed to work, you know?"

"Nothing works as it's supposed to for us, Jeremy," Mary said. "We are important people. And important people carry important responsibilities. Responsibility isn't fun. Responsibility is hard work with often few rewards. But you're lucky. Because you get the best reward imaginable. You get a beautiful family that loves you and that you love more than anything."

It all sounded so simple when she phrased it that way.

"Yeah, I guess. I should probably get back to them. Laila's probably worried I drank all her wine."

She laughed. "I'm going to head out too. They need me back at their house. But I'll see you soon."

CHAPTER NINE

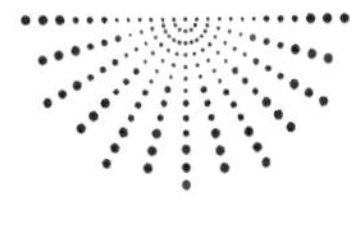

LAILA

Nine o'clock hit, and still nothing on the news. I had two kids; nine o'clock was our bedtime. I couldn't wait up much longer. Part of me was growing concerned. Did something happen to them? Were they okay? Were *we* going to be okay?

Without them, we'd be stuck here. Don't get me wrong, I wasn't ecstatic about taking a voyage twenty-four years into the past. But now that I realized my babies wouldn't be growing up in an apocalypse, I was ready to leave this behind.

I guess ready isn't the right word. I was sad to leave the life Jeremy and I built together. But I couldn't think about the logistics. I couldn't think about what would happen to Moe's in the coming days, or my mom, or the rest of the world. All that I could think of was our second chance.

Our chance to stop all of this before it started. I knew they said that all rivers led to the same ocean, but I still had hope that when we went back, we could keep all of it from happening.

Either way. I was concerned. Then a text slid across my phone's screen from a number I didn't know.

Got a little held up. We'll see you tomorrow. Chamber's meeting at

10:30 their time.

Relief flooded over me. They were alright. We were going to be alright.

Micah lay in the crevice of my arm with his gaze on the TV. Milly slept with her head on my lap. I played with the messy locks of black hair around her face. I stared at *Paw Patrol* on the TV, thinking about how when we went back, my babies would never watch their favorite show again. Because it wouldn't exist for another thirteen years.

But I was also so incredibly grateful I wouldn't have to hear that theme song again. It wasn't so bad the first ten or fifty times. Now though, I'd found myself singing it in the shower.

"Hey," a quiet voice said in the doorway to the living room.

I turned with a smile. Lydia stood there, wearing a sad gaze as she looked over me and the kids. She looked so different than she had when we first met. She was so little then.

Now, her long black curls hung around her maturing face coated in a thin layer of foundation, desperately trying to cover those typical teenage pimples. A thin black line rested above her pale blue eyes. She wore a pink V-neck that made it very clear she was no longer a little girl.

"Hey, kid," I said. Micah stirred beside me, swiveling to meet her gaze.

"Lydia!" He shot forward.

"Shh." I gestured to his sleeping sister. I gently moved Milly to the couch cushion and stood. "You can see her in the morning. You just watch your shows."

His shoulders slumped, eyes on Lydia. "You be here in the morning?"

"Yeah, buddy," she said. "I'll be here."

He smiled and turned back to the TV.

I started toward her and placed my arms around her in a hug. She squeezed me tight. "Can we go talk?"

"Have you seen it?" she asked as I scooped some ice cream into a bowl.

"I didn't watch them, but yeah. I get the picture," I muttered. "Couldn't really stomach it, ya know?"

"Guess I'm glutton for punishment," she said. "I watched them all. Well, parts of them anyway. Micah's was hard. Seeing him kill my mom was pretty rough too."

My brows dropped, and I looked up. "That's out there too?"

She blew out a slow, calming breath. "Yup."

"Oh, sweetie," I murmured, shaking my head. "That wasn't actually Micah. It was Jeremy inside of his head. He'd never—"

"Yeah, kinda figured. And I'm not mad. I get it. She had to die. But it still wasn't a pleasant watch. I saw the one where they put the chips in him and I, well, it made it a little easier."

I looked down at the bowls of ice cream, chewing my lip for a moment. Jesus, we needed to get off of this topic. There was too much going on already, I couldn't think about the path that led us here.

"Do you want whipped cream?" I asked.

"No, just the ice-cream's fine."

"Where's your dad?" I carried the bowls to the dining nook and sat beside her.

"Still getting some shit together. Adam dropped me off and went back for him." She shoved the spoon into the ice-cream. "He took my phone, you know. Like this is my fault, and I'm being punished or something."

It wasn't a punishment. I'd taken the kid's iPads too. They didn't need to worry about all of this shit right now.

"Well, if it helps, Jeremy took mine too."

"Men. They think we can't handle the reality we lived through."

"I don't think that's it." I took a bite. "They just don't want to see us upset. Can't say I blame them, really. I don't want to relive it either."

"Yeah, well, I want to be able to defend myself. All of these kids I go to school with are commenting on the videos, calling me pathetic or saying how 'sad' it is that I lived through that, and I just want to punch them in the face. Fuck them, ya know? They're talking about me like I can't see what they're saying."

At some point along the way, I'd realized that there isn't much use in defending one's honor. People are going to think what they want. They're going to feel how they feel.

Yeah, I knew people were calling me a murderer. I could imagine where it snowballed from there. But it didn't matter. People could think whatever they wanted about me. I didn't want to hear the shit talking and feel less inclined to help them. They were scared, they were panicking. They could call me whatever they want if it made them feel a little better through this.

Lydia took another bite. "It's not like it matters. I'm sure this is all going to blow over. They're going to debunk the videos and everything's going to go back to normal."

I grew quiet.

She and Ray hadn't exactly been in the loop. Lydia was one of us, but her dad wasn't. Not yet, anyway. He didn't hear the rumors moving through the supernatural world like the others. It's kind of fucked up to admit, but they drifted to the back of my mind a lot. I loved them and all, but I wanted them to have the normal life they both yearned for. They deserved it.

On top of that, I didn't want their vision of me to change. I didn't want them to look at me as if they had to kneel at my feet. Yeah, I was a goddess once upon a time. The supreme, top-bitch goddess. But I didn't want to be seen that way. I didn't want them to look to me with fear in their eyes. I didn't want them to know who I was a few hundred thousand years ago. I didn't want them to know what we'd done when we brought our son back from the dead.

"Right?" Lydia said.

I frowned. "No. No, nothing's going to go back to how it was."

"What do you mean?"

I cleared my throat. "It's... it's a long story, hon—"

"Well, make it short," she said with a firm gaze. "What's happening, Laila?"

My gaze turned to the table. "Alright. Well, um." I paused. "I don't really know how to say this. And there isn't really a way to sugarcoat it. So I'll just say it. The world's ending."

Her breath caught. "What?"

"Not for us. We get a little extra time." I scratched my head. "This is the start of the end."

"But...what...I don't understand. What do you... this doesn't make any sense."

"Hey," Jeremy said in the doorway.

I turned and met his gaze. My shoulders softened with relief. He looked better than he had when he left. Still kind of a mess, but better. Definitely not high. And he was always better at explaining things to kids. Maybe he could tell Lydia easier than I could.

He pulled a smile to his lips as he looked at Lydia. "How ya doing, kid?"

"Uh... I don't know."

"Just found out the world's ending?" he asked. Her eyes shifted to her ice cream on the table, nodding. "Bitter pill, I'm still trying to swallow it too."

"Ray'll be here soon," I said. "I just started filling her in. Do you want to help me explain it all to them?"

"Sure. Yeah, but I need to go talk to Celena. I kind of owe her an apology." He gestured toward the steps. "But I'll be back down in a minute. They're gonna be staying with us, right? I think this house is kind of at full capacity."

"Yeah, that's probably best."

"I blew up the air mattresses. Ray can take the couch though. After they get here, we should get the kids back to the house and to bed. Figure they can skip baths tonight."

"Alright. Brody went to get Moriah, but I'm sure she's taking a year to pack her bags. I'll tell him to bring her back to our place."

"That works. Oh, and Papy texted. There's a Chamber's meeting tomorrow morning at their house. Ten—"

"Ten-thirty their time," I said. "Yeah, a little birdy told me. We'll fill these two in and try to get a few hours of sleep."

CHAPTER TEN

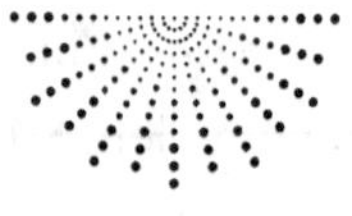

JEREMY

I trudged my way up the steps to my old bedroom. As I stood at the mahogany door, I rubbed from my eyes down to my jaw. It wasn't that I minded apologizing. I didn't. I was pretty good at swallowing my pride. It was just that Celena could be a real cunt when she wanted to be. I loved her and all. But she wasn't as understanding as her sister.

I raised my knuckles and knocked.

"Hang on," Wyatt called. After a long moment, the door pulled open. Wyatt crossed his arms against his chest. "What's up, man?"

"Celena in there?" I asked.

She stood from the bed and made her way to the door. "Where else would I be? Not like there's anywhere else to go when the witch hunts are commencing out there."

"Can I talk to you for a minute?"

She took a step outside, pulling the door shut behind her. "Unless this is an apology, I don't want to hear—"

"It is," I said. "It's an apology. I'm sorry."

She arched a brow. "For?"

As if she didn't know.

I rubbed my tired eyes. "I was a dick, alright? I'm mad at the world, and I took it out on you. And that was wrong. I haven't slept in almost two days, and I'm grumpy, and burnt-out and... I'm just kind of a mess right now. But that isn't your fault. I shouldn't have talked to you like that. I'm sorry."

Her eyes moved between mine. Her stiff shoulders relaxed. "Apology accepted. I get it, this all sucks. But we really have to hang onto any ounce of happiness we have, you know?"

"Yeah, I know." I leaned against the wall. "I know that, I do. But this is just... That part isn't a happy thing for me. Meeting my kid that's my age? My daughter being my wife's age? It's not normal, dude. This isn't something I can be happy about. I get it. They're out there, but that's all that I need to know. I don't want to see them like this. This just isn't how it's supposed to work, and I'm not happy about it. I'm not excited for any of this."

"Why?" she asked. "I mean, I get that it's weird, but you guys are the holy grail of weird. What—worried you're going to be attracted to your daughter?"

Vomit all but spilled from my esophagus. "That's disgusting."

She laughed. "I'm just saying, man. Meeting your kids like this gives you insight. You can get the reassurance all parents want as their kids are growing up. I'm sure you're always wondering what you're doing right and what you're doing wrong, aren't you?"

"I guess."

"Well, they'll be able to tell you you're doing it right. Or what you do wrong before you do it. Either way, it's a win-win, man."

I still didn't see it that way. All that I saw was this being weird and uncomfortable. None of it should have been happening at all. My children weren't supposed to be in their twenties. The world wasn't supposed to be ending. It was just too much.

Regardless, I wanted this conversation to end. I wanted to go home. I wanted to sleep. I wanted to enjoy the time I had left in my life. I knew there wasn't much of it, but I wanted to enjoy what I did have.

"Maybe. I guess, I don't know. But either way, I'm sorry. I'll try to not be an asshole through all of this, alright?"

She gave one of those mothering looks. "Alright."

"I gotta get the kids back to the house. Try and get some sleep. I've got the feeling we have a long day ahead of us." I turned away.

"Yeah, I'm planning on it. But wait," she said.

I turned her way. "What?"

She was quiet for a moment. "I know it's not my place, so I'm sorry if this pisses you off. But that's my sister, and my niece, and my nephew. And whether you realize it or not, you're their rock. They need you, Jeremy. So don't fall apart on them."

It's not like that was in the plans. I was doing everything in my power to not break down. Yeah, I'd gotten pissed off earlier, but I still thought I was doing a half decent job at keeping my shit together.

"I'm not," I said. "It's just been a long day. I just need to get some sleep."

Her eyes shifted between mine for a moment. "Okay. But I mean it, Jeremy. I'll kick your ass if you—"

"Alright, I get the point. Me and Lai are good, the kids are good. They're my world. I'm not planning on fucking it up any time soon."

"Well, you weren't planning on fucking it up the last time you relapsed either—"

"You know what? You're right. It's not your place." My tongue ran along my teeth. "But thanks for your concern."

She raised a brow, crossing her arms against her chest. "Any time."

"I just don't understand how this is possible," Ray said. "You two—you were gods? That's what you're telling me?"

"That is what we're telling you," Laila murmured.

"And the world's ending because you pissed off the real god?" he asked.

"No," I said. "No, the world's ending because the god most of the world worships is a fucker. None of us go to heaven when we die because he destroyed the original heaven. We were going to imprison him for doing so, and he cursed us to live in misery for five-thousand years."

"And he isn't the *real* god," Laila said. "He just wiped the rest of us from history and tried to make it out like he was the only god to ever live."

He tilted his head to the side. "But there is a heaven. Right? I've heard you guys talk about it, there's a heaven."

"Yeah, but it's not where people go when they die. That's just where the Angels live. They won't let humans in there," I said.

"So to avoid the apocalypse, you're going to go back in time. And you want me and Lydia to come."

"Well, we really just need Lydia," Laila said. "But you won't let her come without you, so you can tag along."

"Gee, thanks," he muttered.

She smiled, letting out a quiet laugh. "I didn't mean it like that. I just meant that she'd be a valuable attribute in this war when we have to face it. She's a healer, and she can grow crops. We'll need people like her."

He turned his gaze down. "And I have to become a Werewolf to survive time travel." I nodded, and he rubbed his eyes. "Can I think about it first? Talk to Lydia and see how she feels about it?"

What was there to think about? Not like I was excited about this either, but fuck. The world was about to be a battle ground. He had an opportunity to keep his kid safe. There wasn't much to consider. Avoid certain death for twenty-four years, or deal with the end of the world in the coming days.

"Sure," Laila murmured. "Sure, but don't take too long. We only have a couple weeks left here. And I think all hell's going to break loose before we do."

"But if you haven't already, you should get all the money out of your bank account. We're going to need every penny we all have to get started when we go back."

"I have a feeling banks are going to be gone soon anyway," Laila said.

"I'll take her with me to the bank in the morning. We'll get the money we have out and talk about it on the way home. I'll have an answer for you by this time tomorrow."

"Sounds good." I stifled a yawn. "I'm beat though. I need to get to bed."

"Yeah, me too." Laila stood from the table. "We won't be here when you get up. But if you need anything, call someone in the family. Chris is going to be here with the kids so go with Leah or Brody."

"I'm sure we'll be alright. Thanks though."

"Sure."

***

My eyes had just closed. I was just about to fall asleep when I felt Laila's lips touch my shoulder. Her hand moved along my bicep. "Baby?" she whispered.

"Yeah?"

"Are you asleep?"

I opened my eyes and rolled against the pillow to meet her gaze. "I was about to be."

"Sorry," she murmured with a soft smile.

I smiled back and cupped my hand over hers. "It's okay. What is it?"

"Are you alright?" she whispered. I held my smile and gave a nod. "That wasn't very convincing."

I rubbed my eyes. "I'm not great. But I'm okay."

"You tell me if you're not. Don't hide it, okay? I'll be here for you, but you have to tell me if you need me."

I lifted her knuckles to my lips. "Well, I need you. I always need you. But I don't need you to do anything, alright? I just need to know that we're going to get through this."

"We'll get through anything," she murmured. "As long as we have each other, we'll get through anything. Okay?"

I smiled and touched my lips to hers. "Okay." I pulled back and touched her cheek. "But I'm exhausted. I need sleep."

She kissed me once more. "Alright. I love you, sweet dreams."

"I love you more," I murmured, closing my eyes.

She was right about that. As long as we had each other, we'd make it through anything. It didn't always feel like it. It certainly wouldn't by the day we left. But she and my children were always how I made it through the bad times.

CHAPTER ELEVEN

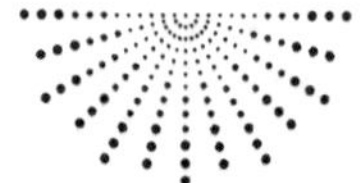

JANUARY 2 - LAILA

My lips pressed Micah's sleeping temple. I ran my fingers through his hair, closing my eyes and breathing in his smell. I straightened up and scratched Tink's head. With a deep breath, I turned and started from the room.

Chris stood in the doorway with a sad smile. "How are you doing with all this?"

"Eh," I said. "Better than your brother. What about you? Are you alright?"

He smiled and lifted a shoulder. "I don't know. Not great, I guess. But it's a second chance. Maybe I'll get around to doing all the shit I wanted to since I was taken, you know? I've got time now. It's kind of like a redo. I can't get the years I lost back, but I get to see what the world was like when I was gone."

"You gonna go back to school?" I asked.

"Maybe. Probably. I wanted to be a doctor though. That's not really the route I want to go any more. We have all these healers now; it's not necessary to have a doctor in the family. Plus, that's at least twelve years. If we only have twenty-four, I'd rather not waste half of it busting my ass. I might go for nursing, I think," he said. "Sucks that

56

we're going back to a homophobic time though. Not looking forward to that part."

I couldn't blame him on that one.

As much as we all loved to bitch about the world we lived in, and as much as so many things needed to change, there were a lot of great things about the modern world. The philosophy of the time was much more accepting. Homophobia ran rampant in 2000, my tattoos were going to get me some nasty looks, and about a million other things.

"Yeah, me neither. And I don't know where we're going to live. It obviously won't be here."

"I hope it's not in the south," he muttered. "God, can you imagine Leah's raging lesbian ass in Texas in the year 2000?"

I laughed. "I don't think Texas suits any of us. It'll probably be somewhere with all four seasons. We're all accustomed to it, and I can't see the wolves being happy in a warmer climate."

"Probably." He rubbed his tired eyes. "I don't know, I guess we'll see. You're going to talk to them today, right? I'm sure they can fill you in on some of those details."

"Yeah, they texted a little bit ago. We're meeting up at your grand-parent's house."

"That'll be fun," he murmured. I huffed, and he smiled. "Well, we'll be here. Let me know how it goes."

"Oh, I'm sure it'll be rainbows and unicorns."

***

"Jeremy, Laila," Papy said as I pulled off my jacket and laid it over the back of my chair. "Before everyone arrives, we need to have a chat."

Jeremy's eyes were as distant and detached as his tone. "Yeah, guess we do."

"How did you two let this happen?" His eyes darted between us. "All powerful, aren't the two of you? And you couldn't prevent a—"

"We had nothing to do with those videos coming out," I snapped. "What—you think that I wanted the entire world to see me being tortured?"

"Well, you could have—"

"There's nothing we could have done. Every compound we found, we cleared. We either took any evidence they left or destroyed it." Jeremy gritted his teeth. "But none of that matters right now. We have more important shit to deal with."

"*More important?*" Papy's face screwed up. "What could possibly be more important than mass exposure?"

"The end," I said. His stiff brow softened, not even realizing he was holding his breath. "We have two weeks. Two weeks, and all hell is breaking loose."

"Well, not literally," Heylel's familiar voice said in the doorway. I turned to him and forced a smile he quickly returned. "Hello, everyone."

"What do you mean?" Papy's wide eyes flickered between us all. "How do you know?"

"That'd be us." Lila and Nick appeared behind Heylel. Her fingertips slid against his shoulder as she brushed past him.

Papy took a quick step back, hand moving to his heart. His other hand erupted with a bright ball of swirling blue energy. "What is going—"

"Have a seat, Papy." Nick gave a soft smile. "And put that out. We have a lot to talk about."

"You bet we do." His blue eyes were wider than the sky is wide. Fast, erratic breaths shook his broad shoulders.

Lila smiled and murmured a slow, quiet incantation. As the words left her lips, Papy's breaths leveled. The swirling ball in his hand gradually receded. His wide eyes blinked as he gently lowered himself to the seat beside mine.

"Nice to see you guys." Nick sent us a cordial smile. "Sorry we flaked last night. Figured we should talk to these guys before we go screaming from the rooftops."

I didn't say anything. My gaze stayed fixed on Heylel as he lifted his jacket from his shoulder and rolled up his sleeves. He stood beside Nick the way that Jeremy stood next to Chris, Adam, or Brody.

The two of them hadn't been introduced recently. That much was evident. They'd been in contact for a long time.

I thought back to all the gatherings we'd had with him since we'd been introduced two years ago. He gave us more insight into who we were than anyone aside from our own subconscious memories. But there was a lot of shit he would have had to have known that he kept from us.

More than kept from us, he'd lied. He flat-out *lied*.

There's no way he didn't know that Jeremy was a necromancer.

But before I could think any longer, people started appearing all over the room.

Brody. But not our Brody. Still in his usual dark washed blue jeans and polo shirt, but his hair was shorter, and he had a full beard, though trimmed close to his squared jaw.

Adam, but he looked a hell of a lot different. Rather than a pair of bleach-stained sweatpants and some decade old band tee, he wore a sensible V-neck and pair of blue jeans. His pot belly was replaced with a broad, chiseled torso.

Beside him stood a woman with jet black hair and a cute denim jacket. I squinted a bit as her gaze met mine. She smiled, and it clicked. Leah. Leah with her real hair. I'd grown so used to seeing it purple, I had no clue how gorgeous she was with her natural color.

Then Chris. His hair was long, longer than Jeremy's. It was pulled back into one dark braid that hung to the center of his spine. And he looked stronger. The years he'd spent in captivity were washed away. He'd been struggling to gain muscle mass from the decade of malnutrition he'd survived. But clearly, he'd reached his goal. He looked a bit more like Adam than Jeremy now that he had some meat on his bones.

Hannah. Sweet little Hannah. I guess she wasn't little since she was technically twenty-four years older than me, but she'd always be little to me. She seemed about the same, but her hair was much shorter. It hung in loose, beach curls at her shoulders.

Kai appeared beside her. Literally nothing about him had changed. He still had some scruff around his cheeks, his muscles were as slender as they were yesterday, and his brown hair still rested in messy waves at his ears.

Connor and Naomi landed beside Lila and Nick. Then Avery and Asher. It'd been a while since I saw the four of them, but nothing had changed except for Avery and Asher's attire. They both wore T-shirts and jeans, contrary to the elaborate, nearly renaissance Fae clothing typically worn on their realm.

"What the hell is going on?" Papy looked around. "What is—I don't —someone needs to explain this to me."

"We will." Brody lowered himself to the table across from his grandfather. "But let's wait until the rest of the Chambers get here."

"It's a long story, Papy," Hannah said. "Too long to repeat."

CHAPTER TWELVE

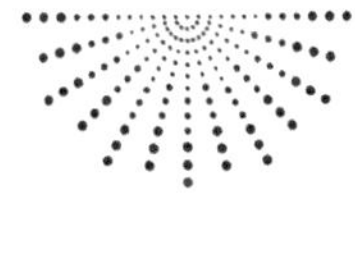

JEREMY

"This is absurd." Eric's wide eyes slammed around the room. "This is—this is unbelievable."

"You two," Dayo murmured, look of disdain moving between me and Laila to Lila and Nick. "You two have been around all of this time and kept all of this from us?"

"We didn't know shit until yesterday," Laila said.

My jaw tightened as I looked at Heylel. We knew nothing. And he played a pretty big part in that. He met my gaze and struggled a friendly smile to his lips. But I clenched my teeth and turned back to Lila.

"We kept it from them." Lila gestured between me and Laila. "And from you."

"But why?" Papy barked. "Why wouldn't you tell us when this was going to happen? We could have prepared, we could have—"

"You knew it was coming," Nick said. "You did have time to prepare. We passed on enough information for you to train your people and to build your stockpiles. That's the only information you needed."

"We should have known *when*," Eric said. "We should have had a timeline—"

"Why?" Lila gave him the look she gave the kids when they threw temper tantrums. Brows wrinkled slightly in question, head tilted. On my wife, I found it soothing and gentle. On her, it looked condescending. "Why did you need the date and time? So you could watch each moment tick by in terror? So you could be petrified sooner than you needed to be?"

"We had the right—"

"You have no idea." Chris let out a huff of a laugh and ran his hand along his chin. "We have lived the past twenty-four years knowing when it ends."

"We also spent the four years prior to that knowing that it would end and hoping that it wouldn't," Leah said. "And trust me. That hope? Praying that there's some chance you could stop it, or that you'd die before it came, that's a lot easier to live with than the knowledge of certain doom."

I guessed I could understand that. And hell, I was grateful for it. Over the last two years since we got Micah back, I'd been able to live. I'd been able to smile, and it felt natural.

Happy. We'd been so happy.

The deadline would've been in the back of my mind had I known. I'd have saturated myself in that date. I'd have stressed, and cried, and probably relapsed. The lack of an exact time gave me peace.

They did the right thing.

But Heylel did not.

He'd lied to my face at least a handful of times. He pretended not to know that I could resurrect the dead. He pretended that he didn't know Lux used to be Laila's husband. He fucking lied.

"By not giving you a date, we gave you hope," Lila said.

"And let's not forget about the fact that we tried to prevent all of this," Naomi stated. "We've spent the last—what? Ten years?"

"Give or take," Nick said.

"More than ten years trying to prevent this," Naomi continued. "We did everything that we could to stop this before it started."

"But if you were from the future, you knew where that man was holding the boy," Blair Martin said. "You could have kept the sacrifice from happening at all."

"We tried," Lila said. "But Peterson was working with Lux—"

"Who?" Roland cocked his head.

"God, whatever you want to call him," Nick said.

He sipped his scotch. "Ah."

"Lux has seen every timeline. He knows every outcome," Lila said. "So when we were close to figuring out where they were, he changed it. He moved them."

"When you can control time and have been around for hundreds of thousands of years, you have a million ways to shift reality to the way you want it to go," Nick said. "He kept fucking with details. He had the time to. He kept changing things so that we had no idea when or where our son was going to be."

"Call him destiny, call him a dick," Leah said. "Either way. He knew exactly what he was doing and how to prevent us from getting what we wanted."

"We fought like hell to find Micah when it was us who lost him." Lila turned her gaze to us. "Then we did the same when it was them who lost him. But no matter what we did, no matter how many times we tried to change it, we turned up at the same end. Sitting in this room with the younger versions of ourselves and all of you."

"If you want to be pissed at anyone, be pissed at your god," Nick said. "He's the one who's responsible for all of this. Not us, not them. Him. He started this shit. And if he hadn't, we wouldn't be where we are. But he did, and we are, so suck it up like we did."

"You keep talking about him. You keep blaming our lord, and he's yet to show his face," Eric said. "Why is that?"

"Why's your God a piece of shit?" Nick asked. He laughed. "Who the hell knows? Pray about it."

I chuckled, and Nick smiled. Stupid, I guess, to laugh at my own joke. But ya know, great minds and all.

Roland gulped down the rest of his scotch. He pushed a strand of salt and pepper hair from his face. "So what's the plan then? That's why you're here, no? To tell us where we go from here?"

Nick nodded. "Yeah, pretty much."

"We are the plan." Avery stood, and Asher followed. "Our land in the Fae Realm is the plan."

"Who are you?" Papy raised a brow.

"My name is Avery Alston. I'm the Queen of the Open Lands in the Realm of Light."

"Bloody hell," Eric muttered.

Avery raised a brow and cocked her head to the side. "And why is that, Eric?"

He laughed. "A bunch of children. We're depending on children to save the world—"

"I'm as old as you are." She had the same tone Lila had. Calm, blunt. Like she was talking to a child. "What are you? Fifty? Fifty-five? I'm fifty-three, sir, and that is this body alone. My soul pre-dates yours by at least five-hundred-thousand years. Every one of us is as old, if not older, than you are. No one looks to Janis and Elijah and calls them children; I would greatly appreciate if you gave us the same respect. Just because I look better than you does not by any means mean that you are my predecessor. I only aged better."

"And how in the hell did you do that? Hmm?" He looked at Lila and Nick. "Why is it that the only way to tell the two of them from the two of you is the way you've styled your hair and the clothes you wear? Why are you twenty-four years older and look as though you're still in your twenties?"

"I control the tree of life," Lila said. "I have the power to grant immortality. But is that your top priority? Or is figuring out what the fuck we're going to do about the alien warship plummeting towards us a bit more pressing?"

He clenched his jaw and leaned back in his seat.

"Tonight, those of us up here will make public announcements with all the governments around the world," Nick said. "We're going to validate the videos that were leaked two days ago and tell the people what we've told you and what we plan to do about it."

"Two days from now, we open portals all around the world to my realm," Avery said.

"Then we encourage the human population to move through

them," Lila said. "The portals will stay open for two weeks until Wormwood touches down. During that time, hell is going to break loose. Unfortunately, only a few million will pass though the portals until they see for themselves what is about to happen. We'll be on the front lines trying to save as many people as we can, but we're talking full on apocalypse here. A lot of people are going to die before the people are afraid enough to start a new life on another world."

"And how do your people feel about this?" Janis asked Avery. "Surely, they aren't happy about the humans joining them."

Avery pressed her lips together. "No, they are not. But our lands are vast. The humans will have their place and the Fae will have theirs."

It made sense. Most Fae didn't give a shit about humans. They looked down on them, in fact. Yeah, it was shitty. But this was—hopefully—a temporary solution until the war was over. A time would come when they'd return to earth and the Fae would have their lands back.

"Segregation. That's what you're proposing," Roland said.

"Unfortunately, it's the only way we can keep them safe for the time being," Avery said.

"It is not ideal," Asher said. "But it is better than Wormwood decimating the human race."

"It is also necessary in terms of illness," Avery said. "We have few viruses circulating our land. Humans have many. If we expose our people with very minute immune systems to all of those illnesses, we'll be fighting a pandemic. So unfortunately, this is how it must be."

"Look, we get that a lot of the humans aren't going to be happy about this," Nick said. "But we have to do what we have to do. And currently, this is our best course of action."

"The Open Lands, that's the Americas proportionally speaking, correct?" Papy asked.

"Aye," Avery said. "Our queendom is about midway between the North and the South. Our northern regions are rather desolate, that's where the portals will deliver the people to."

So where we lived. Canada too. Northern North America. Colder than where we'd visited in the Fae Realm, but still, safer than anywhere on our world would be soon.

It was a lot of land. Proportionally, the capitol of the Open Lands was somewhere near the Bahamas in America. Most everywhere north of there was empty. People would still be close together, but that was still a fair bit of open territory. One that was rich in resources. With the help of some Terra Firma Fae, they could have plentiful crops and plenty of access to clean water.

Also, the Open Lands weren't involved with the wars on that dimension. It was the safest place in all of the worlds for them.

He rubbed his jaw. "It should work. At the very least, keep a vast population of the humans alive while we fight the threats here on earth. That is the plan then, I am assuming. The humans go through, and the supernatural races stay here to fight what's to come."

"Those capable of fighting," Nick said. "And those who choose to stay. We're not forcing anyone to fight."

"Great." Eric stood. "I'll be going to the other realm then."

"All that bitching just so you can run? You aren't going to stand beside your people?"

"Oh, I certainly am. And I'll encourage them to pass through with me."

"Child." Roland rolled his eyes. "I'll inform the other alphas, Laila. We're territorial. We won't surrender our land without a fight."

"Neither will ours." Audrey licked the fangs that had involuntarily fell from her gums. "Not like we'd be welcome in the Fae Realm anyway. But yes, I'm sure my people will feel the same. As we've said before, we stand with your alliance."

"As do we," Elijah murmured. "Our children will not participate in this fight, however. Those under aged will be going to the realm."

Dayo rubbed her temples. "I'll convey the message to the other covens in my regions and to those without leaders. I will stay, but I cannot make promises for my race as a whole."

"Thank you," Lila said. "As for the rest of you, make your decisions. But regardless, the announcement will be made this evening. Decide what you plan to do in that time. And enjoy the time you have left."

"One thing first," Papy murmured. "What type of war will this be?"

Nick turned his gaze downward. "It'll be hell on earth. Put it that way."

"But what does that mean?"

"Primarily natural disaster to start," Nick said. "That's what's coming later this week. Wormwood isn't without physical abilities either, so the type of battle we're used to fighting. In addition to just about every awful thing you can imagine."

"Lovely," Papy muttered. "Just lovely."

As the room got quiet, I pushed my chair back and stood. Laila glanced up at me before doing the same.

"And where are you going?" Blair asked.

"Home," I said. "Can't really go anywhere else since a video of me bringing my wife back from the dead is trending all over the internet."

"We still have—" Eric began.

"I'm not needed here. My kids are waking up soon, and they do need me. So if you'll excuse me."

"Jeremy, could I—" Heylel started.

"And I *really* don't need anything from you," I snapped. I turned to Laila. "I'll see you back at the house."

She slid a hand down my arm and gave a nod.

"I'd like a word before you leave." Papy stood.

"Talk to him." I gesturing to Nick. "It's been a couple decades, I'm sure he's missed you."

CHAPTER THIRTEEN

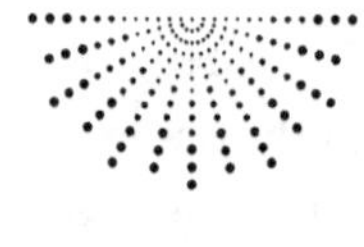

LAILA

"So what do we do now?" Blair said as Jeremy disappeared.

"You go back to your clans and spread the word." Nick brought himself to his feet.

"Be ready." Lila stood. "Six days from now, it begins."

"How?" Papy asked.

"Every major city in the world is going to be under attack," Leah answered. "You can't protect the land, but save the lives that you can."

"Yes, you said that. But *how?*" Papy's voice was edged with annoyance, slight curl touching his lips. "What comes first?"

"Natural disasters," Lila said. "My children and I are going to do the best we can to stop the largest of them. Dulling earthquakes as they begin, slowing tsunamis for the one's we can't. Then the projectiles come."

"Projectiles," Eric said. "What do you mean projectiles?"

"Asteroid isn't the right word," Nick said. "But that's the closest I can get to describing them."

My stomach sunk. Papy leaned back in his seat. Some stared vacantly with wide eyes, others gazed down at the table with unblinking stares.

Lila met my gaze. "That's about everything we have for you. We don't know what happens after they touch down. That's when we went back in time. But for the next two weeks, the world's going to be in turmoil. Natural disasters, things falling from the sky. That's about all we've seen. Sounds simple put like that but things get bad fast. A lot of pain and a lot of death. So... do your best to emotionally prepare for that."

"And make sure you buy the essentials. I'd do that now, actually. Before we make the announcement tonight and everybody rushes to the store to stock up on toilet paper," Nick said.

I stared down at the table for a moment as the others began shuffling from the room. Images of asteroids flying through the atmosphere flashed behind my eyelids. *The stars will fall from the sky,* that's what the Bible said. But for some reason, I never really thought of the logistics there. I never pondered what that would actually look like.

A war ground. That's what we'd see. The world we loved burning. And the people burning with it.

Destruction. Pain. Death.

"Laila." Lila's hand grazed my shoulder. "Can I talk to you?"

Lila turned her gaze up at the cool blue sky. My eyes moved over her, blinking hard as I took her in. People always say you don't actually know what you look like. You see yourself in pictures, you hear your voice in your own ears, but you never really know how others see you. But now I had. And although I'd never had any major self-esteem issues, I realized I'd still been far too hard on myself.

The scars that stood out so prominently when I looked in a mirror were almost unnoticeable on her. You only saw them if you were searching for them. The ink pricked over top was what really stood out.

I never liked my hair color. It always seemed so boring. Brown. The color of dirt and shit. But on her, I saw the thin highlights of red throughout and undertones of near black.

Like most girls in modern America, I criticized my body far more than necessary. I thought my hips were too small and my shoulders were too wide. But they weren't. Not to say that I had a "perfect body," but there wasn't anything wrong with it. She was normal. Her waist wasn't incredibly narrow, her ass was far from voluptuous, and her stomach wasn't flat. But she was beautiful. Not in a supermodel, look how gorgeous I am, sort of way. In a normal way.

As she turned to meet my gaze, I took in her features. I let her smile really sink in. I'd never realized how pretty it was. Jeremy always said my smile could light up a dark room, and I saw that in her. It was infectious.

Still, her beauty was simple. Sweet and soft, like a fairy in a cartoon. Round face, saucer shaped green eyes, and full, soft pink lips.

"How are you doing?" she asked. "With processing everything, I mean."

"You should know that, shouldn't you?" I cocked my head to the side a bit. "You're me. You remember this conversation, don't you?"

She laughed. Her gaze turned to the vineyard. "Yeah, I guess I do. Kind of blends into the noise these days though, ya know? A lot's happened since I was you. I was a different person then. Now, I guess" —she laughed again— "time travel's confusing."

"No shit." My teeth clamped on my bottom lip as I thought. I cleared my throat. "I know you said you tried to stop a lot of things but couldn't. But how hard did you try? Did you... did you do everything you could?"

She lifted hair behind her ear. "Yeah, I did. I like to think I did, anyway. But the thing about time is that if you change too many small details, if you take the wrong lives, if you save the wrong lives, you prevent things that are more important. Or someone else dies in their place only to come to the same end."

"What do you mean?" I asked.

She turned her gaze to the ground. "Think about Martin Luther King Junior. Imagine I went back and pushed him away from the bullet that ended his life. If I had, the riots that followed his assassination wouldn't have taken place. We wouldn't have a day celebrating his life each year, and all the people who found strength and fire because of his murder wouldn't have found that same determination."

I said, "So what you're saying is that the impact his death made was more important than his life."

She was quiet for a long moment. "That's not what I'm saying at all. I'm saying that time is complicated. The impact he made in history is a fixed point in the timeline, like the birth of Albert Einstein. Or like Hitler's rise and fall. And the HIV outbreaks, and the coronavirus pandemic. These things are going to happen regardless of what we do. It's almost as if they *have* to happen. And if you try to prevent it, someone or something else will stand in its place and hold the same level of notoriety and ultimately face the same end." I made a face. "Think about it this way. We could handle the murder hornets, but we couldn't stop the pandemic. Some things can be changed, and some things can't. It's complicated. We may be gods, but we can't control everything. It isn't always our will be done."

I scoffed and licked my teeth. "No, it's always *his* will be done."

She was silent again, gaze in the distance. "Guess that's how it works when you're the God of time."

"That's his title?"

"Not really. He has no title. But that's what I've grown to call him. Among other less friendly terms," she said. "That's how he hides from us. That's how he makes our lives hell. My ability over time is limited but his is omniscient. He can move either direction he wants in any multiple of time. I can only move in multiples of twelve. Twelve hours, twelve days, twelve months, twelve years. If I'm careful, if I do it by myself, I can fiddle with it a bit. I've got some wiggle room. But not like he does. You'll see what I mean in a few years."

"You haven't seen him since he was in Peterson then?" I asked.

"No, I have. But he's a smart little fucker." She paused. "It doesn't really matter though. Bigger fish to fry at the moment."

"Sure," I muttered.

She turned and looked over me carefully. "It's going to be okay, you know. For a while, anyway. For you."

I turned my eyes toward the ground. "Clearly. You're here, so yeah,

I guess things will be alright for a while." I felt her gaze on me but kept my eyes locked on the small puddle by my feet. "I heard their points. Chris and Leah, I mean. I get why you kept it from them. But all those years, all those questions we had. Why didn't you just come to us? Why didn't you tell me? I really... I didn't know if Micah would make it. I didn't know if *I* would make it. Why didn't you at least tell *me*?"

"I did." I looked up in confusion. She smiled. "That day in the hospital. When you got out of captivity. I came to you in that dream. I reminded you what you were fighting for."

Damn. She had. She told me I had to get up, that I had to keep fighting. That I would get the life I craved so badly. That if I gave up, I wouldn't get to be a mother and a wife. But that I had to get up.

"Shit, I forgot about that."

She smiled. "Nick came to Jeremy too. After our dumb ass decided to jump off a cliff while we were pregnant with Milly."

"It was either jump or die. I stand by that decision."

"Almost killed our girl in the process," she muttered. "Granted, he went a little overboard locking you in the basement and everything. But if he hadn't gone to him that day, you would have gotten even more reckless. You would have kept looking and fighting for Micah, and you may have lost Milly in the process. We helped when you really needed us. But this was your story. You had to live it. You had to learn from it. And you have more to live and more to learn before you're ready to face this fight. Your babies have more to live and more to learn."

"I'm grateful for that. That they don't have to grow up during this."

"So are they. Now, anyway," she muttered.

I wouldn't understand what she meant about that last part for a very long time.

We grew quiet for a moment. I rubbed a hand against my tense jaw. "So this whole thing. The time travel thing. That's how we become immortal."

"It is."

"And that's how Avery and Asher appeared back in time in the Fae realm as adults even though they disappeared as children and reap-peared three years later."

That had to be it. Avery grew up on Earth. Then when she was old enough, Lila sent her back in time with immortality. That was why she hadn't aged.

She smiled, head cocking to the side a bit. "Figured that one out all on your own."

"Kai told me that she disappeared and came back a few years later fully grown. I saw her here today and it clicked, I guess."

"To make a long story short, yes," Lila said. "That's what happened."

"We've got one complicated story, don't we?"

"We sure do," she muttered.

"So this is why you asked to talk to me? Just to bullshit?"

"No," I said. "No, I wanted to let you know that you're meeting them tomorrow. The kids, I mean. They're going to be helping us with everything when shit hits the fan. It's better you meet them formally before you see them on some newscast stopping a tsunami or dulling the power of a hurricane."

I'd known that was coming because that's what she had told me yesterday. But it was still a little... odd. In a way, I was excited about it. In another, I was nervous.

"Oh. Right. Sure," I said.

She paused, looking over me for a moment. "And I wanted to tell you to keep an eye on Jeremy. He gets through this. You saw Nick, you saw the two of us together. We really can make it through just about anything. But he just...just watch him. Be there for him."

I stared at her concerned green gaze. "I'm trying. But you know how he is. He has a lot of feelings, and when they're good, he's more than happy to talk about them. But when they're not—"

"He's quieter than a meditating monk. I know. Just be there for him. He won't say it, but he needs you. I know you need him too. But right now, he needs you more."

CHAPTER FOURTEEN

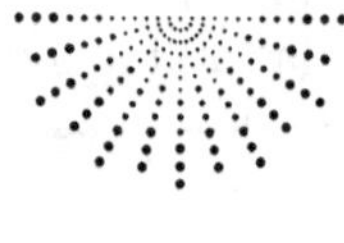

JEREMY

When I got home and the sun still hadn't risen, I realized it was only 6:15. Made sense since the meeting was at five in our time zone. The kids were still asleep, and Chris was pouring a cup of coffee.

As I poured myself a glass, he asked how it went. I responded with a vague shrug and an awkward "It went." I walked to the bedroom to roll a joint. I just wanted to relax. A cup of coffee and a bit of weed usually did the trick.

But I went into the drawer beside my bed and found an empty baggy. I remembered that I bought a bag off of Max at the New Year's show at the diner. I walked around with it in my pocket for a while before Laila smelled it, smacked me in the chest, and told me to leave it upstairs in Adam's apartment.

I asked Chris if he could keep an ear out for the kids until I got back. He said sure. So I teleported to the office, thinking nothing of it. I'd grab my stash, go home, roll a joint, and calm down a little before the kids woke up.

I landed in the office. As I pushed open the door, a cool brush of wind whooshed past me. My first thought was that the heater was on the fritz again. It was an old building; we had issues like that from time to time. But I heard the wind and the flap of flyers that hung on the walls.

I started toward the dining area. As I pushed open the chilled swinging steel door, my stomach dropped.

The five large windows above the booths by the doors were now mere holes in the walls. Thousands of shards of glass laid over the tables and benches creating a blanket like the one of snow outside. A dark red brick sat in the middle of one, a few more were perched on the floor.

Suddenly a joint was the last thing on my mind. Now I was trying to figure out a way to put in five new large glass windows before Laila saw her pride and joy had been vandalized. But that wasn't possible.

I couldn't. I couldn't even walk down the street to the local department store and grab a few sheets of plywood. People would see me. We lived in a small town; everyone knew me. They'd recognize me, and when they did, I didn't know what would happen.

So I teleported to the basement, grabbed my drill from the boiler room, and started searching for miscellaneous items I could cover the openings with. We had two announcement boards down there. Each one would cover a window. Another two hung upstairs in the dining area and one more in the back where the staff hung their jackets.

I unscrewed each and struggled them out the front door. It wasn't until I leaned the first one against the wall as I scrambled for screws that I looked up at the building. Then my heart practically stopped.

Broken windows was one thing. But what could I say? Sticks and stones may damage my property, but hateful words painted on the front of our business felt like a knife to my gut.

Monsters Work Here

My eyes stung with tears, and my chest grew heavy.

This place was everything to Laila. Besides me and the kids, I don't think anything else mattered as much to her. When she saw it, it'd devastate her. Moe left her this place for that very reason, because no one loved it as much as the two of them.

A good portion of her childhood took place behind those broken windows. It was the setting for at least a quarter of our love story. It was where I picked her up for our first date, it was where she told me she was pregnant with Micah, it was the only place she wanted to be after she was kidnapped, it was our home for two years, and it was the place where we got back together after many months apart.

Moe's may have meant more to Laila than it did to me, but it was still the only place that felt like my home outside of our property. Working there is where I learned to be a man. It was the only job I'd ever had aside from a few contracting gigs and fixing broken down cars.

And some asshole destroyed it. Then slandered us.

With cold, shaking finger and a pit in my stomach, I struggled each piece of painted plywood over the holes. It would've been a lot easier with an extra set of hands, but I had to get it done before Laila saw. Or before some little fucker climbed in and stole all of Adam and Jenna's shit, not to mention all of our equipment downstairs. Although, I guess that didn't matter much since the world was ending. Good amps and mic stands weren't exactly a top priority in an apocalypse.

When I finished, I went inside. I scoured the building for other items I could use to cover the rest of the windows, or at least the ones on the first floor. I found a few pieces of scrap wood from the remodel tucked away in the boiler room downstairs. They weren't weatherized, but it was something. At least it'd keep the snow out.

I got the other pieces of wood up and locked the door. I swept up the broken glass and dumped the shards into contractor bags. A heavy breath left my lips as I sat down at the bar. I did what I'd been avoiding since it all started.

I checked my social media.

Laila and I had both been tagged in the videos a thousand times. I had over four hundred notifications, including messages from over fifty news stations and reporters. But telling who was a journalist wasn't exactly easy since I had over two hundred message requests on Facebook alone.

Growing up, everyone talked about it.

You can't risk exposure. Humans don't understand us, and when humans don't understand something, they attack. They'll destroy you. They'll insult you, they'll berate you, they'll threaten you. You can never risk exposure, Jeremy.

That's what Annie said when she bailed me out of jail for freeing a bunch of animals in a testing facility. I argued. I told her what I'd done was right, and she'd never be able to convince me otherwise. She said that I wasn't wrong. But those animals' lives weren't worth risking our entire community. Again, I argued. But now I get it.

They called us every name in the book. I won't waste time going over all of them. But to list a few; demons, aliens, disgusting, trash, evil, despicable, heinous, even witches.

Comments like *Burn them at the stake.* Another read *They don't deserve to share the air I breathe. Kill them all. Rape them like that dude did while you're at it.* And *We better get these freaks in line before they take over.* A few said things like *I knew new world order was coming, this is just the beginning. I bet these animals have been voting in our elections too.*

Oh, yeah, it got political. As if the fact that we had abilities somehow negated our right to take part in choosing our world leaders.

But the worst part? They weren't just strangers saying shit like that. Some were our regular customers. Many were friends from high school.

I'd love to say that I 'acted like a man' and got pissed about those posts. But truth be told? My heart broke.

I bawled. I teleported to the bathroom and vomited into the toilet, I sat down on the frozen seat and shit my brains out. I kept telling myself that I had to breathe, but it felt like someone was sitting on my chest and my throat was sealing shut. My legs trembled, and I broke out in a cold sweat.

It was official. I'd known shit was never going to be the same again. But now I realized why I had to joyously accept what was happening.

Jeremy Skoulda—respected business owner, happy husband, and father of two—was gone. Not like I had a choice in the matter anyway, but it was inevitable now. The only chance of having any life worth living was going back to a time long before this.

CHAPTER FIFTEEN

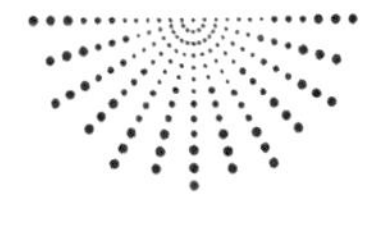

LAILA

I landed in the kitchen and raised my hand to rub my tired eyes. The scent of coffee drifted into my nostrils as I flicked on the light switch above the sink. Tink trotted down the steps, ran to me, and jumped up so her paws rested against my chest.

A heavy feeling sunk over me. I forgot to ask Lila about Tink. I leaned my face down to hers and breathed in her messy odor.

I couldn't leave her behind. I *wouldn't* leave her behind. If I had to strap her to my shoulders like a backpack, then that's what I would do.

"Oh, hey. You're back," Chris said as he walked down the steps with Milly on his hip. "How was it?"

"Weird," I muttered. Tink plopped back to all fours. I turned to pour myself a cup of coffee. "Where's Jeremy?"

"He said he had to run to the diner. Well, teleport, I guess. Can't really get out any other way." He set Milly in her highchair.

I glanced at him. "What do you mean?"

"You haven't been down to the perimeter?" he asked.

I shook my head.

"It's a shitshow. A bunch of reporters, a couple cops. I told Ray when you and Jeremy got back, I'd teleport him to the bank because there's no way out. Couple of the fuckers tried climbing the gate. Then they hit an invisible wall. It's on the news and everything." He frowned. "Never thought I'd see the day. Everyone always talked about mass exposure, but it just... I never thought it'd actually happen, ya know?"

My heart slammed against my rib cage. I stared at the coffee in my cup. "What do they want?"

"The reporters?"

I nodded.

"You. Me. Jeremy, Micah. They want to hear what we have to say. They want our recollection of our time in captivity. I think they want us to confirm or deny what happened in those videos. And I'm pretty sure the cops want to put you in cuffs. That's what everyone on the internet is calling for, anyway."

Like I'd said before, I could handle the berating. But it still stung. I'd spent all of my adult life protecting humanity. I'd tried to do the right thing at every opportunity I encountered. Yes, I'd done awful things. But always in the name of good.

And now, they all hated me.

But that was why I didn't check my phone. Hearing it told and seeing it shown were two very different things. I could do without the details.

"Wonderful," I murmured. "Well, thank God for Helena. One boss ass perimeter spell."

"Yeah, we'd be fucked without it." Chris sat at the bar. "It's so surreal. Everyone always talked about what would happen if we were exposed. And don't get me wrong, I listened and did as I was told. But I don't get it. They saw him torturing us. Beating us, whipping us. You were pregnant. And they saw that too. Yet it's your head they want on a spike?" He sipped his coffee. "It's fucked up. Yeah, you defended your-self. But you begged them to stop first. I just can't believe it. Humani-ty's cruel."

"They're scared. They just want to feel safe. Seeing that people like us exist is a pretty bitter pill." I walked to Milly in her highchair and lifted her sleepy body to my hip. "It's not like it matters. We're leaving soon. And so are they. Then they'll have to accept it regardless of how they feel."

"True," he said. "So what happened at that meeting?"

"A lot of finger pointing. They should have told us sooner, we should have had more time. Then you chimed in. Older you."

His eyes widened a bit. "Really?"

"Really really," I said. "Told 'em they wouldn't have wanted to know. Living life knowing when it ends is worse than anyone can imagine. You were hot though. Muscly. You grew your hair out. You had a long ass braid to the middle of your back. It looked pretty good actually, very hipster."

He laughed. "Wonder if I'll get to meet him."

"Probably," I muttered. "Having a conversation with yourself is some shit though."

"I bet it's cool." He thought for a moment. "Hey, ya know what just popped into my head?"

"No. What?"

"So if you have sex with your older self, does that count as sex? Or is it masturbation?"

I laughed. "I hate you."

"It's a legitimate question. And like, if you were to fuck the older Jeremy, or vice versa, would that be cheating? Because technically, that is your husband. Just another version of him. And—"

"I'm going to go with yes, Chris." I struggled to pull down my unwilling smile. "You perv."

He laughed. "It's not like I actually want to or that I think you should. It's just philosophical, you know?"

"So you wouldn't want to bang yourself?"

"I'm a top. He's probably also a top," he said. "Wouldn't really work. What about you?"

"Nah. Too close for comfort. We share the same DNA. That's like screwing a sibling."

"Ew." His nose curled. "I didn't think about that."

I nodded, laughing.

A sudden ache in my stomach cut me off. My hand lifted to cover my mouth as the sting of acid burned up my esophagus.

"What is it?" Chris asked. "Something wrong?"

"No, just a little nauseous. I'm good." I cleared my throat and glanced upstairs. "So Micah's still sleeping?"

"Yeah, he's out cold. I figured I'd let him sleep in."

"It's early still. He'll probably be asleep for another hour. Wonder why she's up." I gestured to Milly against my chest.

"I don't think she wants to be." He glanced over her and sipped his coffee. "She was crying so I grabbed her. I think she had a bad dream or something."

I turned down to her dopey eyes. "Did you, baby? Did you have a bad dream?"

She nuzzled her head closer to my shoulder.

"She is teething. Might just be feeling crappy."

Another sharp pain stabbed my abdomen. I lurched forward a bit, brows furrowing. Images of a bathroom stall at Moe's flickered in my mind.

"Speaking of feeling crappy, I think something's going on with Jeremy," I muttered. "Here, can you take her?"

"Sure." He stood and walked around the island.

As I passed Milly his way, she turned to me with sad, watery eyes, arms outstretched. "Mommy. Mommy, no. You stay."

"I'm just running to the diner to get Daddy. I'll be back in a couple minutes." I smiled and brushed brown hair behind her ear. "Uncle Chris is here, it's alright."

Her eyes filled with water. "It's scawy out thewe. You stay hewe. It's safe hewe, you stay hewe."

My gaze softened.

I guess that was the first moment that I realized she was listening. Micah paid attention to every word we spoke and had some spunky rhetoric for every conversation. But Milly always seemed to be in her own world.

She didn't talk half as much as Micah did at her age, so I thought she didn't understand yet. I thought grown-up conversations went in one ear and out the other. And most of them probably did. But in that moment, I realized how much tension had been floating around our home in the past couple days. She surely felt it.

"Mommy's safe anywhere." I looked between her eyes and lifted her little fist to my lips. "I promise, I'll be just fine. No one can hurt me."

Her lip quivered. "You suwe?"

"I'm sure. I'll be back soon. You be good for Uncle Chris, alright? Maybe lie down on the couch and take a little nap?"

She rested her head against his chest.

I tightened my sweater around my hips as I landed in the office. It was dark, way darker than usual. There were a million windows scattered from the dining area to the kitchen and office. It was never dark, even when the power was out. The cold air brushed against my nose as I flicked on the light switch.

"Baby." I stepped into the kitchen. "Jeremy, are you here?"

"Don't go out there." He hurried into the kitchen from the staff bathroom. His long black hair stuck to his clammy jaw. The soft white of his cheeks had faded to a sickly, bluish color. He hastily buttoned his pants with shaking hands as he took a few steps toward me.

I walked to him and put a hand on his shoulder. "Are you alright? I felt your stomach doing something, are you getting sick?"

He raised his palm to his cheek, pushing hair from his sweaty face. "No. No, I think I had a panic attack."

My head turned to the side. "What's the matter?"

Jeremy took a few steps toward the office and leaned against the threshold. "I, uh. I left my weed here the other day. And after that meeting, I really wanted to smoke a joint, you know? So I came here to grab it and—" He paused again, blinking hard and turning his gaze downward. "Well, it's cold. So I thought maybe the furnace was fucking up again. But I went out there." He gesturing to the dining area on the other side of the swinging steel door. "And it's... it's a mess."

I stepped back into the doorway and leaned against the opposite support next to the door. "What do you mean?"

His eyes filled with tears. He ran his tongue along his lips and cleared his throat once more. "They... the building... someone... They threw bricks through the windows, they spray painted 'monsters work here' on the front. I can't go to the department store without being recognized so I couldn't get new windows to put up, so I took the announcement boards down and screwed them over the holes. And the other windows, the one's that weren't destroyed. I tried to get up all the glass but—you have shoes on, right?" He glanced down, speaking fast. "Good. Good. I—I wanted to get it cleaned up before you saw it. I did what I could but—but we need new windows on the whole front of the building. I think there's some paint around here somewhere; I might be able to get a coat on real quick. It's so cold out though, I don't know if it'll dry."

Don't get me wrong, I wasn't happy to hear that my business had been vandalized. But that was the last thing on my mind at the moment. I was worried about *him*. The way he struggled to go on, speaking so fast, blinking hard, rubbing his hand against his messy scruff.

I touched his biceps, feeling the tense muscles beneath my fingertips. "Baby, it's okay. Just take a deep breath."

He rubbed his forehead and met my gaze. "I'm sorry. I'm so sorry. I know how much this place means to you and I—"

"It's a diner, Jeremy." I leaned forward and pushed hair behind his ear. "And the world's about to end. Restaurants aren't going to be open much longer. I'm not concerned about some vandalism right now."

His eyes got redder as they filled with tears. "I don't want this place to burn. This was our home. And they just—they butchered it. They destroyed it, and we didn't even do anything. We didn't hurt anyone. I mean, you did when you killed those people, but they were torturing you. You were pregnant with our son. They had you tied down, they were ripping you apart. That piece of shit forced himself inside you and these people saw it. They saw it all and they..." His eyes filled with tears. "Why do they care more about those fuckers than you?" His lips quivered. He pressed them together, wiping his hand against his cheek and shaking his head. "It's so fucked up. They were our friends. They were our customers. We served them, we cared about them. And the moment they realized you were different, they got the pitchforks ready."

I pushed hair behind his ear and searched his gaze. "Who did?"

He turned his eyes to the ground. His hand raised to wipe snot from his nose. "I know I told you not to check your social media, and I wasn't going to either. But I saw this and I... I had to see what people were saying. And they're awful. They're *awful.* People we went to school with, customers we know by name—the things they're saying about us, even things they're saying about our kids..." His lip quivered. He raised his hands to his cheeks, massaging his eyes to rub the wetness away.

I didn't know what to say. I'd never seen Jeremy like this. He'd broken down a time or two, but never to this point where he couldn't recollect himself.

And I was grateful he was being honest about how he felt. So incredibly grateful because I knew what happened when he kept it inside. But I didn't know what to say either. There was no solution I could propose to this.

I placed my hands on his shoulders as his arms fell to his sides.

"I don't know how to do this. I don't know how to get through this. We're losing everything. Everything we worked for is just going to be gone. We have to start over with nothing, and I—I don't know how. I don't know how to be okay with this. I'm not, I'm not okay. We worked so hard for this life. We tried to do everything right. We—we try to be good employers, and we try to be good parents, and we try to be good people, and It all just gets ripped away from us when we did nothing wrong. We did nothing wrong, Laila." His lips pouted forward, water spilling down his cheeks into his beard. "All we ever did was try to be good and kind, and this is how we get repaid. We're the people trying to save them, and they're slapping us in the face. They hate us. The world hates us. And I don't know how to get through this. I don't know how to be okay—"

I leaned onto the tips of my toes and pushed my lips to his. My hands made their way to either side of his face, cupping his jaw in my palms. His hands found my cheeks as he pressed his lips closer to mine. I leaned back and touched my forehead to his. "You lean on me. That's how you get through this. You let me help you. When I lost our son, you were my rock. You were there for me when I needed you—"

"Barely," he muttered. "I lied to you and got high and—"

"But you were still there for me," I whispered. "And I'm here, baby, I'm here. You lean on me. I'll carry *you* this time." His watery eyes moved between mine. "No matter what, you have me. And you have our babies, and our brothers and sisters, and no one can ever take that from us. We have each other. That's how we get through this. We're starting over, and it's bullshit, but we can do this. We can make it through this. We *will* make it through this.

"Some days are going to be harder than others, but we come out on the other end. If the weight's too much to carry, give it to me, and I will. You don't have to be strong all the time. You don't have to carry the weight of the entire world. Give it to me. Let me be the one to be scared and worried sometimes. Some days I can handle it better than you, and that's okay. But you have to let me help you. Don't try and do it all on your own. Let me help. I can help, but only if you let me. You have to tell me; you have to let me be here for you. That's how we get through this. Together. Sometimes it's fifty-fifty, sometimes it's ninety-ten, and that's okay. I'm sure a day's going to come when I need you more than you need me, but if you need me right now, I'm here. I'm here, okay?"

A soft, sad smile pulled at his lips. He gave a fast nod and pushed his lips to mine. He held my face in his hands, and I did the same with his. Eyes closed, he rested his forehead against mine. "I love you."

"I love you more," I said gently. His arms twisted around my back, and he pulled me into his chest. I tightened my arms at his waist, resting my head against him.

CHAPTER SIXTEEN

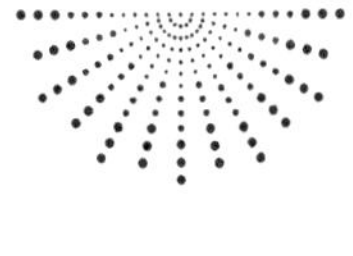

JEREMY

We stood in the office doorway holding one another for a while. It gave me reassurance. But it wasn't one of those moments where the rest of the world faded away. It just numbed the pain a little.

After a while, I splashed some water on my face, grabbed that bag of weed, took Laila's hand, and went home. Before we left though, she told me about what Milly said. That she was worried about Laila leaving. And about the slew of reporters on the edge of our property caging us inside.

I pondered what that must have sounded like to a two-year-old. How scary that must have been. To hear her uncle tell her mother about how those people wanted her head on a spike.

That's when it occurred to me how deeply we had to shelter them from it. From all of it. The apocalypse, the reality of who we were and of what we'd done. They didn't need to know where Laila's scars came from or what she did to make it home. They didn't deserve to grow up living in fear.

All they needed to know was that we'd keep them safe. So Laila pushed that memory to the far cavern of our daughter's mind. She seemed back to her normal self.

We ate breakfast at the large table. I told Micah to put on his snow suit and dressed Milly in hers. Laila laughed, threw on some snow boots, and tugged on her winter coat.

The four of us headed up to the only cleared hillside on our property, far from the perimeter, where my dad had taken us as kids on snowy days. We took turns sledding down the icy mountain.

Maybe it was a bit irresponsible to play and have fun with my kids when the world was about to blow up. But they needed that time. And so did I. I was a father first. Everything else came after. If I couldn't be there for them, if I couldn't have fun with them, I couldn't care less about everything else.

Afterward, we went back to the house and drank hot chocolate with our lunch. Laila's mom joined us, as she did every moment we were at home in the coming ten days. I struggled not to think about the reality we were living in and tried to focus on them. My smiling son, my feisty daughter, my beautiful wife.

They were all that mattered to me. At least, that's what I thought. Until I lived through what came a few days later.

Laila and Rachel spent some time together on the back porch as I sat inside with the kids after dinner. Milly was tucked against my hip, and Micah's head rested in my lap, watching *Spongebob* on the TV. At least that'd still be around when we went back.

When that thought crossed my mind, so did a million others. Would they recognize the difference? A lot was different, but a lot wasn't, at least from a child's perspective. *Toy Story* existed. Just the first two, I guessed. They watched all of them, but *Toy Story 3* was their favorite. I wondered if we'd be able to pull one over on them. Lie and say "this *is* that movie" when they watched one and two. I didn't know though; Milly's mean little ass loved that Lot's-o'-huggin' bear. I didn't think she'd forget it quickly.

The biggest thing with the kids would be the cultural references.

Luckily though, they watched a lot of the movies and TV shows we did as kids thanks to all the reboots. But overall, the world wasn't *that* much different in 2000. Convincing them that we didn't move back in time wouldn't be all that difficult. It wasn't like they knew the year. We still had cars and air conditioning. Amazon had already been up and running for a few years. Not to the capacity it was at in 2024, but it existed.

Cell phones were a lot different though. We wouldn't be passing Milly an episode of *Hobby Kids* on a long drive again. Hell, Bluetooth didn't even exist yet. Or maybe it did but the general public didn't use it.

Damn, we wouldn't have GPSs on our phones either. We'd have to read a map. I wasn't sure I even knew *how* to read a map.

Fuck, I was gonna miss Grubhub and UberEats and Doordash. They were probably the best inventions of the twenty-first century. Granted, I could teleport, but being able to scroll through the options of different restaurants made life so much easier. Soon, we'd have to flip through a phonebook just to find the number to those places. Then we'd have to actually *find* said restaurants. With said map.

Laila's warm lips pressing against my cheek from behind pulled me from my thoughts. I leaned my head against the back of the couch, turning my gaze up toward hers. She smiled and pushed hair behind my ear. "Hey."

"Hey." I smiled back.

"What's going on in here?" She tapped her fingertip against my forehead.

"Just thinking."

"About?" she asked.

"The year 2000," I muttered. "Pre-nine-eleven, pre-coronavirus. Pre-smartphones. A whole other world." Her gaze moved over the kids before she cleared her throat. "How was your time with your mom?"

She shrugged, forcing a smile. "It was good. Always is."

I pressed my lips together and cleared my throat. "Have you checked the news?"

Her head lifted in a nod. "Leah just called. It's on. She paused it; they're waiting on us. Chris is already up there. Mom said she'll watch the kids."

CHAPTER SEVENTEEN

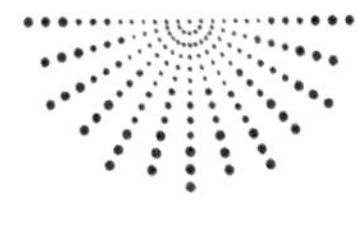

LAILA

When we landed in the living room at the main house, Leah immediately handed me a glass of whiskey. I turned toward the TV and an image of myself stared back at me. Lila, technically. But me. She sat in front of a black backdrop, hair pulled back into a neat, sophisticated bun.

She'd looked so calm, cool, and collected this morning. The day before as well. But I supposed that was her comfort zone. She knew who she was around and exactly what to expect. On that frozen screen though, there was no denying the heartbreak she felt. Her eyes glistened with water she wouldn't allow to escape, and her lips tugged downward at the ends.

I took a long gulp from the glass in my fist. I plopped to the armchair. "I'm ready when you are."

Jeremy sat on the armrest beside me and tucked an arm around my waist.

Leah chugged what remained in her cup. She sat beside Hannah on the couch, grabbed the remote off the table, and pressed play.

"Hello, people of Earth," Lila began. "My name's Laila Callidy. And yes, I'm the girl you saw in the videos that are circulating the internet.

Yes, I killed those men and women. Yes, that was my fat, pregnant ass threatening the man who raped me. And I'm sorry you had to see that. I'm sorry that's how you all see me now because that's not who I am.

"So who am I, you ask? Well, I'm not much different than you. I'm a daughter. I'm a mother. I'm a wife, and a sister, and a friend. I'm a business owner. I'm really a lot like you. I just have capabilities that most of you don't.

"Growing up, I didn't know what I was either. I had a normal life. I went to school. I played soccer. I worried if I'd get asked to the home-coming dance by the boy I liked. But when I was seventeen, that all changed.

"That's when I learned what I was. And I reacted a lot like how you all have reacted. I panicked. I thought that it couldn't be true. I screamed profanities, proclaiming that things like this don't exist. I was an atheist, believe it or not.

"Then a few years ticked by. And I gradually learned how incredibly wrong I was about every single thing I'd ever been taught. Everything I'd believed.

"Truth is, I know that I'm asking a lot of you. Seeing the videos you've seen, I don't blame you for being apprehensive. I don't blame you for being afraid. Hell, I don't even blame you for wanting me dead. But that isn't going to happen. Because it can't.

"I'm not saying that from a place of pride. I'm stating it as a fact. I cannot die. I wish I could. I wish I were like you; I wish my life were simple and ordinary. I wish that I weren't the one to carry this burden. But I am.

"I'm not going to go into the details of who I am and what makes me so important here. If I told you the whole story, we'd be here for hours. And you'd be even less apt to listen to what I have to say."

She pressed her lips together and took in a slow, deep breath. She carefully let it out.

"In eleven days, someone is coming here. And they don't care who any of us are. They don't care about our lives, or our children, or what we want. All they care about is taking back what's theirs. This planet, and your souls.

"Again, explaining the logistics would take way more time than we have here, so we aren't going there. Instead, I'm just going to tell you how this is going to go. And I'm begging you to listen. I'm begging you because I want you to live. I want your children to live. I want the human race to survive, but you won't if you don't listen.

"It will come in waves." She struggled to keep her tears inside of her eyes. "The first starts tomorrow. It'll begin with natural disasters. Tsunamis, earthquakes, hurricanes, tornadoes, volcanic eruptions. And we're going to do what we can to keep them at bay, but we won't be able to stop it all. People living on coasts and near volcanoes, get as far inland as you can. I'm begging you. We'll be there to move as many people out as we can, but if you can get out first, that'd be ideal because there are only so many of us. This is the only warning you're getting because I promise, the planet won't show the signs it usually does.

"Early next week, the second wave begins. That's when the comets are going to start plummeting toward earth. And when a projectile falls from space, it doesn't just leave a crater. It's like a bomb. That's how they plan to put the biggest dent in the population, killing hundreds of thousands of you at once.

"That's when it gets even more difficult because suddenly, our power grids collapse. And I'm afraid that then, the people will start to turn on each other when the dust settles from the first attacks. Looting, fighting amongst yourselves, taking your eyes off of what matters most. Survival. The paradox there is that so many of you will think that to survive, you have to fight one another. But what you fail to realize is that you have to help one another. We are not each other's enemy. They are *all* of our enemies."

Her eyes shifted back and forth between the camera.

"But there is a way to stay safe. There is a way to avoid all of this. But it's going to take a leap of faith. You have to trust me. And I know you don't know me, and I know you have no reason to, but at this point I'm literally begging you. Please. Please, listen to me."

The tears she'd been fighting overflowed from her bloodshot green eyes. Goosebumps erupted over my skin as a lump gathered in the back of my throat. Jeremy's arm tightened at my shoulder. I glanced up at him, seeing the water collecting in his eyes too. I leaned into him.

"Simultaneously, worldwide, portals to another world will open tonight. I know that sounds crazy, I do. And I know many of you won't believe me or even consider listening until it begins and your chances of actually getting out dwindle. But I'm begging you. Pack a bag. Load into your car. And travel to the closest portal near you. Yes, you can bring your dogs and cats. Snakes too, if that's your thing, but there won't be electricity where you're going so if it needs a heat lamp, I'm sorry but there's a good chance it won't make it.

"Every single person will survive if you listen. But only *if you listen.* If you don't, you'll be living through hell on earth. Until you aren't any more. And if you die, when you die, your soul won't go to heaven. Not hell either, but not heaven.

"But not if you take this leap of faith. Not if you believe in me. I will keep you safe if you let me, but you have to let me."

Jeremy's hand at my shoulder stiffened. Lila's teary eyes started drizzling large rivers of water down her cheeks. I felt my hands begin to quiver as I realized I was holding my breath.

"Please. Please, I'm begging you. Pack your bag and go through the portals. The longer you wait, the less chance you stand at surviving. They'll stay open until they touch down, but the moment they enter our atmosphere, I have no choice but to close them. If I don't, this war crosses over to our land of refuge."

Her lips started to quiver. She raised her palms and wiped the water from her cheeks. She cleared her throat.

"That's the last public announcement I'll be making. I won't have time to make another because I'll be a little busy trying to keep you alive. But please. Please, do as I've asked. This isn't about allegiance. This is about survival. You don't have to like me; you don't have to respect me. But I'm begging that you *believe* me. Because if you don't, you'll never forgive yourself."

Then the screen cut to a very confused reporter.

"Well, that was more enlightening than any of you have been since

I've arrived," Moriah muttered from her perch on the chair by the window. "When do we leave again?"

CHAPTER EIGHTEEN

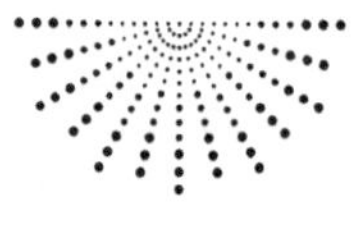

JEREMY

"Jesus Christ." Adam rubbed his fist against his eyes.

"I hate our lives," Leah muttered. "Have I ever mentioned how much I hate our lives?"

"Let it slip a time or two," Laila murmured.

"Why did this have to happen in our time?" She grabbed a joint from the table and sparked it at her lips. "Why couldn't this have happened when we were dead?"

"Because we would have been reincarnated and had to live through it either way," I muttered.

"We should start packing a bag for ourselves too," Brody said quietly from the corner. "Right? I mean, obviously we can't bring all of our belongings. But a backpack would be okay, wouldn't it?"

"I'd think," Laila said. "They had us get all that money together for a reason. They won't need it here, but we will."

"Yeah, but we'll have to carry it," I said. "So pack light. Over two mil cash isn't exactly small carry on."

"I think three briefcases." Leah massaged her temples. "Or one big duffle bag. I can carry it. I don't have much. I just need a couple things. Mom's ring, some pictures. Nothing too big."

"I won't have much either," Chris said. "I got pretty accustomed to living minimalistic."

"We should all get the belongings we want together and bring them back here," Laila said. "Hidden talent of mine, packing a lot of shit into a small space."

"That's what she said." Celena grinned.

Laila rolled her eyes. "You're a child."

"Indeed." She smiled. "But I hear you. I don't have much either. Living in a tiny house will do that for you."

"Me neither," Wyatt said. "Life of a wolf. I do got a couple things, though. Some stuff of my mom's I don't want to lose. Pictures, like Leah said, and a few random things. Think we could drop down to the house and take a look around, darlin'?"

"Yeah, sounds good. I should probably look around there too. Might be a thing or two I wanna grab," Celena said.

"Already said goodbye to my things." Moriah sighed. "I snuck some expensive jewelry into my bag before I left as well. I can sell it when we arrive."

"What about cash?" I asked. "Did you bring any?"

"Enough to get me started."

"You?" Leah arched a brow. "All of our money's going together so that we can *all* get started."

Moriah's eyes lifted a bit. "Darling, I made a deal with your sister a long time ago. I never offered my money to help you all start a new life."

My eyes rolled. She was a La Fay. I expected nothing less. But I didn't particularly want to live with her anyway. She could take her cash and do whatever she pleased. Two million was enough for my siblings and our children to start a life somewhere with a big piece of land that had room to grow.

"Are you serious?" Leah asked.

"As a heart attack," Moriah said. "Look, we had an agreement. I never went back on my end; I trust that Laila won't go back on hers."

"Well, I hope she leaves your greedy ass behind then—"

"Alright, stop it." Laila's fingers pressed into her droopy eyes. "Just like Lila said, turning on each other already. Anyone who doesn't want to contribute doesn't have to. That goes for all of us. If you do, great. We'll find a piece of land with a decent house and find some way to start a new life. But Moriah, if you don't want to chip in, you can find a place on your own and start your own life."

Moriah smiled and sat back in her seat. "I do appreciate a woman of her word."

"My money's going in the pot," Chris said.

"Me too," Brody said. "I don't have much, but I'll pitch what I do have."

"We've got nothing," Kai muttered.

"Yeah. All of my trust fund went to college and then the wedding. I might have a grand or two left," Hannah said.

"That's okay," I said. "We've got enough to buy a nice piece of land with a decent house."

"Shit," Hannah muttered, blinking fast. "Shit, I totally forgot about school. I only have a year and a half left, and now those five years are just going down the drain. What am I going to do? It's not like I can transfer credits from a time that doesn't exist."

"I can help with that," Moriah said. "I can't get you the degree, but I could conjure something up so you could pick up where you've left off."

"Really?"

Moriah crossed her arms against her chest. "It's like none of you know who I am at all."

"I just didn't know that was possible," Hannah muttered.

"Most anything's possible when you have a talented Witch, love," Moriah said.

I turned to Laila and put my hand on her shoulder. "Did you ask her about Tink?"

Her gaze fell to the floor. "No, I forgot. But we're bringing her, damn it. We're bringing her."

We'd better. I loved that psychotic mutt. We weren't leaving her behind. I wasn't sure I'd be able to bring Micah if we did.

"Jenna," Celena said softly.

She looked up from the fixed point on the floor her eyes were glued to. "Yeah?"

"When did you want to do it?" she asked. "The change, I mean."

"Oh. Oh, I don't know."

"Sooner is probably better than later," Leah said. "It isn't easy adjusting to the differences in your body afterward."

"Yeah, I know," Jenna muttered. "I... I don't know. A few days, I guess."

My heart went out to her. We were all going through something similar. But having to become a Werewolf in order to survive? That'd be awful. Especially considering women tended to have a harder time with the change, healthy and young or not.

But I'd make sure she pulled through. She was my sister in-law. If she didn't make it, I'd hold her soul in her body until the change was complete.

Adam moved a soothing hand over her shoulder before pulling her into him. I turned my gaze to the ground. "So we should probably start doing that then. Getting the things we want to bring together, I mean."

"Right," Leah muttered as she stood.

"Probably can't bring Dad's guitar, huh?" Chris said.

"Probably not."

"I'm bringing Mom's music box," Hannah said. "I know it's kind of big, but I'll leave everything else. I just—I have to have that music box."

"We'll make it work," Laila said.

"Start looking for bags, everyone," I said. "We have those hiking packs out in the garage, don't we?"

"Yeah, four of them, I think," Adam said. "We can fit a lot of shit in there."

"We've got a shit ton of duffels too," Leah said. "We'll put clothes in those and belongings in the backpacks. That way if we drop a bag, we don't lose our treasured objects in the vortex. Rather lose a few replace-able pairs of jeans than pictures of Mom."

"But just enough clothes for a few days," Laila said. "We can get new wardrobes once we've settled in."

"Sounds good."

"Ahem." I heard in the hallway. My gaze shifted over my shoulder. Ray stood with five suitcases and two duffle bags. "Someone's going to have to talk to Lydia because she doesn't want to leave anything behind. She says clothes in 2000 were hideous and she refuses to wear them."

"She isn't wrong," Leah muttered. "Ew, remember the jeans under a dress thing? What the hell was that?"

"Masculine femininity, I suppose," Mariah said. "I agree though, an awful time for fashion."

Laila smiled. "I'll talk to her in the morning. So you've decided then?"

"Not exactly thrilled about it. But better than the alternative."

"Depends on where you're standing," Brody murmured.

CHAPTER NINETEEN

LAILA

I stared at the photos hanging above the dresser in our bedroom. Deciding which ones to bring was so much harder than I imagined. We took so many photos in the last few years because we knew a time would come when our reality changed forever, and those frozen images would be all that we had left.

But I didn't realize then that I wouldn't always be able to look at all of those images. I thought I'd be able to look at any picture from any day and carry myself back to that moment. I thought those photos would give me strength on the bad days. I had no idea I'd have to pick which ones mattered most and which ones would be best left in another time.

The wedding photos were beautiful. All of them. The newborn photos of Milly hanging in the hallway upstairs had to come, and so did the one's of Micah from his fourth birthday. Those were the first professional photos I had taken just for him. I wish I had his baby pictures too, but the one picture I did have of him as a baby wasn't one I could frame and hang on the wall, given the situation with Chris's eyes at that time.

Oh, and Hannah's wedding. I couldn't forget those. Those were some of my favorite pictures of the kids. Micah in his tux, Milly in her flower girl dress. And the one with me and Jeremy side by side, each holding our mini-mes on our hips.

But still, I couldn't decide which ones to pack. Sure, they stacked up small, but I wished that I could take every single one of them. But as most people from my generation, I had thousands of photos that meant the world to me. And I could only fit so many in a backpack.

"Hey, hon." Mom gently tapped in the doorway. "Whatcha doing?"

I turned and forced a smile. My hand raised to wipe a tear from my cheek. "Trying to pick which pictures to bring with us."

Her lips vibrated in a trill. She walked across the room and sat at the foot of my bed beside me. "Well, back in the day, we only had a handful of pictures from special occasions. You know, the Christmas card pictures, the birthday shoots. Always had a lot more at weddings, of course, so you can go pretty heavy there. Maybe twenty? But if you want to pass as coming from that time, I'd say pick five from each special occasion and five from each special day."

I plopped beside her. My gaze traced over the photos from our trip to the Eiffel Tower almost two years ago with the kids. Then to the pictures of us at the Grand Canyon, and the Statue of Liberty. And the others, from everywhere else. The Redwood Forest, the Golden Gate Bridge, the Parthenon.

I rested my head against her shoulder. "They were all special days."

"I know." She pressed her lips to my hair. "But I'm sure you have a group picture of the four of you from each one, right? Just go with those. Don't worry about the one's where you look the best, just grab the one's that mean the most. I have a few photobooks you could take with you, too. There's ones of you and Jenna. And me and your dad when we were young. Oh, and Brownie. Remember Brownie?"

I smiled at the memory of my first dog. "Of course I remember Brownie."

"Well, I've got a bunch. Already put together in a neat little album. You can take them out though, so they're easier to carry and take up less room."

I shook my head and leaned it against hers. "That's okay, I'll keep the album. You always wrote in them. Cute little anecdotes about each picture and everything. I want to have those."

She smiled and kissed my hair once more. "Well, it's all yours then."

Mom gazed over the pictures as I looked at the two of us in the mirror. My head on her shoulder. A sad smile across her lips. The inevitable realization that soon, I wouldn't see her again for more than two decades.

"I'm going to miss this," I murmured.

She turned down to me. Her smile receded. "Me too, baby."

"It's not the same for you. For you, it'll be like we never left."

"Not really," she murmured. "Sure, I got to see you and Jen grow up, but those babies…" Her lips sloped in a frown. "They'll be grown. They're going to go from little kids that I see every day, or at least almost every day, to adults who haven't seen me since they were children. They probably won't even remember me."

I frowned and swiveled to meet her eyes. "They won't forget you."

She smiled. "Well, they'll remember the photographs. But no. No, they won't remember *me*. I'm sure they're gonna wonder where I went, too. Make sure they know that I didn't want to leave them, alright? Tell them… Tell them I wish I could still be there with them. And tell them I can't wait to see them again one day. Make sure they know that, okay?"

I swallowed hard. My eyes stung with tears. "I'm not ready for this."

Mom moved an arm around my shoulders. "It'll be alright, baby. You have years before you have to tackle this. And when you do, you'll be ready. Y—"

"No, not that. Well, yeah. The apocalypse too, but *this*. Leaving all of this. Leaving you, and this place. Our town, our time, our home. I never thought that I was a materialistic person, but I guess that I was wrong because I love this house so much. I don't want to leave. I love it."

"Home is wherever you make it, Lai. You know that. We moved before, remember? When we bought the house?"

"But I've already made it." I wiped my cheek. "This place is everything I wanted. It's got the land, and the colors, and the room. It's everything we needed. There's space for the kids. And it's safe, and cozy, and it's perfect. And it means so much to Jeremy. He built it. He planned it all out and made it exactly how we wanted it. It's where we found ourselves. I got my powers here. We got to know each other here, and I'm—I'm not ready to leave. I'm not ready."

"You will be. You'll adjust because you have to, hon. And you'll find someplace else where you'll get to know each other all over again. That's what happens when you're raising kids, you know. You get to know different versions of yourself. And your partner." She smiled as she pushed hair behind my ear. "You'll make your new house your home. You'll make a new life."

"Mommy! Mommy." Micah's voice carried as he approached the bedroom door. I cleared my throat, pulled back, and shooed tears from my cheeks. "Mommy, I..." He began in the doorway before he met my gaze. He frowned and turned his head to the side. "What's the matter, Mommy?"

"Have you told them yet?" Mom whispered as I stood.

I forced a smile. "I'm alright, baby. Where's your dad?"

"In Milly's room. He's getting her ready for bed." He gestured to the steps behind him. "But you're lying, huh? Something's wrong."

I lifted my smile further up my cheeks. "You're an intuitive little man, you know."

"I don't know what that means," he said.

"It means that you pay very close attention." I placed my hands at my hips. "What were you coming in here for?"

"To tell you something."

"And what were you going to tell me?" I asked as I made my way across the room to him.

"That Tink ate one of those bugs. The kinds with a zillion legs. What are they called again?"

"A centipede. And it's not a zillion, it's a hundred. Centi means hundred."

"Oh, right. Centipedes," he said. "Well, she ate one. They're not poisonous, right? It won't hurt her?"

I smiled. "No, it won't hurt her. Dogs eat all kinds of bugs."

"Oh. Good," he said. "I'm hungry though, too. Can I get a snack?"

"Yeah, I'm kind of hungry too. Let's go get something to eat."

"We made some cookies earlier." Mom stood. "In the mood for cookies?"

"Always." I ran my hand over the top of Micah's head. "I'll be right there. Go with Gam, okay?"

He smiled back, giving a nod as Mom brushed past me and took his hand. As they walked through the threshold and down the hallway, I pulled my phone from my pocket. I went into my text messages and opened the conversation from the unknown number the night before.

Question. I sent.

I started down the hallway. A second later, it buzzed. *Shoot.*

Tink. She gets to come, doesn't she?

Read.

But those three little dots to signify typing didn't show up.

A knot stiffened just above my collar bone. No. No, I couldn't leave her. Tink was my baby before I got my real babies. She helped me through the worst part of my life. She gave me a reason to make it through the day. She was something to take care of when I was lonelier than I'd ever been.

Read. And still no reply.

My eyes stung with tears. I sat at the kitchen island beside Micah and slid my phone into my pocket. Tink's fur bushed against my ankle. I leaned down and rubbed her head as her pale blue eyes looked up at me. It took everything in me not to break into a million pieces.

My phone buzzed. My heart palpated as I reached into my pocket. A blurred picture loaded. A furry white husky mix with icy blue eyes, panting at the camera with a smile a mile wide.

Probably the oldest dog alive. We should submit her to Guinness World Records. Does it still count if she went through a portal that makes you immortal? Or is that cheating?

My lips pulled into a grin as tears formed in my eyes. That was too witty to be me, I read it in Jeremy's voice. And that eased my worries about him a tad. This was going to be hard for a while, but at the end of it, we'd still be us.

I quickly typed back. *Thank you. Thank you so much.*

Read. Typing.

It's going to be alright, Lai. Try and get some sleep. You're gonna need it. Long day ahead of us tomorrow.

CHAPTER TWENTY

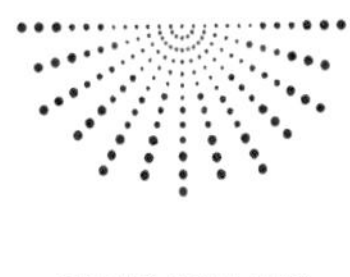

JEREMY

I watched Milly's eyes flutter back and forth as I sang quietly. My hands curled around the edge of the crib, feeling the cool wood beneath my fingertips. I waved my hand over the window, listening to the clang of the metal against the curtain rod as they telekinetically pulled shut. I breathed in the scent of lavender from the wax melting in the warmer in the hallway. Wouldn't be long and we'd have to go back to good old-fashioned candles.

I stared at her a moment longer. All that I wanted for my kids was a sense of normalcy that I never had. But with us as their parents, I came to the inevitable conclusion that they'd never have that.

I kept replaying what Laila told me she'd said early that morning. How worried she was that something would happen to her mother. I remembered feeling the same way when Annie would leave to help Mary or Helena on a case. It's a weight that no child should ever have to carry. They should never have to worry about whether or not their parents are going to come home to them.

Then again, they never would. In a few weeks, we'd be incapable of death. It's ironic to me now, though. How concerned Milly once was for her mother's well-being.

"Hey," Laila whispered in the doorway.

I turned over my shoulder and sent her a soft smile. "Hey."

"She sleeping?" she asked.

I turned my gaze back down to her. "Yeah, out like a light. I think that tooth finally came through; she barely fussed and fell right to sleep. I didn't even give her the Tylenol. Didn't have to rock her or anything. Just sang a little bit."

"She didn't get her usual nap in." Laila's hands moved around my waist and her head rested on my shoulder. "And she got up pretty early. I bet she was exhausted."

I tucked the little purple blanket closer around Milly's chest and traced my finger along her chubby cheek. "Micah in bed yet?"

"He's getting changed into his PJs. He heard you singing to her though; he wants you to play him a song."

"Yeah, sounds good. I want to put my guitars to use a little before we go. I'm gonna miss them."

"Well, maybe we could bring one," Laila whispered as I turned toward her. "If you bring an acoustic, we could shove some of the kid's clothes inside the doodad."

"The doodad?" I smiled, tucking my arms around her waist.

She smiled. "You know, the doodad."

"The sound hole?" I asked.

"Is that the technical term?" she asked. I nodded. "Well, that's lame. It should have some fancy title."

"Musicians probably wouldn't remember some fancy title."

"Well, anything would be better than sound hole. It's too close to glory hole."

I laughed quietly.

In the doorway, Micah said, "What's a glory hole?"

"See what you did?" I muttered.

"Not something you should repeat," Laila said. "Wipe those words from your memory."

He rolled his eyes. "I'm not a baby anymore, you know. I can understand things."

"Well, not that thing," Laila said.

He started to speak again before I cut him off. I was not about to argue with my four-year-old about why he didn't need to know what a glory hole was. "Are you all ready for bed? Want me to sing you a song?"

"Yes, please."

"You brushed your teeth?" I asked.

He nodded again. "*And* I washed my face."

I smiled. "Good job. You go climb into bed, I'm right behind you."

He grinned and disappeared.

I turned back to Laila. "It's alright. I'd rather leave them so we have more room for other stuff. And I don't want it to get broken along the way. I can get a new guitar when we get back there."

She sent me a sad smile. "Alright. If you say so."

"I'm gonna get him to bed if you want to go grab a shower."

"No, that's okay. I'll join you. I could go for a dose of musical medicine too."

I played Micah a few songs as he slowly drifted to sleep. Laila was right, music was something of a medicine. As I heard the chords and felt the vibrations beneath my hands, I felt the stress dissolve slowly from my body. It melted like ice in the spring, gradually turning to water and feeding the dead foliage with new life.

Laila's head leaned against my shoulder, watching him coast to sleep. Her eyes closed as she took in the sound. I was sure she'd fallen asleep too until I set my guitar down to teleport us to our bed. But she opened her eyes and smiled.

"I have to tell you something," she whispered.

"What's that?" I asked.

She slid her phone from her pocket, typed for a moment, then turned the screen to me. A picture of Tink. I looked at the background. She sat on old, mahogany-stained wooden floors. There was a shag white rug behind her. The coffee table she sat in front of was white, and ours was black.

I noted the feet at the bottom of the picture in front of the white dog. If it weren't for the scar just below the big toe, I wouldn't have realized they were mine.

Or his, I guess. Nick.

"Tink gets to come," I murmured.

Laila smiled, lifting her head in a nod. "Tink gets to come."

My face screwed up in a bit of confusion. "She'd be, like, thirty then, right?"

"About. I don't know how old she was when I found her, but I've had her for four years, and the vet said she was probably about two when I got her. So yeah, around thirty."

I chuckled. "So not only do we get to cheat death, but so does our dog."

She laughed. "I guess so."

I looked at her curled against her favorite person. "One lucky mutt."

"Feels a little wrong, doesn't it?" she whispered. "Leaving everyone else when we get an extra twenty-some years?"

I looked over Micah sleeping tranquilly. His chest rose and fell with each breath as his eyes shifted back and forth behind their lids. I thought about agreeing with her until my eyes settled on the scar at his neck. Then the one on his wrist.

I moved an arm around her waist. "No. No, he's four years old, and he's been through worse shit than anyone should ever have to. He deserves twenty-four years of normalcy." I gesturing to Tink. "With his best friend. Milly deserves the peace too. We...even if the world weren't going to shit, they wouldn't get the opportunity to be normal here. Everyone knows us. Every supernatural creature on this plane knows us. Most of them love us, but enough of them don't. And they all know our biggest weakness. To hurt us, you hurt them. Or each other, but we can fight for ourselves. They can't." I frowned. "We weren't even going to send them to school because of how scared we are that someone would hurt them. Or kidnap them and use them as leverage against us. Hell, we were only a few hundred yards away when Thomas La Fay tried to kill them. No. No, we have to do this. For them. And it's actually a benefit to this world, if you think about it. Micah's more powerful than any of us. Milly's more powerful than most, at least as powerful as us. We'll need them. They'll help. They're going to help us save the world."

She nuzzled her head into my chest. "There's something else I have to tell you."

"Which is?" I asked.

"I know you aren't happy about this. But we're meeting them tomorrow." She gestured toward Micah. "Older them."

A slow breath left my nostrils. "Tomorrow, huh?"

"Tomorrow."

I rubbed my mouth. "Well. Better get a good night's sleep then. I don't want to be dozing off when I see them for the first time. I want to be able to capture it. It'll be twenty-four years before we get to see them like that again."

Her eyes searched mine. Waiting for the angst or frustration. But it didn't come. I was slowly coming to terms with it.

They needed to grow up in a more peaceful time than they were born. They needed to live. They deserved a life like we lived before the end came.

But I prayed that it'd have been better than ours had been.

And tomorrow was my chance at finding out.

CHAPTER TWENTY-ONE

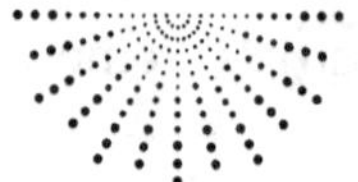

JANUARY 3 - LAILA

My fingers wrapped around the mug of coffee at the kitchen table. The warm scent of java coasted up my nostrils. My gaze shifted from Jeremy at the stove to the rain pouring outside. Yesterday was a winter wonderland. Today looked like a harsh summer storm. I already believed them, but there laid the proof. It had begun.

"After breakfast, you want me to take the kids up to Leah's?" Chris asked.

"Yeah. Micah, anyway. They asked me to keep Mills here." I sipped my coffee. "Said they'd be here in an hour."

"Sounds good," Chris said. "I got my bag packed too. Have you talked to Micah yet? About packing and moving and everything?"

"Not yet," I muttered.

"And keep your voice down," Jeremy said. "Let him have a few more days of peace."

"Right. Sorry." He took a sip from his coffee. "I just didn't want to let it slip if you guys hadn't relayed the message yet, ya know?"

"Yeah, I know," Jeremy said. "I'm just saying. He doesn't know yet, and we want to keep it that way."

"Sure," he said. "But you said Tink is coming, right?"

"Yeah, she is," I said.

"That'll make breaking it to him easier," Chris said. "I'm pretty sure we'd have to drag him kicking and screaming if she didn't come along."

"Yeah, probably," Jeremy muttered.

"How does that work, though?" Chris asked. "They said humans couldn't survive the shift. How can a dog?"

"I don't know, but she did," I said. "I'm not questioning it."

"And she's still kicking? Twenty-four years later?" he asked.

"I guess the shift affected her too," I said.

"Damn. Ya know, being what we are definitely has its low points. But we've got some pretty cool shit too," Chris said. "Remember why Annie never let us get a dog?"

A quiet laugh left Jeremy's lips as he scooped eggs onto plates. "Yeah. Because she couldn't take the heart break of losing another pet after her cat got killed by that raccoon."

"A raccoon killed her cat?" I asked.

"Sure did," Chris said. "Got out of the house one time when she and Leah first moved in. Always a house cat, it had no idea what to do with itself on this land."

"Me and Brody found it a few days later. We thought about just burying it and not telling her, but I got pretty fucked up trying to get the corpse away from the little shit," Jeremy said.

"Ew, it was eating it?" I asked.

"Yup. Still warm when I picked it up too," Jeremy said. "Makes me wonder if we would have gotten there a few minutes earlier, would it have made it?"

"Well, it'd be dead by now," Chris said. "It was near its end then, too."

"Fat ass didn't stand a chance," Jeremy said.

"Well, how'd it get out?" I asked.

"Hannah," Jeremy said.

"Dad always said that animals belonged outside. Guess that resonated with her," Chris said.

"Damn. I'd be so pissed," I muttered.

"Oh, she was," Jeremy said. "But what are you gonna do to a toddler?"

"She scolded her pretty bad though. I think Hannah still remembers it."

"No way she still remembers that," Jeremy said.

"She claims that she does," Chris said.

"She probably formed a memory from it because of us telling the story," Jeremy said. "I watched some documentary about that. People actually create memories from other people telling them the story. That's why the wrong guy goes to jail for a rape he didn't commit. Not because the woman lied about being raped, but because she looks at the line-up and says, 'I think it was that guy,' because he has some similarities to the man that actually did do it. Then the cops say, 'Yeah, we knew it was him,' and it confirms the thought and therefore forms the memory, putting that face on her attacker's body. It literally creates a memory that doesn't exist."

When he said that, the gears in my mind started cranking. That's what we'd have to do our children in a manner of speaking. "What smartphone, buddy? That Leapfrog's the only phone you've ever had." "You never watched this episode of *Fairly Odd Parents* before; it's brand new. It's just a lot like the episode you remember."

I'd have to lie to them. I already knew that, but it really started to resonate in that moment. And although it was in their best interest—so that they could have a remotely normal childhood—it still made my stomach sink.

***

"Do I look okay?" I adjusted my shirt at my hips. "This isn't too, like, young?"

"You *are* young." Jeremy's looked up at me from his seat on the rug with Milly.

"Yeah, but I don't want to look like I'm trying too hard."

"You wear that shirt all the time. Doing something you do regularly is the opposite of trying too hard."

"You know what I mean," I muttered, glancing at myself in the mirror by the front door.

"I don't." Jeremy laughed. "They're our kids, Lai. They've seen you every day for as long as they can remember."

"Yeah, but I haven't seen them. And if I think I look stupid, I'm gonna be self-conscious and say something dumb. That's what I do. So just tell me. Do I look stupid?"

"You look beautiful," he said, stacking a wooden block on top of the other.

My face surely showed my annoyance. "You're not even looking at me."

He laughed. "I looked at you two seconds ago."

"I'm gonna change." I started toward the bedroom, and he shook his head. Just as I was about to turn down the hallway, they appeared.

My stomach dropped as Lila and Nick turned toward the living room. Two figures stood behind them, blocked by their parents. But I saw the top of their heads. A short wave of black curls. And a shoulder-length bob in an ombré from dark magenta to rose gold.

"Woah." Her soft, alto voice danced into my ears. "This place is nice."

"Our house is nice," Nick said.

"Yeah, but this is *nice*," Milly murmured. "It's like, celebrity quality nice."

"It's modern, but it isn't celebrity quality," Lila said.

"Oh, sure. Pretend to be modest," she muttered. "Damn, and you built this place, Dad?"

"Not single handedly," Nick said. "But yup. Sure did."

"I remember it," Micah's deep voice whispered as his gaze shifted around the room. Considering how much he looked like Jeremy, I expected his voice to sound similar, but it didn't. It wasn't quite as husky. It reminded me of my dad. "Vaguely, anyway."

Time seemed to stand still as I tried to look at them through Lila and Nick. I knew that moment was coming, I'd prepared for it. Or at least, I thought I did. But nothing could prepare me to meet my two- and four-year-olds that were older than myself.

Lila caught my gaze and smiled. She took Nick's arm and pulled him a few steps back. I got my first good look at them.

Micah stood an inch or two shorter than Nick. I always thought he looked so much like Jeremy, but now, I could see myself in him. Something in the curve of his lips as our eyes met, and the way they lifted into a smile. But the eyes hadn't changed. Those vibrant, striking blue eyes. Those were his dad's, but the way they squinted when he smiled was mine. He still had Jeremy's strong nose, prominent chin, and chiseled jaw, shaved clean of course.

He wore a neat gray button up and a pair of perfectly pressed khakis. His hair laid flawlessly around his sharp features. But he wore a pair of lace up converse on his feet, just like his dad.

Milly nearly took my breath away. She stood a few inches taller than Lila. But her height was about all she'd gotten from her dad. She looked just like me. But a cooler, edgier version of me.

Her bright green eyes stood out like blooms in the early spring next to her pink hair. The short bob framed her round, pixie face perfectly. Her lips were a bit bolder and fuller than mine, like Jeremy's, but they were the shape of mine. Pouty, almost heart-shaped.

She had more meat on her bones than I did, but she rocked every ounce. Her waist dipped deep between her full hips and bust. She was a lot curvier than I'd ever been, something I was sure she inherited from Hannah. A cute black crop-top rested just above her belly button above her high waisted, ripped black jeans.

Milly smiled as she met my gaze. "Hey, Mom."

I blinked tears away. "Hey, Mills."

CHAPTER TWENTY-TWO

JEREMY

I held my breath, struggling not to cry as I looked at my grown children. No, it wasn't normal. It was far from natural. But it was the best blessing I'd ever received.

From the moment Laila told me she was pregnant with Micah, I prayed to hell and back that I'd be a good dad. That I'd raise decent children who would go on to live their lives as decent people. And that they'd love me because I hated my father, and I never wanted my children to see me the way that I saw him.

But looking at them, seeing how close they stood to their parents, watching the gazes they exchanged, noting the fatherly hand on their shoulders and the smiles across their lips, I realized I'd done it. I was a good dad. Some way, somehow, I pulled it off. I raised two beautiful, perfect creatures. And they loved me. They looked to me with respect and care, the way that I'd look at Annie if she were still alive. The way that Laila and I both looked at Rachel.

"Alright." Nick looked at Milly on the floor beside me. "So how about you each take one of them, and we spend some time with that one."

"I see how it is," Milly said. "You'd rather see her than me."

"Duh." Lila gave her a playful grin before walking across the room and sitting on the floor beside me. "She's cuter."

"Fuck off." Milly laughed.

Lila covered my toddler's ears. "Little ears, Malina."

Micah laughed. "You've cursed around us forever."

"And she doesn't tell us to fuck off." Nick smiled as he came to sit on the floor beside us. "Huh, Mills?"

Milly looked between them and then between me and Laila. She turned up to me. "Daddy?"

"Yeah?"

She stood and walked to Lila. She sat in her lap and met my gaze. "I okay."

"That's a snub if I've ever seen one." Nick laughed.

Lila laughed, moving her arms around Milly's belly and resting her head against hers. Her eyes closed as she took in a deep whiff of her hair. She rocked back and forth a bit as her lips curled into a smile. "God, I miss these days."

I had to chuckle at the irony. There we'd been, bitching about the state of the world we were living in. And completely neglecting to see the beauty of this time when our children were still young enough to enjoy us. When we were still their entire world. Before they turned into those cool, exciting grown-ups standing behind the sectional.

I smiled at Milly. "Well, me and Mommy will be right upstairs."

"I okay," Milly repeated. She turned up to Nick. "What's youw name?"

"Nick." He smiled as he extended his hand to her. "And what's yours?"

She shook it. "Milly. But you know that, huh?"

He smiled. "I do."

She looked at him and then at me. "You look like Daddy."

"I kinda do, don't I?"

She craned her head up to Lila. "And you look just like Mommy."

Lila smiled. "We're related."

"And you have matching tuh-ttoos." She pointed to the tattoos ascending her arm. Her finger slid along the scar at her wrist. "And these too."

"Yeah, we've been through a lot of the same things."

"Damn, I was a smart toddler, wasn't I?" Milly said as I stood.

"I was smarter," Micah said.

"*Was* being the operative word in that sentence," she stated.

He shoved her shoulder, and she laughed.

I laughed, gazing between them.

They were best friends. I didn't have to look twice to see that. They bickered, they shoved one another, but they were best friends. It made me so happy to know that they were still so close.

Micah met my gaze and smiled. "I keep hearing about this balcony. Wanna show it to me?"

My lips pulled into a smile. "Yeah, of course. And your saxophone?"

"Yeah, show him what you can do on that thing now," Nick said from the floor. "Better than we could ever dream to."

I looked back at Micah. "That so?"

"Not to toot my own horn, but..." He shrugged with a grin.

"Toot-toot." Milly smiled.

I saw the resemblance between Micah and me since we'd met two years ago. But now as an adult, it was more of a glimmer than a spitting image. He actually reminded me of Kai a bit. There was this light behind both of their eyes that wasn't in mine. This level of innocence and purity that never existed in me.

He laughed as he looked out over the tree line, tightening his jacket around his shoulders. "This, I remember. Like the back of my hand. I remember waking up there" —he turned to the glass door and gestured to his bed— "in the morning, when you and Mom were still asleep sometimes. And I'd stand right here and just look. I remember the birds, and the trees, and the sky." He laughed. "I do. I remember this."

I'd been dying to know. It was a question that had eaten at me since before we found him. Did he remember that place? Did he remember Peterson as his father?

"What else do you remember?" I asked quietly.

"This day, believe it or not." He turned and met my gaze. "Uncle Cody took me to the main house, and I was so mad that we couldn't go outside. And the house was so quiet. I knew something was wrong, but I knew you guys would keep us safe too. So I wasn't worried. But I was mad about this rain. I wanted to go sledding."

"Uncle Cody. That's Chris," I said.

"Yeah. That was confusing, too. Calling everyone different names and everything. It took some adjustment. I barely remembered it as I got older though."

"I bet," I murmured. "Not really sure how I'm going to adjust to it either."

He smiled. "You will. You slip up every now and then, though." I chuckled, and his smile stretched. "And I remember going back. I didn't realize what was happening, but I get it now. And I remember the night at the diner. The concert. It wasn't on New Year's Eve in our time though; it was just a Friday night show. And Moe's, I remember Moe's. Those veggie burgers are hard to forget." I forced my smile, and he turned back to the trees. "I remember my third birthday party. And I remember meeting Heylel, and Mary. And Gam, I remember her." He smiled wide as he turned back to me. "I'm really looking forward to seeing her again. And her chili. That was some good chili. Mom's is different."

"It's good though." I smiled.

"It is, but not the same. Gam always used the plant-based meat, and Mom leaves the meat out entirely, and it's just not as good." He smiled back. When I didn't return it, he let his smile fall. "But that's not what you were asking, is it?"

I shifted my gaze toward the ground. "No, not really."

"I didn't. Remember my time in there, I mean," he muttered. "I suppressed it, I think. I always knew there was a reason I was closer with Uncle Cody than my other uncles, but I avoided it, I guess. I didn't want to remember."

A touch of relief lowered my shoulders. He didn't remember it. That meant that he always viewed me as his dad.

"But you do now?" I asked quietly.

He frowned. "I do."

"So Peterson..." I searched his gaze. "You... you remember him."

He frowned. "I do. I didn't though, not for a long time. He hadn't crossed my mind in a good fifteen years before it came back."

I struggled to hold his gaze. "And do you... do you remember what we did to him?"

"I remember that I knew he was here. That you guys had him in the basement," he said. "And I remember feeling bad for him. Not because he didn't deserve it, but just... I don't know, he wasn't always bad to me. I cared about him."

A tightness stiffened in my chest as I turned my gaze to the wood at my feet.

"But I knew he had to be stopped. And I didn't want anyone else to feel what I felt. I didn't want him to die, but I wanted it to end. I didn't want him to ever hurt anyone again. And the day that I didn't feel him anymore, I remember being sad because I knew what that meant. But I felt relieved too because I knew he couldn't hurt anyone else again. And kind of guilty for feeling relieved too, I guess. Mom says that's because I love everyone more than I should."

That sounded like my little man. Compassionate, gentle, empathetic.

"She's usually right. If that's what she says, I'd believe it," I said.

"She says I get that from you." He smiled as I turned my gaze up to him. "That our hearts are bigger than the galaxy."

I chuckled. "Well, yours is. But I don't know about mine."

He smiled as he looked between my eyes. "I do. I can feel that sort of thing, you know."

"Not a surprise." I smiled. "You can do just about anything."

"Just about," he said. "But I remember meeting you, too."

"Oh yeah?"

A smile stretched up his cheeks. "I remember wanting to be just like you."

I laughed. "Well, those aren't very high standards."

"You don't give yourself enough credit." He frowned. "I guess parents do that, though. You guys always think you're doing something wrong. That you have to be flawless or something. And you don't. Kids learn from watching their parents learn. You don't have to be perfect. You were pretty close though."

I didn't want to get into the philosophy of my self-esteem issues with my son. He was sweet, and I appreciated it. But time for a subject change.

"Speaking from experience?" I asked.

He laughed. "Dad said you'd do that."

"Do what?"

"That you'd try and get an inside look at our futures from us." He grinned.

I laughed. "Well, can you blame me?"

He smiled still. "No. And no, not speaking from experience. Just a lot of mind-reading over the years."

"So you can tell me that. But what can't you tell me?"

Micah grinned. "I can't tell you what I can't tell you."

Worth a shot.

I smiled. "Fair enough."

"But I can tell you that you did good." His eyes moved between mine as his smile widened. "That you were a great dad. And that we all love you and mom like crazy. There's no one else we'd rather be our parents. Honestly, if perfect parents do exist, you and mom are. I know you need to hear that, but don't think I'm saying it just to make you feel good. You really are great."

I smiled, feeling the tightness in my chest loosen as I looked over him. That was good to hear. But I'd also given Mary a little spiel on this very balcony that wasn't so different.

My smile fell a bit. "I've got another question."

"Go ahead."

"How did you react?" I asked. "When you learned who you were in this story? When you learned what your existence means for this planet?"

"Oh. That." His gaze turned toward the trees. His hands grasped the railing, tightening and loosening. "Well, overall, pretty good, I guess. But I don't know. I mean, it was a lot to take in. It... it hurt. It still hurts."

I swallowed hard, lifting my head in a nod.

"But I was never mad at you guys for what you did. You had to bring me back; I'm your kid. And you lost me so many times; you wouldn't be able to live with yourself if you didn't make sure I survived. It did feel selfish for a while. But I get it. I'm needed here. The hundred or so years it would've given Earth wasn't worth sacrificing me. I'm not sure this battle could be won without me. Not to be conceited or anything, it's just true. I have so many abilities. Giving my soul to them would be more of a threat to this planet than letting them come a century later," he said. "My uncle, I'm mad at. Lux, I mean. Not your brothers from this life."

My heart dropped. "Do you remember him?"

He traced his tongue along his teeth. "Pretty clearly. He wasn't always bad to me, either. But he's a hell of a lot worse than Peterson."

I turned my head to the side. "Have you met him? Here, in this life."

He turned and nodded. "When Peterson had me. I met him a few times. But I remember him more clearly from before. The old life." His eyes came to mine. "Do you remember that stuff yet?"

"Bits and pieces. I don't remember you and your sister, though. Just your mom and him."

"You will. I do. I remember him killing me. And Milly. And M—" He stopped, shaking his head. "My other siblings, I mean."

My heart sunk as my hands grew sweaty. "I'm so sorry. I should have kept you safe that day. I should have—"

"He was your brother. You shouldn't have expected him to kill your kids." Micah shook his head. He pulled a smile to his lips. "It's okay, Dad. It all worked out eventually."

It hadn't. What was about to happen directly correlated to those events.

"But where's that sax at?" He smiled. "I've been waiting twenty-four years to try it out."

CHAPTER TWENTY-THREE

LAILA

"So this is it," Milly murmured, hand stroking the flower petals growing in the windowsill behind her crib. "This is where I was supposed to grow up."

"It is." My shaking hands stroked the thigh of my jeans as I watched her walk through the room.

"It's pretty." She smiled as her gaze shifted to mine. "Guess you've always had great taste."

"Was your house? Growing up, I mean, was your house pretty?" I asked.

She held her smile and leaned against the crib. "Our house is beautiful. But a little old, for my taste. It fits you, though. You're less apt for fancy shit. And our property was gorgeous. Actually, I think I like our land better."

My eyes searched hers. "But we do. We find a nice place for you kids to grow up."

She smiled. "A great place. It has this gorgeous lake going up the drive. Dad used to take us fishing there in the summer. He always threw the fish back in, of course. One died once, and Micah lost his shit. Dad ended up falling in." She laughed. "And you taught me to ice skate on it in the winter."

"It gets that cold?"

"That's Minnesooota, for you." She smiled.

Minnesota then. That's where we were moving. "I've never been. I never saw the allure there. I thought about going a few years ago when all the protests were happening, but there were protests here too, so I just went to the city."

"Yeah, that was probably the most excitement that the place has ever seen. Pretty boring place to grow up. A lot like here, huh?"

"What can I say? I've got a thing for small town America." I smiled. "But you don't have the accent."

"I do with certain words. Dad makes fun of me 'cause I always say di*nt* instead of di*d*n't." She shrugged. "But it's okay. Aunt Lena still lets a yinz slip every now and then."

"God, I hate that word. Anything but yinz. Y'all is better than yinz."

She laughed. "Well, don't act like you don't have a Pittsburghese accent."

"I do not."

"How do you like your eggs?" she asked.

"Dippy," I said.

She grinned. "You do know that's over-easy, right?"

I laughed. "Well, yeah, but you say dippy because that's how you want your yolk. Dippy so you can dip your toast in it."

"And what do you put your groceries in when you go to the store?" she asked.

"A buggy."

She laughed. "A shopping cart. Not a buggy. And it's slippery outside, not slippy. And kielbasa, not kolbusy."

"Alright, guilty. But at least I don't say wersh-cloth."

"You do say spicket though." She smiled. She took a glance over me and laughed. "This is cool, you know. You're nervous because of me for once."

It wasn't that I was nervous. This was just odd. I was looking at my daughter, and she was older than me. But I liked her. I liked her a lot, actually. She was feisty, and bubbly, and adorable. Just like my toddler downstairs.

I chuckled and lowered myself to the edge of the windowsill. "I know I shouldn't be. You know me, but I don't know you. Well, I know little you. But not this you."

"It's alright." She leaned back in the rocking chair, lifting her legs and crossing her ankles on the footrest. "I kinda dig it."

Another laugh. "Your hair's amazing, by the way. It doesn't even look damaged."

"My uncle's a pretty kickass stylist." She grinned.

I tilted my head to the side a bit. "Your uncle?"

Her eyes widened. "Shit, forget I said that."

I thought for a moment. "Well, I know it isn't Brody, Adam, or Kai. And Chris did have pretty long hair when I saw him yesterday, but I still can't see him becoming a hairdresser. So maybe a guy Chris ends up with?"

She tried to will down her smiling lips. "You know I can't answer that."

I grinned. "But that face hasn't changed. Same face my baby makes when she's trying to lie to me."

That'd be nice though, having a cosmetologist in the family. Maybe I'd finally stay on top of getting my nails manicured and my eyebrows waxed.

Milly pushed hair behind her ear and laughed. As she did, I caught a glimpse of a tattoo on the side of her neck descending toward her collar bone. I squinted a bit, gesturing toward it. "What's that?"

"Oh, this?" She turned her neck toward me. Six circles interlocking and one in the middle, connecting the rest. "It's the—"

"Seed of life," I said.

As I'd said before, I wasn't exactly a stranger to sacred geometry. And that was one of the most prominent symbols in the practice. It is the personified symbolization of the creator's consciousness.

She smiled. "Something poetic there, huh?"

That made me smile. It wasn't about a god to her; it was about me and her. The seed of the tree of life. "Also a symbol for eternity," I said.

A grin tugged up her lips. "You can clearly see the poetry in that."

I laughed. "That, I can. The neck hurts like a bitch though, huh?"

"Pain doesn't hurt too bad when you know it can't kill you."

"Yeah, I know what you mean," I murmured. "Do you have any others?"

A bigger smile. "I have the tree of life on my back."

My lips lifted even higher, making my cheeks practically block my vision. "A tribute to me?"

She smiled back, head bobbing in a nod. "The chords to my favorite song on my calf, a few names on my shoulder."

My smile widened. "They say not to tattoo names on your body, you know. It's like a curse."

Her jaw tightened slightly. "You can't curse the dead."

I felt my mouth fall as my stomach sunk. "Oh, damn. I'm so sorry."

"It's alright. Not your fault. We can't all live forever."

"Maybe one day," I murmured.

"Yeah." Her lips pursed, as if struggling to keep from saying something she'd regret. "One day."

I'd look back on that conversation years later and kick myself.

"So," Milly said, fingers stroking the armrests of her chair. "Anything you wanna ask me? Non-specific, of course. I can't say too much, but I can say a thing or two."

I thought for a moment. I cleared my throat. "How'd I do?"

Her head cocked to the side a bit. "What do you mean?"

"As a parent. Raising you guys. How'd I do?"

A quiet laugh left her lips. "Just the star rating, or the editorial review?"

My smile came back. "The latter, if you can."

"Well, I'd have to say four and a half stars. It would be five, but you didn't get me that Barbie Dream House for Christmas when I was eight, and I never forgave you for it." I laughed, and she smiled. "We had a story-book childhood, Mom. You and Dad bent over backwards for us. We had family game night once a week, and you were at every choir concert I was ever in, and you chaperoned every field trip when I was a kid. Of course, I had to tell you to stop when I got to middle school and all the boys I liked had more of a thing for you than they did for me." I laughed again, and she held her smile. "You did everything you should have. You were there for every heartbreak. You told me when I was wrong and taught me to do it right. You... you put up with a lot of shit from me. And you still welcomed me back with open arms, even when I don't think you should have."

Of course I would. My babies were my babies. I'd do anything for them. Nothing they could do would ever make me love them any less than I did the moment they entered my life.

"Bit of a wild child then." I smiled. "I always knew you would be. You had me fooled the first month or two though."

Her smile slowly fell as her gaze travelled to the floor. She grew quiet, and my chest tightened. Did I say something wrong?

She cleared her throat, gaze still averting mine. "I want to tell you something, but you can't ask me what I mean. Just hear it, alright?"

I turned my head to the side a bit but nodded. "Alright."

"I'm sorry." Her bright green eyes glistened with tears. "I'm really, *really* sorry. I should have trusted you, and I didn't, and I'm sorry. And just... when that time comes, just know that I was sorry even as I was doing it. But I get it now. It took me a while but I... I do, I get it now. And I'm sorry."

"What do you—"

"You can't ask me what I mean. Just... just know that I'm sorry. It took me a while but just... just know that I get past it. And when I do, I'm sorry."

Well, what the hell did the little shit do?

But she'd made it clear that she couldn't tell me. When that time came though, I'd realize what she meant instantly. It wasn't exactly a small thing. But she was my baby girl, and I'd forgive her no matter what she did.

And her apologizing that day in 2024 helped me to get through it when she did it. "Okay."

Her gaze softened. She smiled. "So any other questions?"

"A million, actually."

"Well, I don't think we have that much time. But go ahead."

"Do you love yourself? Did I teach you how important that was?"

She laughed. "You were preaching 'body positivity' long before it was a hashtag. Yeah, I love myself. I didn't always, but I do now."

That made my belly feel warm. I told her and her brother every day that they were beautiful, and I hoped that it stuck each time. I didn't want them to have the self-loathing that their dad did. I wanted them to know how great they were even when they didn't think they were.

"Good. That's good. You should," I murmured. "What's your favorite memory?"

She thought for a second or two. "Probably when you and Dad took us to the Open Lands when we were kids. I love it there. They hate me but" —she laughed and raised her shoulder— "I love it. The nature, the way of life. The lack of technology. Never really my thing, ya know? I was always an outdoorsy person."

"I do know that." I laughed. I asked the question I desperately needed an answer to. "Do... do you resent me for anything?"

She frowned. "I did. But I don't now."

"What for?"

"Not telling us what you guys are. That you're basically mother earth and everything. Not telling us who we were. What Micah is." She combed hair behind her ear. "But you did the right thing. I was too little to understand it all; we all were. It's hard to explain to anyone, let alone kids. You and Dad's story isn't just a movie, it's a series."

That made me feel better about the conclusion Jeremy and I had come to. We'd decided not to tell the kids that we were gods. Because we didn't want them to think they were invincible. We wanted them to know they were no better than anyone else. That we were all just people.

And her telling me that made me feel like I'd made the right decision.

I smiled sadly. "Is there anything you wish I would've done differently?"

"I wish you wouldn't have had to work so much. But I understand that you had to. And when I was little, I wished you would've stopped having kids after me." She grinned. "So just know that I get over the sibling resentment eventually. But ya know. I was a pretty mean big sister. We're all pretty good friends now though."

A smile stretched up my cheeks. So there were more. Me and Jeremy would have more kids. I wondered where they were now. It made sense for them not to introduce themselves, because then we might try to map out their existence in accordance with when and how they should exist.

"Can you tell me how many more? Or is that off limits?"

"Off limits," she said. "But more than I ever want, I can tell you that."

I smiled. "And how many do you want?"

"One. Maybe two. Maybe none." Her lips pulled into a smile. "I don't know. I have plenty of time to figure it out though."

"I guess so," I murmured. "Two's nice. Three seems like a lot. Especially now. Knowing about all of this." I glanced out the window. "I don't know. It feels cruel to have kids when you know the world's going to end in their lifetime, ya know?"

"Yeah, but they're pretty happy to be alive. So don't get too hung up on that."

"That makes me feel better," I muttered. "I don't know. I'd probably be pretty pissed in you guys' situation."

She cleared her throat. "So. What else do you want to know?"

I looked over her for a second. "Are you happy?"

"I'm content at the moment. Mindfulness and all that. But I'm not exactly happy about the world ending."

"Sure, but overall. Are you happy?" I asked.

Her eyes moved between mine for a moment, lips curving upward. "Yeah, Mom. I'm happy."

I smiled back. "Good. That's all a mother wants to hear."

"Well, I'm glad to inform you that I am, then."

"Are you in love?" I asked quietly. "Probably seems like a silly question but besides having you guys, nothing in the world feels better than being in love."

A quiet laugh. "I don't know if I'm allowed to answer that."

"But can you?"

She was quiet for a moment. "Yeah, I'm in love. It took me a while to find the right one, but when I did, you and Dad knew before I realized. So trust your gut when that day comes. And persuade me to give him a chance. I'll thank you for it one day."

My lips lifted into a smile. "I will."

Then the sound of a saxophone coasted into my ears. Loud in volume but soft in tone. Gentle, like the waves of the ocean as each note slid into the next.

"And that'd be Micah's one true love." Milly smiled as she stood. "I'm dying to see that damn balcony. Dad talks about it like it's made of gold."

"Come on then," I said, gesturing to the hallway.

CHAPTER TWENTY-FOUR

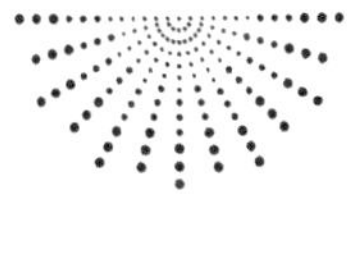

JEREMY

Watching Micah play the saxophone brought me back to the jazz clubs I snuck into before I was old enough to go to a club. He played like a pro. And as he moved his fingers over each key, as he breathed out each note, as his brows crinkled with each pitch; I saw a bit of me in him. Making music brought him the same peace that a guitar brought me.

I'd look back on that moment at every failed attempt he made as he grew up. When he first started to play, and part of me thought that he should give it up too, I'd think back to twenty-eight-year-old him playing as good as Charlie Parker. Better than anyone I'd ever seen in the flesh. I'd remember to push him harder. Because one day, he'd be the best.

A slow clap sounded at the door. I turned to Laila and grown Milly in the doorway. It was surreal to see them beside one another. She looked so much like her mother; I might confuse them if not for the pink hair. But even her hair color made me proud. It was bold and confident. *She* was bold and confident. Like an artist. But not a Bob Ross kind of artist. More of a Van Gogh surrealist.

Micah turned to Laila with a smile. "Thanks."

"No, thank you," she said. "That was beautiful. If little you could see this you, he'd think you're the coolest person in the world."

"I'm alright."

"Oh, shut up." Milly rolled her eyes. "You know you're good."

"It's polite to be modest," Micah said.

"They're Mom and Dad. Just be yourself."

He rolled his eyes.

It made me so happy to see the two of them together. The friendship they'd mustered up as children hadn't faded as they became adults. They weren't just siblings; they were friends. Just like Lai and I were with our brothers and sisters.

"Want to trade?" Laila asked with a look at Micah. "Milly wants to see the balcony too."

"Yeah, of course. Right here." I gestured toward the door.

"Isn't fair, you know." Milly walked across the room. "He gets a door outside, and I don't. I like being outside more than he does; I should have a door too."

"Oh," I muttered. "Well, the wall isn't load bearing. I could put another one in—"

She laughed as she pushed it open, meeting my gaze over her shoulder. "I'm kidding, Dad."

"Oh." I smiled. "Right."

She took a step onto the balcony and leaned against the railing. It is nice. No Fae Realm, but it's a decent view."

"Decent?" I asked. "You can see for miles up here. That's our diner over there. You can't really see it 'cause of the rain, but on a good day, it's clear as the ocean. And that" —I pointed toward the left, standing on the tips of my toes— "that's your grandma's house. And that's the high school you were supposed to go to."

"Ah," she murmured.

"I take it you don't remember that. The diner, I mean."

"No. But I went once."

"Oh yeah?"

"A long time ago though. Well before you worked there," she said. "But I don't remember her much either. Mom's mom, I mean."

"Kinda figured you wouldn't," I muttered.

And that broke my heart. My Milly loved her Gam so much. She followed her all around the house when Rachel was over. Sometimes, it seemed like she liked her grandma more than us.

"I hear she's nice though," Milly said. "You always say she was as much of a mom to you as she is to Mom."

I smiled. "Yeah, she's a nice lady. Loves you kids like crazy."

"She should've come then," she muttered. "We could've done without Ray."

"She felt like he deserved it more than she did. Lydia needs a dad," I said. "Pretty noble thing to do, really."

"Yeah, I guess," Milly muttered. "So how were you cool with that?"

"With what?" I asked, tilting my head to the side a bit.

"Ya know, choosing the guy that fucked your wife over your surrogate mother."

"How do you know about that?"

She smiled, lifting her shoulders in a shrug. "Me and Mom are pretty close. She sat me down and told me the whole story once. How you guys were broken up, how you got back together the day you conceived me. The whole spiel."

I laughed. "And you didn't mind hearing it?"

"Well, it's not like she told me the dirty details." Milly laughed. "But yeah, I wanted the whole story. It's a good one, you know. And we're close."

I smiled. "Yeah, it is."

She smiled back. "So, spill. How were you cool with that?"

"I don't know, because I know your mom. Loyalty's important to her. She chose me over my brother. I'm pretty sure she'd choose me over Ray too."

"Nah, I'd have killed him." Milly laughed. "I'm not as nice as you, though."

I smiled. "Well, I'm glad. Women get hurt more when they're nice. Be mean."

She laughed. "Don't worry. Nobody fucks with me."

I always knew they wouldn't. Milly was a handful even as a toddler, and I loved that about her. She was vibrant and full of life. And anger. So much rage in such a little person.

"I bet they don't." I smiled. "Nobody fucks with your mom either."

"Where do you think I learned it from?" She smirked. "I have a lot of strong women to look up to."

"Yeah. You sure do."

Her eyes moved between mine for a moment. She smiled. "Strong men, too."

"Well. I'm glad you see it that way," I murmured.

"You know, I've got to say. Seeing the way you treat Mom taught me to know how a man was supposed to treat me." Her lips pulled into a smile. "So thank you."

Hearing her say that brought me more relief than I ever knew I needed. It gave me this sense of peace to know that my kids saw how much I loved their mom. It made me think I didn't have to worry about boys breaking my daughter's heart when that time came. Unjustifiably, of course.

"Thank you." I smiled. "Thank you for that."

Smiling, she turned back to the house. "I know this balcony's your pride and joy and everything, but I like the house itself more. Why'd you build it yourself? You could have afforded to have someone else do it, right?"

"Well, yeah. But they would have charged us twice of what we ended up paying. Maybe more, even. I didn't want to drain our account. And I wanted to be in here before you were born, which wouldn't have happened if I paid someone else to do it."

"Makes sense," Milly said. "You did a damn good job though. I know everyone helped, but the idea was all yours. And the layout's perfect. It isn't a boring, cookie cutter, suburb home."

"Is yours?" I asked.

"No. But the layout's stupid. It was built in a time when you still needed a separate set of stairs for your slaves, type of thing."

I sighed. "A colonial."

"Kind of. But you'll see."

"I guess I will," I muttered. "I always loved Victorians, but I was never a big fan of colonials. They're not homey enough, you know?"

"Ours is." She smiled. "You and Mom can make a home just about anywhere."

Maybe that was true. But nowhere else would be the home we'd custom built with our own hands. Nowhere else would be the place where she came into the world.

This was my home. And it hurt that it wouldn't be again for twenty-four years.

"You really don't want to leave this place, do you?"

I sighed again. "No. I really don't."

"Well, maybe you and Dad could do a swap." She grinned. "He'd kill to go where you're going."

Nope. I knew she was joking. But leaving my house was still better than fighting the apocalypse. And I knew that Nix was technically me and all, but he wasn't going to fuck my wife.

Well. I guessed that he technically was. But no. Not happening.

I laughed. "That's alright."

Her gaze shifted over me. "It's not so bad, you know. What comes next for you guys. It's pretty great, if you ask me."

"No, I know. Just kind of sucks. All of this sucks." I leaned against the railing. "I didn't want this for you guys. I wanted you to have normal lives."

"Well, we did. Our lives were damn near human for the most part. We had better childhoods than you did; you tell us that all the time. But normal's boring anyway. This is more exciting. Every great day starts by some abnormal event, ya know? The normal one's all blend together. But the eventful ones are what you remember."

A huff of a laugh left my lips. "Truer words have never been spoken. Pretty fucked up though, don't ya think? Contentment's boring. But chaos is exciting."

"The biggest pitfalls of humanity." Her head tilted. "Or life, I guess. Since we aren't human and everything."

"We never kept that from you, did we? Your powers, we never took them away."

"No. They're as natural as breathing to me."

"Good." I smiled. "Good. I didn't think I'd do that, but I wanted to make sure."

"Yeah, thank the stars," Milly muttered.

I glanced at Micah inside with the saxophone in his lap. I turned back to Milly. "You play something, right? You look like you're a musician."

She smiled and placed her hands at her hips. "What does it look like I'd play?"

"If I had to pick one, I'd say drums," I said, glancing over her a moment longer. "But I've got a feeling you're like me and can play any instrument you pick up."

She grinned. "Except the drums."

I laughed. "Really?"

"Well, I can, I guess. They're pretty easy. But it's a background instrument, you know? More of a guitar kind of girl, myself."

My smile stretched further up my lips. "Electric though. Not acoustic."

"Ding-ding-ding." She smiled. "Bass is my favorite."

Still smiling, I said, "I could see that. What about your pipes? Can you sing?"

"Better than Mom."

"Well, that's not saying much."

Milly laughed. "Yeah, I've been told I'm a good singer."

"What about Micah? He's got the lung capacity."

"But not the vocal chords." She smiled. "I mean, he *can* sing. But he doesn't have much range. He's a bass, you know?"

I made a face. "I'm a bass."

"No, you're not." She laughed. "You can hit bass notes, but you're a baritone."

"Eh, fair enough," I muttered.

I wasn't sure why but talking to Milly felt a little easier than talking to Micah. Maybe because she was a little less awkward and outgoing. Maybe because she was more like Laila and Micah was more like me. Or maybe it was because I knew I did everything right with her.

When Laila was pregnant with her, I was at every appointment. When she was born, I cut the cord. When she cried in the middle of the night, I was who she reached for.

I knew I'd done right by her. Looking back on it, I know I did with Micah too. It wasn't my fault that he was taken. But I'd always feel like I could've done more.

Milly leaned against the railing facing me. "So I told Mom the same thing. But do you have any questions for me? Is there anything you want to know?"

I bit my lip. I cleared my throat. "Was I a good dad?"

"The best." She smiled, crossing her arms against her chest. "All those mugs that say world's greatest dad are liars because unless they're my sibling, they didn't have the world's greatest dad. I did."

Warmth spread through my cheeks. My lips curved into a smile. "You aren't just saying that?"

"I already told you I'm mean. I'd tell you if you sucked." I laughed, and her smile widened. "No, Dad. You really are the best. You may not be a perfect person. But you are the perfect father. There isn't a thing I'd change about you. Not one."

My heart softened as I looked between her eyes. She meant it. She loved me with everything she had.

I'd done it. Or I would do it, I suppose. Her and Micah were my witnesses. I'd be a great dad. Those conversations would carry me on my weakest days.

Because I didn't care about being a perfect person. But I did care about being a great parent. Although, at the end of the day, I'd never believe I was a perfect anything. But they thought that I was. And that was enough.

CHAPTER TWENTY-FIVE

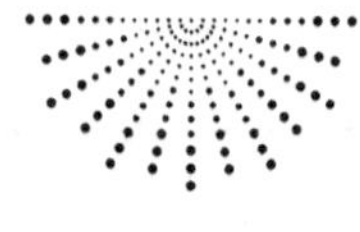

LAILA

"It would've been cool to grow up here." Micah looked around. "But at least I get to live here now, right?" He turned to me with a smile.

He always seemed to smile. Milly did too, but more in a sarcastic, funny-guy way. Micah just smiled to smile. He was a smiley child too. I was glad that hadn't changed.

"I guess so," I said.

"Might need a bigger bed though." He glanced over it. "I think my feet will hang off the end."

A quiet laugh left my lips. "You could take Uncle Chris's. I don't think he'll be needing it." I tilted my head to the side. "But then again, maybe he will. I don't know, have you guys worked out the living arrangements?"

"Not exactly." He sat his saxophone on the bed beside him. "I'm not sure. We have the same spell around our house as you guys do here. He might stay there. Then again, none of us are going to be spending much time at home for a while, I think."

"What's the plan after we leave?"

"You and Dad and the other people like us are going to be on the front lines. Me and my—" He stopped abruptly, careful not to say too much. He gave a quiet laugh. "Some of us are going to travel around, trying to get the people who don't cross over now onto this property and ours back in Minnesota. Once we have a few thousand, we'll open a portal and send them through to the Open Lands. Then rinse repeat. We want to save as many lives as we can. But we don't want to take their free will either. If we force them to go, they'll see it as kidnapping. Not like they have to be grateful or anything, this sucks. But you know how it is. Sometimes, people have to learn for themselves. Humans are stubborn. Most of them won't believe it until they see it with their own eyes."

"Can't say that I blame them," I murmured. "It does seem pretty crazy."

"Well, it is pretty crazy. But it's unavoidable, I guess."

"Yeah, I guess." Silence snuck up for a long moment. My gaze shifted over him. The carefully combed black hair, the bright blue eyes, the collar of his button-up, lifted thoughtfully to cover the scar at the base of his neck. "Can I ask you something?"

He smiled and gave a nod.

"How was your life?" I asked. "Was it... Did you have a good life?"

His lips lifted higher. "Yeah. I did. We all did."

"Good," I murmured. "Good."

"Is that it?" He grinned. "That's all you want to know?"

I swallowed the knot in my throat. "No. No, I want to ask something, but I'm—I'm not really sure how."

He leaned back on the bed and pulled his legs up, tucking them lotus style beneath him. "I'm ready when you are."

I wrung my hands together. My eyes stung with tears I struggled to blink away. After a moment, I said, "Do you... do you hate me for what happened to you?"

His eyes softened as his smiling lips pulled down at the ends. "I'd never hate you, Mom."

"You know what I mean."

Micah's sad eyes moved between mine. "It wasn't your fault."

"It was. We can all pretend that it wasn't, but at the end of the day, I'm the reason we missed the first three years of your life."

He breathed out slowly. "No, Mom. I don't hate you. Bad things happen to everyone. And honestly, it didn't have an impact on me. At least not one I recognized until I was a lot older. But when I did, I don't know. I'm glad I went through it. Because if I hadn't, Uncle Cody wouldn't be here. And neither would Lydia, or Aunt Holly, or the other seven-hundred people you saved. All it did was leave me with some scars. I'm okay with that." A smile moved back up his cheeks. "We all have to make sacrifices for the greater good sometimes."

Never had I seen it that way, and I didn't want him to think that. I wasn't sacrificing him. I was young and prideful, but I would never sacrifice the life of a child—let alone *my* child—for anyone or anything.

"I didn't realize that's what I was doing. I wasn't—I was just stupid. I thought that I could get everyone out long before you were born. I'd never sacrifice you—"

He laughed, gesturing outside. "Clearly." I frowned, and he frowned slightly. "Consider it my sacrifice then. Because if I had a choice, I'd do it again. My scars were worth their lives, Mom. It's okay. *I'm* okay."

I frowned. "Are you sure?"

"I'm sure. I get it, Mom. If I were in your shoes that night, I would have done the same thing. You were trying to keep everyone safe. You did the right thing. And I'd never hold that against you."

It did feel good to hear him say that. Especially considering the honesty in his eyes. But I still felt that weight. It'd never go away, not really.

I cleared my throat. "So Cody's Chris." He nodded. "And Holly is Hannah." He nodded again. "Why'd you guys get to keep your names, but we changed ours?"

He scratched his head. "I don't know, because we're younger. No one knew your kids' names until a few years ago. If there was another Laila Callidy and Jeremy Skoulda out there, it'd be pretty hard to cover your asses once time caught up to you. Callidy and Skoulda aren't exactly common last names, but they are famous ones in this world. Any Demon or Angel that walked through our town and heard about a

Callidy our Skoulda would immediately start drawing connections that could have uncovered your existence. And jeopardized our covers."

My thoughts travelled for a moment. "Do you know if we're going to have to create those identities? Birth certificates, driver's licenses, and all that? Or do they have that figured out?"

"You'd have to ask Dad. I'm not sure how you guys did all that. I do know that no one ever questioned it though. At least, not enough that you had to create new identities."

"And no one questioned our ages?" I asked.

"Well, our friends did when we were growing up. All of my friends had a thing for you. And all of Milly's had a thing for Dad. Teachers made less than kind comments sometimes. But people don't talk about age as much as you think. I think everyone in our town just assumed you got a lot of botox. And everyone thinks Dad's just good looking for his age. The gray hair helps." He smiled. "And you kind of have a baby face, and baby-faced people always look young."

That was true. I supposed there were vamps and wolves that got away with it. Ashley had been in that little West Virginia town for over seventy years before she died. All she did was change employers out of her town every few decades.

"Huh. Guess that's true. No one really questions it around here either. And I really don't look like I'm twenty-five. You don't look twenty-eight either."

"The shift affected us too. Not when we were babies, but once we hit adulthood, we stopped aging."

"I see that. Not a wrinkle in sight." I smiled.

"We're pretty lucky." He smiled too.

I thought for a moment, then my smile widened. "So another question."

"What's that?" he asked.

"Who do you like better? Me or your dad?"

He laughed. "Neither."

"But if you had to choose."

He laughed again, shaking his head. "We're all close. Me, Dad, you. But Milly always says I'm a 'mama's boy.'"

I glanced at her and Jeremy laughing on the balcony. "And what about her? Is she a daddy's girl?"

"I'd say so. You guys butted heads a lot for a while there. I think that's just a girl thing though; women always bicker. Dad says it's 'cause she's just like you. But she outgrew it eventually. She was rough for a while though. Like, the living personification of teenage angst."

I laughed as I looked over her. "Yeah, I'd believe it. She's like three going on thirty already."

He chuckled. "Not much has changed then."

"She told me she was sorry. Is that what she meant?" I asked.

"I can't answer that."

He knew too then. So that meant it was probably a big thing. But what the hell was it?

"Worth a shot."

"Can I ask you something too?" Micah asked.

My lips pulled into a smile. "Sure."

"When I was gone, after you lost me. What was that like? Mom never talks about it, and I know that's because it hurts. But I... I don't know. I've always wondered what that was like for you."

Usually, this was hard to talk about. But for some reason, it wasn't with him. Talking to Micah was always so easy. He was so sweet, and considerate, and kind. And curious. Always so curious.

"It was the hardest experience of my life," I said. "I didn't even get to see you. Never heard you cry, never saw your smile. I dreamed about you though. What you'd look like, what you'd sound like." I exhaled slowly. "And that was when I thought you were dead. But when I learned you were alive..." Tears drizzled from my eyes before I quickly wiped them away. "I felt so guilty. It was like someone was squeezing my lungs. Every breath hurt. Every time my heart beat, it felt like a knife was twisting inside of it.

"I tried to drown it out. I drank a lot. I dabbled in some drug activity. Honestly, I think I hated myself more once I learned you were alive than I did when I thought you were dead because I'd wasted so much time. And every second, every moment, I wondered what he was doing to you. I hated myself for not being able to stop him. I hated myself because I *couldn't* stop him. There wasn't a trail to follow, there wasn't a trace of you guys anywhere. There was... It's like I was looking for a door in a dark room. And no matter where I turned, I couldn't find a solid surface. There wasn't a wall to hold me up or a window to jump from or a knob to turn. There was nothing. But I kept searching blindly because if I didn't, I had no reason to be alive. Honestly, from the moment I lost you in that cell to the moment I gave birth to your sister, I don't think I felt an ounce of happiness. I don't even know why I held on as long as I did."

He looked over me with grief for a moment. He smiled. "Well, I'm glad you did."

My eyes moved over him as a smile lifted my lips. "Me too."

"Sorry to interrupt," Nick said in the doorway. He smiled as he looked between the two of us and Milly with Jeremy on the balcony. "But five-minute warning. We need you guys to open the portals."

"Me and Jeremy too?" I asked.

"No, just them. But take Mills up to the house. We're going to need you guys for damage control. And get the others. Celena and Kai. Pretty nasty earthquake's about to hit the west coast. The four of us and the two of them might be able to stop it before it causes a major disaster. Hopefully, anyway."

"How long do we have?"

He glanced at his watch. "About three hours 'til it hits. So make it quick. We need to get a grip on that tectonic plate before it shifts."

I took in a deep breath. "Gotcha."

CHAPTER TWENTY-SIX

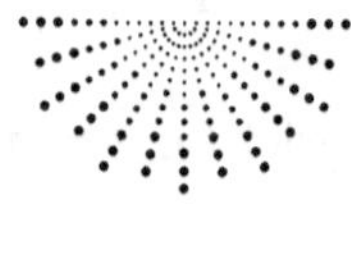

JEREMY

"Daddy," Milly said as I pulled her arms through her jacket.

"Milly," I said.

"Who was they?" she asked.

"Some old friends," Laila said, slipping into her rain boots.

"Oh," she muttered. "I liked that giwl's haiw."

I smiled as I looked between her bright green eyes. The same one's I'd gazed into a few minutes prior. That same boldness lied behind both pairs. Surreal, definitely. But also inspiring. "I bet you did."

I'd thought that meeting them would be so odd. But it gave me so much hope. It made me see myself in a better light to know that I raised those two, amazing people. To know they were my children, grown into amazing adults.

"Can you do that to mine, Mommy?" she asked.

Laila laughed. "Maybe one day."

She frowned. She sighed. "I hungwy."

"Aunt Leah can make you something for lunch when you get there, alright?" I lifted her to my hip.

Milly nodded, pawing hair from her face as Laila plopped her hood to her crown. Laila's hand moved to my lower back. "You ready?"

I gave a nod and teleported to the main house.

"Mommy! Daddy!" Micah yelled, jumping from his seat in the breakfast nook. "Guess what I did today!"

"What'd you do today, kiddo?" Laila asked, kneeling to meet his gaze.

"I made mud pies." He grinned. "Uncle Chris said we couldn't go sledding again because of the rain so we made mud pies."

"That damn rain." I smiled, running my fingers through his hair.

"Did you have fun?" Laila asked.

"Yeah. But Aunt Leah said I wasn't allowed to eat any. They looked good though, like chocolate."

I laughed as Leah walked from the sunroom into the kitchen. "He was not very happy about that."

"But it's okay, cause we're having chocolate ice cream with lunch," Micah said. "Do you want to make mud pies with me after lunch, Daddy?"

"I wish I could, but me and Mommy have to get some work done," I said.

"But I thought you was off work for a while. That's what you said, that you wasn't working because of the new year."

"Yeah, I know, bud, but some stuff came up."

"What kind of stuff?" he said, still glaring.

"Some work stuff." Laila set Milly down. "We're going to be pretty busy for a few weeks, kiddo. But once things settle down, we'll make as many mud pies as you want. Alright?"

He frowned. "Are you going to have lunch with us?"

"I don't think we have time today," Laila said.

"But we'll have dinner together, right?"

"I hope we'll be home by then," Laila said. "But I'm not sure, buddy."

"But—"

"We'll find something fun to do," Chris said as he walked down the stairs. "We could play Candy Land."

Micah looked at him for a moment. "Okay. But you'll be home for bedtime, right?"

I forced a smile. "I'll try, buddy."

He frowned and turned away. "Fine."

Fuck, this sucked.

He had no clue what was going on, and I was grateful for that. I wanted to keep it that way. But he wasn't used to this. Laila or I were always around. Even when I was working, I still made time in my day for him and his sister. I didn't want him to think we were putting him on the backburner. We just had to do what we had to do.

Laila stood and gestured up the steps. "Are Kai and Celena upstairs?"

Leah's jaw tightened. "No one's left today so I think so. Why?"

"We need them." Laila started up the stairs.

Leah met my gaze. *What's going on?*

Earthquake's supposed to hit the San Andreas fault in a few hours. They want to get a grip on it before it does.

Celena doesn't control Earth though.

No. But she does control water.

Her expression remained the same. *An earthquake on the San Andreas fault wouldn't cause a tsunami.*

It doesn't hurt to be prepared, I guess.

Guess not. Be careful. You aren't immortal yet.

Always are.

Nick texted us the address we were to meet at before they left. The Twin Peaks trail at Glen Canyon Park in San Francisco.

San Francisco. The worst possible place in Northern California for the fault to break. A condensed city that's old as shit with aged buildings that would doubtfully withstand a large quake.

I remember learning about the one that hit it in 1906. The city was completely decimated. Over three thousand died. Fires started after the initial quake, which caused more damage than the shift itself. It left hundreds of thousands homeless. The 1906 San Francisco earthquake was still considered the worst natural disaster to ever hit California.

And it was only a 7.9 on the Richter scale. Who know how big that fucker would be.

Unless we could stop it.

———

"I don't see them, do you see them?" Laila asked, using her hand to shield her eyes as she looked from side to side.

"I'd tell you if I did," I murmured.

"I don't get why I'm here," Celena said. "I can't help you with the tectonic plate."

"No, but you have a telepathic connection to back-up," the same voice said behind me. I jumped, hand flying to my heart.

"Jesus Christ," I murmured as I swiveled to meet her gaze.

She didn't look remotely different than her younger self. Messy blond hair pulled into a high ponytail, a pair of faded blue jeans, a short white T-shirt, and a pair of muddy running shoes.

"Same reason I'm here," she said. "I told Lai I'd help open the portals, but she said no. So here we are."

"Woah," younger Celena murmured. She took a few steps toward her, turning her head to the side as her eyes moved over her. She raised her finger and poked her in the cheek. Older Celena smacked it away. Celena nodded. "Yeah, that's me."

"No shit," she said.

"You had to poke her to see that?" I asked.

"Oh my," Kai murmured. "Strange. So strange."

"It's like an episode of *Black Mirror*," Celena murmured, walking a circle around her. As she moved toward her back, she laughed, pointing to her hips. "Damn, my ass is amazing. No wonder I get cat-called so much. If I were into girls, I'd totally wanna do me."

The older her turned to me and Laila. "You guys stay here with me. They'll give us the signal when it's time. Kai, we need you about two miles in that direction." She gestured toward the left. "And Celena, you need to meet Nick and Lila."

"Where at?" Celena asked.

"You can't feel them?" she asked.

"No, these two are all I feel." She gestured to me and Laila.

She took her younger self's hand. "I'll be right back. You two stay put."

Laila and I gave a nod. The three of them disappeared.

"She hasn't changed much," I murmured.

"Celena was born an adult," Laila said. "Aside from the childish rhetoric."

CHAPTER TWENTY-SEVEN

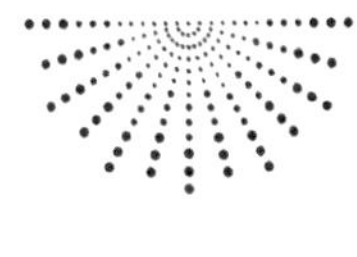

LAILA

I'd only been to San Francisco once. It was on the list of places we had to visit before the world ended. We came last year for a weekend in early May. It rained all day, so we spent most of our time in museums and the hotel pool with the kids. But we did see the Golden Gate Bridge.

We got an Uber to the Roundhouse Café on the edge, had dinner, and walked all of twenty yards before the drizzle turned to a torrential downpour and we had to run back to the restaurant. Jeremy slipped on the steps as we were rushing back to the restaurant and sprained his ankle. After we had dessert, the rain slowed, and we went back to take our picture on the bridge. Jeremy kept bitching that we were going too fast as he limped his way behind us. Micah and I teased him for it the rest of our trip.

Such a simple day, really. But a great family memory all the same. Still, as I looked out over the vibrant city, I wished we would have spent more time there. It was a gorgeous place. Probably one of my favorite cities we'd ever been to. Not one of my favorite places in the world, of course; I hate cities. But of all the cities we'd seen, San Francisco was in the top five. New York and Tokyo were my least favorite. Too many people crammed into too small of a piece of land.

"When you were her, our Celena," Jeremy said to Celena as she drew in the dirt with a stick. "Were they able to stop this?"

She looked up and frowned. "When I was her, a massive tsunami hit the Philippines last night. We were too busy getting people out of the rubble and trying to heal them when this struck. And by the time we heard, it was already too late. The city was destroyed. Thousands died. Maybe tens of thousands. I don't know, there were too many bodies to count."

My stomach dropped as she stood.

She looked over the city. "We were up all night stopping it. And we did. So hopefully, we can stop this one too. But who knows? Time travel's confusing. We prevent one disaster, another's just waiting to happen."

"Do you know what magnitude it was?" Jeremy asked. "This one, I mean. The one we're about to stop."

She frowned. "No one was around to measure it. But above a nine, if I had to guess. Off the charts big. Remember that movie San Andreas? How all the experts say that's not possible?" She tightened her jaw. "Like that. But bigger."

A knot formed in my throat. "Jesus Christ."

"Yeah. And that's only the beginning."

"How the hell are they doing this?" I asked. "How are they shooing the tectonic plates when they're still at least a light year away?"

"How do you have the power to hold a tectonic plate in place? How do I have the power to start and stop a storm? How can we meld people's bleeding wounds back together?" Celena asked. "We just do. And so do they. They built this planet; I'm sure they know things about it that would take humans another thousand years to understand. Things they didn't relay to us for a reason. We made a deal with them, and now we're reneging. This is war. And our casualties are literally money in their pocket. They're going to do whatever they have to to get what they want. But every time the world shifts, every time we go back, we get a little more information and a little more chance at saving our people. Hopefully you guys save even more than we do."

Hopefully.

"Okay, two minutes. You guys know what to do, right?"

"I do."

"I don't," Jeremy murmured.

"Just follow my lead," I said.

I'd done this once before. Also last year. The quake was small though, off the coast of South America. Moriah called one morning and said a Witch from her coven had a vision of mass destruction in a village not far from Lima, Peru. In the premonition, she saw buildings shaking and people being buried alive. It wasn't hard to figure out what that meant. As the Witch had said though, the devastation of an earthquake in a village like that with poorly made buildings would have been catastrophic. The Haiti earthquake in 2010 killed over two-hundred-thousand and injured at least three-hundred-thousand, primarily because it hit an area that was densely populated with poorly constructed buildings.

Before me, when anyone had a vision like that, there wasn't much to be done in those situations. Most Fae don't have the power—nor do they care enough about humans—to interfere with a natural disaster. But Kai and I were different, to say the least.

The two of us teleported to the village from the Witch's premonition and waited. The moment the Nazca plate started to tremble, I felt the power behind it. Kai did too. It only took the two of us to grab ahold of it and keep it from shifting. We were both completely drained afterward, like our life force had been entirely siphoned from our bodies. But we did it.

I'm not sure how big the one set to hit Lima would have been that day. But I do know that we stopped it. And even if it was only one life we saved, it was well worth it.

But the Nazca plate was about the quarter of the size of the Pacific plate.

Suddenly, I felt movement beneath me. My heart picked up as I looked between Jeremy and Celena. "Do you feel that?"

"Nope. But I believe you," Celena said.

Jeremy's wide, unblinking eyes met mine.

"Now," Celena barked. "Now, now. Lila said *now*."

I closed my eyes. Every bit of my focus zeroed in on the ground beneath me. I visualized it, the bedrock of quartz and feldspar miles beneath our feet. The power behind it.

It was stronger than any weapon or creature I'd seen, the power of the earth itself. And yet, I stood there trying to control it. Not even control it so much but maintain it.

My legs began to shake. Not because of the quake itself, but the power I was pushing from my body to keep it in place. I felt blood ooze from my nostril as the vigor of the earth fought against me.

Behind my closed eyes, I could practically see it. The layers of dirt and rock struggling like that of a baby deer trying to escape the grasp of a tiger's jaws. Trembling, quivering, fighting so hard to win. To scrape over the ground beside it.

It wasn't like the earthquake I'd stopped in Peru. It was stronger, almost intelligent. I knew that Wormwood was controlling it somehow, but the force was stronger than anything I'd ever felt. We weren't only fighting the power of the earth; we were fighting the power of a race far more intelligent than us. A group of people strong enough to manipulate the very existence of a planet they were thousands of miles from reaching.

I collapsed to the ground, panting hard. My fingers curved into the dry dirt. I heard Celena behind me, but only the distant sound of her voice over the sound of my heart pounding in my ears.

It hurt. It literally *hurt.* From where I kneeled in that moment, it felt as though my body was deep within the planet, being crushed between two massive pieces of rock. Like somehow, my body was the barrier between a car packed with a million people and a cliffside along an ocean. Not only in a metaphoric sense, although that applied as well. But I could literally *feel* the weight of the world. At least, a decent portion of it.

When you're in that type of agony, every fiber of your body tells you to let go. It begs you to release your hold and catch your breath. But I wouldn't, because I knew that the weight of those lost lives would hurt more than these moments.

I felt Jeremy beside me experiencing the same agony. My eyes stayed closed, so I didn't see the look of pure misery he was also feeling. And I wouldn't, because I may have just released it if I had.

I don't know how long it lasted, but I know that every millisecond that went by, I had to fight the urge to let go. My nails dug deeper into the soil as my quaking body released every ounce of energy it held into that struggling layer of rocks. The weight pushed harder into me, but I kept holding on. It wouldn't kill me. Using my abilities never *actually* hurt me. But I had to repeat that in my subconscious a thousand times.

When my instinct commanded, I let go, I thought about what *would* kill me. Seeing the city burn. Watching innocent people be buried alive by buildings and the earth itself. Witnessing children being crushed by their own roofs. And I grasped it tighter, practically burying my own extremities into that soil.

I felt Celena grip my shoulder. "You did it." I heard her say. "You guys did it. Let go."

Relief washed over me as I released my hold. Like lying in bed after spending the entire day busting my ass in construction. Every muscle soothed, sore still, but softened.

I opened my eyes, seeing only a liquid haze of crimson for a moment. Breaths heaved deep into my lungs as she took my face in her hands. "Laila, are you okay?"

It felt like it did moments after a panic attack, something I hadn't experienced in years. Every cell within me still quivered, but a sense of peace washed over me. A sense of tranquility.

"I'm okay," I murmured. "I just...I just need to lie down."

It all went black.

CHAPTER TWENTY-EIGHT

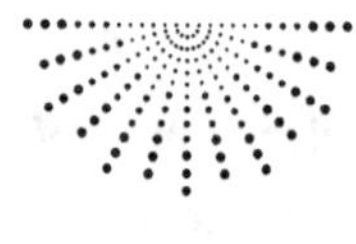

JEREMY

Every bone inside my body felt like it had been replaced with pudding. My limbs were entirely numb, tingling against the dry dirt beneath me. I stared up at the light blue sky, summoning deep breaths into my abdomen.

Jesus Christ.

I knew holding a massive chunk of the planet in place wouldn't be easy, but holy shit.

Nothing in my life ever felt that strenuous. I'd rather run around the country barefoot with no water than do that again. Of course, I knew I'd have to in twenty-four years. But holy fuck, I couldn't even fathom that thought.

So I didn't. I just lay there, staring at a little white cloud inching closer to the bright yellow sun.

"Jeremy," Celena yelled, smacking my face. "Jeremy, are you okay?!"

I swatted her hand as I continued to pant.

"Is this normal?" she said quickly, eyes darting over Laila beside me.

I pushed my numb hands into the ground and struggled onto my knees. The edges of my vision turned black as I waited for my blood pressure to level. I looked over Laila.

Bright red streams of blood descended from her eyes down her cheeks. The creamy color of her face had faded to a pale, sickly bluish. Her lips were almost the same hue.

I reached toward her neck, feeling for a pulse. At first, I felt nothing, and my heart sunk. I slid my fingers a little closer to her chin. A slow thump, thump-thump, pulsed against my fingers, and I exhaled with relief.

"It's never happened before, but I don't think she's used that much energy before," I murmured. "Help me roll her over."

Celena dropped to the ground and shifted Laila's hips as I rolled her shoulders. I took her face in my hands and sent bright white energy into her body. Slowly, the pearly color of her skin restored and the blue tinge to her lips faded. Her bloody eyes peeled open as her pulse gained strength beneath my fingertips.

"Hey, beautiful," I whispered.

She smiled as her eyes slowly closed again. "Can I take a nap?"

I smiled and collapsed beside her, resting my head against her slow-moving chest. Her hand moved to my hair, vibrating the same energy into my body as I'd done to her a moment before. I felt her lips touch my hair as my eyes closed.

"Alright, alright," Celena said. "I'll keep a look out. Five minutes max."

I raised my hand and extended my thumb. I dropped it back to the ground and drifted away.

"Give them a few minutes." I heard Nick say. "It's hard the first time."

"They're going to sleep like babies tonight." Lila laughed.

"Knowing you all just saved millions of lives, I'm sure they will," Celena said.

"I know I am," Lila muttered.

"Well, you know. After we celebrate," Nick said. She giggled, and Celena's eye roll was almost as loud.

I was still too drained to sit forward. Hell, I was still too drained to open my eyes. But I'm not sure I would have if I felt able. It was like a little sneak-preview of who we'd be in a few decades with no pretense or planning to keep us from being influenced.

And it was a relief, hearing them bullshit the same way that we did. Also to hear Nick and Lila still flirting. That was reassuring. At least I knew we wouldn't get old and kiss our sex life goodbye.

"Little me's alright, ye kin?" Kai's voice said.

"That's what Celena said," Celena said. "A lot like the two of them though."

"They're alright," Nick said.

"Yeah, they just need a minute to recoup," Lila agreed. "They aren't immortal yet. Something like that takes a toll regardless, but it's a hell of a lot harder on them than it is us."

Nick's voice grew dreary. "I'd still take that over this."

Silence crept in for a moment. Lila broke it. "It's not so bad. We're going to win. We're going to win, and we already saved a good percentage of the people that died last time around. We'll save more. We will, we'll save more this time. And maybe *they'll* save even more than us. It's okay. It's—it's going to be okay."

"Yeah. I hope," Celena murmured.

"What comes next now?" Kai spoke. "I remember the meteors, but with the quake bein' stopped, I forget the next part."

"Tonight, we breathe," Nick said. "We keep the portals open. The governments are directing people into them, but tonight, we just breathe."

"And tomorrow?" Kai asked.

"Tomorrow, I start teaching her," Lila said. "She's got to know how to use the tree of life."

"Right," Kai murmured. "Sure. But *what's next?*"

Yeah, get on with it. I wanna know too.

"Mount Fuji erupts in three days," Nick murmured. "And It's like a landmine for the rest."

Mount Fuji. That was in Japan. It was in the top ten highest on earth. And it'd been dormant for over three centuries. Good thing too, because if it erupted? It'd devastate Japan. It'd decimate transportation, it'd knock out power. It would virtually cut off food supply to the entire city of Tokyo.

Maybe I shouldn't have snooped on their conversation, because now my stomach hurt.

"After that one blows, they all do," Lila murmured. "But we have a few days in between. Hopefully the masses have moved through the portals by then."

"And next week, the meteors come," Nick muttered.

"If the major cities have evacuated by then, it won't be as bad as it was last time," Lila whispered. "We—less people are going to die. Maybe—maybe none. We're already ahead of where they were when we were them. Stopping the quake last night and this one today, we're ahead of the game."

"Don't get your hopes too high, baby." Nick's voice was gentle. "They did everything they could too, and it still—"

"I know. I know, but I can still have hope."

"Shit," Celena said suddenly. "Shit. Shit, shit, shit."

"What?" Nick asked.

"Wake them up. Wake them up *now*. Kai, go get Celena and Kai," she said quickly.

"What's happening?" Lila said.

"A quake just hit Alaska."

"Was anyone—" Nick began.

"Not yet. But a nasty tide's headed for the northern coast. We have to move. And fast."

Fuck.

CHAPTER TWENTY-NINE

LAILA

"Laila," Jeremy said, shaking my shoulder. "Laila, get up."

"I just..." I murmured. "I just, I need another minute."

"We don't have time. Get up," Lila barked. "Get up now."

"But I—"

"People are about to die," she snapped. "Hundreds of lives are about to be lost. Get your ass up *now*. They need you."

My eyelids lifted, blinking hard at the bright sun. "But we stopped it. We stopped it, didn't we?"

"This one, yes," she said quickly. "But there's a tsunami headed for the coast. We need all hands on deck. Get up. Now."

My eyes felt as though they were coated in sand. But I forced them open and brought myself to a vertical position. As I did, my vision darkened, tunnel forming around the edges. I lifted my hand to my head, rubbing my temples.

"We don't have time for this," Lila snapped. "I know you're tired but—"

"I'm trying, holy shit, dude," I barked.

"Jeremy, come with me. Nick, get her," I said.

"If you'd just give her a minute—" Jeremy began.

"We don't have a fucking minute," she snapped.

"It's alright, man," Nick said, lowering himself to the ground beside me. "I got her. Go help Lila. We're coming."

Jeremy looked at me. I nodded, and he stood. Lila grasped his hand, and they disappeared. Rubbing dried blood from my eyes, I turned my gaze to Nick. "What's happening?"

He twisted the cap off a bottle of water and passed it to me. As I chugged, he said, "There's a tidal wave headed toward the coast."

"But we stopped the quake."

"We stopped *this* quake. Even if we hadn't, it wouldn't have caused a tsunami. And if it did, it would have dissipated drastically before it hit the shore anywhere else. Maybe a few inches higher than normal tides, possibly a couple feet," he murmured. "But another one hit Alaska a few minutes ago. And it rippled, traveling down the coast. Now it's headed for—"

"The northern shore," I murmured. I took another big gulp from the water. "Why didn't you warn us? We could have stationed Celena there."

"This didn't happen in our life," Nick said. "My guess is that they saw us stop the one in the Philippines last night, then this one now. So they struck quick to get their death toll back up. But how are you feeling? Do you need another minute?"

I tilted my head back and chugged the remainder of the bottle. "I'm good. I'm good, let's go."

He nodded quick, took my hand, and we disappeared.

We landed on a quiet beach somewhere a bit colder than we'd been. I didn't realize where we were in the moment, though I now recognize it as the shore of Rockaway Beach.

It looked so peaceful. There wasn't a person in sight, nor a boat bobbing in the distance. Had it not been for the tide receding back into the ocean, I wouldn't have known it was coming.

I turned around, checking to be sure no one was around out of reflex. But no one was there. No people, at least. But I could see the town. A few small restaurants behind the sand. An empty boardwalk. Several hundred feet of oceanfront condominiums. There, I saw the people.

A woman sat on her balcony with a toddler near Milly's age. I couldn't hear what they were saying or make out much of what they were doing, but it broke me to realize they had no idea what was coming. A few balconies to the left, I saw an elderly couple swaying on their porch swing. A man stood on another one a few stories above, gulping down a bottle of water.

But they were up high. That's what I told myself. They weren't at a low enough level that the tides would hit them if we were unable to stop it. Tsunamis aren't what they look like in movies, not when they hit wealthy, well-constructed areas. In a place like Portland where buildings are composed of strong substances of stone and concrete, the worst damage would only be at the ground level. And it would mostly be property damage, not lost lives, which wouldn't matter much anyway since those people would be travelling through a portal to another dimension in the coming days.

Nick gripped my arm, ripping my gaze from the people going about their daily lives. I narrowed my gaze as his wide eyes moved between mine. "Don't think about them. Think about *that*." He gestured toward the ocean. "We stop that, and they'll all be fine. Focus on the water. Do you feel it?"

I turned my gaze back to the ocean. At first, it still looked so peaceful. Any waves crashing in the distance looked just as so. But the closer I looked, the more I could decipher. The crashing waves that looked so calm were rapidly growing in height.

I'd done this before too. I stopped a tsunami in New Zealand just six months prior. But like the earthquake we prevented in San Francisco, this wave wasn't behaving the same. Most tsunamis are larger at sea and dissipate as they approach the shore.

But not this one. It appeared to be getting larger. Taller, more forceful, and moving much faster. They're supposed to slow as they reach the shore, but it wasn't. It was swelling.

I raised my palms and focused on the highest point. From such a distance and nothing in the ocean to compare its size to, I still couldn't tell how big it truly was. But I focused hard on its highest points. I used every fiber of my being to break it, to slow it before it reached the shore. But it only kept growing.

"I need to get closer," I said quickly.

"You take the east side. I'll take the west," Nick said.

I teleported just above the waves, swiftly collecting enough wind beneath me to keep me hovering above the tide. But once above it, I saw how deeply I'd underestimated its size.

It was the same distance from the ground that I had been when I stood on top the Empire State Building. Or at least, it felt the same. It was probably only two hundred or three hundred feet from the still water behind it. But gazing down at the water, seeing large fish and even a few whales caught up in the current, it looked so much larger.

But I focused. I grasped the water with my mind and willed it downward. It worked just fine when I'd done it in New Zealand. The tide was still high that day—it did some damage to the beach and boardwalk—but the people were fine. No lives were lost, and no injuries were reported.

Yet, this wave, the tsunami we'd one day call the Alaskan Disaster, barely responded to my manipulation. I tried pushing it backward into the ocean from the direction it came, only to knock a dozen or so yards off of its highest point.

I started to panic. If it made it to the shore and continued collecting water the way that it was, it would destroy the beach. It'd decimate those people standing on their balconies. The boardwalk would be washed back into the ocean and those small restaurants, as well as the people within them, would be drowned in moments.

Then a thought occurred to me.

A few hundred feet down the way, I saw Nick struggling at the same attempt I was making. I teleported to him, grasped an arm around his waist and thrust us back to the beach.

He yelled, "What the fuck are you doing?"

I started closer to the receding shoreline. He ran toward me, still yelling.

"Just follow my lead!"

He clenched his jaw, nostrils flared.

"It's pulling this water toward it, right?" I asked. He nodded. "So instead of trying to disperse that wave, let's pull it back toward us into our own. There's going to be damage, but it won't be as severe as if that one makes it to the shore."

His eyes widened. "That might work."

"Let's hope."

I summoned the water at my feet toward me. Little by little, it drew closer and closer to the shore until it was at my knees. My hands lifted as my eyes closed, imaging the water those few hundred feet in the distance coming back to me.

It inched closer, water raising until it was at my hip. The higher it rose, the faster my heart drummed in my ears. Soon enough, the water was nearly at my neck. I held my breath as I lost my footing, allowing my body to enter the waves and summoning air into my lungs from the atmosphere above.

My body was completely submerged then. Essentially, I had become one with it. As that realization dawned on me, my eyes opened.

I'd thought I was only a few mere feet off the ground. But I realized, I was entrapped high above the shore, nearly as high as I'd been over top of the tsunami approaching the land.

Through the haze of murky water, dancing with fish, oceanic plants, and debris, I could see the large wave approaching. Heading straight for the massive wall of water Nick and I had created. Gaining speed, large and strong. But I stayed steady, draining more water into the wave I stood within, trying to make it even larger and stronger than the one aimed straight at me.

As it got closer and closer, I focused harder. I allowed my heart rate to slow. If I let myself become anxious, I could drop it. I had to maintain my composure. If I maintained my integrity, the wall of water I'd created would maintain its own.

Then, the impact.

The rolling tide of water smashed into my wall. I felt it struggle, attempting to break at the force that rammed into it. But I fought harder. I held tighter.

I couldn't see if it worked. I couldn't tell if it had rolled over my blockade. But I held my ground. Metaphorically speaking, since I stood within a moving, swirling wall of water.

At least, until I couldn't any longer. Until the impact from the incoming wave stopped. Once that kinetic energy slowed, I gradually lowered the water, trying my damndest to keep it from crashing onto the pier.

I teleported back to the shore.

The water was high, nearly reaching the town behind me. My heart fell with joy as I pushed salty water from my face.

"It worked," Nick yelled a few yards away. "It fucking worked!"

Another natural disaster evaded.

At least, on that town.

I wish I could say the same for the region north of us.

CHAPTER THIRTY

JEREMY

We landed on a cool beach front in Ocean Grove, Washington. I barely had a moment to take in the cliff side to my right before the roar of the wave came billowing toward us. It had to have been traveling at least fifty miles per hour because the moment I saw it, even with the host of extraordinary abilities I had control over, we were already too late.

"No." I heard Lila whisper. Her arms raised. I saw what she was doing and followed just as fast as she did. But the foamy wall of white and gray was only a few yards ahead by then. And despite thrusting every bit of energy we had into that tide, we stood no chance.

Regardless though, I stayed by her side, desperately clinging to any strength I had left to keep that wave from touching us. It made no difference. The wave had gained massive amounts of kinetic energy as it hastily slammed down the west coast.

It was only a few yards before us when I looked at Lila. Her teeth were clamped tightly together, the same way they looked when she brought our daughter into the world. The strong wind pushed long dark strands into her taut face. She was fighting with every fiber of her being.

I was holding on as deeply as she was, but it hadn't hurt me yet the way it hurt her. She'd already watched her world be destroyed and spent the last twenty-four years preparing to stop it. And just as she'd prevented one catastrophe, another unfolded before her eyes. She didn't want to admit that she'd lose her first battle.

So I waited. I held on. I used every ounce of energy I held over water and telekinesis to keep it at bay. But it was unstoppable.

When it was a few feet from touching us, I released my worthless hold, grasped her hand, and teleported us to the air above the disaster, steadying us on a cushion of wind.

She dropped my hand and shoved me away. Not too shocking, I guess. But she knew what I knew. We were about to be pulled under the waves, and there was nothing we could do from inside the rushing tide.

Instead, we watched. I'm ashamed to admit it too. But there was nothing we could do to keep the water from hitting the shore. We couldn't stop it; we couldn't slow it down. All that we could do was watch it slam over the coast.

We watched as it carried boats from the sea onto the town. We watched it tear through homes and businesses. We watched it flood through the community and rip apart everything in sight.

The sound of the wind around us and the roar of the water drowned out the sound of the people's screams. That sickly smell of salt made my stomach churn as wildly as the water ripping through the streets. The taste of iron filled my mouth as I chomped down on my lip to keep from crying.

We'd failed.

All that remained was damage control.

Time moved so fast, yet almost seemed to stand still, as we teleported into the wreckage. Hundreds of people were under water. Homes were completely destroyed. I thought it looked bad from above but at ground level, it felt like a war zone.

I stood in the middle of the street, water whooshing past my waist, trying to pull me down. There was a car a few dozen feet toward my left being carried by the waves. I saw a woman clinging to the edge of a building, screaming, "My baby! My baby!" but there was no baby in sight. Then something slammed into my hip, nearly pulling me down with it.

My gaze shifted toward it, thinking it was debris at first. But I had to swallow down my vomit when I realized it was a man. A middle-aged man in a pair of jeans, wearing a ripped shirt that read *Sam's Sea Shack*. His dead eyes were wide open. A massive slit ascended his abdomen, butchered from some type of debris or another. Beside him drifted several feet of thick red strands. His intestines. Floating in the water beside his dead body.

In every direction I looked, there was someone who needed help. I tried to act fast, but I was frozen for a moment. It felt like it did the day the bomb went off in our backyard five years ago. Like something out of a horror movie. Not even a disaster movie, a *horror* movie. Bodies everywhere, death all around me, and I *felt* it. I felt their souls drifting from their bodies into the abyss, and it made me sick to my stomach.

"Move, Jeremy," Lila yelled before disappearing.

I stared at the man coasting down the river within the street. I heard that woman again. "My baby! My baby!"

I teleported to her, grabbed her shoulder, then teleported to higher ground on the outskirts of the town I'd seen from the sky. She bent over vomiting, trying to scream but unable. Before I could hear her scream again, I teleported back to where I'd been a moment before.

Into that car, the one rushing down the water. A little boy sat in the back seat, probably nine or ten, tears running down his cheeks from his wide eyes. The man behind the wheel was hyperventilating, unable to steer the vehicle that had now become a boat. When he saw me in his rear-view mirror, he gasped. But I grabbed ahold of the headrest on either side, closed my eyes, and lifted the car to the same vicinity I'd teleported the woman to. I could have just grabbed the man and the kid, but the can coasting down the water would have ended up causing more damage and may have interfered with saving another person's life.

Then back to the wreckage.

I teleported back into the disaster and grabbed ahold of someone struggling to swim in the tide. A dog yelped a few feet away, paddling desperately to stay afloat. I flashed to it, still gripping the other survivor, and then back to the place with the car and the woman.

———

It's all a blur from there. I saved more people. I teleported at least five hundred to the outskirts of the town. Some young, some old. Some human, some pets.

But I also moved past a lot that I couldn't save. Like that man with his organs coasting along the water beside him. There were more people like that than I could begin to count.

I didn't find that woman's baby. Not alive, anyway. I did, unfortunately, find a number of dead children floating through the street as time ticked by. One of them may have been her baby.

The coast guard didn't come. Neither did a fire engine or a police car. Not like they could do much anyway, and rationally, it made sense for the governing entities to utilize their resources to help people move into the portals.

Reporters did though. They caught us on camera teleporting people out of the wreckage and healing the wounds we could. Wasting their time, really. They didn't believe what they'd seen Lila say on the news until they saw us trying to save their fellow man. Even so, millions of people were still reluctant to leave their homes. They just watched hundreds die, they watched us save as many people as we could, and yet, they were still full of hesitation.

That's when it clicked. The world was really ending. Life as we knew it was over and would never be the same again. I suppose it would for us, but not for those people.

Laila and Nick showed up shortly after. Maybe twenty minutes into Lila and I moving people to higher ground. Celena and Kai weren't far behind with the future versions of themselves. Even Leah showed. I panicked for a moment because I didn't know who was with my kids, but Leah quickly said Hannah was watching them.

Then Chris, Brody, and Adam came, as did their older selves. Milly and Micah showed too, but Nick told them to get back to the portals. Avery and Asher were there, so were Connor and Naomi. I noted a few other faces that I didn't recognize then but would come to know in the future. Or at least, in *my* future, although it was technically the past.

You'd think that with so many of us there on the front lines, there would have been less lives lost. We were gods, after all. But even gods aren't limitless. There were only so many of us, and although we all had tremendous strength and ability, we weren't heroes.

We were just people. We couldn't save everyone. We did everything we could.

But sometimes doing everything you can just isn't enough.

CHAPTER THIRTY-ONE

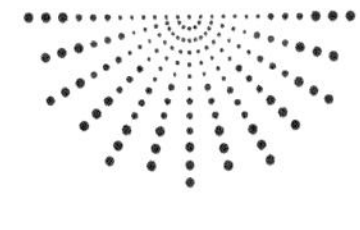

LAILA

"No," Nick murmured as I walked toward him across the beach.

"What's wrong?" I asked.

He frowned. "They couldn't stop it."

"But I thought—"

"I don't know how it happened either, Laila, but it wasn't just this one," he said quickly. "Come on. Follow me."

I picked up on the trail from his energy and hopped onto it. But I wasn't prepared. I wasn't even remotely prepared for what I'd see.

My body was heavy as lead. I needed rest more than I ever had. But when I landed in the murky water of that small town, the last thing on my mind was rest.

It was nearly to my shoulders. Without my ability to teleport, I'd need a boat to maneuver.

I didn't think a wave was capable of doing so much damage that far inland. We were at least a half a mile from the shore, but the entire town was under water. Buildings were literally washed away. Cars were floating next to rooftops ripped from homes and businesses. Bodies were trapped beneath them, many dead from the impact, others struggling for breath as they held onto floating hunks of wood.

I didn't even know where to start. I could barely tell who was alive and who wasn't. It was a war ground. A war with the earth itself. My ability to manipulate it was lost on such a large span of space. For the first time in years, I was humbled at my inability to help.

"Just get as many people as you can to higher ground!" Nick yelled before nose-diving into the filthy water beneath a floating roof..

I teleported faster than I ever had before between the people. I couldn't even begin to count how many shoulders I grabbed ahold of and moved to the outskirts of the wreckage. I teleported into vehicles. I slipped into drowned buildings and moved people out in groups.

But I felt worthless. There were so many bodies. So many dead people. So much destruction.

I let that feeling wash away though. Because we weren't worthless to the people we saved. They were still breathing. And I had to keep the air in as many people's lungs as possible.

It was 10:15 A.M. when we stopped the quake in San Francisco. It was about 11:20 A.M. when Nick and I stopped the tsunami in Oregon. But cleaning up the mess in Washington took nearly sixteen hours.

We kept going until we moved every living person to higher ground. And we didn't stop there. We then moved every dead body to a separate piece of land south of the town.

When the wolves couldn't smell any more bodies in the wreckage, and when Jeremy and Nick sensed no more life in the town, we finally dropped to the ground to breathe.

There were so many of us. Ourselves, the duplicates of ourselves, our family and their doppelgangers, our friends, and others I wouldn't recognize for another five or fifteen years.

Gods. Goddesses. People with more power than humans could even fathom.

Yet, we sat in a dry field above a dead city staring at hundreds of deceased civilians. We didn't speak. We didn't embrace one another for support. We just looked out over the bodies and accepted our defeat.

Those of us with spirit tried to heal those who hadn't been gone long, but it didn't matter. They wouldn't heal. They were gone.

What infuriated me the most was the conversation I'd had with Lux a year and a half before. *'God loves all his children, but you and Nix aren't my children.'* Yet, he was nowhere in sight. The par animarum, the one's he forced into centuries of treachery, were there. Fighting to save the human lives he allegedly loved so much. But where was he? Not there. Not protecting his children. No, we were. Was his heart even broken the way that ours were? Did he even give a shit? Clearly not. Or he would have helped.

I couldn't tell you how long we sat there. It must have been a while, I know that. But I have no idea how long.

Eventually though, Lila, Kai, Celena, as well as their elder counterparts, Connor and I created a small quake of our own. We broke a slit into the earth. Then we gently used the wind to lift every corpse, at least a few hundred, into the ground. We carefully hoisted the dirt we'd ripped from the earth back over top of them, leaving a small mound over top.

I knew the world was ending. But I didn't think about the logistics. I didn't think about the fact that we'd be burying hundreds of people together in a hole within the earth. I didn't think about the fact that hundreds and thousands of people wouldn't be able to have a funeral for their loved one. I didn't think about all the people who were moving to a new world wondering if their brother or sister, or mother or father, or son or daughter, would be close behind. I didn't think about any of that. Not until the moment that I moved mounds of dry dirt over my first mass burial.

And yes, I said first. Because that was far from the last time I'd rip a hole in the ground and move hundreds of carcasses into it.

It was six in the morning our time when we made it home. I didn't say a word to Jeremy. He didn't try to talk to me either. I didn't even take a shower, despite the fact that I desperately needed one.

I just collapsed onto my clean bed and passed out.

CHAPTER THIRTY-TWO

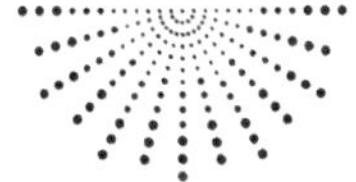

JANUARY 4 - JEREMY

When we made it home, Laila dropped to the bed and fell to sleep within seconds. But I couldn't even think of sleeping. I was completely exhausted. I'd spent more energy in the last twenty-four hours than I had in my entire life. But I couldn't sleep because I couldn't get those images out of my mind.

The bodies floating the streets. That woman begging for her child. The man whose intestines floated beside him in the water.

I looked at myself in the mirror on our dresser. My hair caked against my mudded, bloody cheeks. I'm not even sure whose blood it was because I knew it wasn't mine. Deep dark circles rested beneath my bloodshot eyes. I recognized that expression. It was the same one on Laila's face after the explosion five years ago. Complete defeat. Failure. Pain, agony. For the first time, I truly understood how she felt that day.

We failed. And it was only day one of natural disasters.

I lifted my filthy, sopping legs until I made it to the bathroom. They felt like they weighed a ton each, but I willed them to move. I dropped my jeans to the floor and threw my shirt on top. I stepped into the shower, turned on the water and stood there until it turned cold. I don't even know if I washed my body.

Showers were normally relaxing. They're supposed to be. But after trudging through muddy, waist high water for an entire day, it brought me no relief.

Nothing would for a long time.

I'd been through a lot of shit. I'd seen a lot of shit. But I didn't have PTSD until that day. I had to give Lai credit because it's a bitch of a disease to live with.

When I was finished, I changed into a pair of sweatpants and a band tee. I tried to lie down, but my brain wouldn't stop spinning. Every time I closed my eyes, the events of that day played behind my eyelids like a broken record of a snuff film.

After twenty minutes of struggling, I gave up. I stood, took a few hits off the bowl I kept in my nightstand, and went to the kitchen. I dug in the fridge, pulled out some ham, turkey, tomatoes, and lettuce, set them on the counter, and grabbed the bread from the cabinet. I threw it together and took a bite. But I didn't even taste it.

It was like every nerve in my body had gone numb. I don't know if it was the exhaustion or the trauma, but I could have slammed my head off the butcher block without feeling a thing. But I ate it anyway.

I rolled a joint, lit it at my lips and plopped onto the couch. I saw the sun rising in the distance. No matter how bad things were, that motherfucker rises each morning. It doesn't matter how dark you feel. The world keeps turning and the sun keeps smugly shining.

Until it doesn't.

"Daddy." I heard quietly at the foot of the steps.

I hastily shoved the joint into the ash tray and teleported it to the bedroom. I turned to my son and summoned a smile to my lips. "Hey, buddy."

"Is it time to get up yet?" he asked, rubbing his big blue eyes.

"Are you ready to get up?" I asked.

He shrugged.

"You can sit with me if you want," I said. Micah walked around the couch and climbed to the cushion beside me. He curled up and rested his head against my shoulder. I pressed my lips to his forehead.

"I had a bad dream," he whispered.

"Do you want to talk about it?" I asked.

He turned up to me with watery eyes. "You and Mommy were there. And... and there were all these people. They were... I think they were sick or something because they were sleeping, and they weren't talking, and their lips were blue, and you and Mommy were moving them somewhere safe, but they didn't wake up."

My stomach dropped, and I fought the tears that burned across my eyes. He'd seen what we were doing? He knew what was happening? We'd unplugged the cable boxes and taken the iPads away; I knew he hadn't watched it on the news.

But he didn't need to know what was real. Not for another twenty-four years. So I lied.

I kissed his forehead. "It was just a bad dream, buddy."

Silence set in for a moment. "You and Mommy weren't at the diner, were you?"

"Don't worry about it, alright? Everything's fine."

His eyes shifted between mine. He laid his head back to my chest. "Can you sing me something?"

I tightened my arm around his little torso. Lyrics made their way out of my lips, though I can't remember them. After a few moments, he drifted back to sleep.

I loved my son more than anything. But holding him brought me so much guilt when I heard that woman in my memory crying for her baby. I didn't deserve him any more than that woman deserved her own. Yet, I was the one who got to lie on the couch with my son as the sun rose over the trees in the distance.

And I hated myself for it. I still hate myself for it. But I'd do it all over again. I'd bring him back a thousand times. Even though it meant that woman wouldn't get to see her baby again.

CHAPTER THIRTY-THREE

LAILA

At twelve-thirty, I heard Mom shushing Milly in the doorway. "Mommy will be up soon, baby. Let's go take a little walk, okay?"

"But it's not mowning no mowe," Milly said. "It's time to get up."

"Mommy had a really long night," Mom whispered. "Come on. Let's go see if your brother's hungry. We'll whip something up for lunch."

I started to sit forward until I saw the blood caked to my palm. Milly couldn't see me yet. I had to get cleaned up.

I stared at the wall until I heard the door click shut. I rolled over to a cold bed. Jeremy must have gotten up and let me sleep in.

I stumbled my way from the room. My legs almost felt as though they weren't beneath me as I struggled to the bathroom. I needed a shower, but I didn't have the energy to stand. I was still exhausted.

I teleported into the tub with my clothes still on. Laying on the cold plastic, I struggled my damp jeans from my thighs and tossed them onto Jeremy's pile of clothes beside the shower. I ripped my shirt from my shoulders and started the water.

But I didn't plug the drain. The thought of being submerged in water nauseated me that day. Instead, I grabbed the hose I used to wash Tink and essentially showered lying down.

I couldn't even look at the muddy, bloody water sliding down the drain. Just the thought made my stomach clench.

Once I'd washed the soap from my body and the shampoo from my hair, I just lay there. I didn't have it in me to get up. I needed to. But I wasn't ready to see my kids and pretend everything was okay yet.

I'd lain there for a while when the bathroom door shifted inward. Jeremy forced a smile in the threshold. "Hey."

"Hey," I murmured.

"How'd you sleep?"

"Like a rock." I forced myself to stand. "What about you? Did the kids wake you up?"

He sat on the edge of the bathtub. "No, I didn't. I napped on the couch with Micah for an hour though, I think."

"You must be exhausted." I wrapped the towel around my chest and sat beside him.

He rubbed his eyes. "Just couldn't calm down, ya know?"

I pressed my lips together. "Yeah, if I hadn't used so much energy, I probably would have felt the same way."

He leaned his head against my shoulder. I wrapped my arms around his back, lowering my head to rest on his. "I came in here, and I got cleaned up, and I laid down but I just..." He huffed. "There was this woman. When we first landed, she was holding onto this little ledge against a building. And she kept screaming 'my baby, my baby.'" My eyes closed as my stomach sunk. "I didn't find her baby. Or maybe I did. Maybe I found his body. Or her body. I don't know, baby's a non-binary term so I... Every time I shut my eyes, I heard her. It just kept repeating and repeating, and I had to get up. So I did. I went to the kitchen, and I ate a sandwich. I sat down on the couch to smoke a joint, and Micah came downstairs. He was crying. He had a bad dream."

I pulled back a bit. "Is he okay?"

He inched back. "Yeah, he's fine. But it wasn't just a dream. He saw us...Back there, moving people. He said he saw sleeping people with blue lips."

My stomach dropped. "How? How is that possible?"

"Nothing's impossible with that kid," he said. "I don't know. But I told him it was just a bad dream."

"Did he believe you?"

"He didn't call me a liar." Jeremy moved his thumb and forefinger to his eyes and rubbed them hard.

His eyes looked so heavy. They were normally so big and wide, but they were half of their usual size with the weight of his lids. He needed to sleep.

"Why don't you lie down and get some rest? I'll take over with the kids." I coasted my hand over his upper back.

"No, I'm alright. I'm good. It was just a hard night." He cleared his throat and rolled a kink from his neck. "Nick texted. They were going to come over today to help you see how that tree of life thing works. But I guess they're a little burnt out too. They said to get some rest, and they'll see us tomorrow."

"Have you checked the news?"

"No. And I'm not going to. You shouldn't either. I don't want to know what they're saying about us. All I know is that we did everything that we could. And I don't care what they say. I don't want to hear them call us monsters and become jaded. I'm gonna help them as much as I can, and I don't want to have any hatred for them brewing in the back of my mind, ya know?"

I nodded.

He looked me over. "Where were you and Nick? When the tide hit in Washington, where were you guys?"

"Oregon. There was a tsunami heading to the shore. But we stopped it."

"How?"

"I made this, like, wall of water. I pulled it from the wave, so it made it less powerful."

"Shit, and that worked?"

"Destroyed the beach, but yeah, it didn't make it inland."

I made a mental note to keep that in mind for when time caught up to us. Yes, it'd been tiring. But it was far easier—both physically and emotionally—than clearing the bodies from that little city.

"We didn't have enough time. It was only a couple hundred feet from us when we landed. We tried to push it down or away, but it wouldn't budge. We stayed put as long as we could though. It was right in front of us. Then we teleported to the sky above and we... We watched it. God, I can't believe I'm saying that, but we did. We just watched it wash the town away." He closed his eyes. "We're gods and goddesses. And there were two sets of us. And it still wasn't enough."

"Gods aren't limitless," I whispered. "Fucking hate Peterson, but he was right about one thing. We can't save everyone."

"Maybe that's why you're taking this better than me," he whispered. "I'm just learning that lesson."

I didn't know what to say to that. So I just hugged him and kissed his cheek.

His unblinking eyes stayed heavy against the tile floor. He cleared his throat. "I'm gonna go see what the kids are up to."

"Alright, I'll be out in a minute."

***

The truth is, I wasn't taking it better than Jeremy. Inside, I was a disaster. But I knew that I couldn't let myself fall again. I'd slipped before. I knew what it felt like to fall into that deep pit of depression, and I couldn't allow myself to do it again.

When I went to therapy a few years prior, the doctor told me that when I felt myself begin to stumble again, I had to catch myself. I had to visualize it. When my feet felt weak, I could sit down and take a break. I could dangle my legs along the edge, but I couldn't let myself fall inside. I could reach down and grab a rock protruding from the edge. I could hold onto a branch and take a quick dip. But I had to hold on tight to keep from falling. Because it's a lot easier to climb a few feet from the surface than it is to climb from the bottom once you've fallen and broken a bone.

People died yesterday. Hundreds of lives were gone because we didn't act fast enough. And yeah, I could tell myself that it was my fault. I could let that weight of failure rest on my shoulders. But that wouldn't help anyone.

If I were a depressed, anxious disaster, even more would perish. The world tomorrow would be even darker than it was today. And it was, it was dark. But when you're in the dark, you search for the light. And if you can't find it, you create your own.

That's exactly what I did. I walked from the bedroom to the living room and looked at the two vibrant lights I'd created. I smiled as they laughed at *Peppa Pig* on the TV.

Yeah, it hurt. Life does. Being alive hurts. It's a simple fact of existence. Especially when you have the weight of the entire world on your shoulders. We all wish that we could be happy at every moment of every day. But without pain, we wouldn't be able to appreciate what it means to feel good. We wouldn't know what love felt like if we never experienced hurt.

CHAPTER THIRTY-FOUR

JEREMY

Laila and I were relaxing on the couch with a kid tucked at each of our hips. My head rested on her shoulder and Milly's against my ribs. Rachel sat on the chaise a few feet away. I couldn't tell you which, but some kid's show played in the background.

I'd just begun to wind down. My eyelids were heavy, falling down to meet their lower lids. My arms were gradually growing limp at my sides.

And then my phone rang on the kitchen counter. I'd only checked it a few times in the past couple of days, and when I had, it was exclusively for a message from Nick or Lila. Selfish, I suppose, with all things considered. But everyone, and I do mean everyone, was trying to contact me or Laila either about the videos in the news, the ones leaked online, or the storms that had started yesterday. And I didn't have the energy to deal with it. I didn't have time to explain the story in all of its depth to every person in the supernatural community, nor our employees at Moe's. My mood wasn't exactly chipper, and I felt both physically and emotionally drained.

But it was time to answer some questions. Exhaling deeply, I stood and started across the room.

"Who is it, baby?" Laila asked, tilting over her shoulder to meet my gaze.

I looked down at the phone and sighed once more. A name I hadn't uttered in years. Olivia. I shifted it towards Laila.

"Who is it, Daddy?" Micah asked.

"Daddy's girlfriend," Laila said with a playful grin.

I rolled my eyes.

"I thought *you* were Daddy's girlfriend."

"No, I'm Daddy's wife," she corrected.

"She's an old friend," I said as I started toward the patio door with the phone.

"An old *girl*friend," Laila said.

I shook my head with a smile. "I hate you."

"Oh. You guys have a lot of old friends," Micah muttered.

"Well, that tends to happen when you're old," I said.

As I pulled open the patio door and slid the green bar on the screen, Laila spoke. "Tell her whatever she needs to know."

I stepped outside. Holding the phone to my ear, I answered, "Hello?"

"What the fuck is going on, Jeremy?" she snapped.

"I've been great, how have you been, Liv? I got the Christmas card, by the way, congrats on the new baby," I said.

A low huff. I could practically hear her shaking her head. "It doesn't really seem like we have the time for pleasantries."

I rubbed my eyes. "Guess not."

"What's happening? What the hell is going on?"

"You saw the news. You know what's going on. The world's ending."

"And you knew about this?" she growled. "You knew that the world was about to fall apart, and you couldn't have taken five minutes out of your day to give me a heads up? I have kids, dude, I have a life and—"

"I assumed your dad had." I made a face. "He's been pretty damn vocal at the Chamber's meetings. We never made any attempt to hide an ounce of this, we told everyone what we knew."

"My dad." She scoffed. "In what world have I ever been on good terms with my dad?"

"It's been circling the community for more than a year now. Everyone knew this was coming, or at least suspected it. Did you just ignore it? Because we've been talking about this for—"

"I'm not a part of that world anymore, Jeremy, damn it," she said quickly. "I haven't cast a spell in months, and I haven't even seen my family since my wedding day. So no, no one gave me the four-one-one. I know that we aren't best pals or anything, but I'm at least part of the reason you have your kid back. You could have shot me a text. 'Hey, Liv, just a heads up. The world's going to end soon. Just letting you know so you can get your ducks in a row.' That would've been perfectly sufficient."

Ah, shit.

Well now, I did feel bad. No, we weren't friends, but if I knew she didn't know, I'd have told her. But I assumed that Eric had. She was his daughter. If you hear the world's going to end for certainty, why wouldn't you make contact with your kid, even if you are estranged?

Then again, we're talking about the same fucker that said I should kill my three-year-old.

I leaned over the railing and rubbed my eyes. "I'm sorry. I didn't know. I really thought Eric would have told you."

"Yeah, well, the last thing he told me was that he'd rather see me dead than marry a human and have 'watered down, useless grandchildren," she said.

"Sounds like your dad," I murmured. "I really am sorry. I didn't know about all that."

"I guess you wouldn't." A long pause drew in. She cleared her throat. "Will, my husband, until that video played on the news, he didn't know about any of this. I didn't even tell him about what I am until this morning. He saw you in the news. Two of you, actually, and he recognized you from pictures on my Facebook. It was a whole big thing. He's freaking out. For good reason, I guess but I just—I don't know what I'm supposed to do. I don't know what to do, Jeremy."

I gazed out over the foggy morning. "Do you want to keep your family safe? Or do you want to fight?"

She scoffed again. "You know good and damn well that I have no skills in battle. I can cast a couple spells, and I have good intuition but there's no way in hell I can do even a fraction of what I saw you guys doing last night. And who was that, by the way? How were there two of you?"

"It doesn't matter. But what does is keeping your family safe. And the only way for you to do that is to listen. Do what your local officials are saying. Go through the portal."

"I'm not Fae, Jeremy," she snapped. "That is where it's going, right? Because I know it isn't Heaven, and Hell seems about as bad as this so I'm assuming that's where it's going. The Fae Realm. And I can't live there. I can't live without toilets with running water and electricity and-and—"

"None of that's going to be around here for much longer either, Olivia." My voice was sharper than the tip of a dagger. "You're more concerned about shitting in a hole than your entire family being wiped out by a natural disaster or a meteor? How is that even a concept in your mind right now, dude?"

"Well, clearly, I haven't had as much time to prepare for this as you have!" she yelled.

Silence crept in, and she drew in a long breath.

I closed my eyes and did the same. It wasn't fair. None of it was fair. She didn't deserve what was happening. As much drama as she'd caused over the years, she'd still been a hero to me more times than I'd care to admit.

And she'd done it all right. She went to college, she got a good job, she married a nice guy and started a sweet little family. She was living the American dream. And suddenly, it was being torn out from under her.

That was the case for most of the world. Everyone had a life, one they loved, whether they bitched about it constantly or not, and now they had to leave it all behind. They had to start over in a place where they'd be foreigners. The lesser race, quite literally speaking.

It wasn't that the Fae *hated* humans, but they had no respect for them either. They were powerless and—in their eyes—destroyed everything they touched. The humans were graced with a world almost identical to the Fae aside from a few beasts and plants. And while the earth realm was a dying planet, the Realm of Light flourished with beauty and growth—and had for just as long. Yet, in only the past hundred years or so, humans had completely destroyed their own home.

It's like that old saying about picking out a new dog. If you go to the shelter and the little bugger shits where he sleeps, that's not the one you want to bring home. You want the one that at least knows to defecate on the other side of the kennel. And in the eyes of the Fae, humans not only made the mistake of shitting where they slept, but they also defended it because of their false illusion of a better life with fossil fuels and convenient transportation. Regardless of the fact that even in one of the so-called 'first world countries' on this planet many places still drank water that contained lead and uranium.

"So that's the best advice you've got." Olivia broke the silence. "Pack a bag and jump into a world where my entire family will be unwelcome."

"You're a doctor, Liv. You'll be revered there."

"I'm a PA. I'm not a doctor," she said. "And they have a million healers on that plane. I'm not any more useful than them."

"Maybe not, but how do you think a human who breaks their arm going through the portal is going to feel about someone with green skin and glowing white hands holding them down to heal a broken bone when you can wrap it up with a stick and help it heal on its own? Naturally, the way they're used to," I said. "You'll give them a sense of normalcy. You'll matter there as much as you do here, maybe even more."

It got quiet again. I ran my hand along my tense jaw. "Or stay. But that's a bigger risk. One I doubt you want to take with a newborn and a one-year-old."

A heavy breath sounded through the speaker. "Thanks for the

advice. I—I have to go pack. Are there going to be any freak storms before I can make it to the portal?"

"Not that I know of. Two days and there's going to be a lot of volcanoes erupting though, so I'd move fast."

She sighed once more. "We'll be in the other world by nightfall as long as the line isn't too long."

"Well, good luck. And don't be surprised if you puke on the way through. It's not exactly pleasant."

"Thanks, I'll keep that in mind. And Jeremy?"

"Yeah?"

"Fuck you."

The line went dead.

I was sure I'd be hearing that a lot in the coming days.

CHAPTER THIRTY-FIVE

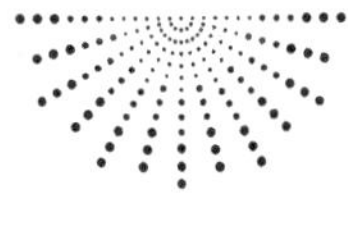

LAILA

While Jeremy was outside talking on the phone, I picked up my own. And my stomach dropped.

Over the past few years, I'd become something of a pillar in our community. After destroying two compounds where nearly a thousand of us were being held captive, our people started referring to me as a savior. But I was dealing with my own trauma then, and I wanted no part of that notoriety.

When word came out that some few thousand years ago, Jeremy and I were once gods ruling the planet, the people turned to me. I can't say that I was worshipped, but I was definitely looked at as a leader. Not that I truly wanted that either. Nonetheless, I wore the crown. And things weren't exactly organized.

I'd given my number to nearly a thousand survivors and a few of each of their family members. That was the type of person I was. *Call me any time. Day or night, I'll do whatever I can to help you,* I'd said.

With an impending apocalypse on the horizon, that was a really bad move.

Because while I was trying to pick up the pieces and figure out what the fuck life meant from here, I also had thousands of text messages from numbers I'd never seen before. I'd remember their faces, at least vaguely, but it all turned to a blur of chaos.

Someone recognized me from the videos, what do I do?

Is this really happening? Hello? Laila? What's going on? What am I supposed to do?

They tried to kill me. I need help. I'm at (so-and-so location), please send help.

I'm scared. I'm so scared.

They hate us. How did you let this happen?

You said you'd help us, where are you?!

They're after me.

My sister's hurt. We need a healer. Where are you?

We can't get through your property line, and we need you.

You said you'd always be there but where are you now? You're no better than God.

Wtf?! Where are you?

Why are you helping them and not us? You swore you'd help us.

I know I owe you nothing, you saved my life once, and I'll always be in your debt, but we need you too. The humans are turning on us. They don't trust us. What makes you think we can persuade them to move to another dimension?

So is that offer just for the humans? Or am I supposed to sacrifice my life for a world that hates me?

I have a family. I have people counting on me. I can't fight in a war, Laila. I know you need all the help you can get, but I'm just not the type of help you need.

Damn it, Laila, I've been calling you for hours. Where are you?

How is you forcing us to fight your war any different than Peterson strapping us to a table to make us use our powers for him? Fuck this and fuck you. I'm going to the Fae Realm.

Overwhelmed doesn't begin to touch how I felt in that moment. My body flooded with panic. They were right, I said I'd be there for them, and I wasn't. I was too busy sleeping and meeting my future children while their lives were in peril.

I didn't even know where to start. What was I supposed to do?

Argue with them? They weren't wrong.

Help them. That's what I had to do.

I lifted my head from my phone. "Mom."

"Yeah, baby?" she said from her seat on the couch.

"Can you watch them for a few hours?" I asked. "I have some things I need to take care of."

She gave a concerned expression. "Yeah. Sure, of course."

Micah's head peeped over the back of the sectional. His big eyes pulled open. "You're leaving *again?*"

I forced a smile. "Some people need my help. But don't worry, things are going to settle back down real soon."

He crossed his arms against his chest and turned back to the TV. "Whatever."

I closed my eyes and released a slow, calming breath. The clunk of the patio door pulling shut forced them to open. I met Jeremy's gaze. "Everything alright?"

"Yeah, they'll be fine."

"Are you staying, Daddy?" Micah asked.

Jeremy raised a brow at him then looked back at me. "Where are you going?"

Everywhere. I spoke into his mind. *The survivors, their families, everyone's going through a shit storm. Humans are attacking the ones they recognized, others don't know who to turn to. They're scared. And I built this army, I need to lead them.*

He chewed his lip, clearly debating within his mind. I knew he was burnt out; he should have stayed home and gotten the rest his body needed. But he turned to Micah with a sad smile. "I'll be back later, alright? You be good for grandma."

You don't have to, I said into his thoughts. *I can handle this. You need to rest.*

I'll sleep when I'm dead.

I smiled. *So never.*

He sent back a bare smile.

"But, Daddy—" Micah began.

"Relax, bud," Jeremy said, squatting down to his level. "I'll try and be home for dinner. But, if I'm not, I *promise* I'll be home to put you to bed and sing you a song."

Micah's arms stayed crossed. "Only say that if you really mean it."

"Have I ever broken a promise I made you?" He gave a playful grin, leaning forward and tickling his side. Micah let out an unwilling giggle, pushed his hand away, and crossed his arms back to his chest. Jeremy held his gentle smile. "I *promise* that I'll be home to put you to bed. I'm going to try really hard to get here for dinner, but if I can't, I swear on my life that I'll be here for bedtime. Okay?"

"You better," Micah said.

He laughed. "I will. You're gonna be good for Gam, right?"

Micah crossed his arms and lifted his chin. "I'm always good."

Jeremy smiled, eyes moving between Micah's. "You sure are." He leaned forward and touched his lips to his forehead, then did the same with Milly. I walked around the couch and gave each of them a hug and kiss, took Jeremy's hand, then teleported to the main house.

"Jesus Christ," Leah grumbled as we landed. "What? What now?"

My gaze shifted over her. Dark, tired circles sat below her eyelids. Her skin looked ghastly compared to its usual warm, radiant brown. The pink to her lips faded into a nearly white color.

"A lot of our people are hurt," I murmured. "Do you have it in you to do some healing?"

She rubbed her tired eyes. "Yeah. I guess. Let me pee first."

"Where's everybody at?" Jeremy asked.

"Laying around somewhere." She stood and started to the powder room. "Grab who you need."

"We need someone to stay here," I said. "There's some people at the gates."

She glanced at me from the bathroom door. "So we're bunking now too?"

"Well, we do have the toboggan," Jeremy said. "But we don't have a furnace set up there, and it is pretty cold—"

"Fine," she snapped. "Fine, but I'm staying at your house. I do not have it in me right now to play hostess."

"That's good. Maybe Hannah and Kai can stay here, and everyone else can move in with us for the time being. That way, everyone has a safe place to stay, and we can all be together still."

"Whatever. Not like this is going to be our home for much longer anyway. Might as well kiss it goodbye sooner than later."

I pressed my lips together as she started into the bathroom.

That thought sent a shiver down my spine. I knew this home meant more to the siblings than it did to me, but it'd been my home for a time too. And I didn't want to leave it. I didn't want to think about it not being our home anymore. But it was true, even if it did break my heart.

"I'll get Kai and Celena," Jeremy said. "You find Adam and Brody. See who's willing to come."

CHAPTER THIRTY-SIX

JEREMY

Just as I was about to knock on Hannah's door, I heard hushed whimpers seep out from beneath, thinking it was Kai at first. I heard his condolences.

"It's all right, love," he whispered. "Everything's going to be all right. We-we just have to make it a few more days, and then all of this, all of this pain is going to stop."

"It won't stop. It's just being put on pause," Hannah said between gasps. "You don't understand. You don't know how it feels. The void is so much brighter, and it's not meant to be bright. The brighter it is, the more people who die. And soon, soon it's going to be brighter than a sun, and I-I-I can't help them. I can't bring them back. I-I—"

"Shh," he whispered.

My eyes closed as a shaking breath left my nostrils. I knew exactly how she felt. Feeling so many souls leave their bodies at once the day before felt like my body shifting to a black hole. A pit was forming within me. It physically hurt.

When you have the ability to bring people back from the grave, you feel obligated to return every soul to a body. Still, I didn't spend much time in that space we go when we die. Primarily because being there was like floating through a graveyard. Sure, the souls aren't dead. But they're striving for a body. They want to live again. Sitting in space isn't life; it's literally purgatory. It's just... nothing. Emptiness. Souls aren't meant to float amid the abyss; they're supposed to be cradled within flesh and blood.

"Fuck," Celena said behind me. "What's wrong?"

I turned. "Laila checked her phone. A lot of people need us. The survivors, others in our community. Some of them are hurt. Do you have it in you to help?"

She ran her hand over her blotchy pale face. "Yeah, do we need Wyatt?"

"Not with us. But he could be helpful here. There are people at the gates; they need a safe haven. He and Hannah can man them."

"Alright. Let me get dressed. Text me where you need me."

I frowned, then the door behind me pulled open.

"Bloody hell, what now?" Kai said.

I turned to him. He looked as drained as the rest of us. "We need you if you have the energy."

"I got enough rest."

Jenna opened her bedroom door with Luka at her hip. She looked me over. "What is it?"

"Others, like us. They're under attack. Humans, they're turning on our kinds. They need somewhere safe to stay, and a lot of them need healed."

She pulled Luka closer to her chest. "I'll wake Adam up."

I gave a nod as Hannah stood from the bed behind Kai. Kai sent her a smile then brushed past me to the bathroom as Celena and Jenna walked back into their rooms. She wiped her red cheeks.

"How are you holding up?" she asked.

"Hanging in there. What about you?"

"I don't know. I was okay. But... you felt it, right? When all those people died?"

"Yeah. I felt it."

She frowned. "A blessing and a curse."

"Our lives tied up in a single sentence."

An unwilling smile pulled at her lips. "Guess so."

"We need you, too. There're people at the gates. They need a—"

"Yeah, I heard you," she said. "I'm going down with the Jeep now."

"Wait for Wyatt. There might be some people hiding in the woods to get away from the reporters if they're still there. He can track them down."

"Will do. Necklaces in the basement?"

"Yeah. We might need to make some more though."

"Sure," she said. "I'll call Helena."

"Thank you," I said.

"Least I can do. Not like I'm actually out there saving lives."

"You were. Older you, I mean. She knew how to use Kai's powers. She was a badass, actually."

A sad smile tugged at her lips. "Well, that makes me feel a little less worthless."

I smiled. "You've never been worthless."

She looked between my eyes for a minute. "Thank you. Do me a favor though?"

"Depends on what it is."

She gestured toward the bathroom. "Watch out for him out there. He's only seen the good side of humanity. He doesn't know what he's walking into."

"That's my brother. I've got his back. And more importantly, so does Laila."

I said things like that a lot. That Laila's the one with the power. But I don't say that to stroke her ego, I say it because it's true.

She's the one concerned with the greater good. She's the one who wants to save everyone all of the time. And she's the one who can deal with it when she can't.

I cared about the greater good too, but when I cared about something, I cared too deeply. I let it consume me. That's why I focused on the family. Because when I thought about the big picture, it overwhelmed me. Thinking about the weight of the entire world on my back was all consuming, and at that time, I wasn't strong enough to bear that weight.

So I focused on her. Because if I carried her, she could carry the world.

I guess that's another lesson Peterson taught her when he took Micah. She had to live with the guilt of losing her son to save hundreds of others.

Had it been me in her shoes, I'd have left everyone else for dead to save my son. But Laila was different. She had to save them all. And somehow, she actually did.

***

"Have you ever been here?" Laila asked, turning the phone toward me.

I squinted at the address. "No. Canada was never my thing."

"Well shit. I can't teleport somewhere I've never seen." She typed quickly, telling the person on the other end we were on our way.

"Google earth it," I said. "If I see the place, I can get there."

She typed at the speed of light.

"Where am I going?" Celena asked.

"Go grab Helena," I said. "Bring her back here, and we'll text you where to go from there."

She disappeared. I turned to Kai, pulling up another Google earth image of a home in Spain. "They ken I'm coming?"

"They know someone's coming," I said. "Go into the home though; don't knock outside. Land and teleport in once you see through the windows. Heal who needs healed, then bring them back here. We'll go from there."

He examined the image. "See ye soon."

Laila turned her phone to me. A suburban house. Typical, manufactured home. Blue shutters on white vinyl siding, cute picket fence, a Suzuki parked in the drive. Without an inside view, we had to do the same as I'd told Kai. Land in the yard and go inside once we got a view from a close vicinity.

They said in their message that people were gathered around the perimeter, but I didn't realize what they meant until we landed.

Immediately, before I even got a glance in the house, we were met with shouting and gunfire. Their aim was shitty though. I pulled Laila closer and teleported to the outskirts of the home across the block. The mob of mostly white men with guns and baseball caps began screaming, "Fan out!"

"Jesus Christ," Laila muttered, hand moving to her heart. "Judge, jury, and executioner brought to a new level."

"At least they're moving," I whispered. "I need a glimpse inside. I'm not familiar with this area at all."

She peeked around the edge of the bush. "I think I can see in that window right there," she murmured. "But I don't want to move us in there between two pieces of drywall."

"Can you hear their thoughts?" I asked. "Because if you can see what they see, we can get in no problem."

She closed her eyes. After a second or two, her head shook. "There's too much chatter. All these people, they need to shut up."

"Well, you could text them and have them send a picture—"

"Don't move." I heard behind me, followed by the clicking of a rifle. I closed my eyes and released an annoyed huff. "Don't move or I'll—"

I teleported behind him, stuck an arm around his neck, and grasped the gun in his hand. He gasped as I tightened the crease of my elbow into his neck. Laila stood, ripped the gun from his palm, and looked firmly between his eyes. "You're really tired. You need a nap, don't you?"

I felt his body soften in my arm. Laila smiled. "Take a nap then." His blubbery body went loose in my arms, and I struggled to get him on the ground without falling myself.

"Fucker," Laila muttered, kicking his outer arm as I balanced myself.

"Text them," I said. "As fast as you can. The more of them we have to deal with, the longer this is going to take."

She slid her phone from her pocket as we lowered ourselves back to the bush.

I turned behind us, scanning the area as she typed. Groups of two to three roamed in different directions. They snuck around the edge of cars like cheap actors in a shitty cop show. I had to fight the urge to laugh.

It was pathetic. They saw us teleport. They saw videos of Laila incinerate a man and erupt a tree from a concrete floor through another's body. How they possibly thought their skills hunting deer and elk was even close to hunting down a pair of gods was beyond me.

Sure was humorous to watch though. A bunch of chubby middle-aged men and drunk hicks jumping around the edge of trash cans in pursuit of us.

Makeshift militias like theirs didn't work. They're just a bunch of lazy shits who have no physical skill needed for battle. War takes training. And I was no Jackie Chan either, but any one of us, even my four-year-old, knew better than those jackasses.

"Got it," Laila said, grasping my hand and teleporting inside.

The smell of vomit immediately touched my nostrils. It was dimly lit, struggling to avoid being seen from the outside between the blinds. As my vision adjusted, I heard the shattering of glass followed by a shriek. "Get it back up! Put it back up now!"

"I'm trying!" another voice yelled.

"Sarah?" Laila called. "Sarah, where are you?"

"In here, in here!" a woman's voice called.

Laila started fast through the house, following the sound of the girl's voice. We rushed through a hallway into a living room. My stomach sunk as I realized where the smell of vomit was coming from.

A young guy lay on a brown couch with his limp arm resting in a pile of blood colored vomit on the ground. His face was purple, every orifice nearly swollen shut. His head lulled to the side, breaths barely moving in and out of his exposed, bruised chest.

"Laila," a woman said beside him, tears rushing down her cheeks. "Laila, heal him."

"Yeah. Heal him," a young girl said sharply at his feet. "You're the savior, right?"

She ignored the tone in the girl's voice as she kneeled beside the boy. "Have you ever been healed before, sweetie?" she asked, pushing short black curls from his cheek.

His head shifted back and forth a bit. Laila looked at me. I moved to his head and took each of his arms in my palms. As she spoke to him, I turned to the women. "Grab his legs."

"Why?" the girl snapped.

"Being healed hurts. He's reflexively going to hit when she starts," I said.

"But—" the young girl began.

"Do you care about him?" I asked, eyes shifting between hers. "Because she'll save him, but she can't do that if he's throwing punches."

"I understand that," she snapped. "But he's a wolf. He's stronger than all of us combined."

"I'll try." The man coughed. "I'll b-be still."

"Why aren't you healing then?"

"They shot him up with something," the older woman said.

I clenched my hands around his. Laila glanced at me with a look of panic but started the process.

The girl wasn't wrong, it took a lot of willpower to hold him down. But all that I kept thinking was how in the hell did they know about wolfs bane? And where did they get it on such short notice? The average person doesn't grow Aconitum napellus in their garden.

It occurred to me that I'd only seen a video or two. I knew there were thousands, but I didn't realize Peterson exposed our weaknesses in them. I recoiled back to the question I'd thought of days ago.

Why the fuck did he release those tapes? He did all of this to prepare us for the war. Giving the humans a way to destroy our army was opposite of preparing for the war.

But then another thought dawned on me. The Angel the night it all started. The one who tried to kill Laila.

Lux.

Fucking Lux.

It wasn't Peterson, it was Lux that released those videos. But again, why? Why prepare us to fight this war and expose our weaknesses to the enemy? The wolves made up at least thirty percent of our army. And why did he send Angels after his best soldier?

"Hold it, Nat," the older woman said.

"I'm trying, damn it," the girl yelled from the man's feet. "It's a little hard to focus at the moment."

"Do you have a shield up?" I asked her.

A gunshot fired outside.

Laila looked up at me. "Can you finish healing him?"

"What are you going to do?" I released my hold and moved to where she stood.

She ran her tongue along her teeth and started toward the front door.

CHAPTER THIRTY-SEVEN

LAILA

As I opened the front door, they screamed, "Now! Now, fire!"

I raised my hands on either side. Bright violet flames licked through the air like a blow torch. Each piece of metal fell to the ground before me in a pile of melted copper, still bright red from the heat. The men stared at me with gaping mouths.

One screamed, "Again! Again!"

I slammed the air behind them into the back of their legs. They fell to the ground, dropping their guns on the way down.

"What the fuck is wrong with you people?!" I yelled. "What did we do to you? Why are you acting like pathetic children when all that we're trying to do is help your dumb asses?!"

"You're a monster!" one man called. "All of you, you're Demons!"

"You wouldn't know a Demon if it slapped you in the face," I barked. "We're trying to save you. We're trying to keep you safe, and this is how you repay us? With bullets and beatings? Why?! *Why?!*"

"We don't want your help," a man toward the back yelled.

"Fine, then stay here and die. Maybe you'll be a little smarter in the next life. If enough of you survive to repopulate after what's coming," I snapped. "But why attack us? Why do you hate the people trying to save you? Because we can do things you can't? Because we're—"

"Because you're evil!" a man screamed. "Because you're the devil! Because you're murderers!"

I huffed as my jaw clamped shut. Out of the corner of my eye, I saw someone reach for the gun they'd dropped. I teleported in front of him and put my foot over the barrel. His hand trembled as I kicked it away.

"Like you?" I looked over the crowd. "Like all of you? Like you were just about to be? Tell me, if I hadn't stopped those bullets, which one of you was going to take credit for my death? Or would none of you? Would you all pretend that you're better than me? That you hadn't just killed a woman? A mother, a wife, a business owner. That's what I am, and you were going to kill me. Why—because I killed a man who strapped me to a table and ripped my skin to shreds? I know you couldn't hear it because the audio was of my victimizer, but I was begging them to stop. I was controlling my abilities. I was fighting with everything I had to keep from hurting those bastards, but they wouldn't stop, and my body instinctively reacted—"

"That's the problem," a man a few people down murmured.

My eyes narrowed. I took a few steps down until I stood over him. "What did you just say?"

He said nothing, staring at the tops of my feet. I telekinetically pushed his head up to face mine. "What did you just say?"

"That's the problem," he whispered. "You lose control, and you murder people."

I narrowed my gaze. "Is that what I'm doing now? Am I losing control? Because I feel steady as a stone."

His body trembled as he looked into my eyes.

"Stop looking at me like that. I'm not going to kill any of you," I said. "But listen to me you bigoted, idiotic shit heads." I took a step back and darted my gaze over the crowd. "Me and my people are trying to help you. I am putting lives on the line to save yours. If you don't want our help, then fine. Die. Fucking die. But leave my soldiers alone. Killing my people is like killing your own because our mission here is to save the planet. We want to save the human race. We are Guardians. Our existence is to protect yours from outside sources that want to hurt you. If you want us to help you, if you don't want to go through the portal—"

"The portal to hell," another man murmured.

"Hell?" I asked, walking toward the right where the man had spoken. "No. No, if you stay, *then* you'll be living in hell. Those portals go to a land more beautiful than anything you've ever seen. A land you don't deserve. But one that has been graciously offered either way. And no, I'm not going to force you into the portal. If you want to see for yourself, then fine. You'll see. And you'll die. But stay the fuck out of my way.

"We're about to be in a real-life war of the worlds here." I side stepped, looking out over the men on their knees. "And once it starts, I won't be able to do much to help you. So either go now or regret it later because if you stay here, your days are numbered."

"Laila." I heard Jeremy say behind me, holding the partially healed man against his hip with the middle-aged woman from inside. "We have to go. Back to the house, now."

"What is it?"

"Celena," he said. "She's hurt."

When we landed in the sunroom, my heart hammered so hard that it hurt. Celena was sprawled out on the couch not much different than the man Jeremy were helping to the armchair. Her eye was black and blue, her lip busted open. Blood dribbled down her cheek from a gash in her forehead. Wyatt sat beside her. His thumb pushed matted hair from her cheek as she struggled to keep her bloodshot eyes open.

"What the hell happened?" I kneeled beside Wyatt.

"They weren't ours," she choked out. "It was a set up."

"What do you mean?" I asked.

"What the fuck do you think she means?" Wyatt's wide eyes darted to mine. "They were human. They tried to fucking kill her. What were you thinking? Why didn't you—"

"Wyatt," Celena murmured, head shaking a bit. "Stop it."

"No." His gaze snapped to mine. "What the fuck, Laila? You didn't even check to see who you were sending her after. You led her straight into a trap. You didn't even confirm their identities, you just fed her to the wolves."

Jeremy chuckled. Wyatt turned up to him with a tight jaw and deep, angry pants. "Sorry," Jeremy muttered. "Just ironic since she's the wolf and all."

Celena's lips curved upward, bruised hand raising for a high five. Jeremy tapped it as Wyatt's furious gaze came back to mine. "This ain't funny. This ain't a damn joke. She could have died. I can't teleport like you. I had to wait for Brody to get back before I could even—"

"Baby," Celena said.

"No, Celena, Christ. God damn it. This isn't okay. This shouldn't have happened." His angry eyes were still on me. "Don't send us out there unless you can promise our safety. You're the one who preaches about always going with backup, and you sent her out there alone and no teleporters here to help in case something like this happened. You didn't think shit through."

"I was just trying to help—"

"Who? Who were you trying to help? We don't owe these people shit. You sacrificed your kid to save them the first time, and that was your choice, but you don't get to sacrifice—"

"Watch yourself, Wyatt," Jeremy said.

He glared up at him. "It's the truth—"

"Stop it," Celena snapped. "Damn it, Wyatt, you're not helping anyone. No one sacrificed me. I went out there on my own free will. Because like Laila, I want to help. I was human once. I know you weren't, but I was, and I understand why they're reacting like this. I panicked when I learned about all this too if you don't remember. And I didn't need backup to heal a few people and bring them back here. I'm not a little girl, I can fight my own battles—"

"And this wasn't your battle—"

"This is *all* of our battle." She shot him a look. "Just because we don't remember it doesn't mean that we aren't equally as obligated to protect the souls we brought to this planet."

"I—"

"I'm in a lot of pain, and I don't have it in me to argue with you right now, damn it," Celena blurted. "So shut up so my sister can heal me."

He slammed his jaw shut and brought himself to his feet. He started toward the kitchen, and Jeremy tailed after him.

I looked over Celena again, and my stomach dropped. He was right. I shouldn't have sent her out there without being sure I was sending her to allies. The sacrificing comment went right over my head, honestly. I knew he meant it figuratively, and he had the right to be mad. I'd be mad too if he sent Jeremy out, and he came back looking like Celena did.

"I'm sorry," I murmured. "I didn't know—"

"Oh, stop it," Celena said. "You know how Wyatt is. He doesn't like taking risks, and he's overprotective. You were trying to act fast, and that's a risk we have to take right now. This is war. War means making split second decisions. And I'm fine. A little wolf's bane hasn't killed me before, it won't kill me now. I'll be out of commission for the rest of the day, but it's not a big deal. By morning, I'll be good as new."

"I'm still sorry."

"Don't be. This is my war too. And I could handle those fuckers. They were all on the ground before he even showed," Celena said. "Just heal this shit for me, would you?"

I brought glowing white light to my hands.

"And I'm sorry for what he said about Micah," she said, reddened blue eyes moving between mine. "He didn't mean that."

I simply shrugged.

I handed Celena a bottle of water. She took a sip and moved a hand to her stomach with a wince.

"Shit, did I miss something?" I asked.

"No, just the wolf's bane. Kind of feel like I've got a cold. But I'm alright. It's metabolizing. I'll be better soon."

I turned to the others we'd brought back from Canada. "How are you guys? Feeling better?"

The man nodded. "Yeah, I'm okay. Same as her."

I looked at the women. "And you guys?"

The older woman said, "We're alright. I'm Sarah, by the way. My daughter, Natalie, and her boyfriend, Mason."

"I remember. You were in the first compound with me. Witch, right?" I asked.

She nodded.

"Well, I'm glad you're okay. All of you. You can stay here until things settle down. There are others though, so I've got to head out."

"Sure," Sarah said. "Sure, thank you."

Natalie scoffed a bit. I knew what she was thinking. She heard the things Wyatt said too, and they filled her with disdain. Although, I wasn't sure what disturbed her more. His comments about not owing the survivors anything or hearing that I'd sacrificed my son to save them.

"Where is she?" a sharp voice said in the kitchen.

"Lila," Nick's voice said. "You need to calm down—"

"Don't start," she snapped.

I let out a breath and stood.

"What's this about?" Jeremy asked. "What's going on?"

"Your wife," Lila snapped as I started into the kitchen.

"You mean you?" Jeremy said.

"Well, I was never this dumb so no, not me," Lila said.

What had I done wrong? I just saved three people. Surely she hadn't heard about Celena yet.

"You're seriously overreacting," Nick said.

"I'm overreacting?" she said as I stepped into the doorway. "Really? Am I? Because from where I'm standing, it feels like you're *under*reacting."

"What's going on?" I asked, looking between them in confusion.

Lila turned to me. "What the fuck were you thinking?"

"What are you talking about?"

"Why were you in Montreal?" she snapped. "And why'd you force a group of humans to bow to you?"

My face screwed up in confusion. "What?"

"It's all over the internet." She reached into her pocket and turned the screen of her phone to me. "You standing in front of almost fifty dudes that you pulled to their knees as you lecture them about how they should be grateful to you?"

"I didn't say that," I said. "And I didn't make them *kneel* to me. I just yanked them to the ground to get their guns out of their hands. I didn't even hurt anyone—"

"A picture is worth a thousand words. And what does this one say, Laila?" She gestured to a picture of me standing in front of the men on their knees. "This says bow to me, I'm your queen. This says to hell with your rights. You do as I say, or you die."

"I didn't mean it like that—" I began.

"But it's what you said, isn't it?" she barked. "You told them if they didn't listen, they'd all die—"

"That's almost verbatim what you said on CNN—"

"But not after forcing their guns from their hands and throwing them to their knees! This is some Khaleesi shit. This is some season eight, let's slaughter a damn city shit—"

"I didn't hurt anyone," I said quickly. "All I did was tell them to stay out of my way and to quit fucking with my people—"

"Why?!" Her eyes glowed. "Why didn't you just get the guy and leave? Why'd you have to make my life so much harder? Now everyone's calling us a dictator. They're saying this is new world order. Resist the monster uprising is trending on every social media network. Because you had to go assert your authority—"

"I had just healed a man who'd been beaten to a pulp," I snapped. "My phone is still blowing up with people begging me to come help them because the people they're supposed to be protecting are terrorizing them. They're destroying our army's inhibition—"

"Yes, but you just made them feel like following us is scarier than what's coming. If they're worried about fighting us, then they're not going to listen and save themselves before it's too late—"

"And if they kill our army, what difference will it make?" I asked. "If they kill our people, we won't be able to fight them, and the people who've sworn their lives to us will turn on us for failing to protect them—"

"You could have protected your people without cutting those guys balls off—"

"Their ego is more important than my followers feeling like they have a reason to fight for me?"

"Of course not, you idiot." Lila's voice was like ice. "But you could have done it without making a crowd of grown men piss themselves. You didn't have to show them how strong you are. They already know that that's why they're fighting back in the first place. All that you did was make shit worse. You could have just taken the guy and come back here. You didn't have to play the 'my horse is bigger than your horse' bullshit. You have a tank, and they have spears. They know what you're capable of. What you did just made them hate you more. They would have backed down after the volcanoes—"

"You mean when more people died?" I stared her down. "Those lives are less important than those assholes' egos?"

"Is this what it's like to be inside your head?" Hannah said as she came down the steps. "Because it's making my head hurt just to watch."

"Give me your phone," Lila said, hand extending in front of me.

"For what?"

"I'll handle the survivors. Clearly you can't do that without acting like a child, so I'll handle it. Just sit fucking still and recoup today like we told you to."

"What are you going to do with them?"

"I'll heal the ones who need it and get those who need refuge somewhere safe. I'll fucking handle it. Just stay home and don't make my life any more difficult. I'm the one who has to stay here when you go back. I'm the one whose reputation you're destroying. I'm the one has to deal with whatever mess you make. So let me fucking clean it up." She wiggled her fingers, like a mother confiscating a child's cell phone.

I slid it from my pocket and slammed it into her palm. She disappeared.

Nick exhaled slowly as he met my gaze. "I'm sorry. You know how she is. Always harder on herself than she should be."

I wasn't sure if that the 'than she should be' line was accurate now that I thought about it.

"She'll get over it. Just relax today. We'll see you in the morning." Nick glanced between me and Jeremy. "Just get some rest."

He disappeared too.

Jeremy turned to me. "Baby—"

"I'm fine. I'm fine, but I need a minute to myself. I'll be home soon."

I landed in the cold diner.

I looked at the plywood over the windows. One of the announcement boards hung facing me. The banner on the front nearly slapped me in the face. Max and I had made it when I first took over Moe's. We thought it was funny and represented our place, the place that we all considered home. But suddenly, it felt bitterly ironic.

> *We're All Family Here*
> *Feel Free to be Yourself*
> *(Just don't be a dick)*

CHAPTER THIRTY-EIGHT

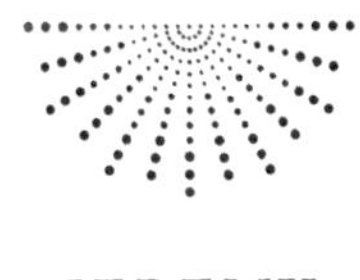

JEREMY

I laid my head on my arm against the counter, expelling a slow, deep breath. Today was supposed to be better than yesterday. But turns out it was almost as shitty, just in different ways.

Hannah grabbed a water from the fridge. "Your hair looks good like that. I never thought I'd say it, but you can definitely rock the pretty boy fade."

I flipped her off, keeping my head against the cool granite countertop.

"What the hell was all that?" Adam's voice said, appearing in the doorway to the sunroom. "I just got back from dropping a couple people off at a camp in one of the underground hospitals, but it sounded like World War Three in here. No pun intended."

I straightened back up, grasping the counter to keep me vertical. "It's been a really long day."

"Basically," Hannah said, "Laila was fighting her with herself."

"Well, she always does that. But usually not so loud."

"Laila was arguing with Lila," I said. "She probably went to the diner. I should go check on her."

"No, you should give her the space she just said she needed," Hannah said. "You *should* go see your kids though."

"Yeah, I promised Micah I'd be home in time for bed. It's barely after dinner now. Maybe I can get their baths done too."

"Good idea." Hannah tugged her black locks into a ponytail. "And I'll take care of everyone here."

"Do you have some clothes I can borrow, man?" I asked Adam. "I don't want to go home with blood on me."

"Yeah, I'll go grab you some. And me and Jen'll be down soon with Luka. We're giving our room to some of the survivors."

"Sounds good. I'll wait to get the kids a snack then," I said.

———

"Daddy!" Micah exclaimed from the kitchen as I landed in the living room. "You're early!"

Milly smiled at me from her seat in the sink. I smiled back as Micah teleported in front of me. "Are you hungry? We just ate, but Gam just put the leftovers in the fridge. They're warm still."

I couldn't help the grin that pulled at my lips as I messed up his hair. He pushed my hand away but smiled up at me. "Yeah, I'm starving."

"Go ahead and grab it then, hon." Rachel rinsed Milly's hair with a cup of water. "This one made a big mess so we're getting her bath done early. Micah's filthy though so he'll still need one too. But he wants to go make more mud pies first."

"Oh, great, thank you." I started to the fridge. "And thanks for watching them. We really appreciate it."

"I don't mind." She gave Milly a wan smile.

"We made more cookies," Micah said as I pulled the warm soup from the fridge. "They're in the oven now. Gam said they'd be cooled when I'm done playing outside. Do you want to play outside with me? I'm bored and I—"

"Yeah, buddy." I laughed. "Yeah, I'll play outside with you, but can I eat first? Is that alright?"

He smiled. "Yeah, that's alright."

Rachel laughed at the sink. I sat at the island with the soup, teleporting a spoon to my hand. "Give your dad a minute, kid. He looks a little tired."

"Sorry." Micah climbed into the chair beside me. "I had fun today, Dad. Me and Milly and Gam watched movies, and then we made a pillow fort. Have you ever made a pillow fort?"

I smiled and gave a nod as I took a bite of the soup. Rachel laughed and shook her head. "He's missed you guys."

"It's alright. I missed them too." I tucked an arm around his shoulders.

Micah continued talking quickly and asking me silly questions. But it wasn't annoying; it was pleasantly distracting. It was the first time all day I wasn't anxious.

It's funny how quick that switch flipped. Going from nervous warrior to happy father in a matter of seconds. Kids are excitable, and I know how that can cause anxiety, but it did the opposite for me. It reminded me what I was fighting for.

Adam, Jenna, and Luka arrived with sleeping bags and Luka's pack-n-play shortly after Micah and I were done making mud pies in the yard. Leah, Brody, Celena, Wyatt, and Moriah landed a little while later. We lit a fire in the living room and sat around making smores with cookies instead of graham crackers.

When it hit nine, and Laila still hadn't made it home, I started to worry a bit. I reached for my phone out of instinct before I remembered that Lila had taken hers. I tapped into her mind telepathically and asked if she was okay. She gave some generic response, saying she was fine and would be home soon.

By nine thirty, I lay Milly down and got Micah his bath. He chatted away, proudly proclaiming how great of a day he'd had. He hadn't mentioned Laila since I'd first gotten home, and I was relieved because I wasn't sure what I'd say if he had.

But as I tucked him into bed, he did just that.

"Daddy," Micah said.

"Micah." I lifted the blanket around his shoulders and tucked the comforter down his body. Tink jumped onto the bed beside him.

"Where's Mommy?" he asked.

"I think she's at the diner."

"Why didn't she come home with you? Is she mad at you?"

I laughed. "No. No, she isn't mad at me. She's just having a tough time and needed some time alone."

"When I'm having a hard time, I don't like to be alone."

I sat on the bed beside him. "Can I tell you a secret?" He nodded. "I don't like to be alone when I'm having a hard time, either. But everyone's a little different. Some of us like to work through things on our own. And some of us like to be surrounded by people we love when we're working through something. But both are okay. Good, actually. Working through stuff is good no matter how you do it."

His puzzling eyes moved between mine for a moment. "What is she working through?"

"Ask me that in twenty years, alright?"

"But I'm asking you *now*. I won't remember in that many years."

My lips lifted in a smile. "You're too smart, you know that?"

"You didn't answer the question." I was about to speak but he continued before I could. "I know something's wrong. I can tell you're scared. But I'm—I don't know what it is, and it's scaring me, too."

Of course he was. Why wouldn't he be? His life was just turned upside down too. He was sheltered from the physical risks, but I knew this was taking a toll on his mind. In a week or so though, life would be better. For him, at least. Not so sure how I'd feel by the time this was over. But he just had to make it a little longer.

I brushed hair from his face "You don't need to be scared. Everything's okay—"

"No, it's not, you're lying. Something's wrong."

My tongue ran along my lips. "You're right, buddy. Something is going on. But you're too little to understand all that—"

"No, I'm not." His lip curled down. "Milly's too little, but I'm not. I can understand things—"

"I know you can. I know. But I'm your dad, and I also know that what's going on out there is too big for you to understand. Not because you aren't smart. You're the smartest kid in the world. But you're too little for this. And you have to trust me. I'm not telling you what's going on to keep you safe. I'm good at that, right? Keeping you safe?"

His annoyed gaze moved between mine. He nodded.

"Alright then. So for now, all you need to know is that you're safe. And I will continue to keep you safe, just like always. Mommy and I are doing everything we can to keep you and your sister safe."

"What about her?" he asked.

"Who?"

"Mommy. Who'll keep Mommy safe?"

I smiled. "Mommy's pretty good at keeping herself safe. But if she needs me to, I'll keep her safe, too."

He nodded slightly. "And who's gonna keep you safe?"

"Mommy will." I held my gentle smile. "We keep each other safe. That's what marriage is all about."

He looked over me for a moment. "When I go to sleep, can you make sure Mommy's safe? Because she didn't look good today."

"I sure will," I said. "Now you go to sleep so I can go check on Mommy, alright?"

He rolled onto his side and nodded.

I stood and started to the door. As I flicked off the light switch, he spoke again. "Daddy?"

"Yeah, bud?"

"Tell Mommy I said I love her and sweet dreams."

I smiled. "I will, kiddo. Goodnight."

"And, Daddy?"

"Yeah?"

"I love you. Sweet dreams."

My smile widened. "I love you too. Sleep tight and sweet dreams."

CHAPTER THIRTY-NINE

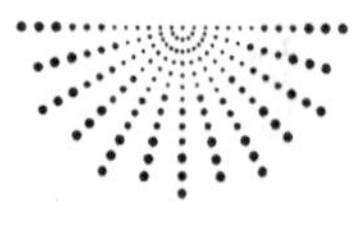

LAILA

I sat on the floor below the cash register. My fingertips slid over the cool bottle of Jack Daniel's resting on the tile floor. I shook it, watching the bubbles rise from the base of the bottle to the neck I'd put a decent dent in.

It wasn't the worst day of my life. But it wasn't great either. Lila was right. Wyatt was right. Even Micah was right.

Weighing the struggles of others against my own was never my strong suit. Thinking about myself and the people closest to me often came second. I never asked to be a leader, but now that I had to be one, I had to do it right. I couldn't be a shitty ruler. Good leaders put the needs of their followers above their own, and I'd covered that base as best as I could. But I put my greatest attributes at risk for that. I lost my son for that. Now I felt like I was losing him again.

It was starting to feel like being a good ruler meant being a shitty friend and a shitty mother. And it was ironic, because being those two mattered to me more than being a good ruler. I was just so torn.

I wanted to do this right. I wanted to do it all right. I wanted my people to have a good person to look to for guidance, but I wanted to be the mother I'd been to my children since I had them. The mother that bakes cookies and plays hide and go seek for hours.

216

It was like walking a tight rope made of fishing wire. I was trying so hard to stay balanced. My family on one end and the rest of the world on the other. They were equally as heavy, but the surface holding me up was so unstable, it could hardly bare my weight, let alone the cargo I was carrying.

"Laila?" Jeremy called from the back of the house. "Are you here, babe?"

"In here," I said.

The stainless-steel door swung open. He leaned against its frame and sent me a gentle smile. "Hey, you."

"Hey."

"Having fun sitting alone in the dark?" he asked.

"I'm not alone. I've got my friends Jack and Daniel right here." I lifted the bottle.

He chuckled. "Care if I join you? Not really interested in Jack and Daniel though."

I smiled as I set it on the shelf behind my head. He took a few steps forward and gripped the counter to steady himself on the way down. "We should really clean back here a little better."

"Yeah. I think that's a speck of Moe right there." I gestured toward the red droplet on the cupboard across from me.

He licked his thumb, leaned forward, and scrubbed it a bit. "Nah, just ketchup."

I took a long glance over him. His hair wasn't as messy as it'd been earlier. His eyes looked less dark and a little more sparkly. He had a bit more color than he'd had this afternoon. "You look better. Did you get a nap in?"

"No, just hung out with the kids. They've got a way of lifting me up, ya know?" I gave a nod. "I was waiting on you to turn in before I did."

I frowned. "Yeah, I was gonna go home earlier. I realized I had blood on my shirt, and I didn't want Micah to see it. So I poured a drink. I really didn't want to go home because I'd smell like alcohol, and I didn't want Micah to think I was out partying or something. So I just sat down and took another drink," I said. "Probably not the most responsible thing to do in the midst of an apocalypse. So I just sat here."

"She did tell you to relax. Having a couple drinks is kind of the definition of relaxing," Jeremy said. "You needed a break, so you took one. There's no shame in that. It's not like you drank the bottle."

"I guess," I said.

He glanced over it. "If I were you, I probably would have downed the bottle."

I noted the lustful gaze in his eyes. "How are you doing with that? The cravings, I mean. I know they're stronger when you're stressed, and you've been pretty stressed."

His gaze came back to me. "I want to. I'd love to get drunk right now. But I know that I can't. I don't want to do that to my kids. I don't want to do that to you. So I just... Ya know, I just look at you guys, and I have a reason not to."

"But you're okay?" I asked.

He smiled. "Yeah. I'm okay, baby."

I saw the genuine expression in his eyes and nodded back. I rested my head against his shoulder. He moved his arm around my shoulders until my head curled against his armpit. I buried my hands into the faded gray T-shirt and closed my eyes.

His lips touched my forehead as his fingertips traced my bicep. "What about you? Are you okay?"

"Yeah, I guess."

"What's on your mind?"

"I don't know," I said. "They were right, you know? I jumped, I just acted. I didn't even think. I just sprang into action. Save the people, show those bastards who they're messing with. Intimidate them into backing down. But that was stupid. Lila was right. I risked lives today because I didn't think. I just—I thought the same tactics we use on our typical enemies would work on the humans too, but that was stupid. I could see how scared they were. And I—I should have given them a reason not to be scared. I should have showed them that I'm not just trying to protect our kinds, I'm trying to protect them too. They're not the enemy. They're just scared."

"She was a bitch," Jeremy muttered.

True, but that kinda stung. She was me. And my husband just called her a bitch.

"She's me. And if I could tell my younger self some shit, I would have been just as harsh. I see her point. She wasn't wrong. I should have handled it better."

"That's the problem. Like Nick said. You're too hard on yourself. You always have been. You need to give yourself a break sometimes. You don't have to be perfect."

"But that's just it. If we're going to save the world, if I'm going to be a leader, I *do* have to be perfect. And I just always fall short. Some way or another, I always miss the target. If I'm not disappointing my people, I'm scaring the people I'm trying to protect. And if I'm doing right by both of them, I'm hurting my kids. I just keep fucking up. I'm not ready for this. I can't be a leader. I'm a mess. I don't know who I'm supposed to put first. My instinct tells me my babies, but even if I'm keeping them safe, I'm hurting them by not being the mom they're used to having. It feels like I have to choose between being a good mom and sister and wife or being a good leader, and it's just too much pressure, and I'm not ready for it."

It got quiet for a moment as he kissed my forehead and played with a piece of hair hanging against my chest.

His fingers found mine. They slid between the gaps and clasped tightly around my palm. "Well, the good news is, you don't have to be a leader for another two and a half decades. And you get all the freedom you need to be the parent you want to be in a couple of weeks. Besides, according to our grown children, you were a perfect mother. So I wouldn't worry too much about that part."

"I guess."

"Not just that, and I hate to even say this, but according to Peterson, you turned out to be a hell of a leader. So much so that he was obsessed with you his entire life."

My gaze narrowed. "Yeah, that's very inspiring, Jeremy."

"I'm sorry. I'm just trying to help," he murmured.

And now, I was being a bad wife too. Granted, that was a shitty comparison. But it was a valid point too. One way or another, I'd get it together. Didn't know how in the hell I'd manage that, but I would. I'd get it together.

"I know," I said. "I know, it's okay. I'm just stressed."

"I'm here if you need me." He kissed my forehead once more. I turned and met his gaze. He touched my cheek before cupping it in his palm. "And no matter how much this sucks right now, I know you're going to be great. You're always great."

A smile pulled at my lips, and I touched them to his. His hand holding my cheek slid to my neck. He pulled my face closer.

I brought myself to my knees, lifting one over his lap until I kneeled above him. His hand around my shoulders shifted to my waist, tugging until our chests touched.

"Thank you," I whispered at his lips.

"It's the truth," he murmured.

I kissed him again. "Not for that. Just for being here. For being by my side no matter what."

"That's what marriage is all about." He pushed my hair that hung in my face behind my ear.

I touched my forehead to his, nodding as my arms moved around his neck. "I love you."

"I love you." He smiled.

My lips moved back to his, basking in the relief they brought. His hands found my waist, pulling my body closer to his chest. I slid my hand from his neck down his side, curving my body back to find the buttons on his jeans.

He laughed and pulled away. "What are you doing?"

"Trying to relieve some stress." I smiled. "Are you down?"

He smiled, gripped the buttons of my jeans, and yanked them open.

I guessed he could use some sexual release too.

CHAPTER FORTY

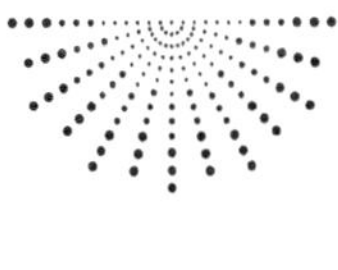

JEREMY

Laila's head fell to my chest, panting out deep breaths as my arms circled around her waist. I pressed my lips to her hair and laughed as I struggled to catch my breath. "Correct me if I'm wrong, but I think this is the first time we fucked on the counter."

"Yeah, but we did fuck on that table over there once. And that booth seat in the corner."

"No, I think it was just hand stuff in the booth," I said.

"Maybe." She laughed, pulled back, and hopped to the ground. She stepped into her jeans and shimmied them up to her hips. Her fingertips tapped the countertop. "First and last time."

"Well, we don't know that," I said. "Might take us twenty-four years, but we'll bang on this counter again eventually."

"You think Lila and Nick still fuck?" She put her hands at her hips. "'Cause I don't think she'd be so bitchy if they did."

They were flirting yesterday. They still fucked. The god and goddess of fertility don't just stop fucking because they're older.

"I really hope so." I laughed. "I'd like to think that we don't get old and suddenly hate sex."

"Sexless marriages are pretty common when you reach your forties and fifties," she said. "Wouldn't surprise me."

"It'd surprise me." I gave a playful smile, hooked my fingers in her belt loops, and pulled her into me. "I know you. And I know me. A time is never going to come when we aren't having sex at least once a month."

"Once a month." She scoffed, arms twisting around my neck. Her lips pulled up a grin. "It better be once a *week*. At least."

I smiled and touched my lips to hers. "You've got yourself a deal."

She grinned and kissed me once more. She pulled back, picked my shirt up off the floor, and tossed it to me. "C'mon, get dressed. If we get home now, we can get close to eight hours of sleep before the kids come charging in."

Laila pulled the blanket up to her face and closed her eyes. I plopped down beside her and moved my hand to her cheek. "Babe?" I asked.

"Yeah?" she said, eyes still closed.

"Micah told me to tell you he loves you and sweet dreams."

She smiled, and her eyes lifted. "So he doesn't hate me for missing dinner?"

I smiled back. "No. He just missed you, that's all. It's been a long week for all of us."

"True. Unrelated, but how do you think the humans knew about wolf's bane?"

"I don't know. I didn't watch all the videos, but I'm assuming Peterson mentioned it in there."

Granted, I wasn't sure how they got it so fast. But it wasn't like the plant was illegal. It's a flower. Anyone who lived near a nursery could go grab some, juice the stems and petals, and suck it into a syringe.

"Why though?" she asked. "Why would he want the humans to know how to stop some of our most valuable assets?"

"I don't know. He was working with Lux though. And I know he said he didn't want to hurt his own people but considering the fact that the Angels have no part in our alliance—and that one tried to kill you the other night—I think he's leading all of us in different directions. The *why* part is over my head, though."

"Not unless he never cared about the people here," she murmured. "He clearly hasn't for the past few thousand years. Why would he start now?"

No, he did. I knew that even then. He loved the humans. He just had a trick tucked away in his back pocket.

"I don't get it. He's a mysterious little fucker. He's always working for himself, you know? It's never about the common good. It's always about what *he* wants, and what *he* thinks is best."

"Yeah," she said. "Yeah, I guess. But it just... I don't get it. Hating us, I get. But letting the humans stay here to be massacred, that doesn't add up to me unless he doesn't care about their lives."

I didn't know what he was planning. But I was exhausted. Tomorrow would probably be as shitty as today had been. It was time to recharge.

"I need some sleep," Laila said. "And so do you. Let's talk about this in the morning."

I touched my lips to hers. "Alright. Goodnight."

"Night," she murmured.

"But, hey, one more thing," I whispered.

"What?" she grumbled.

"If you're worried about being a decent leader, give Roland a call."

Her eyes opened. "Why?"

"Well, he's a dick. I'm not a big fan of him personally. But he is a good leader and has been for some hundred and fifty or sixty years. He's fair, and respected, and his people love him. They fear him, but they also love him. He may be an asshole sometimes, but you can't say he isn't a good ruler. And lord knows he *loves* you, so I'm sure he'd be happy to give you some pointers."

"Hm," she muttered. "Yeah, that's a good point. I will."

I pulled the blanket closer to my face. "Alright. That's all. Good night."

She smiled and touched her lips to mine. "I love you. Sweet dreams."

"I love you, too."

CHAPTER FORTY-ONE

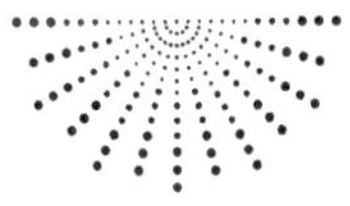

LAILA

It had been so long since I had a retrocognitive dream that I didn't realize what it was at first.

I sat on a wooden chair at a round table littered with cups, little handmade trinkets, and a baby in my lap, speaking softly in Elvan. Her bright green eyes turned up to me with a wide smile, and I immediately knew who she was.

My Milly.

The first image I'd recalled of my daughter from my first life.

She had the same dark brown hair and round, chubby cheeks. Her lips were a bit wider, and her nose a bit more prominent, as mine had been then too. She wore a white gown that made distinguishing her gender almost impossible had it not been for the fact that I knew my daughter's face.

I heard a bang upstairs followed by a young boy's voice calling, "Sorry!" in Elvan.

"What was that?" I yelled.

"Nothing!" the boy yelled back. His voice sounded different in another language, but I still knew it. Micah.

I chuckled.

I'm not sure what I expected our home then to look like, but I did find myself a bit shocked at the modesty. It looked like a home inside a village I'd visited on a class field trip in grade school.

The walls appeared to be simple logs stacked on top of one another. A wood burning fireplace sat in the middle of the room, separating the kitchen area from the living area. There, a few benches sat in a circle with instruments I didn't recognize leaning against them.

All in all, it reminded me of our home before we renovated. A cabin. It made sense considering that memory took place sometime around 2,000 B.C.. But beside the home I'd lived in on my home world, this place was a slum in comparison. Although surprising, I can't say it was shocking. I did find peace in simpler living. And Jeremy would probably be content to live in a tent.

A knock sounded at the door. I looked out the open window, noted the cool wind and dark night sky, and felt my brows fall a bit. I knew that Nix wouldn't knock, and I guessed I hadn't been expecting visitors.

I stood from the table and shifted the baby to my hip. She fussed, and I hushed her. I made my way across the creaking wooden floor to the poorly constructed door. I pulled it open, and my heart skipped a beat.

Lux stood on the other end of the threshold. The whites of his dark eyes were streaked with red. The alcohol on his breath filled my nose when he opened his mouth.

"Nix isn't here," I said in Enochian, pushing the door shut.

"I know." He caught it and held it open. "I know, I'm here to talk to you."

"I'd rather not," I said, grasping the door and pushing it further toward him.

"Please." His sad eyes moved between mine. "Please, Vèa. I only—I need someone to talk to."

"And I have two children I need to get to bed. Not that you care but I do," I snapped. "We can talk when Nix returns. Excuse me."

I went to push the door shut again, but he dropped to his knees and stared desperately into my eyes. "Please. Please, Vèa."

I supposed it was odd for Vèa to see that man on his knees too.

"Who is that?" Micah asked behind me. He laughed and rushed past me, wrapping his arms around his uncle's neck.

I fought the fire burning within me as Lux tightened his arms around his little waist. His eyes closed, and he whispered something in his ear.

My fingers wrapped around my son's shoulder. I pulled him back to face me. "Go upstairs, mi lim."

"But—"

"No buts. It's time for bed. And take your sister," I said, lowering her into his arms.

"But Lux just—"

"Listen to your mother." Lux brought himself back to his feet. His fingers traced over the young boy's black hair, and I telekinetically pushed them back. He caught my accusative gaze and took a step back. He smiled down at my son. "Time for bed, esiasch."

The boy shot me an annoyed gaze, situated his sister against his hip, and teleported away. When he was out of sight, I looked back to Lux. "Do not touch my children when Nix isn't here."

"He ran to me. Was I supposed to push him away?"

"Aye." My voice was deep and harsh. "Just because he doesn't remember what you did doesn't mean that I've forgotten—"

"I understand," he murmured. "I understand. I'm sorry."

I continued to glare.

"May I come in?" he asked.

I took a step back and moved the door further inward.

He smiled and took a step inside.

I sat on the bench opposite of Lux in the living room. He had a hand over his face, rubbing his eyes hard and taking in deep breaths. He shifted his gaze to the ground and wrung his hands together. I noted the ashy color over his cheeks and the dirt and dried blood around his fingernails.

A knot formed in my throat as I slid a steaming ceramic cup across the table.

"What's happened?" I asked quietly.

He stayed silent for a moment, looking down at his shaking hands before tightening them to fists. Then cleared his throat. "I've… I've done an awful thing, Vea."

"I'm not surprised," I muttered. He shot me a look before he turned back down to his lap. I sighed. "I only meant it wouldn't be the first time. What is it? What have you done?"

He stayed quiet for another long moment. Then his head moved from one side to the other. "They don't care about our people. They didn't—they never wanted their souls to return."

"What are you talking about?" I asked.

"Those bastards," he said quickly. "This was all about politics. It had nothing to do with developing new life and helping them grow into a better race. They never wanted better for them than we've had, it was about power."

I tilted my head to the side. "The Conclave?"

"Yes. I—I went to adjust the logistics. And they were incredibly vague. They kept evading my questions, and I—I pressed. I told them I needed more than they were giving. I needed numbers, and assurance of housing once they arrive. And they told me a little town north of the capitol," he said. "I said that wouldn't be enough room, and I suggested the lower continent, somewhere near Altum Babage, and they… They laughed at me."

I tilted my head to the side. "But we have millions. We'd need at least that."

His gaze turned up to mine. His brown eyes filled with tears. "That's what I said. And they said no. That we could only use that piece of land."

"And what of the others?"

His lip trembled.

I blinked hard. "We're to leave them?"

"Not leave them. *Give* them. They are the payment for the allotted time we've spent here."

"But the deal was—"

"The deal was a sham," he said quickly. "We made the agreement without hearing all of its details. They lied to us, Vèa. They used us. They used our creations. We were nothing more than shepherds to sheep waiting to be slaughtered for meat. They—"

"Were? What do you mean *were*?"

He turned his gaze downward.

My heart picked up in my chest. I watched him squeeze his hands together. I noted his legs begin to quiver as his hands moved to his cheeks.

"What did you do, Lux?"

"I told you," he whispered. "I've done something awful."

"And what is it?" I said quickly.

His unblinking eyes stared at the ground.

"Damn it, Lux." I leaned forward and gripped his chin. Turning it up to me, I looked deep between his watery eyes. "*What did you do?*"

His lips began to quiver as his eyes overflowed with water. He struggled to form words. After a moment, something barely louder than a whisper left his lips. "I killed them. I killed them all."

CHAPTER FORTY-TWO

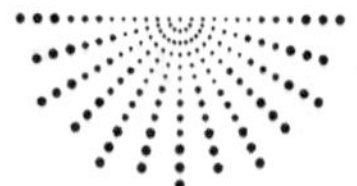

JANUARY 5 - JEREMY

Early that morning, Micah's finger tapping my shoulder pulled me from my sleep. I glanced out the window to the dark morning.

"Did you have a bad dream?" I whispered.

He shook his head with a smile. "Come here. Come here, I have to show you something."

"Can't it wait a few more hours?" I asked. He shook his head and pulled my hand. "Buddy, I'm really tired."

"C'mon, Daddy," he insisted, pulling my arm with all of his strength.

I rubbed my eyes and sat forward. "Alright, what is it?"

He bolted to the door and turned back to me. His hand moved in a quick wave, smiling over his shoulder. "Follow me."

I stood from the bed and stepped into my slippers. "Right behind you."

He grinned and darted down the hallway. I followed a few yards behind, walking through the bedroom, then down the hallway, past my group of sleeping relatives in the living room. "Up here, Daddy, come on," Micah said at the top of the steps.

I started up the stairs, still rubbing crusted goop from the corners of my eyes. Each step felt like a hike. I'd gotten close to eight hours of sleep in the past two days and really needed more rest. But kids are like a dose of insomnia.

"Hurry up!" Micah demanded in a whisper. "Hurry, hurry."

I teleported to his bedroom. He turned to me with a smile and pulled the balcony door open. "Look, Daddy. Look!"

"I'm coming, geesh." I walked across the room. I took a step onto the balcony. "Alright, what is it?"

"Look, over there." He pointed over the trees. "Do you see it? Over there, by the diner. Do you see it?"

I squinted a bit, still blinking to see through my typical morning haze. I did. I saw exactly what he was so excited about.

In the distance to the right, I took in the swirling of colors in the sky. Dark green with hints of purple and blue. They danced just above the tree line at the local high school. In the fall, that same area was lit by the lights of the stadium at the football field. But tonight, a dozen colors danced in the sky like the northern lights of the arctic.

"Aren't they pretty?" Micah grabbed my waist and craned his head as high as he could.

I lifted him to my hip. "Yeah, they are pretty."

"I thought that couldn't happen here. You said we had to be somewhere else to see that oar lights."

"The *Aurora* lights," I muttered.

"Right. Aurora lights," he said. "So why are they here?"

I looked a little closer. I saw the crowds of people moving down the steps of the stadium. It all began to tie together then. The portal to the Fae Realm was creating them.

It gave me some relief to see how many people were gathered in that stadium. I couldn't tell how many, but clearly a decent chunk. About the same amount that attended the games on Friday nights. It wasn't the whole town. But it was at least a few hundred, maybe close to a thousand.

"I don't know, buddy," I whispered.

"Can we go look?" he asked. "Can we go see them up close?"

"I think we've got a pretty good view right here." I pulled him a little closer and kissed his forehead.

"Well, we can watch them, right? I don't have to go back to bed?"

"No, you don't have to go back to bed. We can watch them."

He grinned and wrapped his arms tighter around my neck. "Thanks, Daddy."

I smiled. "Any time, kid."

The lights didn't stop until the sun rose and made them invisible. By that time, Milly was crying in her crib. I walked to her room, lifted her to the changing table, changed her diaper, put her in some clean clothes, and started downstairs. Micah got dressed and met me in the kitchen.

Adam was up with Luka, giving him a quick bath in the sink. I set Milly on the floor and started to the fridge. I grabbed a dozen eggs, a pound of bacon, and started up the stove. Adam brewed the coffee while I mixed up pancake batter.

Before long, everyone was awoken by one kid or another. Micah had this habit of approaching people that were asleep and peeling their eyelids open to wake them, so he was the primary culprit. Leah hated it and smacked him away, but he just laughed and moved to his next victim.

I knew the world was burning out there. But damn, it felt so right for a minute. Surrounded by family, cooking up breakfast, drinking a cup of coffee with my brothers and sisters in the home they'd helped me build.

I wanted to stay frozen in that morning. My young, healthy, oblivious children harassing their aunts and uncles. The smell of bacon filling my nose, coffee brewing in the pot behind me.

It just felt like home. And soon, this place wouldn't even exist.

Two hands curved around my waist as I flipped a pancake at the stove. Laila's lips touched my shoulder as I laughed quietly. "Morning." I turned to meet her gaze.

"Morning." She smiled.

"Mommy!" Micah darted from the living room into the kitchen. His arms wrapped around her legs while hers rested at my waist. "Mommy, did you sleep good?"

An unwilling smile curved her lips. She kneeled down to meet his gaze, pushing waves from his face behind his ear. "Yeah, I did. Did you?"

"I did, too. But the lights woke me up."

She cocked her head to the side. "What lights?"

"The oar lights," he said.

Laila turned up to me.

"The *aurora* lights," I said.

"Oh, yeah. *Aurora* lights," Micah said.

She looked back to me and tilted her head to the side.

Above the portal to the Fae Realm at the football field in town. It wasn't really aurora lights, but it kind of looked like them. I didn't have the heart to tell him otherwise.

"I thought about waking you up too, but Daddy said you had a hard day, so I let you sleep," Micah said.

Her gaze moved back to him, and she smiled. "Well, thank you. But you could have woken me up. I would've loved to see it."

"If they're there tonight, I'll wake you up, okay?"

She smiled. "Yeah, I'd like that."

"And I'm sorry," he said.

"What for?"

"I was mean yesterday. I said whatever, and I know you don't like when I say that. So I'm sorry. I know you had some stuff to work on, and it's okay for you to do that by yourself. I just missed you."

Laila's lips higher into a smile. "Thank you for that, but you don't have to apologize. I'm sorry, buddy, I know I've been really busy lately. I'm just trying to do the right thing."

"Well, I bet you *are* doing the right thing." Micah grinned. "You're the smartest person in the whole wide world, Mommy."

I smiled too. He really was a sweet kid.

She laughed and shook her head. "Well, I don't know about that. But I'm trying."

"Are you going to be busy today? Or do you have more work?" he asked. "It's okay if you do. I won't be mad. Me and Gam can make another pillow fort."

"I will be busy later. But I think I have some time to spend with you and your sister first. Maybe we can do something together after break-fast, how's that sound?"

"Can we play in the yard?" he asked. "It's a little rainy, but I like the rain sometimes. Maybe I could push the clouds away for a little bit. Sometimes they're too heavy though. Yesterday, they were too heavy."

"We'll see what we can do about those clouds. But can I talk to your daddy for a minute?"

"Okay. I'll go try to wake up Uncle Brody. He's not very good at waking up."

I laughed as he took off to the living room.

Laila turned to me and exhaled slowly. "Can we talk in the bedroom for a minute?"

CHAPTER FORTY-THREE

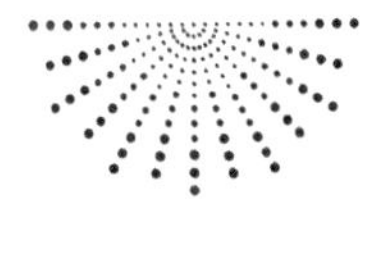

LAILA

"Bout we knew all of that," Jeremy said. "We knew he destroyed the old worlds. I don't really understand how one man was capable of that on his own, but that isn't new information."

"We *heard* it. From him, not from our own memories," I said. "And honestly, I wasn't sure I believed him until I saw that with my own eyes."

"But all you saw was him. You didn't see the ruins or any evidence—"

"No, but I saw the genuine remorse." I closed my eyes and sat on the bed beside him. "Last night, and the other day... when I saw all the damage in Washington, I was so angry at him. He let our people die. He knew this was coming, and he wasn't out there on the front lines with us. He wasn't fighting. He's capable of killing an entire planet. More than just an entire planet, a couple of planets. Mine, yours, his. He destroyed them all to protect these people, and he didn't show when these people actually needed him."

"He destroyed them in a childish tantrum. Not to protect our people," Jeremy muttered.

"My point exactly," I said. "*Our* people. *All* of our people. He's a dick, but he loves these people. He *loves* the humans. So why is he letting them go through this? Why is he letting them die?"

Jeremy combed his fingers through his messy black waves. "I don't know, Lai."

"I just don't get it. I don't understand that fucker. Why? Why can't he just come out of the woodwork and explain what the fuck he's doing? This is the apocalypse; we need to know what his plan is so that we can act accordingly."

"But that's just it." Jeremy rubbed his eyes. "I don't think he has a plan. His plan was to keep us locked up long enough so that he wouldn't have to explain shit to us. So that we woke up just in time to stop the world from ending. He's hiding for a reason. He never wanted this responsibility, he wanted to do whatever it is he wanted to do and leave us to clean up the mess. That's all he's ever done. He causes problems, makes a mess, and expects us all to do the dirty work."

"Yeah, I guess."

He looked me over for a long second. "What—Do you feel bad for him or something?"

A huff left my lips as my gaze narrowed. "No. Of course I don't feel *bad* for him. He's done nothing but cause us problems for hundreds of thousands of years."

I'd never feel bad for that man. But when I saw him in that dream, I didn't see a malicious, evil god. I saw someone that was pissed and burned a construct that was against the best interest of his people to the ground. And I could relate to that.

But that was just it. It wasn't that we were on the same side. It was that we only knew a drop in all of this.

"What is it then? Why are you making that face?"

"Because I think there's a lot more to the story than we're seeing. I think he does have a plan. And I think that we're big players in his little game. I just don't know what he's working toward. I don't know if we're his allies or his enemies."

"I think that's pretty obvious," Jeremy said.

I chewed on loose skin along the inside of my lip. "I don't. Nothing with him is obvious. He works in the shadows behind closed doors. He's always been a devious politician, and that's what politicians do. They lead you to think they're working toward one thing or the other, but there's this giant scheme going on behind the curtain." I thought for a moment. "I *know* that he loves these people. I know he does. And he's not going to sit idly by and let those fuckers come and take them. He's doing something. He's got a plan. I just don't know what it is."

That morning flew by. I spent the day in the back yard with the kids, Jeremy, and the rest of the family.

The kids played on the swing set and chased one another through the yard. As I watched Milly toddle after Micah chasing Tinkerbell, the strangest flashes passed through my vision. Although, I suppose it wasn't that strange in comparison to most of the things that had happened in the past few years.

The backdrop was a bit different. The sun was shining brighter than I'd ever seen, and the trees looked fuller. Instead of a few inch high grass, they trudged through a field of wildflowers.

Micah was a bit older though, maybe eight or nine, and Milly, perhaps five or six. She wore a white dress, something like a long pajama shirt that she kept tripping over. Micah wore a pair of near potato sack looking trousers and a flowing white shirt that reminded me of something a pirate would wear. Both of their skin was a few shades darker which I accredited to the lack of sunscreen in such distant times.

Jeremy, or Nix, I suppose, chased after them. He laughed as he hoisted them into the air and dropped them, only to catch them in an echo of gentle, childish giggles.

It wasn't the three of them that left me blinking hard at the world around me, trying to distinguish between the present and the past. But the two young toddlers struggling to keep up. I couldn't make out their sexes, nor what they really looked like.

Still, that was the first glimpse I got at the other lives Jeremy and I created some five thousand years ago.

But just as quick as they appeared in my mind, the images drifted away.

Around eleven, Jeremy tapped my shoulder as I wiped sticky juice from Milly's cheek. He passed me his phone.

Tell Laila to meet me at Moe's at 12:15. You stay back and watch the kids. And pack your damn bags already.

That was definitely me, not Nick.

I tightened my jacket around my hips as I scanned the cold, empty diner. The heat was blasting. but it was still freezing. I guess plywood on broken windows doesn't supply much insulation.

My gaze kept resting on the narrow walkway between the bar and the drink station below the serving hatch. So many memories flashed behind my eyelids.

I stood in that very spot when Jeremy picked me up for our first date. I found Moe's body in the same place. I poured Moriah a cup of coffee there the day that she brought me Nastya's letter, detailing how my son was to be used as the lamb in the biblical prophecy of revelation.

A lot of good happened inside these four walls. But a lot of bad did, too. The diner had been my place of refuge and solitude for years. And it made my chest hurt to know that I was going to leave it behind.

But I reminded myself I'd find a new place of refuge and solitude. We'd build another business, one that could never harbor the amount of pain that this diner had. One that would mean just as much, only in a different way.

"Would you look at that," Lila said behind me. "I'm the one that's late this time."

I swiveled on the bar stool and met her gaze. She sent me a sad smile as she lowered herself to the seat beside me. "Sorry for the way I talked to you yesterday. I could've made the same impact without being such a cunt. I wasn't really mad at you. I was mad about the fact that we stopped a disaster and a new one manifested just as quick. But that wasn't your fault."

"No, you were right," I said. "It did look bad. I didn't even think about it in the moment. I was just annoyed. These fucking humans. I love them, I do, but I hate them sometimes, too. They're going after the people that are trying to save them, and it just—"

"Infuriates you?" she asked. I must've made a face, and she nodded. "Yeah, me too. But what are we gonna do, ya know? If we force them into humility—"

"We'll have no stable ground to keep them safe," I muttered. "I get it. And if I could go back in time and yell at my younger self, I would too."

A sad smile tugged at her lips. She took in a deep breath. "You say that now but, in all actuality, we had to make mistakes. We had to learn from them. Including that one you made yesterday. When the roles change, when you become me, you can keep her from making that mistake." Lila glanced at her watch. "But no use in sitting here arguing with ourselves. We have work to do. You ready?"

"As I'll ever be."

She took my hand, and we disappeared.

As we landed, cool air brushed my cheeks, sending a shiver through my extremities. My teeth chattered as my vision adjusted to the bright sun. I squinted hard, unable to see anything but sparkling white snow.

I looked around the wooded area and tilted my head. "Where are we?"

"My home." Lila lowered herself to a broken log and gestured behind me. "Your home soon."

I spun around and felt butterflies dance in my stomach. It wasn't the cottage in the woods I was so accustomed to. But not a place I'd mind living either.

A massive white farmhouse with a beautiful porch that wrapped around the entire home. Dark blue shutters framed each of what looked like a thousand windows. On the second floor, a snow dusted balcony overlooked the property.

The landscaping around the home was detailed and still exploding with foliage, despite the frozen temperatures. Ferns hung on the rafters of the porch, blooming flowers sat in pots, and gorgeous bushes flourished around the perimeter. One section of the stunning porch to the right was encased in glass, surely providing for a beautiful sunroom.

"Woah," I murmured.

"It was a total shit hole when we bought it. When I walked inside the first time, the place looked like a tornado moved through it. But it was cheap for all the land it's on. And I could see the potential. I'm sure you will too. And now you know how pretty it turns out to be." Lila smiled. "So don't be discouraged when the realtor shows it to you. It really did have great bones."

"You aren't kidding," I murmured. "It's so big though. I can't imagine cleaning this place."

Even so, I could feel the comfort of it. Big or not, it looked like a beautiful place to raise my children. The kind of place you'd see in a family movie.

"There were a lot of us. We needed the space. Jeremy didn't want it, though. He said it was a money pit, and we didn't have the cash to blow. But I remembered seeing it today. When I was you. And I told him this is it. This is our home. We're getting it, and we're fixing it, and this is the place where our kids are going to grow up. Turned out to be a great place. Micah did most of the convincing though."

"He's got him wrapped around his little finger." I turned over my shoulder and met her gaze. "Do you still call him that?"

"What—Jeremy?" She smiled. I nodded. "Usually. Sometimes he's Jeremy, sometimes he's Nick, sometimes he's Nix. Sometimes I'm Lila, sometimes I'm Laila, sometimes I'm Vèa. Most of the time, he's Jeremy and I'm Laila. But it'd be a little confusing for you guys, so we've been trying to use Nick and Lila for the most part. And we always tried to use Nick and Lila around the kids as they got a little older so they didn't get confused. But we're Mom and Dad to them anyway. Kids don't pay that much attention to their parents' names."

"Yeah, I didn't realize Mom and Dad had a name until I was in, like, fourth grade. I just thought they were Mom and Dad, you know?"

She smiled, chuckling. "Yeah. I do know." She stood. "Alright, we can chit-chat later. Let's get to work."

I placed my hands at my hips. "Alright. Show me what to do."

She grinned. "You sure you're ready?"

"No. I don't have a clue what the fuck I'm doing. But I'm a visual learner. So show me."

Lila took a few steps back and extended her hands out in front of her. I watched carefully as her palms ignited with a dark green dancing ray of light. Licks of violet began to stream into it, forming lines throughout that resembled something like veins.

The purple pulsed through the orb like blood to a body. Her hands pulled slightly apart, expanding the green orb until it was nearly the size of a basketball. Her eyes opened, and her gaze met mine.

The emerald color of her eyes resembled the ball within her palms. Cascades of purple pulsated through them. I began to grasp the *tree of life* concept.

It wasn't a tree, not by any means. But the pulsating violet throughout resembled something close to branches. The way it moved through the emerald color could be equated to leaves if you squinted hard enough.

"So do we eat that or something?" I asked.

"Why would you eat it?"

"You know. Eating from the tree of life and all that."

"No, dumb ass." She tossed the ball to the ground a few feet away. "You don't *eat* it. You travel through it."

"Oh. Okay." I took a step toward it before she grasped my hand.

"I really have to give you a step-by-step tutorial, don't I?" she asked.

"Well, yeah, that's generally how you teach someone."

She frowned. "You know, I don't remember being so dumb."

"Fuck you, bitch," I said.

Her lips curved up. "I'm fucking with you. Get a sense of humor."

"I have a sense of humor." I put my hand to my hips. "You're just mean."

"Well, keep that in mind the next time you make a joke, bitch, because we literally have the exact same sense of humor."

I huffed and crossed my arms against my chest. "Alright, well, if I'm not going through it, then what are you doing with it?"

She outstretched her hand and murmured something in Elvan. A yellow lily blossom appeared in her palm. She pulled off two petals and handed me the flower. She gesturing to the whirling portal on the ground. "Throw it in."

I tossed the flower into the swirls. She outstretched her palm toward the green and purple light. Her fingers wiggled in an almost a stirring, upward motion. Then the lights gradually receded into her skin.

On the spot on the ground where the lily had disappeared, there now laid that same yellow lily.

"Go ahead. Pick it up," Lila said.

I bent over and lifted it to my palm.

She took the petals in her palm and smoothed them to pieces. A yellow film rested on the tips of her fingers. She gestured toward the flower. "Go ahead. Pull off a petal."

I tugged one off and did the same as she had. Crushing it between my fingers and watching the yellow tint slide across my fingertips. As I dropped the wrinkled petal to the ground, she smiled and gestured to the bloom. "Now watch the spot where you just pulled that petal off."

I turned my gaze to the Lily. The petals she'd ripped off looked no different. They hadn't regrown or come back to life. But I squinted.

It was like I had done a thousand times, only it was happening on its own.

The petal I'd ripped off was growing back. Slowly, but it was certainly growing.

"How could this flower survive if Jenna couldn't?" I asked.

"How did Tink?" she asked. "Your guess is as good as mine. But if you asked me for my *best* guess?" I nodded, and she said, "Tinkerbell is innocent. This flower is innocent. And in their own way, both carry with them a bit of magic of their own. They're in touch with the universe in a way that humans aren't. In a way that those of us gifted with abilities are born to be."

"Huh," I muttered. "Didn't have to go all Yoda there, but I get what you're saying."

She laughed. "But keep in mind, we can't do this to everything. There are cycles at play in an ecosystem. Dirt is composed of dead organisms. To keep it rich, we have to allow that natural cycle to function. So don't go preserving all your anniversary flowers this way."

I supposed that made sense. It would essentially make all things non-biodegradable. Basically, we'd just made that flower plastic. But an unbreakable plastic that could not break down.

Although, I supposed it could. With the help of my husband.

That brought with it an interesting question though. Did this mean that plants had a soul, or some other form of spirit? Maybe I should enlighten Micah that being a vegetarian didn't make him any less of a murderer than me.

"Do you want to try?" Lila asked.

"What? Making that thing?" I raised a brow.

"If you think you're ready for that, sure."

"I don't know how the hell to do that." I moved my hands to my hips.

"Didn't think so." Her eyes closed, and she did it again. I watched closer that time.

It reminded me of the smoke that came off of my body when I tapped into the power of my soul. But that purple, spinning light always seemed to nearly erupt around me. This was different.

Instead of jumping from her skin, it seeped out. Like hair growing or sun darkening the color of my flesh. It was free forming and natural, ever so gentle in the way it flowed from her body.

As her eyes opened, she met my gaze with a smile. "Open your hands."

"But you said I wasn't going through it yet."

"You aren't. You're feeling it."

I looked down at it. "You sure I'm ready for that?"

She smiled. "I didn't think I was either. But once I felt it, once I held it, I knew exactly what I was doing. I knew how to summon it from inside. I knew how to hold it. Hold it, and your body will know exactly what to do."

CHAPTER FORTY-FOUR

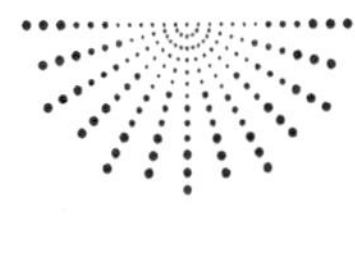

JEREMY

The cool, dewy smell of rain drifted to my nostrils. Water had just begun to drizzle from the clouds above as I watched Micah chase after Milly and Luka on the muddy lawn. Her loud laughter filled my ears and my lips lifted in a smile.

A familiar, even more pleasant smell drifted up my nose. Brody lowered himself to the stair beside me. He outstretched his hand with a slow burning joint.

"Thanks," I said as I lifted it to my lips.

He nodded, blew out some smoke, and gazed out at the kids. "How ya doing?"

"Pretty good at the moment. Not great overall, but I'm alright. What about you?"

"About the same," he said. He gestured toward Micah and Milly. "Have you told them they're moving yet?"

I took a hit and passed him the joint. "Not yet. We will soon though. I don't want them to have to be stressed out yet, you know?"

"I don't know, man. I think Micah knows something's up." He gesturing to him. "He asked me why we were all here this morning."

"What'd you say?" I asked.

"I didn't. I kind of fumbled for a second, he just stared at me. You know that face he makes when he knows you're lying? The scrunched-up eyes and the thing where he raises one eyebrow?" I laughed, and he nodded. "Yeah, he did that. And then Adam told him to come eat. But you're gonna have to tell him soon or he's going to figure it out on his own."

That couldn't happen. But I could see it now. Me and Laila teleporting out to another tsunami, then him teleporting after us to see what was up.

We needed to address it. But I just wanted him to enjoy his life here for as long as he could. I didn't want him to know what was coming. I wanted him to have some peace before he had to leave everything he loved behind.

"Yeah, I know. Maybe me and Laila will tell him tonight. We've only got a week now. He should have some time to think about what he wants to bring with us."

Brody nodded. "Not a bad idea."

I looked over him and caught an expression in his eyes I hadn't seen in years. His skin looked pastier than usual. He hadn't shaved in a few days. I think he was even wearing the shirt he'd worn the day before—which was not common with my uppity little brother.

"You sure you're alright, man?" I asked.

He took a hit off the joint and huffed. "I don't know. I mean, yeah, I'm okay but I just..." He bit his lip, shaking his head. "I don't know."

"Have you heard from Gwen?"

"Yup. Yup, I sure did," he muttered. "I called her last night. I missed her, you know? And I just wanted to talk to her for a minute. Even if I am leaving, it's not going to happen for a few days. And the last few days have been literal hell. I just needed someone."

I gave a nod.

"And I heard someone in the background. A dude." He huffed again, jaw tight. "So I asked who it was. She told me not to call her again and hung up. Just... hung up. And I know we aren't together anymore, and I can't be upset about her being with another guy, but it's only been four days. Four fucking days."

Damn. Four days was fast. I didn't blame him for being upset. No matter what, this was painful. But she couldn't have waited twelve days until he was gone? That was a slap to the face.

"That bitch," I muttered.

He took another long drag off the joint. "Of course she's gonna move on. I get that, I really do, I get it. But… but we were together for three years. It'd be four in August. We saw each other almost every day, and I always called her on my drive home from work. She'd call me any time she had a night terror, and I'd be there in a second. When she had a panic attack, and no one else could calm her down, I showed up. Any time she needed me; I was there for her. And she was always there for me too. I'd call her if I had a bad day at work, and she'd tell me to come over, or to come pick her up…" He took another hit and turned his gaze to the trees in the distance. "And I know she doesn't owe me anything, but if she called me and said she needed someone to talk to, I'd be there in a heartbeat. No matter what, I'd drop whatever I was doing, and *I'd be there.* But she just dropped me in less than a week like I meant absolutely nothing to her. Like the life we've had together means absolutely nothing."

"I'm sorry, man," I murmured.

He frowned. "She's my best friend. She's been my best friend for three years. And that's what sucks the most. I didn't just lose my girl-friend; I lost my best friend."

Brody extended the joint out to me, but I shook my head. "I think you need that more than I do, man."

"Yeah, I guess so, huh?" He grew quiet for a moment. "Before Milly came along, when we didn't know Micah was alive, and you and Laila were broken up. Did you ever try to call her?"

"Yeah. I did."

"Did she answer?" he asked.

"If she didn't, she called me back within a few minutes."

"Did you… Did she listen to you when you needed her?"

That was a weird time between me and Laila. She wouldn't see me in person. Probably because she knew that when she did, it'd end the way it did when we finally did see one another. With my dick inside her.

But she was there for me to an extent. We talked periodically. It was like we were internet friends.

"Yeah. She did. We'd text back and forth, and I sent her memes a lot." He chuckled and waited for me to go on. "She didn't always reply, but she always reacted to them. And she'd call me occasionally. This one time, she was shit faced, I don't even know if she remembers it. But she video-called me at, like, three in the morning. And I could tell she was drunk, and she asked me to come over. It was the first time in months that she had, and I *really* wanted to say yes. But I knew she'd regret it, and I didn't want to be that guy, you know?"

He nodded, and I shrugged. "So I told her to just talk to me, and if she still wanted to see me in the morning, I'd be there. She said okay. And we talked. Not about us, not what I really *wanted* to talk about. But it was nice. I had my best friend back for the night. It got kinda deep after a while though. She asked if we'd still be together if Micah lived. If I wouldn't have chosen drugs over her if she hadn't got our son killed." I pressed my lips together as I glanced at him in the yard. "And I told her we'd still be together if I wasn't a little douchebag." He laughed, and I smiled. "She fell asleep. And I stayed on the call for like, two hours. Kinda creepy, I guess. But I missed her. That was as close to seeing her as I could get, and I couldn't bring myself to hang up."

He rubbed the back of his neck. "I want that."

I knew what he meant. Not that he wanted where we were in that time, no one in their right mind would want the relationship we had then. But it looked like a good time to make a joke.

"Sorry, man. I'm not good at sharing." I grinned. "And she's already turned you down once."

He shoved my shoulder, and I laughed. "Not Laila, asshole."

"I knew what you meant."

"It's just frustrating. I was genuinely good to Gwen. Like, I'm a damn good boyfriend. I'm not just talking out of my ass; I know that I did everything right." His throat bobbed with a swallow. "We never even argued. Maybe about where we were going for dinner or what movie we were going to watch, but we never fought. Ever, not once. She always said that she wished she met me when she was a teenager because the past hundred years felt wasted on the other guys she'd been with." He ran his tongue along his teeth, still looking out into the yard. "I just want what you and Lai have. And what Hannah and Kai have, and what Wyatt and Celena have. I want to be with someone who loves me as much as I love them."

"I'm sure she's out there somewhere, man," I muttered. "And, look, I don't know if you want to hear this. But I know Gwen loved you. Maybe even more than you loved her."

He bit his lip. "You don't put someone you love through this shit. I'd never do this to her. Never. I'd *never* hurt her like this."

Little did he realize, that's exactly what he'd do.

CHAPTER FORTY-FIVE

LAILA

"**H**old it," I repeated. "I just have to hold it."

Lila chuckled, giving a nod. "Open your hands and hold it."

"And I'll know how to do it?" I asked.

"We'll still have some kinks to work out. But yeah. After I held it, it was like all the puzzle pieces snapped together. So go ahead. Open your hands," Lila said.

"Is anything crazy going to happen? Am I gonna, like—"

"Damn it, Laila, just open your fucking hands."

I raised my palms. She extended her hands out to mine and gently rolled it to my fingertips.

It hit me like a twenty-ton truck. An audible gasp heaved into my chest, and my eyes shot wide open. Never in my entire life had I felt so much power.

Suddenly, I felt weightless while still feeling the weight of the planet in my arms. It doesn't sound like it makes sense, but that's how I felt. I couldn't feel the weight of my body—it was almost as if I *had* no body in that moment—but I felt the heaviness of that energy.

It reminded me of the sudden rush of power I felt when Micah was born. A strong, encompassing amount of love wrapped up with innocence, joy, and even a touch of fear.

But it felt similar to traveling through the dimensions, too. Airy and beautiful, yet dangerous. It was an amount of power I'd be terrified to see in anyone else's hands. Hell, it was even terrifying within my own.

And that was only what I *felt.*

A cascade of visions followed the initial eruption of strength.

Literally, I was looking at Lila. But in my mind, I saw Nix. I felt his lips touch mine before he pulled back with a grin, murmured something about seeing me on the other side in Elvan, then jumped into a swirling vortex of green and violet on the ground like the one I held in my hands.

I saw Lux. He smiled at me, lowered his upper half in a bow, and jumped in after his brother.

Another face. Stella. She sent me the most gleeful expression, said she loved me in Enochian, and followed Lux.

Then another face. One I hadn't met in my memories from that life but bearing these eerily familiar, dark green eyes against mahogany skin. She cocked her head to the side, smiled the biggest, shit eating grin I'd ever seen, and jumped.

Venark's gaze met mine as he smiled wide. He leaned forward and touched his lips to my forehead. He took the hand of a short girl with jet black hair and light brown eyes. She smiled at me just as exuberantly. And they leaped.

Then a man whose shoulders were nearly twice the width of my own. One with dark brown hair, skin the color of a tree's bark, and eyes as sweet and inviting as honey. He held the hand of a woman with short blond hair and pale, piercing blue eyes. They grinned my way, closed their eyes, and stepped into the vortex.

A woman whose skin was darker than night with undertones of silver took my face in her hands and whispered a language I didn't recognize. Yet the phrase translated instantly. *I and our people will forever be within your debt.* I smiled at her and gestured toward the vortex. She smiled back, gave a nod, took the hand of a red-haired man with high pointed ears, and they hopped inside.

Those were just the faces I recognized. Jeremy. Lux. Stella. The mystery woman who I wouldn't connect to her current body for quite some time. Kai. Hannah. Wyatt. Celena. Avery. Asher.

Another fourteen followed. I was able to figure out which ones were Connor and Naomi. But the other twelve all faded together in a messy blur. Those that I *had* met in my current life that moved through that vortex didn't look as they did in their first life, so I didn't recognize them as who they were until a while later.

Seven were men.

There were two more blonds with light skin. They reminded me of Lux, but not similar enough to be related. One more white appearing man with brown hair and blue eyes similar to Nix's, but not so much that I thought they were kin. Then a man who looked a great deal like Wyatt, but shorter and not quite as buff. Another dark-skinned man with inviting brown eyes and a friendly smile that I recognized but couldn't pinpoint to any person in particular. Two more men passed through, one who appeared similar to a light skinned Asian man and another with skin the same color as Avery's and eyes nearly as dark as his flesh.

And another five women.

Another dark skinned, dark haired girl who looked a hell of a lot like Avery. Two more women with light skin that appeared Chinese, although I'm sure that isn't the correct terminology since this took place somewhere far from earth. Then a woman who looked not much different than the last woman, but with darker skin and softer features. And the last, a woman with skin as pale as her white hair and minty green eyes.

I took in a deep breath and stepped in after them.

The jolt sent me back to my reality, dropping the ball of swirling energy to the ground.

I fell to the snow behind it. My chest heaved up and down as I relived the memory that just moved against my eyes.

Lila laughed as she lowered herself beside me.

"What the fuck was that?" I said with fast blinking eyes.

"Oh, come on. You know what that was."

I tried to regain my breath. "The par animarum."

She smiled. "Every last one of us. The moment we gave them eternal life."

"Here." Lila passed me a bottle of water. "Just breathe for a second."

I twisted off the cap, tilted my head back, and chugged until only a few sips remained. My breathing began to return to normal as I wiped cold sweat from my brow. "You said nothing crazy was going to happen."

"I didn't, actually." Lila smiled. "I interrupted you and told you to open your hands."

I rubbed my tense forehead. "Well, I don't magically know what I'm doing now."

"We'll try again in a minute. It felt familiar though, didn't it?" She grinned.

"I guess," I murmured. "But different."

"Because it isn't just your ability anymore. Technically, in this body, we're Lux's granddaughter. We have the ability our soul carries combined with his."

"That's what you meant when you said the tree of life is wrapped up with time," I said.

Lila nodded.

"Fucking creepy, isn't it?" I curled my nose. "He was our husband once. He put our soul into his granddaughter's body."

"Guess he finally realized that ship had sailed. And he did it to give us more power. So that we'd be stronger than anyone this world's ever seen, himself included. Not that we needed much help, really. Even then, we were stronger than he was. Still though. It helped. There's only a few people alive equally as powerful as we are."

"Micah and Milly."

"And a few others."

That settled it then. We'd have more children. I'd seen two more in the visions earlier that morning, but were there more?

I looked up and moved my gaze between hers. "A *few*?"

She laughed. "I can't tell you everything, Laila."

"What can you tell me then?" I asked.

"That depends. What do you remember?"

I lifted my shoulder. "Not much, but enough. More than I need to see, I know that."

Lila huffed. "No, there's a lot more that you need to see."

"I've seen everything I need to."

"No, you really haven't. It's just bits and pieces now, isn't it?" she asked. "The beginning, when we were married to Lux."

I cringed a bit. "Yeah, and that was plenty."

She tilted her head to the side a bit. "You didn't do anything worse than he did. You know that, don't you?"

"Of course I know that. He killed my kid. Kids. Many times. Obviously, he's done worse than I did—"

"But you almost understand it," she said. "Because when you thought that Jeremy cheated on you, a part of you wanted to kill him, too. You can almost sympathize with his reaction because there have been times when you didn't feel much different." I opened my mouth to speak, but she said, "You don't have to lie to me, I remember thinking that way. I remember being exactly where you're sitting right now. But I remember a lot more than you do. And that's why you do need to remember the whole story. Because it gets a lot deeper than that. What do you remember, two interactions with Lux from that life? Maybe three or four?" She shook her head and laughed. "Look, you'll see it all when the time comes. But he did us dirty too. Yeah, we fucked his brother. But let's just put it this way. His reaction was more than just hypocritical, alright? He did horrible shit, Laila. You don't have to give him your sympathy because he doesn't deserve it."

"It's not about sympathizing with Lux. It's about the principle. I'm not Vèa. That isn't me, that's a whole other person. I'm not her. I don't do shit like she did, I'm—"

"You are," Lila said. "*We* are. We're Vea, and Jeremy is Nix, and—"

"I *was*. You *were*," I said. "We aren't now."

She was right. And I was lying.

I did feel disgusting for what Vèa had done. It wasn't that I felt bad for him; it was that I was ashamed of myself. Infidelity is wrong, and it was hard for me to grasp that I had done that.

But Lila was right about the other part too.

We were no worse than he was.

She grew quiet for a few heartbeats. "Are we the same girl that climbed into that van? Are we the same girl who had the opportunity to send Jeremy our location and didn't? Are we the same girl who missed out on the first three years of our son's life because of a decision that *we* made?"

I turned my gaze to the ground.

"Yeah. We are. We are that girl. We've grown, and we've learned from our mistakes, but that doesn't change the fact that we are that same girl. We may have done some shitty things when we were Vèa, but we can't deny that we were her. Growth means taking accountability for who you are and what you've done. Yes, Laila, we cheated on our husband. Yes, we let him manipulate us. Yes, there was a time when we practically bowed to that piece of shit, but we *learned.* You can't discount the past because you don't like it. We made mistakes, but we overcame them. Don't judge Vèa based off of who she was when she was young. Judge her by what she became. You haven't seen it yet, but I promise you, she wasn't always that contradictory young queen. She grew. Just like we did in this life. And I am *proud* to be her. You should be too."

I turned my gaze to the house a few dozen yards away.

Lila closed her eyes, hand rubbing against them. "Whatever. Subject change. What is it that you want to know? I'll try to answer as best as I can."

My mind traveled back to those images that moved against my open eyes this morning. I turned over my shoulder and met her gaze. "I saw something earlier. It came after a dream. The first time I saw my babies in their first bodies."

Her lips slowly lifted in a smile. "You saw the others." I nodded, and she smiled wider. "That's early. I didn't see them until I was a few months pregnant."

"It got me thinking... Micah and Milly travel through the portal with us. They become immortal because of it, right?" I asked. "My future children. Will I have to send them through a portal one day too?"

"No. No, the shift changes something in our body. It mutates our DNA, I guess. They'll be immortal, too, the same way Heylel is immortal because of his parents. But they could, I guess. Travel back in time to evade what comes next. They didn't though. They could do it on their own if they wanted to but... well, they want to be here, too."

"I know you can't tell me much. But can you tell me what they're like?"

With a grin, she pulled her knees to her chest. "When I was you, Lila didn't tell me."

"So is that a no?" I asked.

She looked over me for a moment. "What are they like?" Her lips flapped together in a trill. "Well, first of all, I love all of my kids equally. But your next little one's the best. Not that I have a favorite because I don't, but she's a good girl. And incredibly smart. Like, ivy league smart. Not as powerful magically speaking though. Not that she's power*less*. Just not quite as strong in that regard. She's more of a thinker than a warrior, you know?" I smiled and gave a nod. "She's gentle, like Jeremy. But very soft spoken. She kind of grew up in Milly's very large, very headstrong shadow. She's beautiful, too. In a very sophisticated kind of way. Not the messy, hippie kind of pretty that we are. Kind of like Hannah in that way."

"And the other one?"

She released a huff of a laugh. "Remember when Dad used to say, 'I hope that when you have a kid, you have one *just like you*?'"

"Uh-oh," I muttered.

She laughed again. "Yeah, well, we got that with Milly. But that one?" A slight smile toucher her lips. "He's like that for Jeremy. Like... okay, you know how Micah got the great traits of both me and Jeremy? Really sweet for most part, but really passionate when he wants to be?" I nodded, and she said, "Well, that little shit got the worst of both of us. He's more like Jeremy than me or you though. Really emotional. All sad and mopey, 'woe is me, no one has it as bad as I do' sort of thing. I love him, love him with my whole heart. But I thought he'd outgrow his bullshit by now. He's still a raging pain in my ass. Definitely a mama's boy too. He and Jeremy didn't get along really well in his teenage years. They've gotten better now, but it's still pretty rough sometimes. Probably because they're so much alike. But stars forbid you tell either of them how similar they are." She laughed. "That whole tortured musician bullshit is, like, engrained into that kid's DNA."

Great. So I had that to look forward too. My husband was my best friend, and I loved that he was in touch with his emotions and all, but she was describing my next son as a step further in the tortured soul department.

"Oh," I murmured.

She squinted slightly. "You didn't want me to lie, did you?"

"No. No, thank you," I said. "Just sucks to hear, you know?"

"Eh," she said. "He's young. And yeah, he's a sad little dude. But so was Jeremy. Once he had something to live for, that changed. I mean, just think about it. Micah has this concrete, important destiny that gives him a drive. And Milly's" —she laughed— "Milly's the definition of female empowerment. And M—" She caught herself, careful not to give away her name. "And his other sister's always been really fucking smart. But he... I don't know, he just hasn't found himself yet. He will one day. I know he will. He just has a lot of soul searching to do."

I grew quiet for a long moment. I cleared my throat. "So four? We have four?"

"Is that all that you've seen?" she asked.

"Is that a trick question?"

She smiled. "I've already said too much. I'm not going to confirm or deny anything else. And we're immortal, anyway. Maybe we'll have a million more one day. Maybe we won't. I don't know, I haven't seen past 2024 either."

"Right," I muttered. "Sure."

"Anything else you want to ask me?" she asked.

I stared at the Lily on the ground. "Yeah, there is actually. I... last night, I had another dream. A memory, I guess."

"Yeah. I remember it."

"And Lux... Micah, or whatever his name was then," I began.

"Miorbhail." She smiled. "That was his name. It means miracle."

I smiled slightly. "He... when Lux came to the door, he came running downstairs, and he was so excited to see him. He knew him, and he genuinely loved him."

"And you're wondering how we got past what he did?" she asked.

"No. Well, yes, that too. But no. No, I just... That fucker. He knew how much our children loved him, and it seemed like he loved them too and I just..." I looked up and met her gaze. "How could he kill them?"

She ran her tongue along her teeth. "I wish I knew. But that man never ceases to do the exact opposite of what you expect. And he rationalizes. He says 'nothing ever dies,' as if that makes it any better." Lila bit her lip. "All that I do know is that I'll find a way to kill that fucker before he ever gets the opportunity to take my babies away from me again."

"I second that," I said.

"But come on." She stood and extended her hand out for mine. "We have work to do."

CHAPTER FORTY-SIX

JEREMY

"Pssst," echoed from around the corner of the house. My head turned that direction. Nick was stooped behind a bush along the side of the porch. He sent me a half smile and made a 'come here' motion with his hand.

Adam sat beside me at the wicker table. He looked from me to Nick. "Jesus Christ, this is weird."

Nick chuckled, then made another gesture for me to come that way.

I gestured to the kids. "Watch them for a minute, would you?"

Adam nodded as I stood. I walked across the patio, glancing at Micah and Milly to make sure they weren't paying attention. I looked at Nick. "What's up?"

"Are you busy?" he asked.

"Not really, why?"

"Do you have time for a walk?"

It was so fucking strange to see myself without looking in a mirror or at a photograph. You think you know what you look like, but you really have no clue, not until you see yourself from an outside perspective.

I never had an issue with the way I looked. Not that I was conceited, but I knew I was attractive. Although, I started to realize I may have been a little full of myself after all because, although he was a good-looking guy, he was no model.

His eyes were striking against his light skin and near black hair, dusted with strands of grey. He had an attractive, diamond shaped face. His beard was trimmed a lot closer to his skin than mine, and he actually shaved around the edges with a razor to keep it looking maintained.

But when I looked in the mirror, I never really noticed how big my nose was. Not that it was ugly, and it probably would have looked weird if his face were even a tad bit smaller, but seeing it on someone else made me see that it wasn't anywhere close to dainty. Annie used to say that we had Dad's Roman nose, but I'd describe it as a slightly hooked Grecian shape.

"Stop it," Nick said.

"Stop what?" I asked.

"Judging me," he said. "I get it, you're humbled. But stop staring."

"Did you just read my mind?"

"I don't have to; I remember this conversation."

"Oh. Right."

He took a glance over me as we strode down the snowy driveway. "So how are you doing?"

"Well, if you remember this conversation, then you know how I'm doing."

He smiled. "Well, humor me. How are you?"

I let out a quiet laugh. "I don't know. I'm alright, I guess. At the moment anyway."

"Good," Nick said. "That's good. But overall. You're hanging in there?"

"Yeah, I'm good." His eyes moved over me carefully for a moment, almost accusatively. I laughed again and rubbed my hand over my mouth. "I don't know, maybe good isn't the right word. But yeah, I'm hanging in there. The kids help. Kind of just throwing myself into Dad-mode to get through this."

"Yeah, that's usually our method. Tested and approved." He smiled. "It's funny how they kind of just make the rest of the bullshit fade away, isn't it?"

"Strange," I said. "Weird how two tiny people have this magical ability to make me feel better. I never really thought about that part of parenting before they came along, you know? The financial aspect was always what I thought about. The money, the time they need, and the lack of sex with my girl." He laughed, and I smiled. "But I never realized how good they could make me feel. It does something to you when another person looks at you like you're the greatest thing in their world. Nothing feels better."

"Not even heroin," Nick said.

"Eh, maybe about the same as heroin."

It was intended as a joke, one I thought he of all people would understand, but I guess he didn't remember that part of the conversation. Or maybe he didn't say that when he was me. I'm not sure, but he stopped and met my gaze.

"No, not even heroin," Nick stated.

"Yeah, I know. It was a joke."

"And it's not funny," he said. "You wouldn't let the world burn for a high, but you would for your kid because that's love. Addiction and love aren't the same thing, Jeremy. Don't get them confused."

My brows furrowed a bit. "I'm not. It was a joke. Sorry, I thought we'd have the same sense of humor, dude."

His gaze moved between mine. After a moment, his expression softened. "Right." He picked up the pace, and we continued down the path. "Not about the same, but heroin's a close second." I laughed, and he smiled. "I don't know though. I think sex might just be one rank above drugs."

"True. True, but only with her. Not *just* sex."

"Oh, yeah. Definitely," he said. "You'd think fucking the same person for five hundred thousand years would get old, but it never really does."

"Almost like it gets better, right?"

"Eh. I don't know, sometimes are better than others. Any time we've been apart for any length of time, it's always better. And certain times throughout the month are always better."

"Yeah, when she's more into it," I said.

"Oh, and when she's pregnant."

"Yeah, she's horny as shit when she's pregnant," I said.

"And her boobs are bigger. I don't even mind the belly, you know? Not until she's, like, *really* pregnant."

"Gets a little creepy, right?" I asked. "I mean, I know the baby's way up there, but it's just kind of cringy."

"Yeah, remember when she was pregnant with Milly—"

"And I had to stop because I saw her moving?" I asked.

"It was like her whole fucking foot was kicking me away." He laughed.

Call me a narcissist, but it was actually pretty nice to talk to myself. He got it. And it didn't feel grimy to talk about my sex life with him, because he was me. It was like having a conversation within my own mind.

I chuckled. "Ya know, you should've just told that story when you showed up. Wouldn't have had any doubt you were me after that."

"Really?" he asked. "Everyone knows that story."

I stopped walking. "Nuh-uh."

He laughed again. "What—You don't think she told all of the girls about that?"

That was the sort of thing Laila would do. Everyone in the family knew the grotesque details of Ray's dick after their hookup that one time. Even though I hadn't asked, nor had any desire to know.

Ew. I bet they knew the grotesque details of mine too.

My lips curled down. "Damn, she probably did, huh?"

"Oh yeah, she definitely did. It's an anecdote she tells at Christmas dinner."

"Bet the kids love that," I muttered.

He chuckled and lifted his shoulder. "They're kind of used to it. We were those embarrassing, super affectionate parents you never wanted to bring to school functions. But they're grateful for it now. And they're glad we aren't prudes."

A slow breath left my lips as they lifted in a smile. "Always wanted parents like that."

"Yeah. Me too." He was quiet for a moment. "But ya know. You try to do better for your kids than what you had. And we did, they had a pretty damn good life."

Had. They *had* a pretty good life. But that was over now.

I frowned.

"So. We need to talk about something."

"What's that?" I asked.

"Me," someone said behind me.

I swiveled around. Heylel began to speak, but I cut him off. "There's nothing to talk about."

"Yes, there is," Nick said. "You need to—"

"No, you fucking lied to me," I snapped. I looked at Nick. "That's what this little chat was for? To ambush me into—"

"This conversation is so that you can hear my side of the situation," Heylel said.

"I don't really give a shit what you have to say," I said. "We were friends. I came to you for help, and you lied to me how many times? You knew who I was, you knew what I was capable of, and you kept that from me—"

"No, *I* kept that from you," Nick said. "Lila and I are the ones that told him what to and what not to say."

My jaw tightened. "You said you did everything you could to help. Keeping the fact that I could resurrect the dead from me is the opposite of helping, it made things worse. If I would have known, then—"

"Then what?" Nick said, returning the same expression I was making at him. "If you were *told* you could resurrect the dead, what difference would it have made? If you *knew* you could use Laila's powers, what would that have done?" I opened my mouth to speak, but he cut me off. "Jack shit, that's what."

"Well, maybe Laila wouldn't have died in that fucking cell—"

"Oh, please." Nick laughed. "She's died a million times. It wasn't that much of an inconvenience."

"The entire point of Peterson holding us captive that day was to teach me something he already fucking knew," I said. "Come to think of it, something *you* already knew."

"Yeah, exactly. To *teach* you," Nick said. "You had to be forced into learning your ability, Jeremy."

"Oh, so you agree with Peterson?" I snapped.

"Yeah." His eyes opened wider. "Yeah, actually, I agree with that fucker on a lot of things. He was a piece of shit, and I hate the little bastard, but you know what, yeah. He was right when he made that move. Because the only way you were going to learn was if someone took the person who mattered most to you away. And the only way to hurt Laila was to hurt Micah so he used him as leverage to get you to use your fucking head. You weren't going to tap into that ability for anyone but her or your kids. You wouldn't have remembered how to unless you *had* to."

My jaw tightened. "That isn't true."

"Really?" He raised a brow. "Because I haven't seen you tap into that ability at all in over a year. You don't use it unless you have to. And you wouldn't have *discovered* it unless you had to. So yeah, I told Heylel to keep it from you because you had to learn on your own. Just like I did. Just like Hannah did."

"Then you're an asshole."

"Ooh, that hurt." He laughed, and I suddenly realized just how well I could pull off a fuck boy, snarky grin. "You know, you spent all that time bitching about how Laila wouldn't learn her powers, and you've done the exact same thing. You have one of the most important abilities that exists, and you don't even use it. For the exact same reason too, because you think you're strong enough without it, and you don't need it. But you're wrong." He looked over me for a moment. "Now, I'm gonna go so you two can talk. And if Heylel comes to me and says you blew him off, I'll be back, and we'll go through this whole spiel again. Alright?"

I crossed my arms against my chest. Like my toddler when I told her she had to wear pants if she wanted to go play in the yard earlier this morning. Because that's what I was to him. A child. He was almost double my age, he knew what he was talking about, and I needed to listen.

He disappeared.

Heylel met my gaze and summoned a smile. "So where would you like to begin?"

CHAPTER FORTY-SEVEN

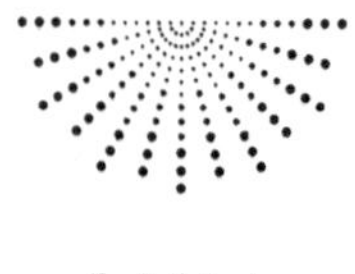

LAILA

"Now you've felt how powerful it is." Lila conjured the energy to her hands. "You know what to expect when I hand it to you. So just hold it for as long as you can. Get used to the way that it feels. But don't drop it this time."

I extended by hands out for hers. "I'm ready when you are."

"Here it goes then." She started passing it to me. "But I'm serious, Laila. Keep holding it. Don't let it go."

"What happens if I do?"

"Nothing. But we'd have to restart. You have to get used to the way it feels in your hands." She dropped it to my palms. The energy rushed through me like a bolt of electricity. "Don't think about it. Notice how it feels, observe the feeling, but stay relaxed. Find a comfortable place with the power. Exist *with* it."

She was right, mindfulness was the way I had to focus on this ability. It didn't come from a place of fear or protection; it centered around peace.

But it was so fucking powerful. I imagine it felt a great deal like holding the sun. A beautiful concept of creation but also a weapon powerful enough to kill thousands if anything came just the slightest bit too close.

"Don't think about its capabilities," Lila said softly. "Don't think about what it has done or will do. Just feel it. Acknowledge it as a part of who you are. Like a limb. Of course your leg could do some damage if you used it for that, but its purpose isn't to harm. Its purpose is to help you walk. This is the same. It's simply a part of you. Feel it, acknowledge it, and accept it."

I gaped deep into the swirling colors. Images started to flash against my open eyes.

Nix lifting our son above his head and tossing him into the air. Micah's bubbly giggle dancing into my ears. I felt the smile across Vèa's lips and then my own began to do the same.

Then another vision moved against my eyes.

Vèa's stomach felt like an empty pit twisting into the abyss of outer space. Her chest hurt as if a sword had been thrust through it. The legs keeping her on her feet went entirely numb as she collapsed to the marble floor of the Elder's Hall.

That same little boy with brilliant blue eyes and golden skin lay in a puddle of crimson that poured from his neck. Beside him was my little girl. Her head faced the cool pond of red, dark brown waves restful with that purple Elvan Ore necklace that hung in her jewelry box back home.

Vèa screamed for help. Over and over, she begged for someone, anyone that could hear her. Still bawling, she struggled the children from the ground to her lap, screaming for Nix.

Over the sound of her pleas, she didn't hear the footsteps that tiptoed behind her.

A hand grasped her shoulder. And a stabbing pain radiated just below her ribs. A gasp left her lips as her blood coated hands slid to her abdomen. Her fingertips grazed cool metal. She blinked hard and fast, just as the knife slid out of her from behind.

Yet somehow, that didn't hurt as much as it did to see her children bled out on those marble floors.

"No." I pushed that memory from my mind and pulled my hands apart.

But before I could release the orb, Lila grabbed my palms and held them in place under the energy. "Feel it, acknowledge it, and accept it, Laila."

My head shook again as tears poured from my eyes.

"Feel it, acknowledge it, accept it, and move past it." Lila's voice was firmer that time.

I struggled against her hands. "I can't. I can't, it hurts. It hurts too much."

"It did hurt, but you're thousands of years past that. That's over, Laila. You need to feel it, acknowledge it, and accept it."

My teeth began to chatter, and she squeezed her hands around mine to keep them steady, thumbs soothing them gently. "Close your eyes. And *feel* it."

I clamped my teeth together and brought my top lid down to meet the bottom.

The man with the knife whispered into Vèa's ear. He spoke in Enochian. "You are no queen. You are no god. The one true god has won. You will never rule again. Goddess of mothers, and look at you. Dying beside your dead children. Pitiful."

The blood pouring from her chest didn't hurt as much as those words. Or perhaps, that knowing he was right. Not only had she lost power to save her people, but even her own children. If she couldn't even protect the lives that came from her womb, how could she protect the people of earth she also called her children?

Despite her apparent grief and tremendous pain, she grabbed ahold of the man's throat. Her fingers lit aflame as an ear-piercing shriek left his lips. He struggled against her fingers, but her strength was magnified by a thousand. His screams quieted as he tried to pry her palm away, but she persisted.

Still holding him in place with one hand, she reached for a blade at her calf with the other. I only saw it in a passing glance as she thrust it into his face, but its color in her peripheral vision sparkled an iridescent, purplish black. She pulled it back and stabbed him again.

Elvan ore.

His hand at her shoulder released, and he fell to the ground behind her. Holding a hand over the wound in her stomach, she brought herself to her knees and leaned over the man's body. I couldn't make out his features through the stab wounds to his face, so I couldn't identify him, but his hair appeared as light as Lux's and his palms against the thick armor were a warm golden color.

But she just kept going. She stabbed, and stabbed, and stabbed. Through his face, through his chest, through his abdomen. She kept going and going until she couldn't anymore.

She collapsed beside her children and pulled their bloodied bodies to her chest, tears gushing from her eyes as she screamed in agony. Not from the physical pain, but the mental affects.

"Vèa!" Nix's voice carried as he ran toward her. "Vèa." He collapsed to the ground and pulled her body into him. He stared at the wound in her stomach, then at the children. His breaths grew uneven. "Why aren't you healing? What's happened?"

Then nothing. Only the usual black haze that rested behind close eyelids.

I slowly lifted them open. My cheeks burned from the salty water pouring from above. But my teeth were steady.

Lila gently pulled the energy back into her palms. It absorbed into her skin like some sort of glimmering lotion. Her hand moved to my shoulder.

"Sit down for a minute," she whispered gently.

My knees pulled up to my chest, and I wrapped my trembling arms around them. Lila sat beside me and tugged her arm around my shoulders. Her palm slid up and down my bicep as I struggled to get my breaths level.

"Are you okay?" Lila asked.

I didn't answer. I just stared at the yellow lily in the snow. My fingers flexed and released, adjusting to the tingling sensation the orb had left radiating through my flesh.

"Why did it show me that?" I whispered after a long moment.

"I'm not sure. But it showed me the same thing," Lila said. "The moment we became immortal. And the moment we lost that eternal life."

"But that doesn't even make sense," I said quickly. "If we were immortal, how did they kill us? Does that mean you can be killed?"

"Technically, *everyone* is immortal. Nothing ever really dies," Lila paused. "But yes, technically, it *could* be done again. It won't though. We know how they did it now, and I'll be damned. The twenty-four of us will destroy that bastard before we ever let that happen again."

"How?" I asked, turning to meet her gaze. "How did he do it?"

"Heylel should have told you that." Her head tilted. "Our souls give our bodies eternal life. If the soul is removed from the body, then the body rots."

"Yeah, he did tell me that, but I still don't understand. My soul was still inside that body, or I wouldn't remember that."

"He was siphoning it," she said. "Lux was gradually pulling our soul from our body. We were too caught up in the emotion of losing our children to fight back. That's why we lived long enough to kill Metatron, because our soul was still hanging on trying to heal our body. And even so, we couldn't have done it without Nix."

"What do you mean?" I asked. "What does Jeremy have to do with it?"

"Jeremy and Lux both have power over the afterlife. They can manipulate souls. That's how Micah's soul ended up in Mirobhail's body even though we lost him in our first pregnancy. Nix stashed it away and moved it into our womb when we conceived him."

I thought long and hard for a moment. "But we couldn't have done that?"

"No. No, unfortunately that's the only power of his I can't get a grip on. Maybe one day I will, but Vèa couldn't then, and I still can't now. There's been a lot of arguments about it over the years." She crossed her legs into a lotus pose. "He can't use this, either. The tree of life. He can travel through time without me, but he can't grant eternity. No one else can. Not Micah or Milly, not even Lux. That's why Angels can be killed. Their lives can span thousands of years, but they can be killed far easier than we can."

Well, I supposed that did make sense. It also explained why I was so significant in every life. No one had the power to grant eternity but me. It also explained why I was able to kill Metatron. Heylel said he was immortal because both of his parents were eternal, but not all Angels were. Just Heylel because *both* of his parents were immortal.

But at least now I knew how to kill them.

Elvan ore.

I focused hard for a moment. I cocked my head to the side. "Then why do we need him and the kids for the shift?"

"Because of how many people we're sending back. Like I said before, we have some wiggle room when we do it alone. But in a group, things get more complicated."

I huffed and rested my head against my knees.

So confusing. I wasn't sure I could even attempt to grasp it all. But I would eventually once everything settled down.

"But are you ready to go again?"

"Again?"

"Yeah, bitch, you have to know how to create it. Feeling it and accepting its power is only a fraction of the process here."

"Jesus," I said. "Well, what's next? Seeing him behead my brothers and sisters?"

"No. Not for me anyway. Next, you just let it flow from you."

"Sounds too easy," I muttered

She laughed. "Drink that water. Then we go again."

CHAPTER FORTY-EIGHT

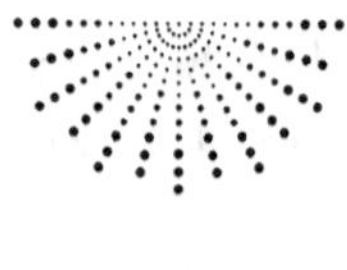

JEREMY

"Lucy!" Micah ran out the front door to me and Heylel on the front porch.

Heylel laughed, leaned down, and wrapped his arms around his chest. He pulled back after a short moment and gripped his shoulders. "Hello, little one. How are you today?"

"Good," Micah said. "I don't like this rain though. It's boring. I like the snow better."

"Well, hopefully it clears up soon."

"I hope so," Micah said. "Are you staying for dinner? Aunt Leah's making chicken with Gam. I helped peel the carrots."

"No, he's not," I said.

Heylel turned his disappointed gaze toward me. As Micah opened his mouth to object, Heylel spoke, "Your father's right, I have things to do this evening. I'm not sure I can stay. But maybe one day soon, alright?"

Micah frowned. "Alright."

"Go ahead inside. I'm coming in in a minute," I said.

"But—"

"No buts, Micah. Go inside," I repeated.

That wasn't usually the way that I talked to Micah. But apparently,

I had to have this conversation with Heylel. I wanted to get it over with so I could enjoy the little bit of time left I had in my home with my kids. This asshole would be around where I was going, and evidently, we'd have plenty of time together then.

Micah crossed his arms against his chest and huffed. "Fine." He stomped his way to the door and slammed it shut behind him.

Heylel sat in the wicker chair beside the wall of windows into the living room. "Can I be frank with you, Jeremy?"

"Oh, you mean for the first time since we've met?" I cocked my head to the side. "Yeah, that'd be great."

"I understand why you're angry. In your shoes, I would be angry with me too. But you have to believe that I never kept these things from you with any ill intent. And I never truly lied—"

"Bullshit." An ironic cackle escaped me. "Bullshit, dude. You lied to me from day one. You could've told me I was a necromancer the day we met, and you didn't."

"I told you that you were a god that day, Jeremy," Heylel said. "I told you that you were a leader of the world. Would you have believed me if I told you that you could raise the dead, too?"

"Yeah. Fuck yeah. My sister's a necromancer, my mom was a necromancer. It would have made sense if you told me I was too. Hell, I believed you even though nothing you *did* tell us that day made much sense. I *always* believed you. I believed you when you told me you were my nephew. I believed you when you told me I was God's brother. I believed every word that came out of your mouth, why wouldn't I have believed something that actually did add up? Something that could be proven, something that wasn't a massive stretch to the imagination."

"That's just it." His eyes softened. "You are my superior, Jeremy. You weren't just my uncle; you were my leader. You called the shots then. You were a commander of armies. You were the closest thing to a father that I've ever really had, and I lost you." His eyes glistened with tears. "I lost you and Vèa. I lost two of the only parental figures that ever mattered to me."

Yeah. That sucked. But I still didn't see how that justified lying to me.

I crossed my arms against my chest. "What's your point?"

"I spent five-thousand years searching for you. I investigated each and every rumor of par animarum, and not one of them was the two of you. Never, not once after that first life did I find you again." He ran his palm over his tense jaw. "Eventually, I gave up. I stopped searching because I figured he found some way to destroy you all for good. I thought you were gone, and I thought that when these days came, my people would have to fight Wormwood alone. It wasn't ideal, but I came to terms with it. I built an army of my own. I grieved every day, but I accepted it. There was no other choice. Then twenty-four years ago, you showed up."

I leaned against the railing, licking my teeth with a stiff jaw. So like I thought. He was going to be around plenty, he didn't need to waste my time here and now.

"Laila, actually. She came to me with that beautiful little girl in there. That sweet child, only a few months older than she is now. And she told me about the time she came from. She explained how Milly knew me already although I hadn't seen her in eons. She told me about you and your past that wouldn't even occur for another two decades. She told me the date that they arrive. January 12, 2024. She warned me. She told me everything, Jeremy."

"So you've known about all of this for almost as long as I've been alive," I said. "You kept all of this from me when you could have helped me prevent it from happening altogether."

"You told me not to," he said. "I thought the same as you do now, but I am not a master of time. The concept of altering a timeline was too complex for me to grasp. It still is. But I accept that with grace because it is not my duty to make decisions about this plane. It is my place to direct and control the Demons, and I do the best I can in that regard. But it isn't my place to step on your toes. And I didn't question keeping it from the child you were then because it was an order from *your* lips."

Almost had me there for a minute. He had to go and call me a child. Sure, I may have been when he initially learned all of this in 2000. But I wasn't now. I wasn't when I met him. He could've given me a little fucking more than he had.

"*The child I was.*" I laughed. "You didn't have to tell me about Peterson kidnapping my pregnant fiancé when I first met her. But we aren't talking about who I was ten years ago, Heylel. We're talking about who I was three years ago. The day you called me for a meeting, or any of the hundred meetings we had after that. Or maybe the person I was two years ago when I found my son, and I asked you why you didn't tell me Nix was a necromancer—"

"I didn't lie to you that day. I told you that you and Nix were different, and I wasn't sure what those differences entailed—"

"But you did. You knew that I was capable of necromancy before I went into that hell hole and felt my wife die in my arms for the millionth time—"

"And I kept it from you because you asked me to!" he yelled.

My gaze hardened as he looked up at me like my son had five minutes prior when I told him to go inside.

He took in a few deep breaths to regain his composure. He closed his eyes and rubbed his mouth.

"Jeremy, I am *sorry.* I am so deeply, incredibly sorry that you watched Laila die that day. It hurts me that I hurt you. I am so deeply sorry. Truly, I am. But I told you what the older you told me to tell you. And still, if you told me today to keep a secret for you, I would. Even from another version of you. Even if you asked me to keep something from Laila. I would do anything you asked me to because you are the only person alive that I trust to carry the world's burdens. And because I hate myself for not being there the day that I lost all of you. But when I got you back, when I had my *family* back, I would have done anything to keep it. If I broke my promise to you twenty-four years ago, or two years ago, I would have risked that. I would have risked losing my family again."

I took in a deep breath.

Maybe I saw his point. Maybe I was just mad at my life. Maybe I was mad because I had to leave my entire life behind, and I wanted this conversation to end so I could go back to be with my family in my home.

But damn it, one way or the other, I was mad.

"To keep your family in your life, would you keep a secret from someone you love?" he asked with dewy eyes.

I thought back to the months I spent lying to Laila about using. I thought back to the day I said 'I do' with six oxies rushing through my veins. I thought back to the day that she learned what I'd kept from her. I thought about that look of betrayal in her eyes.

"Yeah, I would. I have. And you know what I learned?" I asked. "That lying to the people you love is no way to keep them."

He frowned, closing his eyes. "Jeremy—"

"No. No, I don't want to hear it. I'm pissed at you, dude." He frowned, and I laughed a bit. I ran my hand through my hair. "I get it, alright? I get why you kept it from me but that doesn't make me any less pissed at you. But clearly, I get over it. You're proof of that. At the moment though, I'm mad. So you go see the version of me that isn't pissed at you and I'll... Well, I'll see you in a few months my time."

"But—"

"No. This conversation's over. I'll see you when I see you."

CHAPTER FORTY-NINE

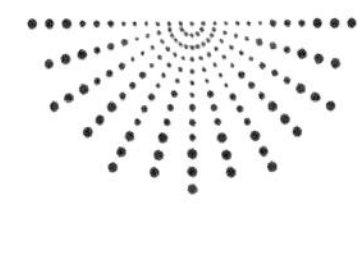

LAILA

"So what's it gonna be this time?" My hands moved to my hips. "Am I gonna see my home planet explode?"

"No, this is the easy part."

"Why do I feel like you're lying?"

She chuckled. "I'm really not."

"Well, what happens?" I asked. "Am I gonna have any visions? Any terrible things I need to prepare for?"

"No. I didn't, anyway," Lila said. "You might be different. I doubt it, but we'll see. You've adjusted to how it feels. You just need to know how to summon it from within you now."

"And that's the easy part?"

She smiled. "Always has been the easiest part, right? Using the ability isn't what's so bad, accepting it is what's difficult."

The memories of the first time I tapped into my earth and water abilities drifted through my mind. When I sprouted a tree through a man's chest, when I drowned a man in his own spit.

"Yeah. Acceptance is the hardest part."

"But you've done that. So now..." She raised her palms and summoned that green and violet energy to her palms. The orb was smaller though, no bigger than a tennis ball. "You just tap into it."

I outstretched my palms. Closing my eyes, I tried to feel that energy slide from my own. I focused hard on how it felt and tried to summon it myself.

"What are you doing?" Lila asked.

I opened my eyes. "I'm trying to create it."

"Not like that, dummy," she muttered.

I huffed and dropped my arms back to my sides. "I'm never going to get this if you keep being so elusive. Just—"

Lila laughed. "Okay. Okay, I'm sorry. You had the right idea. Lift your hands up like that again." I sighed and raised them. "Now, I'm going to hand this to you. And when I do, adjust to it in your palms, okay?"

I nodded. She smiled and gently set the ball into my open hands.

The same exuberant, spilling energy flooded over me. But as she'd said, no vivid memories washed across my eyes. No fear surged through the pit of my stomach.

"How do you feel?" she asked.

My gaze scanned the orb. I felt the tension in my face and stiff shoulders loosen. The green slid through the pulsing lines of violet, and I exhaled a slow, calming breath.

"Tranquil. Soothed, and relaxed. Almost euphoric, but not high. Clear," I murmured. "It feels like tranquil clarity."

Her lips raised higher into her full cheeks. "The best description I've ever heard."

I looked from the orb back up at her. "What do I do now?"

"Let that same tranquility flow from you," she said.

"Do you have to talk like Yoda?"

She laughed. "If you aren't ready, that's okay. You can sit down and hold it. That helped me."

My left hand shifted to hold it as I used my other to ease me to the ground. I sat in the snow with my legs crossed lotus style. I watched it carefully. I tried to visualize the ball within my hands expanding, but it stayed the same. My brow stiffened as I focused harder.

"Don't think about it." Lila sat before me. "Don't think about the energy itself."

"What do I need to do then?" I asked.

"Close your eyes," she said softly. I pulled my lids together. "And now, just don't think. Not about the energy, not about what's happened in the past few days. Just focus on your breath."

"You want me to meditate?" I asked.

"Yeah. Exactly. Take a deep breath in." She spoke in a soothing manner, like one of those women on a meditation video. "And slowly, let it out. Focus only on the breath. As each breath pulls into the lungs, think 'in,' and as each breath eases out, think 'out.' Just—"

"I know how to meditate," I muttered. "I got this. Shut up."

"Duly noted," she said.

My mind began to zoom in on the focal points of my body. The heaviness of where my seat met the ground. The way that the cool snow pricked through my wet jeans tingled my warm calves and thighs. The way that the lack of warmth almost burned.

I pulled myself back to the breath. The strongest point, deep in my abdomen. I focused on the way that the air felt seeping into my lungs, filling my entire chest, and soon every limb with oxygen.

After a moment or two, the point of contact started to feel weightless. I didn't feel the heaviness of my bottom beneath the cool earth. I felt light and airy, as if floating on a cloud.

Still, between my open palms, I observed the sensation of power. The strength of worlds within my hands. But I didn't think about what it was capable of, as Lila had mentioned. Instead, I focused only the sensation of it.

The way it tingled up my arms. The warmth collecting around me. The familiarity.

In that moment, it began to bring back another feeling. It reminded me of something, something I couldn't quite place. It almost felt like... like home.

But not home as in my renovated cabin in the woods. Not home as in my mother's house. Not even like the home of her embrace, nor my dad's.

It felt like a home I didn't remember.

But it reminded me of something else, too. Something that I felt every day. Something I first felt four and a half years ago in a tiny cell when I pushed a glowing ball of white light into the world.

Motherhood.

An uncontainable, massive amount of love and joy.

"Laila," Lila whispered. "Open your eyes."

I slowly lifted my eyelids.

Instead of seeing Lila beside me or the large home in the distance, a layer of green energy throbbing with veins of purple engulfed me in a globe. Rather than holding the orb, it was holding me.

It was almost like one of those massive hamster balls you climb into at festivals and the mall. Only, I floated within it rather than stood.

I marveled at it for a moment, mouth agape and eyes wide. I couldn't believe it. I mastered it. I mastered it quicker than any other ability I'd ever tapped into. I was proud of myself.

For that split second, anyway.

"I'm doing it! Look, look, I—"

The energy snapped back into my skin like a rubber band. I fell to the snowy floor, wind knocking from my lungs as my butt slammed the iced soil.

Lila laughed, extending her hand out to me. "Good job. Now, let's do it again."

CHAPTER FIFTY

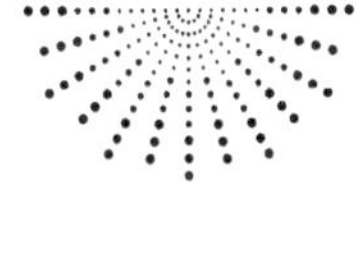

JEREMY

"Daddy." Micah scooped a bite of rice to his lips.

"Micah," I said.

"When's Mommy coming home?" he asked.

"I'm not sure, buddy. Hopefully she'll be home soon. But if she isn't, I'm not going anywhere. I'll put you to bed tonight."

"But you got me to bed *last* night," he muttered. "I want Mommy to got me to bed."

"*Put* you to bed, not got me to bed," I corrected.

"Whatever," he said. "I miss Mommy. Where is she anyway?"

I swallowed the bit of food I'd put into my lips four sentences prior. "She's working on some stuff."

"The same stuff she was working on yesterday?" he asked.

"No, some different stuff."

"What kind of stuff?"

"Grown-up stuff," I said.

"What *kind* of grown-up stuff?"

"Grown-up stuff that you don't need to be concerned with," Leah said as she filled up his glass of juice.

"But—"

"When you're a grown-up, I'm sure she'll tell you all about it." Leah placed her hands at her hips. "But you aren't, so it's not your business."

He huffed and took another bite of rice. "Whatever."

I smiled. Truly, I loved that kid more than anything in the universe next to his sister. But sometimes, I thought that I'd like him a little more if he were quiet once in a while.

Still, it made me happy to sit beside him and share a meal in our home. I knew it might be a while before we got to do that again. Even though this would be over in a week, we'd still have to *find* a home when we got wherever we were going. We'd be living out of a hotel for a few weeks at least, maybe a couple of months before we could close a sale.

"Why was Lucy here?" Micah asked.

"We had some stuff to talk about," I said.

"What *kind* of stuff?"

Across the table, Celena laughed. "You're gonna give your dad an aneurism, kid."

"What's that?" he asked.

"Alright, you know what." I twisted an arm around him and roughed up his hair. "No more questions. No more questions for the rest of the night."

He laughed and pushed me away. "But you said asking questions is how we learn things."

"It is," I said. "But it's been a long couple of days, and I don't feel like being a teacher. So for the rest of the night, statements only. No questions."

"You're no fun," he muttered.

I laughed.

On the other side of the table, Chris cleared his throat. I glanced his way, and he tapped the side of his head.

What's up? I said into his mind.

Have you and Laila talked about when you're telling him yet? He asked.

I shook my head.

Well, if she gets home before they go to bed tonight, maybe you should. Why?

He said something today. He saw the suitcases in your bedroom and asked why. If we were going on a trip soon. I told him I didn't know; he'd have to ask you or Lai. And he said you wouldn't tell him because you're lying to him about something. He made that determined face and said he's going to figure out why. We only have seven days left, and I think most of us are going to be away from home during that time. He'll be here, with Rachel. And if he teleports out to investigate...

I closed my eyes and blew out a careful breath.

This moment was coming, I'd known that. And it was exactly what I was afraid of. It was bad enough that some way or another, he'd seen the tsunami hit the west coast. They said the volcanoes came next, and I certainly didn't want to be chasing my son away from molten lava and ruining the chances of saving someone else.

We'd have to tell him within the day.

Alright, we'll tell him tonight. The last thing we need is him teleporting to follow one of us when we go to stop a volcanic eruption tomorrow.

He nodded. *I was thinking the same thing.*

The other side of the table all glanced behind me. Milly grinned and excitedly kicked her feet. I turned over my shoulder. Laila stood a few feet behind Micah with a finger over her lips. My mouth heightened into a smile.

She grasped his shoulders, and he jumped. He turned around, loud bubbly laugh echoing from his lips. "Mommy, you scared me!"

"That was the idea." She smiled and wrapped her arms around his torso. She leaned down and touched her lips to his forehead. "What's for dinner?"

"Chicken, rice and vegetables," Leah said. "Want me to get you a plate?"

"Nah, I got it. Thanks though." She pulled away from Micah and touched her lips to mine. "Hey, you."

I smiled. "Hey. How was your day?"

"Good." She smiled. "Really good." She walked around the table and kissed Milly's forehead. "What about you?"

"Can't complain," I said.

"Mommy, are you staying home now?" Micah asked.

"Yeah, kiddo, I'm in for the night."

"So you can put me to bed?"

She smiled. "Yeah, I'll put you to bed. But after dinner, I've got to get a bath real quick. I'm a mess. I have mud all over me. But when I'm done, we'll get you and your sister's bath and changed into your pajamas. We might even have time to read a story, what do you think?"

He grinned. "I think that's perfect."

———

"How was your day, babe?" Laila asked from the master bathroom, peeking her head around the corner of the door. "Anything crazy happen?"

"No, not really." I pulled on my sweatpants. "Talked to myself for a few minutes. Heylel came by."

"Oh," she muttered. "How did that go?"

"I don't know," I said. "I'm just... I don't know, man, I'm pissed."

"Understandably," she said. "What'd he say? Did he apologize?"

"Yeah. But apologizing doesn't change the fact that he lied to me for as long as I've known him."

"Well." She ran a brush through her hair in the doorway. "I mean, we kind of lied to ourselves. That's why he didn't tell you what you could do, right? Because we told him not to?"

I rolled my eyes. "Yeah, and I get that. But it still doesn't change anything. He didn't just lie to me before we found Micah, he lied to me after the fact, too. He said he didn't know what Nix and I had in common. Looked me dead in the eye and lied."

"I guess. But he did have a good excuse for it. We told him to keep it from us."

"That isn't the point," I said. "I lost you in there. I almost lost our chance at getting Micah back. And he could have prevented that."

"But you got me back. And Micah. You got us both back. It's not that big of a deal, really. He did it for—"

"It's a big deal to me," I said firmly.

She raised a brow and looked me over for a minute. I knew that expression. She thought I was being petty. And honestly, I knew that I was too. But I was frustrated. No, it wasn't fair to take my anger out on him, but it's not like it'd really affect him. He was probably hanging out with older me in that very moment. My anger may have been pointless, but it wasn't hurting anyone.

"Alright. Point taken."

As she turned back to the bathroom, I released a deep breath. I cleared my throat and changed the subject. "So what about you? What'd you do all day? Work on that tree of life thing?"

"Literally, all day," she said. "It wasn't easy at first, but I think I've got the hang of it. I mean, I'm no expert yet. I figure it'll take time and practice to get to that point. But yeah, I think I've got it."

"That's great," I muttered.

"It was so cool." She walked into the bedroom. "I mean, it was pretty scary the first couple of times. It's so powerful. Stronger than Micah, if you can believe it. Kind of bugged me out at first."

"Yeah, sounds pretty sketchy."

My apathy makes it sound like I wasn't happy she'd figured it out, and that wasn't the case. I was. But I was just... I don't know. Burned out. Stressed. Dreading what would come by nightfall this time tomorrow.

"Oh, we're meeting up with Lila and Nick at the diner in the morning. That's why I told Micah we're getting him to bed soon; we've got to get to sleep early. They want us there at seven our time."

"Seven's sleeping in around here." I managed a smile. "But yeah, it wouldn't be a bad idea to head into tomorrow being well-rested."

She rubbed lotion up her arms. "But you know what else happened today?"

"No, what?" I asked.

"I saw it. The day I made the twenty-five of us immortal. God, it's so fucking weird. But it was exciting too, ya know?"

I smiled. "I bet. Did you recognize anyone?"

"Yeah. You, of course. And Lux. I saw Avery and Asher, and Venark, who I'm now certain is Kai, with Hannah. She didn't look much different, but she didn't look that much like Nix, so I'm not sure if she was your sister then. Oh, and Connor and Naomi, I saw them too. And I saw Celena and Wyatt for the first time, too. Wyatt's eyes are a tell-tale, ya know? The way he looks at her, that hasn't changed."

"Not surprising," I said.

She sat on the bed. "I don't know, it was just so weird. And I." She paused. "I saw something else too."

"What's that?" I asked.

"I know you said you saw me dead that day in the Elder's Hall. But did you see the kids?"

"No, just you. You, and all the blood on the floor. Then Lux on the other side of the room. Why?"

"It wasn't just my blood," she muttered. "I... I collapsed beside them. They were right there."

I blinked hard a few times.

That was odd. Why had I only remembered her? But It seemed obvious. Seeing my dead children would've hurt too much. Seeing her that way hurt too, but not like seeing them would have.

I sat on the bed. "I don't know. Maybe my subconscious didn't want to remember that part."

"Maybe," she muttered. "But I saw that, too. The second time I touched it. I saw them on the ground, and I saw one of the archangels kill me. I'm not really sure why, but I did."

I wasn't a huge fan of this conversation, and here seemed like a good place to change it. "Speaking of the kids. We need to tell Micah."

"Yeah, I know. I just think he needs some more time. He deserves some peace and—"

"We all need more time." I cut her off. "But we only have a week left. And he knows something's up. We're going to be gone a lot more in the next few days and he's getting curious. The only one watching him is going to be your mom, and if he decides to teleport after one of us, then we're going to be chasing our four-year-old through a natural disaster. We have to tell him."

She arched a brow. "What do you mean 'he's getting curious?'"

"He said something to Chris. Something about how we're lying to him and how he's going to get to the bottom of it."

Her eyes closed. She drew in a deep breath and carefully let it out. "What do you think we should tell him?"

I pressed my lips together. "I don't know. You're better with words than I am."

"Fine. I'll be the bearer of bad news. *When* do you think we should tell him?"

"Tonight. I think we should tell him tonight," I said. "It'll give him some time to decide what he wants to bring. He can pack his own bag. You know how he is about his clothes."

She pressed her lips together. "Alright, tonight."

I tucked an arm around her waist. Hers moved around my torso. "So how's that tree of life thing work? Do you grow a tree we all hop into?"

She pulled away, lifting her palm in front of her. "Don't touch it, alright?"

I nodded.

Her eyes slowly sealed shut. After a moment or two, a green, almost smoke like material drifted from her skin. Threads of violet thumped through in organic, swirling lines. It gathered an inch or two above her palm, gradually turning to a perfect sphere.

I squinted a bit, watching the lines of violet throughout it. They twisted and turned around one another, almost like the plasma balls every cool kid had in elementary school had. But instead of vibrating toward the outer sphere, it danced *through* its perimeter. The harder I focused, the more I realized why it was called the tree of life.

The purple lines looked like branches of an oak swaying in the wind. That green smoke like energy could easily be equated to leaves dancing on a breezy day. The only thing that it was missing was a trunk.

"I really wanna touch it," I muttered.

She snapped it back into her palm. "Well, I don't know what would happen to you if you did. So let's not."

"Mommy!" Micah yelled in the doorway. "Mommy, the lights are back! Come on, come look!"

She laughed and started to her feet. "Alright, I'm coming, buddy."

CHAPTER FIFTY-ONE

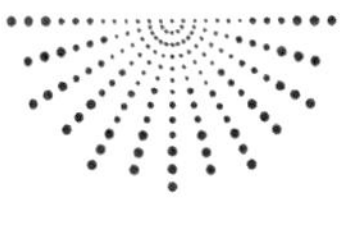

LAILA

We followed Micah up to his bedroom. With Milly at my hip and Micah on Jeremy's, we stood on the balcony for a while. Micah marveled at the beauty of the colors as I tried not to panic over the people standing in the bleachers waiting for their turn to walk into another dimension.

Although, it wasn't *them* that made me anxious. It was the fact that our small town had a population of around ten-thousand people, spread out over large farms and condensed suburbs. Our county housed over seventy-thousand total. And that stadium, although it was about halfway full, couldn't have held more than three thousand people. Even if it had been full the night before, that still was a grand total of no more than five thousand. Even if they set that one specifically for our town rather than the county—which I doubted because we had the largest stadium in a fifty-mile radius—that still meant that half the citizens weren't leaving.

If only half of the population left earth to the Fae realm, that meant that three and a half billion people had no intention of leaving their home.

And we couldn't save them all.

After a while, I cleared my throat and told Micah it was time to get a bath. He objected at first, but I insisted, and he eventually conceded. Jeremy and I took turns; I bathed one kid while he entertained the other.

Milly fell to sleep pretty quick while Jeremy helped Micah get dressed. Then came the conversation I'd been dreading for days.

I stood in the doorway as Jeremy swooped Micah into his bed. He giggled as his dad plopped him onto the covers and tickled his sides. I smiled, but felt my heart falling. This could be the last time we lay him to sleep in the bedroom we'd designed just for him.

Jeremy glanced over his shoulder in a mess of black waves and sent me a sad smile.

"Mommy, you're still gonna read me a story, right?" Micah situated the comforter beneath his armpits. Tink brushed past my calf and hopped onto the bed beside his legs.

"Yeah, I'll read you a story." I walked to the bookshelf and looked over the titles. "What are we in the mood for tonight?"

"The silly pom one." He grinned.

"The poem one, you mean?" I asked, reaching for *Falling Up* by Shel Silverstein.

"Yeah, that's it. Po-em," he annunciated.

I chuckled as I sat on the bed next to him. I laid the book in my lap. "But before we read this, Daddy and I need to talk to you about something."

Jeremy pulled the chair from the desk to the bed and sat. Micah looked between the two of us with an expression of concern. "So you're going to tell me why you've been gone so much? And why we had to leave the diner the other night, and why you don't want me to leave the house?"

I pressed my lips together and tried to figure out how to answer that. The reality was, I couldn't tell him the truth. Not the whole truth. He was four. You can't tell a four-year-old the world's ending, and you really can't tell him that his existence plays a big part in why.

"Yeah," I murmured. "That's the goal here. But I'm not really sure how to say it in words that you'll understand, kiddo."

"I'm not so little anymore." His eyes moved between mine gently. "You can tell me, Mommy. I'll be okay."

I smiled. "I know you will. You're one tough kid. It's just…it's hard for grown-ups to understand. It's even harder for kids to understand."

"I'll try real hard," he said.

"You shouldn't have to," Jeremy said quietly. "That's just it, buddy. You're a kid. You're not supposed to have to worry about what's going on out there."

"But it's okay, I don't mind," Micah said.

I chuckled. "Alright, well you want to know what's happening out there?"

Jeremy shot me a *what the fuck are you about to say?* expression as Micah nodded.

"Well, there's a lot of bad storms going on right now. And it's getting kind of scary. That's why we want you and your sister to stay home, because the barrier we have around the house can keep you guys safe. That's why we left the diner the other night, a really bad storm was coming."

"But I… I saw your hands, Mommy," he murmured.

"Yeah. You did, huh?" He nodded. "Well, someone did get hurt. They got hurt pretty bad. But a friend of ours took care of it. We just didn't want you to worry, that's all. But everything's okay. You're gonna be just fine. So am I, and your dad, and your sister, and all of your aunts and uncles. Everyone's going to be just fine in a week or two."

"Is that when the storms are going to end?" he asked.

I pressed my lips together and looked at Jeremy. He met my gaze then shifted his eyes out the window for a moment. He turned back to Micah. "Kind of."

"What do you mean?" he asked.

"Well." I paused to clear my throat. "Well, next week, we're all going to go somewhere else. Our whole family. We're going to move somewhere that's safe from the storms."

He turned his head to the side a bit. "But you said we're safe here at home, right?"

"We are," Jeremy said quietly. "We are safe at home. But the storm that's coming next week... It's going to be a lot bigger than these storms have been. And it won't be safe here anymore."

Micah's lower lip began to tremble. "Where will be safe then?"

"We're not exactly sure *where* yet," Jeremy said. "But we are sure about one thing. Mommy and I are going to keep you safe no matter what. That's why we're leaving because the place that we're going will be much safer than where we are now."

"So we're moving, but you don't know where?"

Jeremy nodded, and Micah turned his gaze to me. "But I love this house. You told me I'd never have to leave, that's what you said when I first moved here. That this is my home, and I'd never have to leave."

My heart throbbed. He was right, I had said that. I had told him he'd never have to leave the home he loved. And it was true when I said it because I had believed it to be true.

"Because that's what we thought at the time," Jeremy said. "But things changed, buddy. And I wish they hadn't. I wish we could stay here forever. I built this house. It's my favorite place in the world. This is my home too. I don't want to leave it. But some things are out of our control."

"And no matter what, we're going to be together," I said. "And as much as I love this place, I know we'll find another place we love just as much."

"But you don't even know where," he asked. "We're moving, and you don't even know where."

"That's part of what makes it exciting." Jeremy pulled his lips into a grin that barely looked fake. "We'll buy a new house, and you can even help us pick it out. But while we're waiting to buy it, we'll get to stay in a hotel. We can find one with a big pool, and a hot tub, and we can fill up on free breakfast in the mornings, and we'll check out some cool new town. And I bet we'll find some awesome new playgrounds we've never been to before."

A little pitter patter of joy crept into my heavy heart. The smallest smile lifted my lips. Lila had said that. That Micah loved the house, and he played a big part in convincing Jeremy to buy it.

Micah smiled. "And I can help pick the new house?"

Jeremy smiled wider. "You sure can."

He looked down at Tink at the edge of the bed. "And you'll keep Tink safe too, right?"

I smiled. "We will."

He thought for a moment. "Will I get to go to school? You said I can't go now because it's not safe, but the place we're going, will it be safe for me to go to school?"

"It will," I said.

"Well, as *safe* as an American school can get," Jeremy muttered.

Micah's eyes widened, and his smile got wider. "But I can? I can go to school?"

That meant so much to him. He wanted to go to school so bad. He wanted to learn, and read, and make friends. He wanted normalcy. And this was a way to give it to him.

That realization brought me some peace.

I smiled. "Yeah, buddy. You can go to school."

"That'll be so much fun. I'll meet other kids, and we'll play outside and…" Micah grinned. After a moment with airy eyes, he said, "See? I'm not so little, I can understand things."

I laughed as I pushed hair behind my ear. "But listen for a second, okay?"

He nodded.

"For the next few days, things are going to be pretty crazy out there. Daddy and I are going to be really busy helping people. We might not be home for dinner and to put you to bed. A lot of your aunts and uncles won't be here either. Gam's going to watch you and take care of things around the house. But we need you to stay here so you don't get hurt out there, okay? We need you to listen to Gam and do what she says. It's dangerous outside of the perimeter. Let me and Daddy handle it. You just handle things here at the house, okay? Can you do that?"

His face grew serious. "You keep those people safe, and I'll keep Milly and Gam safe."

I laughed, and Jeremy smiled. "That sounds like a good plan."

"Can you read me the book now?" Micah asked, gesturing to my lap. "I'm getting sleepy."

My lips pulled upward as I climbed up the bed and curled beside him. Opening to where we'd left off last, I quietly read the poems, submerging myself in the sound of his sweet giggles at the funny stories.

Ultimately, I hadn't lied to him. Nothing I said was untrue. There were bad storms out there, and a worse one was arriving in a week's time.

The only thing I didn't tell him was that my mom wouldn't be joining us.

CHAPTER FIFTY-TWO

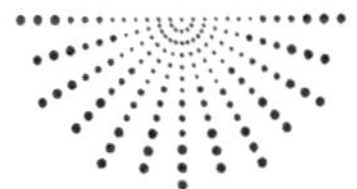

JANUARY 6 - JEREMY

I turned on the spigot of the bathroom sink. As the water splashed to the bowl, I scooped it into my palms and lifted it to my cheeks. The temperature jolted me from my slumbered haze, but as I pulled my hand from my cheek, it trembled before me.

Today wasn't going to be a good day. It was going to be as bad as Wednesday had been, maybe even worse. I was trying to prepare myself by saying I'd done it before.

But in every battle I'd fought prior to this week, there was an end game. Save the guy and kill the Demon. Slaughter the Vampires and burn their nest to the ground. Find my fiancé and bring her home. Break down the doors and free the survivors. Find my brother and get him to safety. Hold my son and kill the bastard that stole the first three years of his life from me.

But there was no endgame here. Today would be just as the tsunami had been. Damage control.

Then rummage through the wreckage for bodies and give them a proper burial.

My stomach ached. I wasn't ready to do it again.

I always *thought* that I had PTSD and some form of generalized anxiety before that day. But I didn't have a clue what that really felt like until Tuesday morning after the Chamber's meeting. Sure, I'd had depression and the same mild anxiety every living creature copes with when they fear for their life.

But I had no idea how debilitating anxiety could truly be. My heart thudded against my ribcage in a way I'd only experienced in active battle before. My stomach hurt worse than it ever had, which means a lot coming from a recovering heroin addict. My hands and feet felt almost numb from how tingly they'd become.

It made me think back to the way I reacted when Laila came home after three months in captivity. And it flooded me with guilt. I'd had no idea what was going on in her head or the way that she felt inside of her body. I had no idea what it was like to live in a place where you have to constantly be on alert for the next threat. I had no concept of how hard that must have been for her.

Still, I never would. What she went through was far different than what I experienced during those twelve days. But I got a *glimpse* into how it felt when she struggled not to crawl out of her own skin.

"You ready?" Laila asked in the bathroom doorway.

I clenched my trembling hand to a fist at my side. "Yeah, I'm ready. Is everyone up?"

"Yeah. Celena and Wyatt are already at the diner. I think Kai is too. Brody, Adam, and Chris are waiting on us. I asked Moriah if she was coming, but she practically laughed in my face." She rolled her eyes. "Guess she figures her part in fighting the apocalypse was that letter and a few bags of blood."

I huffed. "Why are we taking her again?"

"A deal's a deal," she said. "I'm a woman of my word. Honor and all that."

A long breath eased from my nostrils. "I'm so sick of honor."

She smiled and extended her hand to mine. "C'mon. We should get going."

"Looks like we're all here," Lila murmured with a look around the diner. Okay, good. Good, I took everyone into account. Good. No Lydia though, huh?"

My expression hardened. "She's fifteen."

"Yeah, I know. Just used to her being a lot older. But that's okay, we can make this work. Okay. Okay." She glanced around again. "Okay, so Celena and Wyatt, you're going to Mount Kaeptu."

"Where the hell is that?" Wyatt asked.

"Korea," Lila said.

Wyatt raised a brow. "*Which* Korea?"

Nick tried to stifle his laugh.

Lila's hands went to her hips. "North Korea."

"You've got to be shitting me," Wyatt said. "Those fuckers—"

"Their leader is not the population," Lila said. "Believe it or not, many of those people are prisoners to their own land."

"We're Americans. They hate us," he said.

"So does the rest of the world," she said. "But when you're about to fall off a cliff, you don't give a damn whose hand is reaching out to grab yours. Just help the civilians, alright? Can you handle that?"

He huffed. "Guess I have to."

"We'll be fine." Celena slid her phone from her pocket. "Let me just find some Google earth images here and... alright, got it. When's it gonna blow?"

"About two hours? Somewhere in there. We're not sure about the exact time. Just get people back and try to persuade as many as you can to travel through their portal. It might surprise you how easily coaxed they are. The women will be easier. Try them first."

Celena said, "We'll do what we can."

Lila dipped her chin. Wyatt and Celena joined hands and disappeared. She turned to Adam. "Alright, you and Leah are at Mount Vesuvius. I know you don't have much options in the way of directing the spread of any lava, but you can move people and that's all we really need. Just get people out."

Leah rubbed her eyes. "Pompeii. We get Pompeii."

Nick smiled. "It was pretty mild compared to Mount Fuji and Saint Helens. We're handling those two."

Adam rubbed his closed eyes. "Let's hope we don't get turned to statues."

"You'll be alright," Lila said.

Leah put her hand on Adam's shoulder, and the two of them disappeared.

Lila turned to Kai, Chris, and Brody. "Alright. You three are going to Mount Merapi in Indonesia." Nick pulled his backpack off and undid the zipper. "This volcano's been erupting for centuries. People are sticking away from the eruption itself, which is good. So your primary focus isn't going to be the people."

"The pyroclastic flow is the issue there." Nick pulled out three large gas masks and tossed them to them.

"The what?" Kai asked.

"The smoke," Chris said. "The ash and soot. Breathing quality's gonna be bad."

"Oh," Kai murmured. "Where do I take it then? I can move the air, but where should I take it?"

I wasn't an expert on volcanoes. But I knew a thing or two.

"That's not really it," I said. "Yeah, breathing quality is going to be close to nothing. But the issue isn't the air; the issue is what happens when the shit flying out of the volcano falls back down to the earth."

Nick nodded. "It looks like it's just ash, but it's actually a landslide of hot air full of rocks and shit. Like a flash flood of boulders smoldering at a thousand degrees. It's gonna be hotter than hell, and I mean that in the literal sense."

Brody said, "Then what the hell am I doing there?"

"Kai's going to handle the pyroclastic flow," Lila said. "Brody, Chris, it's your jobs to move as many people a thousand miles from the mountain before that happens. But yeah, once that baby starts spewing, you get the hell out."

"Whatchye mean I'm gonna handle it?" Kai asked. "I'll do what ye need me to, but I'm the brawn, not the brains. You've got to tell me what it is that I've got to do."

"Slow down the momentum of the flow," Laila said.

Kai huffed. "I know ye all had classes where you learned what these words meant but I—"

"When you see a bunch of shit flying in the air from the mountain-top, slow it down before it hits the ground," Nick said. "It'll try to gather in large floods of debris that slam down the mountain very fast. Don't let that happen. Slow it down as best as you possibly can."

Kai inhaled deeply. "Very well. Now, was that so hard?"

Lila laughed. She looked at Brody. "You know where you're going?"

"Rough idea." He grabbed ahold of Kai's shoulder.

"Just remember," Nick said. "You aren't invincible, guys. If you have to teleport out, you teleport out. We can deal with the damage afterward. And as awful as it sounds, losing one of you is worse than losing a thousand of them. We're going to see loss of life today. That's inevitable. But don't let it be one of you. Because without our family, thousands more lives will be lost."

That sent a shudder down my spine. It was true. I knew it was true. Like when you're in an airplane that starts going down. You put your own oxygen mask before your kids, because you know how to put it on them once they pass out from lack of air. It seems selfish, but it really isn't.

Still. Right or not. That was a hard realization to come to grips with.

Brody pressed his lips together and let a sigh escape his nostrils. "See you later." They disappeared.

"Then there were two," Laila muttered.

"Well," Lila said. "Four."

I exhaled slowly. "So where do you want us?"

"I'm going to Mount Fuji," Lila said.

"And I'm going to Saint Helens," Nick said.

"But Jeremy, you're going to Mount Shasta in California," Lila said.

"And Lai, you're going to Kīlauea, Hawaii," Nick said.

"What? Why?" I asked.

"Why what?" Lila said.

"Why are we splitting up?" I said. "Everybody else went in pairs."

"We aren't everybody else," Nick said.

"But—"

"All four of us are immune to fire. All four of us can teleport, and fly and redirect airflow," Lila said. "We're outnumbered with these volcanoes already, but the four of us can protect ourselves. They all had to go in teams. We have to handle this alone."

"That's the climax of every horror movie in history," I said quickly. "We split up, and we die—"

"You don't die." Nick outstretched his arms and gestured over his body. "We're proof of that."

My heart picked up speed in my chest. I clenched my trembling hand to a tight fist at my side. Laila touched my bicep. I looked down at her, and she smiled. "We got this."

I huffed. Sure, she'd probably handle this fine. As she usually did. Laila could handle just about anything that came her way. But me? I was not so sure that I had this.

She reached onto the tips of her toes and touched her lips to mine. I held her cheek for a moment. She pulled away with a smile. "I'll see you tonight."

She sent Lila and Nick a wave and disappeared.

"You'll be alright, man," Nick said. "But pull your hair back. It's gonna drive you crazy if you don't."

CHAPTER FIFTY-THREE

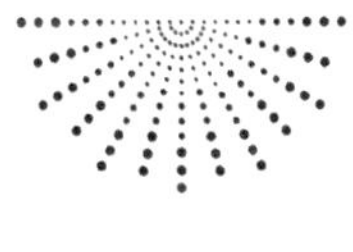

LAILA

I pulled my knees to my chest and looked out over the warm island from my seat next to the simmering volcano. A beautiful view, really. To my left, a short cliff side into a bubbling pit of red magma. A few miles in the distance to my right, inviting lights of blue and green danced a couple dozen yards above the ground. The smell of sulfur from the volcano wasn't exactly pleasant, but the stars shined as bright as ever. So calm and peaceful, I almost didn't blame the people for failing to believe the world was about to end.

I brought myself to my feet. I spun the air beneath me, using it to lift me higher above the mountaintop. I wanted an aerial view.

Everyone had already been well informed of the danger at hand. They heard Lila tell the world to get away from the volcanoes. They heard her tell them to enter the spinning vortex I saw swirling off the coast a few miles in the distance.

But no one was lined up to cross into the other world. The village nearby was lit by porch lamps, people sitting outside enjoying the warm, humid breeze. I heard music billowing from a resort on the other side of the island. They'd decided to blissfully enjoy their paradise.

No one was taking it seriously. There was clearly a swirling vortex on the other end of the island—one I'm sure they'd all heard of, one I could see with my own eyes, so I'm sure they had too.

Yet, they didn't believe it. They hadn't seen any evidence of the world ending firsthand. They'd rather sip their cosmos and pina coladas and pretend that the evidence of something far greater than them wasn't just a few miles away. The power of disbelief is a sickeningly potent thing.

I remembered seeing the viral videos of Kīlauea's eruption in 2018. I remember my heart skipping a beat as I watched the rivers of lava rushing through the streets. I remember the controversy of people purchasing masks to deal with the smog, despite experts saying they wouldn't help. I remember telling Jeremy that we should do something. And I remember him asking, "What though? What can we do?"

Compared to what today would bring, the damage that day was minuscule. A few dozen people were injured, but no one died. The air quality was bad but even so, there wasn't anything that I, or he, could really help with. It was a matter of repairing the land once the dust had settled.

That was more than a year before I had all the abilities I have now. I couldn't teleport. I couldn't manipulate air, not at the capacity I could these days. I could read minds, but I hadn't learned how to comb through a vast number of thoughts. I could create fire, but what good would that have done in a volcanic eruption? Sure, I was impervious to lava. But I was a five foot three, small woman that couldn't exactly be used as a shield. Without being able to teleport people out, I was practically useless then.

But I was far from useless now.

I couldn't keep that lava from spewing once it began. But I could do just about anything else.

My eyes moved over the land, scanning the area to devise a plan for once that lava launched from the earth. People aren't dumb; they tend to build their homes a safe distance from the actual volcano. In 2018 though, the problem wasn't Mount Kīlauea itself but the lava vents in its vicinity. I think it was somewhere around two dozen simultaneously started spewing. And it all started after a quake.

I figured that when I started to feel the earth shake, I'd try to stop it as I'd done on Wednesday. But considering Lila and Nick's prior knowledge, I figured that wouldn't be easy, if even possible. Although, even if I could bring a level 6 quake down to a level 4, it'd minimize the amount of lava that would erupt.

At least, I hoped. The most knowledge I had of volcanoes and earthquakes was my geography class in freshman year. Truthfully, I was winging it.

<hr>

By three a.m., I was growing antsy. I'd been waiting for almost two hours and I felt nothing. No tremble, beneath the ground, no lava squirting from the mountaintop. It was no wonder we had to go back in time to prepare for this, because the planet didn't give us any of the warning signs it's supposed to when a natural disaster strikes. The only way to know that it was coming was Nick and Lila's prior knowledge.

Just as I huffed in annoyance, tired of waiting, I felt it. Barely a tremor at first. But definitely something. Not something people sleeping in their beds would feel, definitely not something the vacationers would notice in their drunken haze on their patios.

But It intensified. The ground began to shake violently beneath my feet. I closed my eyes and tried to feel the weight of the tectonic plate miles beneath me, but no sooner than I felt the tremor did the pressure let up.

I opened my eyes and turned my head to the side a bit. Confused, I wondered if that was all. I'd hardly even felt the strength of the plate, I hadn't stopped it.

Then a loud rumble roared behind me.

I spun around, and my jaw dropped.

It was nothing like the videos from 2018. It wasn't a black field of obsidian with geysers of red spewing a dozen yards into the air.

The mountaintop was like the jaws of a dragon vomiting bright red, liquid fire hundreds of feet into the air.

"Holy fuck," I murmured.

CHAPTER FIFTY-FOUR

JEREMY

Mount Shasta, Northern California. I remembered this place pretty clearly. It's where we found our son. Not on the mountain itself but along the same ley line the mountain was seated on. We were a few hundred miles south of the mountain, to be specific.

Still, when Nick and Lila told me Mount Shasta, the first thing I did was google 'What would happen if Mount Shasta erupted?'

The results were somewhat comforting. It said the town of Mount Shasta, Dunsmuir, and Weed Yreka were the most at risk because they were within thirty miles of the volcano, each only populated by a few thousand people. As Nick had told Brody for the one he and Kai were assigned, the biggest concern was pyroclastic flow, not the eruption itself.

Of course, that was based on the simplistic views of seismology as naturally occurring disasters. But I knew better. It wasn't the planet running through natural cycles. Everything that was happening was at the hands of the people who *created* the planet and knew it better than any scientist alive. It wasn't close to natural; it was the equivalent to a beekeeper stealing honey from their witless pets.

I tightened my jacket around my cold shoulders. My eyes shifted over the mountaintop, waiting for the rumble or roar I knew was imminent. I found myself really wishing I had a cigarette right about then. Couldn't smoke a joint, I needed to be on my toes. At least the nicotine might calm my nerves a bit.

I teleported to the sky above the mountain, catching myself on a cushion of air. I looked out over the towns in each direction. Shasta, Weed, and Dunsmuir in the distance. Shasta was closest, I was sure it'd be the one to get hit the worst.

But I wasn't really sure what I'd do when it started to erupt. I knew I had to control the pyroclastic flow, but I didn't know how to do that. Air, I guessed. That was how. But I'd never used air on a scale that big. Using it to hold my body weight was pretty simple. Using it to push some curtains shut or to blow away a cloud on a dreary day was easy peasy. But using it to slow down molten hot boulders that weighed more than cars was far from my area of expertise.

The roar louder than that of a jet engine made me jerk, hand flying to my heart as I nearly dropped my hold on the wind beneath me. So high above the air, I didn't feel the quake. But I saw it. I literally *watched* the earth quiver.

A cloud darker than anything I'd ever seen billowed from the frozen mountaintop. It cut through the dark blue sky faster than I knew possible. So dark in color, it almost instantly slashed the light from the twinkling stars above.

The warmth from the ash touched my skin, yet my body felt colder than it ever had.

My heart picked up speed in my chest, bursts of adrenaline rushing to my extremities. My arms and legs went numb, and my breath stopped.

I just froze.

Perhaps the worst moment in all of history to freeze in fear, but I can't explain it any better. That's what I did. I just fucking *froze.*

I told my legs to move. I told my arms to flail. I told my body that it had to stop what was about to happen, but I just couldn't.

Instead, I did as I'd done three days prior. I *watched.* I watched that cloud of burning ash and smoldering rocks start to race down the mountainside.

And still, I was frozen in place. The pressure was on, harder than it'd ever been. Yet, I was just sitting there. Hovering uselessly above the smoke when I was supposed to be down there stopping it. Even writing these words brings me to an angry sob because I still don't know why I didn't fucking *move.*

It wasn't until that black cloud of smog was halfway down the mountainside that my body felt free from its momentary paralysis.

I teleported to the ground beneath the landslide of debris. My arms outstretched before me, and I pushed. Wind rushed from behind me. My ponytail flung forward and slapped me across the cheek.

And it worked. It *worked.* I was holding off the black cloud from heading toward the town. For a half a second, that is.

But the earth trembled again, only for a second or two, but just long enough for another puff of black smoke to push up from the mountaintop.

I caught myself clutching my breath again. I was holding a massive cloud of hot ash from sliding any further down the snowy mountain, but another one was about to fall on the other side.

I felt my breath began to heave in and out of my chest as I watched the next flow of smoke fall down to the earth in slow motion. I didn't know what to do. Hold back the one I had a handle on, or move to the other side and stop that flow.

Fuck. *Fuck, fuck, fuck.*

I wasn't frozen that time, but I may as well have been. No matter which option I took, a flash flood of hot air and rocks was headed toward a town.

Which one do I stop? The one headed for Weed or the one headed for Shasta?

Fuck, fuck, *fuck.*

A thought occurred to me. Create a wind tunnel around the foot of the entire mountain. Like a wall of air pushing upward around its entire base, similar to how Laila described she did with the tsunami.

With wide, alert eyes, I took in a deep breath and teleported to the other side.

The landslide of hot ash was headed straight toward me, just as it'd been on the other side. I summoned the air from behind me and surged it toward the black cloud.

And it worked. It worked; I kept the flow at bay on that side too.

Simultaneously, I was holding two black clouds of heat and ash from slamming toward the towns nearby.

But then, the ground quaked again.

And it wasn't just smoke that time.

I looked up, watching lava spew a hundred feet in the air.

My heart started beating so fast, I don't know how it didn't break through my ribcage.

My stomach ached as I tried to figure out which way to direct the white-hot magma.

I tried to tap into fire, to somehow manipulate that hot liquid spitting from the mountaintop. But as I focused in on fire, I lost my hold on air.

Hot gray smog slammed into my body from the opposite side of the volcano. The pyroclastic flow headed for Weed.

And sure, I could tolerate the heat. It didn't even phase me. But what I hadn't considered was the air. I may have been superhuman, but I still had to breathe.

I coughed, trying to summon clean air into my lungs but only pulling more smoke into my body.

Holding the flow before me with one hand and shooting the smoke away from behind, I tried to hold my breath. But it wasn't clean air in my lungs. It was thick, black, ash.

I had to breathe. But I had to hold that ash back from hitting the town. I heard Nick's voice in my head. "One of you is worth a thousand of them."

One of you is worth a thousand of them.

I didn't agree. I hated that thought. I wasn't that kind of god; I didn't want to put myself before the masses.

But I had no choice.

I was no good to them dead.

So with tears in my eyes and a chest full of smoke, I teleported to the wooded area two miles from Weed.

CHAPTER FIFTY-FIVE

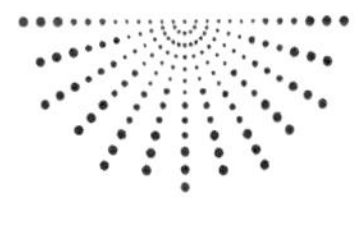

LAILA

As the lava started spewing from the volcano's lips, I drew in a deep breath and braced for impact. I'd seen a few small homes on the mountainside, but I checked earlier, they weren't occupied. So as long as I kept the lava in that general vicinity, everything would be okay.

But Lila and Nick wouldn't have sent me here if it were going to be that easy. They would have sent Leah and Adam if it'd be that simple. No, it was about to get bad. I just didn't know how.

The lava shooting from the volcano was almost identical to a diorama kids make with vinegar and baking soda for class projects, but instead of oozing from the top, it was shooting. It had to have flown at least two-hundred feet in the air.

I stared up at the molten liquid then out over the vicinity. I couldn't figure out what about it would be so bad. There were a few hotels a couple of miles away, but this lava wouldn't reach them. Even with the loud roar and temperature rising, it felt anti-climactic. I should have been *doing* something. But there was nothing to do. No one was hurt, no lives were at risk.

Honestly, it was boring.

Pretty, but boring.

I was admiring the lava sliding down the mountainside when the ground suddenly shook beneath me. Not a slow build into a large quake, but a fast tremble I didn't have the chance to grip.

Then another loud growl from the mountain. A puff of dark black smog erupted from its top, encasing a massive wave of glowing red.

The climax I'd been waiting for.

It's almost hard to describe. The first eruption was as bright and large as any volcanic eruption I'd ever seen. But that vomit of red had to have been three times as powerful.

It reminded me of Luka in his colic days. I was holding him in my lap once in the breakfast nook, bouncing up and down after he'd eaten. Out of nowhere, his little mouth opened and launched puke across the room at Jenna on the other side of the island. We all gaped, wondering how such a little guy held that much liquid inside of his tiny belly.

I looked up, shaking my head with my mouth wide open as the lava drizzled down around me like rain from a cloud. Spots of lava touched my skin. I wiped them away quickly, then looked out over the towns in the distance.

My stomach dropped.

Only specs hit me, but I watched in slow motion as massive, white-hot boulders soared toward the ground in every direction. The resort fifteen miles away, the cottages a few miles to my left, the little bed and breakfast to my right.

Time seemed to stand still for that moment. I didn't know where to go first. I didn't know which cottages were inhabited. I didn't know who to save because that was the impossible decision I was faced with.

Who do I save?

In a split second, I had to make a life dependent decision.

The resort.

It had the most people. If I stopped a boulder the size of a truck from hitting that cottage, I may have saved five or ten lives. But it I stopped it from hitting the resort, I saved at least a hundred.

I teleported into the air just below the boulder. Levitating hundreds of feet above the ground, I ripped the air from behind me and directed it to the rock, pushing it with every fiber of my being. It soared through the air and plummeted into the ocean off the coast, creating a wave that slammed the shore.

Still hovering in the air above the resort, I turned.

My heart slammed through my stomach and fell to the ground beneath me as I watched the boulders I couldn't stop fall to the earth.

They plunged to the ground.

Boom. Boom-boom. Boom-boom-boom.

Like missiles, flying through the air and destroying everything close to where they landed.

I saved the resort. But I couldn't say the same for the rest of the island within my view.

I blasted further into the sky, looking for which area was hit the worst, all while the volcano continued to erupt. Instead of massive flying boulders though, it was mostly lava that stayed relatively close to the mountain itself. Never thought I'd say I was relieved for only lava to spew from a volcano, but there was a first time for everything.

To my left, a cloud of black smoke seeped up from the ground. I'd scanned the area and hadn't seen any evidence of life there. No lights, no campfire, no noise. But now I heard screams.

I teleported to the ground there, landing in a mass of ash and smog. I couldn't see them, but I could hear them. Their screams, their cries. I closed my eyes and held my breath, focusing on the sounds of their minds. Not the words themselves, as their minds were a jumble of panic and pain, only their locations. I teleported to them, unable to even make out their appearance as I gripped two shoulders and teleported to the beach a few miles away.

The people bent over vomiting as I teleported back to the place I was just in. More voices, crying, screaming names, searching for their loved ones. But I grabbed them too and took them back to the beach.

I didn't see their faces, I didn't catch their names, I just kept going. Teleporting to the sound of someone's thoughts and taking them somewhere with clean air.

Honestly, I went into autopilot. I didn't speak; I didn't think. I just grabbed and teleported. Healed, and teleported. Flew, and teleported.

Then the ground shook again. More lava spewed into the atmosphere, more boulders flew miles from the volcano, more smog filled the clean air.

But I was stuck in a revolving door. I couldn't stop every rock from flying toward a home or campsite. I couldn't keep the lava from erupting. The quakes were happening too fast for me to grip the tectonic plate.

The paradise on the Big Island was quickly deteriorating. Within an hour's time, it'd become what humans describe as hell. As hot as the sun. Molten lava falling down like rain. Excruciating pain in every direction. Fear writhing through every soul in sight.

On my fiftieth or so trip to the beach where I was moving people from the damage of the island, a woman grasped my arm before I could teleport out.

I can't even tell you what she looked like. I don't remember the color of her hair or the complexion to her skin. All that I can recall are two eyes the size of saucers darting between mine and the sound of her crackly, smoke tainted lungs.

"What do we do now?" she pleaded.

I looked to the swirling pit of vibrant lights a few hundred yards down the beach. "Jump."

That's all that I could think to say. That's all that I had *time* to say. There were roughly 150,000 people living on that island, and I didn't have time to convince each and every one of them to go through the portal that had been open since before the volcano erupted on a scale history had never witnessed.

All that I could do was help the people I saw who needed it and pray that the rest would listen.

CHAPTER FIFTY-SIX

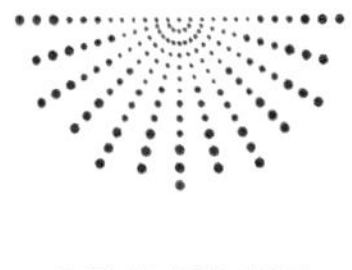

JEREMY

I lurched forward hacking, watching black smoke escape from my mouth as if I'd just taken a hit off of a four-foot bong. My hands gripped my knees as I coughed and coughed, trying to see through my oxygen-deprived haze. I didn't have time to catch my breath to its full capacity, but I just needed to breathe for a moment.

I leaned against a pine tree. My hands raised to my burning eyes, rubbing hard before I looked at the plume headed toward the town behind me.

In that split second, watching that cloud of death race toward me and the thousands of lives I stood before, a million thoughts chased through my mind.

I had so many abilities. I was so strong. Because of Laila's powers, and who I was five-thousand years ago, I was one of the most powerful creatures to ever walk the planet. I was unstoppable. I was practically limitless.

But I'd found my limit.

Killing me wouldn't be easy. Soon, it'd be close to impossible. But you didn't have to stab me to kill me. Putting thousands of lives into my hands and forcing me to accept that I was powerless to save them was essentially the same thing.

It got closer, and I summoned the air behind me toward it, but I couldn't stop thinking.

I thought that my family mattered more to me than the world. Fuck the world as long as I can keep my family safe, I'd thought. But I was wrong. I was *so* wrong.

Those people mattered. They each had a life to live. They each had families they loved as much as I loved my own, and they were about to be gone in the blink of an eye.

And I was trying. I was trying so hard to keep the cloud from rushing into the city behind me.

It occurred to me that this wasn't the only pyroclastic flow headed down the mountain and my stomach sunk.

Dunsmuir. Shasta.

I felt so sick.

What do I do? What the fuck do I do? Let this plume slam into Weed to teleport to Dunsmuir or Shasta?

There were twenty-four of us, more even, when you account for the doppelgangers, and it still wasn't enough. All of us and our seemingly limitless array of abilities weren't enough. We were all divided around the planet, fighting clouds of demise just like the one headed toward me, and it wasn't enough. We all had to make decisions like I was faced with in that moment.

Who do we save? Who do we let die? Who do we help? Who's more important?

Ultimately, no one was. All of their lives mattered equally. It was just a matter of availability and closest proximity. The tree line closest to Weed was the first I saw. It looked like a nice forest to catch my breath in. And that was it.

That simple decision cost thousands of lives in the neighboring towns.

Tears rained down my smog, dust covered cheeks as I wafted air into that cloud of dust, forcing it to disperse. My hands shook, and my stomach ached as I blasted clean, cold air into it with every cell inside my body.

It was like using a dust blower over a filthy fire pit. At first, it didn't do much but move the mess around. But the longer and harder I slammed it with clean air, it gradually began to drift away.

It must have been ten minutes of constant slamming of the air flow before it looked somewhat clean enough for breathing.

I released my hold and fell to the ground. Dust and crystals of frozen ash drifted past me as tears poured down my ashy cheeks. My hands shook like the wings of a hummingbird as they raised to cup my face.

I couldn't see it. I couldn't hear it. I couldn't smell it.

But I felt it.

Thousands of souls lifting from their bodies a few miles away.

I'd saved one town.

But I lost two.

When I brought myself to my feet from my trembling knees, I debated which town to teleport to first. Which one got hit worse? Who needed me more? Shasta was closer; it probably got hit harder.

I closed my eyes and teleported to the city. As I landed, I forced them open.

My mouth dropped. Tears burned across my irises. I lifted my hands to the sides of my head, knowing I should move, but feeling as I had when the volcano first erupted.

Frozen. Paralyzed in place. But that time, not because of fear. This time, I was frozen in shame.

Smoke billowed into the sky in the distance. The smell of burned plastic and flesh drifted up my nose. Hot air radiated against my skin. Screams and pleas filled my ears from the outskirts of the damage. But I couldn't move. All that I could do was sob.

It wasn't the joyous town I'd visited two years ago. It was the same place, but not a single feature I remembered still stood. Not the hotel Laila and I had stayed in with our daughter. Not the ice cream shop we stopped at on our way to the airport. Nothing was the same.

Nothing.

Nothing the plume of ash touched survived. The city was a flattened, smoldering, empty field.

A few structures remained. A hospital, perhaps, or maybe an office building. A car dealership appeared to be somewhat unscathed, but the lot of vehicles was a pit of ash, although a few were still intact. Flipped, windows shattered, but intact.

I knew what pyroclastic flow was. I knew what it was capable of. But I had some sugar-coated image of it in my mind. When it'd hit me, it burnt the clothes from my body and left my lungs feeling as if they were on fire. But I survived. It was hot, and it hurt a little, but I survived.

My body was more flame retardant than an entire town. And rationally, I knew that. But standing at the foot of that mountain, bombarded by that smoke, with the weight of all three towns on my shoulders...

I wasn't strong enough. I was impervious to heat, but I wasn't fucking strong enough.

And thousands of people died because of my weakness.

I was on the edge of a break down, a full-on panic attack. I heard a child screaming. I'd heard plenty of screams when I first landed but the sound of that little boy yelling, "Daddy! It hurts! Daddy! Where are you?! *Daddy*?!" ripped me back to reality. Guess that parental instinct kicked in, even if it wasn't my kid.

Thousands were dead. But hundreds weren't and they needed help. So I sprang into action.

CHAPTER FIFTY-SEVEN

LAILA

The next eighteen hours were some of the most strenuous of my life. It was a living hell. I'm sure that the sun rose at some point, but there was no evidence of light casting down from above. All that I saw when I looked up was a dark black cloud, shimmering with smoldering ashes and drops of molten liquid. The people on the beach who were still debating entering the portal made makeshift shields from boats and miscellaneous items found on the shore to protect themselves from the droplets of raining fire.

The volcano erupted again, and again, and I did everything that I could. But I couldn't see, it was hard to breathe, and I was exhausted.

No one else came. Not the National Guard, not FEMA. Nothing and no one lent a hand. And I understood. We were in the start of the apocalypse. The government believed us, even if the masses didn't, so all of their resources were allocated to helping the people who weren't being stubborn. It was me against a volcano, trying to save the lives of people who barely believed they were at risk.

I didn't sit once from the moment it started spewing to the moment I moved the last living person to the beach. At least, I hoped it was the last person on the Big Island. I didn't exactly count, and I had no clue how many people were actually there. I had a rough idea of the population but that didn't account for tourists.

I didn't have a moment to drink some water. I didn't get the chance to take a piss. I didn't have the opportunity to be anything other than a rescue boat from the moment it started.

But every time I landed back on the beach, less people were there than the last. They were doing it. They were jumping into the Fae Realm.

It was a shame that it took losing so much for the people to listen. My heart broke because I couldn't save them all. But at least they were finally listening.

It was about 11:30 p.m. their time when the island was finally cleared. The only sound for miles was that of the volcano roaring, spitting and spewing lava and dust into the sky.

By that point, I was so lightheaded that I could barely stand. I'm sure my oxygen levels were dangerously low. I wanted to stay and try to contain the spread of the rubble and save the wildlife that remained.

But the adrenaline was wearing off. I was having a hard time standing upright, and my stomach felt like it was going to explode if I didn't get to a toilet. My legs were practically twigs beneath me. I was having a hard time lifting my arms, let alone walking.

There was nothing left that I could do. So I teleported home.

I landed in the shower, not wanting anyone to see me in my current state. Taking in that breath of fresh air after hours of inhaling hot, black smoke almost hurt. The sudden jolt of oxygen sent me stumbling to the cold ceramic seat inside the shower.

After a few minutes of gripping the shower to keep me steady, I sent a telepathic message to Jeremy.

Are you okay? Do you need me?

Instantly, his thoughts echoed back to mine. An ironic huff of a laugh. *Not exactly okay, but yeah, I'll be alright. I should be finished here soon. Don't know how much more I can do. Are you home?*

Yeah, just got here. You sure you don't need me?

I'll be alright. There isn't really much you can do. Not much anyone can do.

I know what you mean. I'm gonna get a shower and lie down then.

Alright. Love you. Sweet dreams.

Love you, too.

My arms felt so weak that even pulling off my smog covered clothing was a chore. Turning on the water was just as difficult. Standing was almost impossible. I ended up sitting to take that shower.

Once I got the worst of the ash off of me and bathed myself as best as I could, I teleported to the closet. I struggled myself into my pajamas. I teleported to the bed.

I lay down and lifted my phone from the side table. I knew I didn't have much time left here, and didn't know how much availability I'd have in the coming days, but I wanted that meeting with Roland.

Quickly, I typed, *Sorry I know it's late. But think we could meet up one day soon?*

As I closed my eyes, it buzzed on the nightstand. *Of course. When are you free?*

No clue.

Ah, me neither. Just give me a call when you have a moment to spare then. If I answer, I'll squeeze you in.

Great. Thanks.

See you soon, mon ange.

I rolled my eyes, shuttered the screen, closed my eyes, and instantly fell to sleep.

CHAPTER FIFTY-EIGHT

JEREMY

I wish that I could put into words how awful January 6th, 2024 was for me the first time I lived it. I wish I could explain how bad it hurt. But it was unlike any pain I'd ever felt. Losing Micah hurt like a son of a bitch, but it wasn't the same. There was no guilt attached to that pain.

It wasn't my fault Laila climbed in that van. It wasn't my fault that we believed he was dead for the first year and a half of his life. I resented myself for not being there to help her, but it wasn't my fault.

I wasn't a dad yet then. I loved the idea of having a child, but it wasn't for me what it was for Laila. I didn't feel him inside of my body for eight months. I didn't hold him the moment he was born. Losing him hurt because I lost the idea and theoretic responsibility that came with having a kid. But most of all, it hurt me because it hurt *her*.

My *losing Micah moment* was landing in that ashy field and feeling the weight of thousands of souls—souls I was responsible for—filling the abyss.

Then picking up the pieces of my failure.

I spent hours combing through lifeless bodies, healing burn wounds, and searching for life. My ability to sense a soul helped in that regard, but it was still the most difficult thing I'd ever done.

For almost twenty hours, I teleported breathless people to hospitals and dug children and pets from destroyed homes. It wasn't even the physical exhaustion that tore me apart; it was the emotional turmoil.

I moved a boy around Lydia's age from beneath a beam weighing at least a ton. His left leg detached upon impact, and the large hunk of wood on top of his thigh was the only thing keeping him from bleeding out. And he couldn't feel the right one.

Burns and gashes, broken bones, and bleeding wounds; I could heal. But I couldn't grow his left leg back. I couldn't heal his paralysis.

A kid no more than seventeen would never walk again, and that was on *me.*

A woman around Rachel's age was trapped in a vehicle on the outskirts of the town. It flipped into a bank, and the pyroclastic flow busted out the windows. I'm not even sure how she survived. Regardless, her entire upper body was covered in third degree burns. I healed them. But once I was done—and I was just about to teleport out—she grabbed my arm and begged me to heal her granddaughter in the back seat.

I looked behind her. I'd spend the rest of my life wishing I hadn't. Had the child just been dead, I would have brought her back, regardless of the consequences that come with necromancy. But the body left there was entirely indistinguishable. The closest thing I could equate it to is a pig at a lū'au.

It took everything in me to keep from vomiting. But just as she was about to turn around, I grasped her face and told her she was gone. She screamed. Over and over, she screamed at the top of her lungs. I told her I was sorry, and she punched me in the face. I teleported her to the group of survivors at the swirling vortex a few miles south.

I saw a thousand more situations like that before I was finished. Most of them blurred together, but the ones with the kids engrained into my mind like a tattoo. One that still stings as much as it did that day all these years later.

Once the area was cleared, I ended up going back to that car. I carried that little girl's burned corpse outside. I wish I could forget the way her skin sounded as it cracked and fell to black char on the ground. I had to stop to puke at that point.

But I dug a shallow grave. I lay the small body, not much bigger than my daughter's, into that hot soil and carefully lifted the dirt over top of her. Marking the spot with a large rock, still warm from the eruption that ended the young life, I kneeled beside her and cried.

Still, I think back to that little girl. I often wonder what her story was. Were they on their way home from some fun activity in a neighboring town? Were they headed to visit family? Why was she with her grandmother? Where were her parents? Were they addicts like me, is that why she wasn't with them that night? Were they dead? Was her grandmother to her what Annie was to me? If that weren't the case, if she were just on an overnight stay with her grandma, how would they feel when they reunited with their mother, and their daughter was nowhere in sight?

Up until that day, January 6th, 2024 was the worst day of my life.

But January 8th would be even worse.

The 9th, 10th, 11th and 12th weren't much better, either.

When I made it home, it was close to five A.M. our time, January 7th. Close to twenty-four hours, and although I was exhausted, I didn't want to sleep. I was starving, and filthy, and too afraid to close my eyes and see that little girl's dead body.

Instead, I took a shower, spending the entirety fighting back tears. I pulled on a pair of sweatpants, kissed Laila's sleeping cheek, and walked to the kitchen. I grabbed an apple from the counter and leaned against the fridge, enjoying the cool feel against my still hot skin.

I looked over the crowded living room. Leah, Brody, Adam, Jenna, Chris, Ray, and Wyatt were out cold. I figured Kai was back at the house, but I wondered where Celena was.

Then quiet chatter sounded on the patio. I headed toward the door and took a step outside.

Celena sat on the cement, staring distantly out into the trees. Kai rested his head against her shoulder, lip trembling as he pulled in a drag off the joint between his fingertips. His gaze shifted to me when he heard the door click shut.

"Bout ye, brother?" he barely murmured.

I shrugged a bit, unable to answer that honestly. "Been better. What about you?"

He lifted his head from his sister's shoulder and wiped the corner of his eye. "Not my best."

"Bad there too?" I asked.

His lip quivered, nodding. He turned his gaze to the ground.

"Mind if I." I gestured to the joint.

He raised his fingers and passed it my way. I leaned against the railing, pulled in a long drag, and looked down.

"What did it feel like?" Celena whispered, frozen eyes locked with something in the distance.

"What did what feel like?" I asked.

"All those people dying at once." Her voice was barely above a whisper. "I know you felt it. You're a necromancer. What did it feel like?"

I took in another deep hit. "Like a shotgun shell to the chest."

More like a bomb exploding within me. Or a thousand knives stabbing me at once. Like being bludgeoned all over at the same time.

But it was difficult to verbalize. Even that doesn't come close to describing it. That was just the best comparison I could make.

She didn't even blink as I handed her the joint. Her breaths were slow and even, but her eyes were so vacant. Some would say like she'd seen a ghost, but that would have been less pained and more fearful.

"I coul'nt believe it," Kai whispered. "I've seen volcanoes blow before. It's not an uncommon weapon where I'm from. When I was a lad, folks like me were a big deal, being able to heal and all. I healed soldiers brought down by those mounts. But that... I've never seen anything like it." He looked up with watery eyes and met my gaze. "If this is just the beginning, how are we going to win?"

"That's a problem for future us," I said.

"It's a good point though." Celena murmured. "We don't stand a chance."

I huffed. "No. No, we do. *We* do. We can't die. It's all them I'm worried about." I glanced out to the world behind the protected tree line. "They're the ones who don't stand a chance."

"What—do you think that's better?" Celena's gaze shot up to mine. "All of their lives are less important than ours?"

Of course I didn't. But I supposed it did come out apathetic. It was just the only way I could say it aloud. It wasn't like she sounded how she felt either. We had to keep from breaking down because if we didn't, we wouldn't be able to fight the next day.

"No." I took a hit off the joint. "No, that's the worst part. They get peace. They get death. We're the ones who have to live with the guilt. We're the ones who have this blood on our hands for the rest of forever."

Her gaze softened. She reached for the burning herbs in my hand. I passed it her way. "But I don't know how we'll win either. If this is just the beginning, I don't want to see the end."

"Me neither," Kai said.

"Might be the only ones left *to* see the end," Celena muttered.

"I can't believe that. I saw people going through the portals. There's going to be survivors. There's going to be a lot of survivors." I nodded hard. "There has to be."

"I hope so," Kai whispered.

"That'd be a pretty picture," Celena said. "But look around you, dude. The world's ended. They're pillaging this planet. Even if we win, which isn't looking like a strong possibility, there won't be a home for them to return to. They're destroying our home."

"We can rebuild," I said. "We can build a new world—"

"Look around you, Jeremy!" Celena gestured outward. "Aren't you wondering why it's so dark? Have you even looked up?"

My heart dropped.

"Go." She pointed ahead. "Look up."

I started off the porch. As I stepped out from under the roof, I lifted my chin toward the sky.

My legs instantly went numb.

It wasn't unusual to look up at the night sky and see a layer of thick clouds where we lived. We rarely had a cloudless night. It was almost impossible to find the moon, let alone the stars, most nights.

But I'd never looked up at utter darkness either. No light pollution in the distance. No illumination outside whatsoever of the fairy lights Laila hung over the swing set.

Just a thick, black dust cloud stretching miles in every direction.

A moment of derealization washed over me. It almost felt like I was high, but without the euphoria. More like a hangover, I guess.

The world spun, and my body felt like I didn't belong within it. Even the T-shirt hanging on my shoulders felt like it weighed ten pounds. I had this almost indescribable urge to drop out of my skin and let my soul float into the abyss. It didn't feel natural. Nothing looked real. I couldn't be looking at a black sky. I couldn't be. It felt like a nightmare, one I prayed I could awaken from.

But I didn't.

"So much for the solar panels, huh?" Celena said.

I didn't say anything, just stared at the sky. Black as night. Blacker than night, blacker than anything I'd ever seen.

There was a great earthquake. The sun turned black as sackcloth...

The voice of the deranged zombie we kept in the basement almost five years prior echoed in my ears.

"This happened before," Celena said. "Some two-hundred years ago. A volcano erupted, and the sun was blacked out for an entire year. There was famine. People had to resort to eating cats and shit because they couldn't grow crops. But this wasn't just *one* volcano, Jeremy, this was hundreds. Maybe more, I don't even know. We're half a country away from the closest eruption an—"

"I know, Celena," I barked, head twisting to meet her gaze. "I know."

Her expression was empty as she lifted her shoulders. "I'm just saying. We're fucked."

I swallowed hard and turned back to the sky. I heard the creak of the patio door pulling open. I thought that it was one of my brothers or sisters, maybe Laila, so I didn't turn. I heard a quiet little voice.

"What awe you doing, Daddy?" Milly asked.

My gaze turned to the porch. She stood just outside the door with her purple blanket tucked beneath her arm pit and her thumb in her mouth. Her dark hair rested in a braid against the back of her head. Her nightgown hung to her short knees, and a lump gathered in my throat.

She was so little. So tiny, so innocent. Just like that little girl I'd buried whose body was barely more than ash.

I forced a smile, heading to the porch. "Nothing, Mills. What are you doing up?" I lowered myself to her level.

"I heawd yewwing." She glanced at her aunt. "And I heawd you. And I missed you."

That thump in my throat got thicker. I forced my lips higher. "I missed you too, kiddo. But how'd you get out of your crib?"

She grinned, burying her red cheeks into her plush blanket.

"You know you're not supposed to teleport out of your crib." I smiled.

Milly shrugged. I laughed and moved my hands beneath her armpits, lifted her to my hip, and breathed in her soft baby smell, ignoring the memory that cascaded through my mind of burned flesh.

I turned to Kai and Celena. "I'm gonna get her back to bed, guys. We should all try and get some rest."

Kai said, "Didn't mean to wake you, lass."

"Yeah, sorry, Mills." Celena forced a smile. "Go to sleep for your dad, alright?"

She nodded against my chest, tightening her arms around my neck.

As I tiptoed through the dark living room, I held my daughter so close to my chest. She probably thought I was hugging her so tight because I missed her, and I did, but that wasn't why. I was just so happy she was alive.

I'd seen so many dead children that day. Five years before when we lost Micah, I thought I knew how bad it hurt to lose a baby. But I didn't know him yet. I loved the idea of him, but I didn't love *him.*

But I loved them more than life now. I'd do anything for them. I'd fight for them, I'd kill for them, and I'd die for them.

And yet, that love brought us to the end of the world.

As I glanced out the black window at the top of the stairs, looking at the utter darkness outside, my heart sunk.

I'd fight for them. I'd kill for them. I'd die for them. Yet, I helped bring them into a world destined for death. I planned to curse them into the same unfair responsibility I was faced with.

Immortality. Living forever with the burden of millions of lost lives on those two tiny shoulders.

God's a real fucking comedian.

CHAPTER FIFTY-NINE

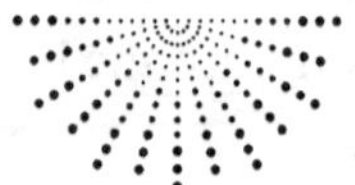

JANUARY 7 - LAILA

When my eyes drifted open, I looked at the clock on the nightstand. 1:32. I noted the lack of light coming in through the window, and my eyes widened. I shot up in the bed, tapping Jeremy's shoulder. "Baby. Baby, get up. We slept the whole day, we have to get up."

"What?" he grumbled.

"It's 1:30, we have to get up," I said.

He opened his eyes and glanced at the clock. He reached for his phone plugged in by the pillow. He passed it my way.

1:33 P.M.

I stood, rushed to the window and pulled the curtain aside. It was pitch black. The only light outside was cast from the windows inside the house.

"What's going on?"

"The volcanoes." Jeremy sat up in the bed. "There was a great earthquake. The sun turned black as sackcloth," he quoted.

My stomach swirled. I heard him, but it hadn't settled into my mind.

I looked back out the window, staring out at the utter darkness.

Black. Pitch black. Even with a lantern or flashlight, you'd only be able to see a few feet ahead of you.

Jeremy's footsteps echoed toward me as I tried to grasp it. I knew that the end was coming. I'd seen it with my own eyes all week. But I hadn't thought about this part. I knew that even one massive volcanic eruption could do something similar to what I was witnessing. I'd read an article about it a few years prior. Experts warning of a single volcanic eruption that could make daylight invisible, hidden by a cloud of ash and sulfate. How it would interfere with navigation. How planes world-wide would be grounded. How you'd be stuck wherever you were.

I could still hear the zombie in the basement uttering those words, staring up at me like the goddess I didn't realize I was. Deranged smile plastered across his rotting face. Hands reaching out to grasp me.

I thought I knew how bad it'd get. A biblical apocalypse would be a total shitstorm, I knew that. But it wasn't until I looked into total darkness at one o'clock in the afternoon that it really sunk in.

"Couldn't sleep last night," Jeremy said. "Kai and Celena were sitting out on the patio. I followed them. Then… I saw this." His hand moved around my waist. He rested his head on top of mine and shook it a bit. "It's bad. It's really bad."

"And it's about to get worse," I whispered.

His warm sigh radiated against my neck, sending a shiver down my spine and a fog to the pane before us.

A quiet tap sounded at the door. "Come in."

"Hey, guys," Max whispered at the door. "How ya doing?"

"Seen better days," Jeremy muttered.

I didn't speak, just continued staring out ahead.

"Yeah, I know what you mean," Max said. "Never thought I'd see something like this. Reminds me of the pandemic, ya know? Driving down the empty highway, all the lights out, how quiet it was."

"Does feel similar," I murmured. "That only lasted a few months though. A cloud like this… It could take years to dissipate."

"You don't think you all could use that shit you do with the air to break it up?" Max asked. "I mean, you *are* gods."

"Even gods have their limits," Jeremy said.

Max got quiet for a moment. He cleared his throat. "Rachel told me to come see if you guys wanted something to eat. She and the kids spent some time picking and growing in the garden yesterday. Got a bunch of tomatoes, and I guess there was some bacon in the freezer. So BLTs for us and tomato sandwiches for Micah. She sent a boatload to the others back at the main house too. Getting low on bread though."

"I could eat." Jeremy touched his lips to my hair and released his hand at my waist. "But I think we have a bread maker packed away somewhere. And there's tons of flour and yeast in the basement. I'll find it after lunch and bring it up to the main house."

"That ought to work," Max said. "But can I talk to you for a minute, Lai?"

I turned from the window and met his gaze. "Yeah, sure. What's up?"

Jeremy brushed past him. Max walked to the bed and took a seat at the bench on the end. His fingers ran through his hair, and he cleared his throat. "You aren't going off to save the world today, are you?"

"Lila made contact before I came home yesterday. She said I'd be needed here. Why?"

His hand reached up to rub the back of his neck. He massaged a knot, head shaking slightly. He cleared his throat again, as if fighting off tears. "I, uh... Jenna and I. Ray, too, I guess. We're... Celena and Wyatt. They're gonna change us today."

"Oh," I murmured. "Right. Almost forgot about that."

He nodded, blinking eyes turned down to the carpet. "I guess this sounds stupid considering everything you're dealing with right now. But if you have the time... I mean, Ray has Lydia to sit with him. And Jenna has Adam. But I... I'm pretty scared about the whole thing. Celena told me what it was like for her the first time. When she was changed. And I know she didn't have time to prepare for it and I did. A little time, anyway. But I don't know, I just... This is a lot. I know it must seem like nothing to you, but it's a big deal to me and I..."

"You want me to sit with you?" I asked quietly, lowering myself to the bed beside him.

His bloodshot brown eyes turned up to mine. "If you don't mind."

Max was my best friend since I was around Micah's age. I'd made his mom a promise the day she died, that I'd take care of her baby boy. There were a lot of people whose babies I couldn't be there for. But I would be there for him.

I lifted my lips to a smile. "I don't mind at all. I'll have Jeremy watch the kids."

He forced a smile. "Thank you."

"Of course."

As I stood and started to the door, Max barely whispered, "Laila?"

I turned over my shoulder. "Yeah?"

His dopey eyes looked up to mine, glistening with tears. "Am I gonna die?"

I chuckled. "What?"

"The change," he murmured. "I heard Wyatt talking with Adam once a while back. He said something about how dangerous the change can be for humans. That some people die. And I... I don't want to die." His lip quivered, eyes rimmed with water. "I don't want to die, Lai."

My eyes softened. I walked across the room and sat on the bed beside him. I took his hand and shook my head. "You aren't going to die, Max."

"Do you know that?" he asked. "Do you know for sure? Because I-I'm not ready to die. I can handle being turned into a wolf, but I don't want to die. I know that the world's dying anyway, but I-I don't want to die."

I squeezed his chubby, calloused palm. "You aren't going to die. The change is dangerous for some, that's true. It's harder on a female's body than a man's though. And it's most dangerous for someone who isn't in great health. Older people. People with heart conditions, mainly. They can go into cardiac arrest easily because the venom is pumping through your body rapidly. Wolf heartrates are higher than humans, too. It's very hard for some humans to tolerate that change. But you're young, and you're a man."

"But I'm not in the greatest health, Laila." He gestured over his torso, hand resting on his chunky stomach. "I'm, like, eighty pounds overweight. I don't know of any problems with my heart, but that doesn't mean they aren't there and I—"

"Max." I squeezed his hand tighter. "I'm gonna be right there. I won't let anything happen to you."

"But you couldn't heal my mom," he whispered. "What if—"

"I can't heal cancer. But that's only because what I do when I heal is accelerate growth and that's the opposite of healing cancer. With cancer, you need to slow the development of new cells, not accelerate them," I said. "But if your heart stops beating, I'll get you back to your body. I promise you."

"You can resurrect the dead?" he asked.

"I can't. But Jeremy can. He doesn't often. There are major ramifications when he does. But if that's what it comes to, we'll deal with the consequences afterward. I'm not losing another one of my best friends. I won't do it, Max. I won't."

A long pause drew in. "Jeremy can do that. Just bring dead people back to life."

"It isn't black and white," I said. "The body has to be intact and in good health. But yes. He can. And for you, he will."

He stared at the ground for a moment. "That's what happened in that video then. When you were in that cell together. You died, and he brought you back."

"He did."

"What was that like?" he whispered. "Death, I mean. What does it feel like?"

"I don't know. Kind of hard to explain. Peaceful, I guess, is the best word for it. The dying part is hard. The pain. But once your heart stops, and you move into the afterlife, it's just... Peaceful."

He thought for a moment. "The afterlife, you said?" I nodded. "What is that? Is it heaven?"

"No. No, it's more like purgatory. Just your soul suspended in the darkness. Space, I think. Or maybe not, but that's what it looks like. You see the other souls, but they all look like stars."

He thought hard for a moment. "We become stars when we die?"

I arched a brow, head tilting from side to side. "I don't know. Maybe. That's how souls look there. But I don't know for sure."

He nodded softly. He cleared his throat. "Well, I guess I won't have to worry about that, huh?"

"I guess not." I smiled. "But c'mon. Let's go eat."

"My last meal as a human," he muttered.

CHAPTER SIXTY

JEREMY

"Daddy." Micah darted from his seat at the kitchen island. He ran toward me full force, arms encircling my hips and resting his head against my stomach.

I laughed quietly and kneeled to meet his gaze. "Hey, buddy. How was your day yesterday?"

"It was good. We were in the garden. Me and Milly picked so many vegetables. Gam said she can make a stew tomorrow. And there's no meat! Just veggies."

I laughed and smiled wider. "That's awesome, buddy. I can't wait to try it."

"And we have our own herbs too. There's garlic and thyme and rose dairy. Gam let us tried some. I liked it so much."

"Rose*mary*, kiddo. Not rose dairy," I muttered.

"Oh. Right."

Rachel turned from the stove with Luka on her hip and met my gaze with a sad smile. "He's really excited about his herbs."

"I see that," I said.

"Where's Mommy?" Micah walked back to the kitchen and hoisted himself to the bar stool.

"She's in the bedroom talking to Uncle Max. She'll be out in a minute," I said.

"Oh, good," he said. "You're going to be home today then?"

I smiled and gave a nod. I walked to Milly in her highchair. My lips pressed to her forehead as she scooped handfuls of tomatoes to her mouth. "Yeah, I will be. I'm not sure about Mommy though. But then we'll both be gone for the rest of the week."

"That's okay. I'll handle it here."

I laughed, and Rachel smiled. "He's a good little protector, you know. He saw that cloud rolling in yesterday evening and teleported us all inside."

A quiet laugh left her lips, and I looked to him with a questioning gaze. "Is that right?"

He nodded. "You told me about the storms, and I knew they was dangerous so I got us in the house. I told Gam we should go to the basement, but she said no."

My little hero. This really was the right thing to do. Because I knew he was playing a big part in helping us fight what was going on out there.

"Between dry heaves," Rachel muttered. "Not a big fan of teleporting."

"Laila didn't like it in the beginning either," I said. "But good job, buddy."

"So we was okay up here?" he asked, big blue eyes searching mine. "We didn't have to go to the basement?"

"No, Gam was right. You didn't need to go to the basement. Coming inside was a good idea though." I roughed up his hair. "You're good at this whole Guardian thing, you know."

His grin stretched up his cheeks as his shoulders straightened. He turned to his applesauce on the counter. "I know."

A quiet laugh left my lips. I reached for a sandwich on the counter. As I took a bite, I heard Adam and Jenna coming down the steps talking quietly to each other. I glanced that way, noting Jenna's foggy glasses as she wiped her wet, reddened cheeks.

Adam met my gaze and breathed out slowly. Deep circles rested beneath his dull eyes. His typical clean-cut beard looked a bit messier, grown an inch or two longer than I was used to.

"Can I talk to you for a minute, man?" he asked.

"Yeah, sure," I said.

Micah huffed. I laughed and kissed his forehead. "I'm coming right back, kid."

"Yeah, yeah." He pushed me away. I stood with the sandwich, took another bite, and gestured outside. Adam followed me to the patio.

Holding the door open with my hip, he took a step outside and tightened his jacket around his torso. I let the door go. "How ya doing?" I asked.

"Shitty," he said. "Real shitty. What about you?"

I wiped my lip. "About the same. Just kinda rolling with the punches at this point."

He glanced out over the dark yard. "Fucking bizarre, isn't it? Dark at one in the afternoon."

"To put it mildly." I took another bite of the sandwich. "How bad was it where you were?"

His lips pressed together. "Saw things I'd never want to see in a million years. And you?"

I swallowed the food in my mouth. "About the same. Better just leave it at that."

He rubbed the back of his neck. "Yeah. I don't particularly feel like talking about it either."

"What's up though?" I asked. "What'd you need to talk to me about?"

He swallowed. "Celena's biting Jen today."

"Oh," I said. "Right."

"Yeah, and she wants to do it at the diner. It's our home, ya know?"

Probably best. I didn't want a bunch of mid-turned wolves around my kids. They were practically candy to anything that liked to drink blood.

"Right," Adam said. "Well, she's worried. She knows there's risks when a human's turned. I tried to tell her it'd all be fine but she... I don't know, man, she's scared."

"Sure," I muttered. "I wouldn't want to go through that either."

He rubbed his tense jaw. "She wanted me to check with you before she goes through with it. She wants Lai there too, so I'm not that worried. I know there's risks and all, but she's worried about dying and I..." He shook his head. "She wants me to make sure you're gonna be available today. For a worst-case scenario situation, you know."

"So I can bring her back if she dies."

Fair enough. I'd brought back my brother in-law when he died, and my brother. I'd bring Jen back too if she didn't make it.

He nodded. "I know Han could too, but she's a little busy with all the people up at the main house. But I just wanted to make sure you're on-call if we need you."

"Yeah, sure. If Laila's there, she can get me a telepathic message if things start to go wrong. I'll be there, don't worry. Laila would never forgive me if I let her sister die."

"That's what I told her," Adam said. "But she just wanted me to make sure. I don't blame her. It's something like twenty percent of females that don't survive the change. But we've got a million Fae on hand and two necromancers. None of our people are going down today."

"Yeah, we won't let that happen. Let her know she has nothing to worry about. Rachel will be here with the kids too, so if I need to flash out, I will. She's young and healthy though. I'm sure she'll be fine."

"I think so too," he said. "But ya never know. Thanks though. That'll put her mind at ease. She was worried you guys were going to be off stopping a hurricane or something and she..." He sighed. "Well, if your schedule's clear, she has nothing to worry about."

"Yeah, Nick and Lila said this was our last quiet day until we go back. So as long as you guys do it soon, everything'll be alright."

"Alright, good. Thanks, man." He patted my shoulder and started into the house.

I took another gaze at the darkness in the air. Wolves usually howled at the moon the night that they're changed. But they wouldn't tonight.

CHAPTER SIXTY-ONE

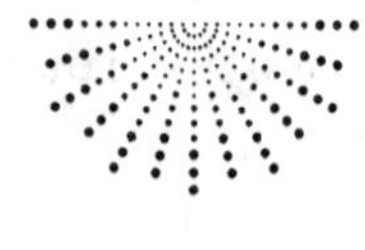

LAILA

"Mommy," Micah said as I walked into the living room. "Mommy, you're home!"

I smiled and leaned down to give him a hug. "I am, kiddo."

"Are you gonna be here all day?" he asked with excited, vibrant eyes. "Daddy said he'll be here."

I frowned. "No, I have to leave soon. But we can have lunch together first."

"Are you going to save people?"

My lips lifted higher. "Something like that."

He smiled, nodding. "It's okay then. Did you save people yesterday?"

"I did," I murmured. "I tried my best, anyway."

His smile fell. "Someone got hurt?"

"Let me talk to your mom for a minute, kid." Jeremy's fingers touched Micah's shoulder.

"Wait." Micah turned back to me. "Did someone got hurt?"

Not exactly the conversation I wanted to have with my four-year-old. But he'd know if I lied. So I'd tell him the truth.

"Yeah. Someone did."

He shifted his gaze to the floor. "Is they okay?"

"They will be," I murmured. "One day, they will be."

Once this war was over. When they were reborn. I hoped they would, anyway. It's not like I knew it with certainty, but I believed it was true when I said it, so I wasn't lying to him.

A sad gaze washed over his sweet little face. "But you tried real hard?"

"I did," I said. "I tried as hard as I could, buddy."

He nodded slowly, eyes finding mine. "Well, good job trying, Mommy. You'll do better next time."

My eyes stung with tears I quickly blinked away. "I'll try to."

He smiled. "You will. Practice makes perfect, right?" I smiled back. He turned up to his dad. "Okay, you can have her now."

Jeremy laughed as he pranced off. His eyes met mine. "You're going to the diner with Jen and Max?"

"And Ray, too. Max really wants me there. I was gonna ask if you could watch the kids."

"Yeah, of course." His voice lowered, and he leaned in. "But Jen's really worried. She needs you too. She's worried she's not gonna come out on the other end."

"So is Max," I muttered. "I'm sure everything's going to be fine. But just... You know. Stay available. Just in case."

"I'll be here. Send the message, and I'll be there."

"Sounds good," I said.

"Mama." Milly's arms outstretched for me with a big smile. "Mama, come hewe!"

I grinned and teleported to her. "And what are you doing, little miss?"

"Mine eatin totatoes." She grinned, lifting another to her lips. "They's good."

"Are they?" I smiled. "Can I try?"

She raised the sloppy tomato slice from her plate and extended it outward. I leaned forward, opened my mouth, and took a bite. "Ooh, those are good. Slobber and all. Do you mind if I..."

I started gathering them off her plate into my palm. She laughed and shook her head. "They's mine!"

"Oh, I'm sorry." I smiled, setting them back to her tray. "I should get my own, huh?"

"Yeah," she grumbled. "Get you's own."

I laughed and touched my lips to her forehead.

After lunch with the kids, we all teleported to the diner. It wasn't exactly fun. But I was sure this would be easier than the past few days had been. And honestly, it'd be nice to spend some time in the apartment before we left. It had been my home for quite some time. I wanted to say goodbye to it.

"So... how do we do this?" Ray pulled off his jacket. "Do you go for the neck or what?"

"Well, where do you want the scar?" Wyatt asked.

Max said, "It leaves a scar?"

"The last one you'll ever get." Celena pulled her shirt down to expose her upper breast. "But yeah, it scars."

"Maybe the back then," Ray said. "If I get another job as a cop, I'll be changing in a locker room a lot. Might be a little hard to hide on the neck."

"Can you go for the leg on me?" Max asked. "I wear short sleeves a lot when I cook."

"Ugh, I don't want hair in my mouth," Celena muttered. "You do him, babe."

"Yeah, I'll get Max and Ray then. I'm starving. You get Jenna."

Celena sat on the couch beside her. "Where do you want it, Jen?"

"Uh," she muttered. "Uh, I don't know. I don't know, where's best?"

Celena said, "Doesn't matter really. The closer to your heart I am, the shorter the change will be."

Jenna's hands trembled. Adam ran his hand up her forearm and kissed her hand. "I... I guess the boob then. I want it over as soon as possible."

"The boob it is," Celena said. "I'll try to not make this weird. Just FYI though, I'm not into girls so this won't turn me on or anything."

"Good to know." Jenna tugged her shirt down a bit. "But before you... before you do it. Can you just... what's it going to be like?"

"It'll hurt when my teeth sink in." Celena lifted her hair to a ponytail at the nape of her neck. "But It'll feel good. Really good, actually. While I feed at least. You'll feel euphoric, like the best high you've ever had. Then the venom will start spreading through you. You'll faint. When you wake up, you'll be disoriented but won't be in too much pain. It'll come in waves. Almost like contractions. It'll hurt, and It won't be too bad. It'll really hurt. Once the pain stops dissipating, you'll be close to the change."

"How long?"

"'Til you change?" Celena asked. Jenna nodded. She turned to Wyatt. "What was it for me? About two hours?"

"Maybe a little longer but somewhere in there," Wyatt said.

Jenna said, "So three hours max?"

"I'd say four." Wyatt kneeled down beside Max. "Celena wasn't human, that might have helped her transition faster."

"Four is still like a fraction of Luka's birth," Jenna said. "I think I can handle that."

"You can." Celena gave her an assuring smile. "You're gonna do fine."

Jenna forced a smile back. "I think I'm ready."

"Alright. Lean back then." Celena gestured to the couch.

"Here." Adam situated himself and patted his lap. "Lie down."

Jenna lay down and relaxed her head against his thigh. He took her hand and soothed her hair with the other. He smiled down at her. "You're gonna be alright, baby."

"I'm scared," she whispered with watery eyes. "I'm so scared."

I knew that she was too. But I wasn't worried. I had a pretty decent gut feeling about this sort of thing, and I didn't have any bad ones here. She was gonna be okay.

"Don't be," he murmured. "I'm right here, and Lai's right there. Jeremy's just a blink away. You're gonna be okay, I promise."

Her lips quivered as her hand reached up to stroke his jaw. He smiled, leaned down, and touched his lips to hers. Her shaking palm held his face for a moment. He pulled back and touched the hair resting along her cheek. As Celena kneeled over her chest, Jenna's gaze met mine. "Make sure I get home to my son, okay?"

I smiled. "I will."

Her desperate eyes searched mine for a moment. She turned to Celena and nodded. "Okay. I'm ready."

Celena canines expanded from her gums. She pulled Jenna's shirt further down her chest and lowered her mouth to her breast. Jenna's brows crunched down, and Adam touched her cheeks. "It's okay, you're okay."

"Alright, you ready, Max?" Wyatt asked. "'Cause I'm just getting hungrier by the second and I—"

"Yeah, yeah," Max said. "Yeah, I'm ready. Get it over with."

I sat beside my oldest friend on the love seat. He reached out for my hand. Wyatt dropped to his knees and lifted Max's foot to the coffee table. I cupped it between mine and sent him a smile.

"Never thought we'd be here, huh?" Max forced a smile. "You being the goddess of the earth and me getting turned into a Werewolf?"

I laughed. "I can honestly say that I never thought anything like this would happen."

"Life's fucking weird." He leaned his head back onto the cushions. He grimaced as Wyatt's teeth sunk into his calf. "Just imagine if Adrian could see us now."

I managed a smile. "She'd be cracking jokes about how you're about to be super turned on by another man."

"And you'd be telling her at least I needed a catalyst to get turned on. Unlike her horny ass."

I laughed. "Yeah, it'd probably go something like that."

His eyes closed, lips rising in a smile as the euphoria set in. "I miss her mean ass."

"Yeah," I whispered. "Yeah, me too."

"Something like this isn't how she went down, is it?" he asked quietly. "Not a wolf change gone wrong?"

Adam glanced at me with fear in his eyes. Jenna went unconscious in his arms. "No. No, it was nothing like that."

"What was it then?" he muttered. "You never told me, and I've always wondered."

He was right. I'd never told him because it wasn't something I liked to talk about. But the whole family knew. And sure, Max had been a part of the family for a long time. But this was about to make it official.

Adam kept his gaze on me, shaking his head.

But Max had the right to know. "She tried to kill me. She went down when we tried to get the knife off of her."

His eyes opened. "She tried to kill you?"

"Stabbed me in the back."

His eyes grew disoriented. "Why'd she do that?"

"I wish I knew."

He thought for a moment. "Well. I'm glad it was you that came out on the other end." His head clunked to my chest. "Wouldn't be escaping the apocalypse without you."

CHAPTER SIXTY-TWO

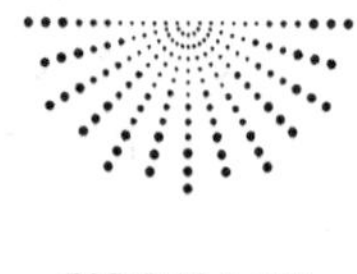

JEREMY

Luka kept asking where his mom and dad were, and we kept lying. Telling him they were at work. He knew Jen didn't work at night. He knew Adam hadn't worked all week. But he was used to spending time with Rachel daily, and he didn't mind chasing after his cousins.

Micah asked to make a pillow fort. All the adults happily obliged. It was a good distraction, one I think we were all grateful for. Even Moriah joined the party.

We spent the rest of the day playing with the kids, struggling with all our might not to look out the window at the dark sky. When a heavy downpour slammed to the puddles in the yard, I felt an ounce of relief. I'm not sure why. I didn't know if it'd have any effect on the cloud of dust and ash that spanned the planet. But it felt normal. It's supposed to be dark when it rains.

Chris and I got our guitars out and sat in the living room with the kids. Brody teepeed some branches in the fireplace and let Micah spark them to a flame with his fingertip. Rachel got some graham crackers, chocolate, and marshmallows from the pantry, and we made s'mores with smiles and laughs as if the world wasn't crumbling down around us.

Although nothing was normal, we strived to give them the sense that it was. We didn't talk about what we'd witnessed the day before. We didn't let them see the terror coursing through our veins when we caught a glimpse of the darkness outside.

At 6:30, I got a message from Nick. He said they'd talked to the Chambers about what tomorrow would bring. They had a plan in place for the cities that we couldn't cover, but that he and I would be taking New York City. I told him okay and pushed that thought to the back of my mind.

Around 9:30, I told Micah and Milly it was time to get to bed. They objected, which admittedly, gave me a sense of joy. My kids wanted to soak up every minute with me. But it was still time for bed. Keeping things close to normal for them meant staying on their schedule. We'd busted our asses to get them on one, and they were gonna stick to it.

Milly was a breeze to get to bed. I changed her into her pajamas, handed her a bottle, and sang her a song. By the time I'd made it to the chorus, she was out.

Micah wasn't so easy. Being the chatterbox that he was, there was always some rhetoric that came with every bedtime conversation. He'd do just about anything to fight his sleep. Like me in that way. I loved sleep once I was doing it, but actually falling to sleep was never my strong suit.

"I can bring my sasophone when we move, right?" Micah asked as he wandered around his room. "I really like my sasophone. I don't want to leave it."

"I don't think so, buddy," I said. "We don't have much room. But maybe we'll come back for it one day."

Micah frowned. "But I really want to bring it."

I sat at the foot of his bed. "I know you do, buddy. But if you bring that, you can't bring much of anything else. Wouldn't you rather bring a few things than one big thing?",

He thought for a moment, frowning as his gaze shifted to the floor. "I guess."

"It'll be here though," I said. "We'll come back for it one day. I promise."

He looked up. "You promise?"

I smiled, thinking about watching twenty-eight-year-old him play it on the balcony. "I promise."

He plopped onto the bed beside me. "I don't want to leave, Dad."

"Me neither," I muttered. "But the storms are getting worse out there. We only have a few days until we have no choice."

He rested his head against my shoulder. "We're all gonna be okay, right?"

"We are," I murmured.

His eyes turned up to meet mine. "You promise?"

"I promise."

He raised his pinky up toward me. "You pinky swear?"

I smiled, raised my pinky, and interlocked it with his. "I pinky swear." He smiled. "But it's late. You have to get to bed."

"But I'm not gonna see you all week. I don't want to go to bed yet."

"After this week, we'll have the rest of our lives to see each other." I smiled. "Come on. It's time to lie down."

He huffed and scooted up the bed, wiggling under the sheets. "Fine."

I laughed and stood to kiss his forehead. I started to the door. "Goodnight, buddy. Sleep tight."

"Wait," he said.

"What is it?" I asked.

He looked over me for a moment. "Mommy said people got hurt yesterday."

I frowned. "Yeah. They did."

His eyes moved between mine silently. "Is that why you feel how you do?"

My head tilted to the side. "What do you mean?"

"You're sad, Daddy," he whispered. "Mommy's okay, and we're all okay. So is that why you're sad?"

I grew quiet, head turning toward the ground. "Yeah, that's why I'm sad, buddy."

"Did you hurt them?" he asked quietly.

I looked up. "No, of course not."

"Then why do you feel like you did?" he asked.

I forced a quiet laugh. "You ask a lot of big questions for such a little guy."

He didn't say anything, just waited for me to go on.

"Well, it's more complicated than that. I didn't hurt them. But I didn't protect them, either. And it... It kinda feels like I may have been the one to hurt them."

"But you didn't. It wasn't your fault." Micah's expression was so wholesome and gentle. "It was the storm's fault."

"Yeah. You're right, buddy."

And he was. But that didn't change that I felt the abyss filling with light. That didn't change that I'd buried a toddler yesterday. That didn't change that I'd carried people from burning buildings and dropped them into a portal to another dimension.

Whether it was directly my fault or not, nothing changed how much it hurt.

"So you can be sad, but you can't be mad at you," he said. "That's not fair to you."

I smiled. "I'll keep that in mind."

He lifted his lips in a smile. He rolled over and patted the bedside for Tink to join him. She hopped up and settled in. He looked back up at me. "Okay. Sweet dreams, Daddy."

"Sweet dreams, Micah. I love you."

"Love you too."

I flicked off the light, pulled the door shut, and started downstairs.

With each quiet step, I thought about how smart he was. Had it not been for meeting the older version of him, I'd have been worried about what all the trauma he'd faced thus far would cause. He understood concepts far too large for his little head.

Even now, despite his gentleness and naivety, he's still centuries wise beyond his years. It's ironic really. Considering how young his soul is compared to the rest of us. We'd lived thousands more lives than he had, but he understood things better than any of us. He has this all-knowing sense of the universe and the way that things work, and always has.

Maybe that's why his soul was worth a million lives. Because innocent kindness is worth so much beside jaded misery.

Just as I rounded the corner to my bedroom, Laila's voice echoed in my mind.

We need you. Now.

CHAPTER SIXTY-THREE

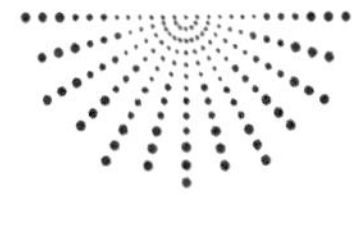

LAILA

Max gripped the trashcan before him, head jutting forward as vomit soared from his mouth. I ran a cool washcloth along his forehead while he struggled to catch his breath, ejecting even more from his stomach. The smell wafted into my nostrils, and I had to swallow down my own baby-barf. I held my breath and traced my hand over his upper back.

"Ah, fuck," he grumbled. "Fuck me, man."

"Told you it wouldn't be pleasant." Celena ashed a cigarette into the sink across the open floor plan.

He raised his middle finger, now coated in a layer of mousy brown fur.

"It'll be over soon," I murmured. "Just hang in there."

"Jesus Christ." Ray kneeled on the hardwood floor. His hands held either side of his head as Lydia rubbed his back.

"You alright over there, bud?" Wyatt asked.

Ray lifted his head quickly. "Yeah, my head's just killing me."

"Not uncommon," Celena said. "Your skull is shattering and reforming. Hurts like a bitch the first time."

"How about the second?" he murmured, shaking hands moving to the ground before him. His fur covered face shifted up to meet her gaze.

She said, "Not quite so bad."

"Hardly feel it now though," Wyatt said.

"Holy fuck," he murmured, shaking his head as he panted out deep breaths.

"High-key want to take a picture of you right now." Lydia grinned. "You look like Chewbacca."

He glared up at her. "Don't you dare."

She laughed. "I won't. Just really want to."

"So who's gonna feed who?" Wyatt asked with a look between Lydia and I.

Max made a face. "What?"

"You have to get blood in you before the change is over," Wyatt said.

"I got a transfusion my first time. But I wish it would've been oral," Celena said. "It's always better that way."

"Might be a little weird for you, Lydia." Wyatt glanced at Ray. "You probably don't want to get turned on by your dad."

"Ew." Her nose curled. "Yeah, I'll go with Max. Still weird. But not so creepy."

"Uh, no." Max's lips pulled down. "She's a baby, dude, I'm not about to get a hard on with a fifteen-year-old in my mouth."

"Odd phrasing," Celena muttered.

"*You* won't get turned on," Wyatt said. "Unless eating gets ya going, man."

"Just the blood bag that gets aroused," Celena said. "I mean, it can be arousing for the wolf too. But only if you want it to be. Think of it like a whipped cream foreplay situation. It can be hot. But you can still enjoy whipped cream without pitching a tent."

"No." Ray's voice sharpened. "No one's feeding off of my daughter. She's Fae. I know what that means. I don't trust me or Max enough for that."

I really should've paid more attention when he said that. But I was just focused on making this easier on Max.

"She's a half breed. Not that hard to resist," Celena said. "Tasty, but not delectable."

"We'll be right here," Wyatt said. "I know you think you're tough, Ray, but even as a wolf, I can take you."

Ray narrowed his gaze. "It's not happening."

"Dad—" Lydia began

"No." He almost yelled, warm brown eyes shining as his head shot toward her. "It's not happening."

"It's alright. I'll do it," I said. My eyes shifted to Celena. "Heal me in between?"

Celena said, "Will do. Should probably do the bleeding in the guest room though. The moment you start dripping, these newbies are going to be in an all-out bloodbath."

"You do smell really good." Max's puke scented breath got closer to my hair, sniffing. "What is that? Honey?"

"Yeast, actually," Wyatt said. "I know, Fae smell like cookies, right?"

"I think it's more like warm bread," Celena said.

"Literally." Max's eyes closed as his nose got closer to my head. "But almost citrusy, too. Like... like strawberries, almost."

"You're making this weird." I tapped him in the face. "Stop it."

His eyes opened, anger flashing through them for a second. He blinked hard. "Right. Sorry."

"Thought about biting my head off for a second there?" I smiled.

His cheeks reddened beneath his fast-growing fur. "Little bit."

"It's the Angel." Wyatt gestured to me. "That's what that sour-sweet smell is." His eyes shifted over me for a moment. "C'mon, Lai, they're all getting a bite. Can't I get a taste too?"

I said, "I'm not just food, you know."

"Yeah, I know. I know, but." His gaze fixated on the thumping pulse at my neck. "You just taste so good, dude."

"Wyatt." Celena raised a brow at him. "Stop looking at my sister like she's a cake."

"But she practically is," he said.

"Ya know, I may have said yes if you weren't being such a dick the other day." I stood and placed my hands at my hips.

He cocked his head to the side. He thought for a long moment. Then his head straightened back out, and his eyes softened. "I meant to apologize for that."

Well, he hadn't. And granted, I hadn't taken it to heart all that much. But still. Nah. He wasn't getting my blood. He had a full belly anyway.

"Uh-huh," I said. "No dessert for you."

"No, really. I am sorry about that. I didn't mean it how it came out. I was just mad." His southern drawl came out a little heavier than usual. "I wasn't trying to say you sacrificed Micah. I know that ain't how it went down. I was just worried about my girl."

"Well, thank you for apologizing. But still. No cake."

He frowned. "Fine. But when we go back to 2000, you're gonna be feeding me on the regular. You know that, don't ya? We'll be shit outta hospitals we can break into to steal blood, trying to stay on the down-low and all."

"I figured as much. But you're gonna be waiting a little while for dessert." He huffed, and I smiled. "They don't need to eat yet, do they?"

Celena said, "Another half an hour for Ray, maybe an hour for Max."

"I'm gonna go check on Jen then." I started down the hall.

As I walked, I ran my fingertips along the cream-colored paint. I remembered picking it out at the local department store five years before. Mountain Crest White, that was its name. I remember saying that even the *name* was pretty. Jeremy laughed and said it didn't matter how pretty the name was if the color sucked. But I said anything beautiful had to have a beautiful name.

I remembered rolling the paint onto the walls with him. I recalled panicking when we put up the first few strokes and they came out bright white when I intended to have a *warm*, inviting white. I remembered Jeremy shaking his head with a grin and saying that it'd dry darker. I tossed paint at him across the hall.

His eyes widened as his lips lifted in a grin. He teleported the feet between us, lifted me to the air by my hips, rubbed my back against the fresh paint and kissed me hard. Then did something else to me pretty hard.

I smiled at the memory, reminding myself how young we were then. How I thought that I was grown because my ID said so, and because I was running a business all on my own. But I had no unearthly idea how immature and naïve I truly was. A child, essentially. An old soul trapped within a simple span of twenty-four years for centuries, forgetting the lessons I needed to recall for growth.

Just a baby really. Even when we went back, I wasn't too far from childhood. It wasn't until I truly melded with the memories of my first self, my eldest self, that I grew up.

I knocked quietly on the bedroom door. "Who is it?" Adam called.

"Me," I said. "Just wanted to check on Jen."

"Come on in," he said.

I turned the knob and took a step inside. Jenna was down on all fours, body quivering as quiet grunts left her lips. A blanket covered her naked body. An old gray, cleaning bucket sat between her outstretched palms, half turned to paws.

A layer of sandy colored fur erupted from her peaches and cream skin. The round apples of her cheeks had broadened beside the pink, dewy nose protruding to a snout. Her small forehead was half collapsed, long mane of blonde shortening by the moment.

Adam sat beside her on the floor, running his hand over her broken forearm, curved halfway toward her breast like some sort of dinosaur. His concerned gaze shifted up to mine. "She just fed. I don't think it'll be long now."

I looked over his bleeding forearm, squinting a bit. "You let her bite you?"

His lips heightened to a half smile. "Not like it's the first time." I chuckled. "She won't have venom 'til the change is complete anyway."

"Sure," I said. "Might want to have Lydia or Celena heal that up for you."

"Is that okay, baby?" Adam asked her quietly. "Or do you want me to stay?"

She leaned forward, vomiting into the bucket. Once she stopped, she tried to make out words, but only odd, half-groans left her jaws. Her mouth quivered as she struggled, shaking her head. She looked up at me with a desperate gaze.

"I think that's a yes." I walked into the room and sat on the floor beside her. She collapsed sideways, dropped her head to my chest, and buried her half palm, half claw into my shirt.

He looked over her carefully for a moment, stroking her shoulder. "I'll be right back, okay?"

She nodded, water pouring from her eyes. I slid my hand over the top of her head and smiled up at him. "I got her. Go ahead."

As the bedroom door clicked shut, Jenna turned to me. Her mouth opened, and an odd sound—something between a whine and a bark— left her lips. She shook her head vigorously, hands clutching either side of her hair in fistful's.

I focused on her mind, trying not to read her thoughts, but zeroing in on them. *You're okay, Jen.*

I can't talk. I can't talk, this is terrifying. This is so scary. Everything hurts—it hurts. It hurts. I feel like I'm dying. It—

"I know. I know it hurts, and I know it's scary, but it's going to be over soon. Then the only time you'll have to do this is when you choose to. And it won't be so scary the next time. You'll grow to love it."

You don't know that. You aren't a wolf. You don't know what this feels like.

"No, but I know plenty of them. Have a whole army of them, actually. And they're fairly proud of who they are. They love what they can do. Just look at Celena. She didn't want this. But now she is, and she couldn't imagine it any other way. She loves her abilities. She loves being an animal."

I don't even like dogs.

"Sure you do." I smiled. "Just, ya know. Not my dog."

She turned away and stared down at her trembling paws. *Is this how you felt? When you learned what you are?*

"Was I scared, you mean?" She nodded. I huffed. "I was a maniac. You should have seen me. I started flipping the fuck out. I ripped out an IV. I punched a nurse in the face. I set Jeremy on fire."

An odd huff echoed from her mouth.

"That's how fear manifests for me," I muttered. "I get cocky. I go into warrior mode. I start hitting, and screaming, and I punch people in the face." She tried to tighten her shaking paws to fists and whined when she couldn't. I took them in my hands and rubbed them gently for a moment.

As her trembling slowed, I continued, "But yes. I was terrified. I couldn't calm down. I destroyed an entire hospital room, and I wasn't even trying to. I was just... I was scared. And I couldn't stop. That scared me even more. Jeremy was trying to talk to me, and I didn't really want to hurt him. At first, I did, for a second. But he caught fire, and I smelled the flesh burn on his arm, and I felt it too, like I'd done it to myself. I just... I could see him through the flames, and I could hear him telling me it was okay, that he'd be fine, but I was a walking bomb, you know?" She leaned her head closer to my chest. "I just wanted to calm down. But I couldn't. Then another nurse walked into the room, but she was in this, like, almost fireman suit. And she was telling me it was okay too, but it scared me even more and the flames got bigger. I saw a needle in her hand, and I heard Jeremy telling her to wait, to let him talk me down. But she made it through the room and cornered me. She jabbed me with the needle. And it all went black."

Jenna looked up at me with watery eyes. *What happened after that?*

"I woke up in Jeremy's bed," I said. "He was talking to Leah in the hallway. We'd been at one of the underground hospitals. The only way in and out was through teleportation. I was trapped. That's what made me panic so bad in the first place. But I was still freaked out. Thought I'd stumbled into a weird, Witch cult or something."

You kind of did.

A quiet laugh left my lips. "Yeah, I guess so. I didn't know what was... I don't know, I thought that they were kidnapping me or something. Adam was one of my best friends, and I was in love with Jeremy, but I felt so betrayed. Like I didn't know them at all. They could do all of these crazy things, and neither of them told me. I guess Jeremy had hinted here and there. Odd little phrases or whatever. But they kept something so big from me. I couldn't trust them. I needed out of there. So I jumped up and started looking for my shoes. He realized I was awake. He came back into the room and said something like *hey, beautiful.* I told him to get away from me. He kind of just...." I trailed off, remembering that look of grief over his face. "He nodded and took a step back. I was surprised, actually. I thought he was going to tell me I had to stay there, but he didn't. He just nodded and told me he understood. He stepped aside."

And you left?

"I did." I laughed, still holding her hands. They'd stopped shaking somewhere in the midst of my story, serving as a gentle distraction from her treachery. "I walked past him and practically ran downstairs. Leah stopped me in the living room. She told me I had to stay, that we had to talk about what happened and what I was. I said that they were all crazy and ran away, but Brody was blocking the door." I laughed. "I thought they were going to kill me or something."

I probably would have too. Who the hell does that? You were just trying to leave.

"No, I get it now. I would have stopped me, too. I was exposed to them. They had to cover their asses. I wasn't going to tell anyone; I'd be institutionalized in a second. Mom was already worried about me after the accident and everything."

Well, seeing your dad die is pretty traumatic. If my kid came home saying her boyfriend had superpowers a few months after something like that, I'd probably lock her up too. Not now that I'm about to be a Werewolf, but before, I mean.

"That's why I wasn't going to tell anyone. That's why it took so long for me to tell you." She looked up, eyes moving back and forth between mine. "But they didn't know that. Not for sure anyway," I said. "I heard Jeremy at the top of the steps. He told Brody it was fine. I wasn't going to tell anyone, and it was fine. But Brody kept insisting we all had to talk before I left. I started to panic again. My hands lit on fire, and I started yelling. Then Jeremy was in front of me. He grabbed my shoulders, and I felt like I was inside a washing machine. Spinning, breathless, disoriented."

The first time you teleported. I nodded. *That's how it felt for me too. Like I was spinning but sitting still at the same time. I knew it was coming, and Adam told me what to expect, but it was awful. I got so sick. I puked all over him.* I laughed. *Did you puke too?*

"More than if I'd drunk a bottle of Vlad to the face."

A laugh echoed in her mind. *What'd you do after that?*

"Well, after I puked my guts out, I realized we were at my car. At the cabin. Half a mile from where we'd just been." I chuckled and shook my head. "I thought I was losing my mind. I said I didn't know how I'd gotten there. I started accusing him of drugging me and he just… I don't know, he looked sad. For me, I think, because I was going through that. He said he hadn't. But he did teleport us there. I told him he was crazy. He just stayed quiet. He listened to me rant about how it all was insane. That there was no way he was my soulmate. That I was losing my shit. That none of it was real. I'd lost my mind; I'd had a break down. Something was happening, but it wasn't supernatural. It was insanity. I was an atheist, I knew that nothing like that could be possible. I just kept going, and going, and he waited. Once I'd stopped, he reached his hand out and showed me his forearm. I'd burned him when he grabbed me."

Then you believed him?

"I told him it was in my head. That it wasn't really happening, it was in my head. And he wrapped his other hand around the burn and squeezed. I gasped, and I looked down at my own hand, but it was fine. He said that delusions are just in your head. They don't hurt. Not physically."

And then *you believed him?*

"And I had a panic attack. I got down on the ground, and I started rocking back and forth. He tried to comfort me, but I pushed him away. He waited. Once it stopped, he moved in front of me because I wouldn't look at him. And he got really serious. Really gentle too, but serious. And he said that it was okay if I wasn't ready for this. Any of it. That I didn't have to use my powers if I didn't want to, and I didn't have to join the clan. That he was young too. He didn't think he was going to find a soulmate at all, let alone then. And if I wasn't ready for that, then great because neither was he. He said I could leave, and I didn't have to come back. He wanted me to, but I didn't have to. And if I needed him, he'd be there. They'd all be there. They'd help me figure out what I was. They'd help me learn to control my powers, or he'd hire a Witch to bind them if I didn't want them. But either way, I owed him nothing. Not an explanation, not a phone call. Nothing. He handed me my car keys. He told me whatever I chose was okay, that it was up to me. But he was going to give me space to figure it out," I said. "He kissed me, told me that he loved me, and disappeared."

Her eyes shifted between mine. *So what'd you do?*

"I went home. I took a shower. I sat by the creek and tried to do it again. I focused and I focused, but I couldn't get it to work. I said fuck it and went back inside. Then Mom started a grease fire in the stove. She caught her sweatshirt on fire, and without thought, I put it out. Didn't even touch her. I just wished that it'd stop and it just stopped. Poof. Gone. Barely even burned her. And I went to bed. I laid there for a while. I thought about how handy it'd be if I knew how to use it on command, if it was even what I thought it was. I thought about Jeremy. How he wouldn't have given me the chance to leave if he was a part of some weird cult. How well he'd always treated me. How he never pressured me into anything. How he let me take the reins on everything. How much he loved me. And how much I loved him. I'd only known him a few months, and I loved him so much, more than I loved anything." A slow breath left my nostrils as I smiled. "I showed up on his doorstep at three o'clock in the morning."

She looked over me for a moment. *Well, that sounds a little more traumatic than what's happening to me.*

"Not really. There was no pain on my part."

Yeah, but it was scarier. You didn't know what to expect. I do.

"True. But it happened on a normal day. I got to go back to my normal life. It wasn't in the middle of an apocalypse. I had a choice to get out and go back to how things had always been. You don't get that choice." I felt her hand quiver in mine and squeezed it a little tighter. "It's okay to not be okay through this. It's okay that I wasn't okay then. It's always okay to not be okay. No one has to be strong all the time."

She stared down at her hands. *But I'm gonna be okay, right?*

I smiled. "You're gonna be perfect. When this is over, you're going to feel better than you ever have."

Jenna stayed quiet for a moment. She looked over her oddly misshapen legs. *My fur's a pretty color, huh?*

"Your fur is a gorgeous color." I grinned.

She turned her eyes up to mine. *We're gonna be okay. You guys aren't going to let the world end. I know it's bad out there right now, but this is temporary. The world isn't gonna end, end. Right?*

It caught me off guard. I turned away, unable to meet her gaze. "I wish I could say we're going to fix this. I hope we do. But I don't know, Jen."

Her head tilted downward. *Can only do what you can do, I guess.*

Just then, a glass shattering scream cut through the silence. "Stop! *Stop*, it hurts!" I heard.

My stomach sunk as I sat forward. "I'll be right back."

Jenna scooted back so I could stand. As I darted from the room, the screams got louder and higher in pitch. I couldn't tell whose they were, but I knew they weren't a man's.

"Get them off!" Adam screamed.

"You're killing her," Celena yelled. "Stop it, damn it, stop!"

I sprinted down the hall, stomach dropping.

Gurgling screams. The smell of urine in my nostrils. A pool of blood on the hardwood floor.

Wyatt ripping Ray from the girl in the puddle, hands wrapping around his wolverine like neck. Celena slamming Max to the floor, fist repeatedly clunking into his cheek.

Lydia.

Pale blue, vacant eyes frozen in terror. Face splattered in blood. Neck chewed open. Half-eaten organs hanging out of her torso.

Adam collapsed to her as I teleported beside her.

"Start compressions." I told Adam. He nodded fast as I jumped into Jeremy's mind.

We need you. Now.

"I told you to stop." Wyatt squeezed Ray's throat. "I told you to fucking stop."

"You fucking listen to me." Celena's hand was tight in Max's blood drenched hair. "When I tell you to do something, you fucking do it, boy."

"Look at what you did!" Wyatt lifted Ray by his throat and angled him toward his dead, blood drenched daughter. "Look at what you fucking did, Ray. Look!"

He didn't look like Ray. He looked like a half wolf, half human, deformed animal. The way Werewolves and wendigos are depicted in old movies. But his eyes looked so human. Filled with grief and shame.

"Don't make him look at her like this," I yelled.

Wyatt's furious amber eyes met mine. "Don't tell me how to handle wolf shit, Laila."

"He—"

"He needs to know why you listen to your fucking alpha," he spat.

CHAPTER SIXTY-FOUR

JEREMY

I'd had it in my head that I was going to the diner for one of the wolves. Maybe Jenna's body couldn't handle the shift. Maybe Max's clogged arteries couldn't bare the rapid acceleration of his heart. Or maybe Ray was just a little too old to be changed.

A fifteen-year-old girl strewn out on the wooden floor with intestines overflowing from her slit gut was the last thing I expected.

She was gone. No doubt about it, she was gone. Not even the best emergency surgeon in the world could repair what the wolves had done. Regardless of the fact that her heart wasn't beating, no science in the world could repair what'd happened. Truthfully, I wasn't sure we could either.

But I'd seen too many kids die in the past few days. And that little girl's existence was the reason I had my brother back. I owed her. I was going to do any and everything I could to get her back.

I collapsed beside Laila. "What the fuck happened?!"

"I don't know," Laila said.

"Are you fucking kidding me?" Celena yelled, one fist burying into Max's hair as the other gripped his throat. "You're gonna try and get out of my hands? After what you just fucking did?"

"Get them out of here." Laila's piercing gaze darted between Ray and Max. "Both of them. Get them back to the house. And stay far away from my house because on god, I will kill you both if you get within a hundred feet of my babies."

"I..." Ray whispered, blood dripping from his lip as he looked over his daughter. Tears spilled from his eyes. "I didn't—"

I looked at Celena. "*Now.*"

She disappeared. A second later, she reappeared and disappeared again with Wyatt and Ray. As she did, I looked over Lydia.

Her typically dark skin looked so light. But the whites of her crystal eyes were redder than flames. I could literally see the inside of her neck. The torn muscles, the ripped tendons, her flooded esophagus.

"We're going to need Kai," I said. "You can't heal this by yourself."

"And Brody and Chris to hold her down." She looked up at Adam. "Go get them, and come back for Jen."

He nodded fast, fists pumping hard into her chest as he looked to me. "You ready?"

I took Lydia's hand and closed my eyes.

My mind drifted away. Deep into that black pit, using her palm as a guiding tool to her soul. But it wasn't as easy as it'd been with Laila, Chris, or Micah. Laila was my soulmate; finding her soul took less time than it took to blink. Chris and Micah were my blood. They weren't hard to find there either.

But Lydia and I weren't exactly close. I loved the kid, but she was more of a friendly acquaintance than family. Focusing on her soul wasn't easy because I didn't know it very well. Familiarity is everything when travelling at inhuman speeds through a graveyard of black light-ened by billions of bright souls. Especially since it'd filled so rapidly in the past few days.

It was brighter than ever. Human souls were a bit duller than any of the other races, and few of us had died recently. But it was still blinding.

Anxiety began to creep over me. The longer I searched, the longer her body was deprived of oxygen. The longer she went without air, the less her body would be worth returning to. I knew it hadn't been long, but any span of time is too long to be away from a corpse. Especially one that needed so much healing, healing I wasn't even sure we were capable of.

Then a thought occurred to me.

"Call to the soul," Hannah had said in one of our trainings. *"It isn't as simple as speaking, but that's what I did when I brought Laila back the first time. I called to her. When I yelled her name in my head, I almost heard her call back. She pulsed in the abyss. That puff of light was like a beacon. It guided me to her."*

It'd worked for Hannah. I prayed it'd work for me.

Lydia, I thought hard. *Lydia.*

In the distance, far from where I floated, in the middle of a cluster of bright souls, I saw it. Just as Hannah had said. A pulse. Almost a flash, but it didn't fade. It grew brighter.

The color of her soul reminded me a bit of my own. Hints of dark gray smoke a few shades lighter than mine vibrating with soft hues of baby blue. Specks of white sparkled through it, like Laila's pinpricks of gold.

I rushed toward her and enveloped my essence around hers.

I heard a gurgle. "Now," I told Adam.

He stopped pumping and disappeared.

My eyes opened. Lydia's wide, bloodshot eyes jerked back and forth as if in REM. Her body writhed side to side. Laila flashed to the other side of her, gripping her seizing body in place.

"I don't know where to start," Laila said. "The neck's bad but the gut isn't any better and I—"

"Kai can do one and you can do the other," I said quickly, eyes shutting as I felt her soul struggling to leave the confines of my own. "Just help me hold her down until they get here."

"Okay," Laila said.

As awful as that experience was, I can't say it wasn't good practice. I'd evaded that ability since I'd learned it. Even when I did try to do it, I only understood the *how* part when I had to. It was in that moment, holding Lydia's soul into her body—existing within the abyss and the earth at the same instant—that I understood why older me told Heylel not to tell me what I was.

It was one of those things that couldn't be taught. It had to be self-learned. Like learning to walk or how to chew food. Some part of you instinctively knows how to do it. But no amount of coaching can teach you. You just have to learn it on your own through practice and repetition.

Regardless, I wouldn't admit that to him. I knew he was right. But my pride was more important.

"The hell happened?!" Kai dropped to the floor beside me.

"Lydia stubbed her toe on the back of the couch," Adam said. "A few drops of blood, and Ray just charged her. Max followed suit."

"Jesus Christ," Brody said.

"You get the legs, I'll get the arms," Chris said.

"I'll take the throat while you do her stomach, Kai," Laila said. "It'll heal faster. I'll help you down there."

"Sure." His hands glowed bright white above Lydia's stomach.

Her shifting eyes steadied as a gurgling, ear piercing scream filled the small apartment. Laila's hands wrapped around her throat shining bright energy into her bloodied neck. Lydia's head shifted back and forth rapidly. Her body must have been filled with the worst pain already from her wounds, and the healing on top of it could only be described as hell on earth.

I held her hand tighter and tried to focus. Over the sound of her bubbling cries, it was nearly impossible. I closed my eyes to try to zone in on my hold over her soul.

<hr>

It took Laila about thirty minutes to heal Lydia's neck. All the while Kai struggled with her torso. His hands were physically inside of her. He said something about how her liver was practically gone. It took him the entire time to replenish that one organ as it'd taken Laila to repair her throat.

And that was just one of the many things they'd destroyed.

All five feet of her intestines were butchered. Torn into a thousand pieces—some just floating through the muck of blood, some digesting in Max and Ray's bellies. Kai said her stomach was gone, as were her kidneys. Honestly, I had no idea how we were managing to keep her alive.

I guessed that was the power of gods, though. But what the myths don't tell you is that it takes a host of gods to save even just one human life. We were depicted as limitless because that's how the humans viewed us. We have vast capabilities, but it takes a group of us to do anything substantial when situations become dire.

Once her neck was intact though, the screams got so much worse. She was still coughing—or maybe vomiting—blood. She kept screaming for them to stop. That it hurt too much. To just let her die.

When she said that, I scooted up to her pale face. She kept screaming, instinctively fighting against Brody and Chris's hold. Her head writhed in every direction. I teleported a pillow from the couch beneath it to keep her from giving herself a concussion. I lifted her shaking head and shoved the pillow underneath.

"Lydia," I said. "Lydia, look at me."

She screamed again, desperate cries filling my ears. Tears poured from her bloodied eyes as I took her cheeks in my hands. "Lydia, look at me."

Her head fought my hands, and I let that relaxing, calm energy of my soul flow from my hands into her. She kept crying, but the angry flailing lessened. I struggled a smile. "That's better, huh?"

Her lips quivered, eyes overflowing with more anguished tears. "It h-hurts. It hurts so bad."

"I know," I said. "I know. The kind of pain you're in is unbearable, right?" Her blood coated nostrils flared. "But look at you. You're bearing it."

"I don't w-a-a-ant to," she whispered. "Let me die. Please let me die."

"That's just the pain talking," I said gently. "But this is gonna end. The pain's gonna stop. I know it hurts right now, but it *will* stop."

"I don't want it to hurt," she murmured. "I just want to die. It was better than this."

"It is pretty peaceful there, huh?" Her lip quivered as she nodded. "But it isn't pleasant. You can't be happy there. It's just nothing. Living when you're healthy is better, isn't it?"

"I just want to di—"

"But answer the question. Living is better, isn't it?" I asked quietly. Her jaw trembled, and more tears rolled from her eyes. "It is. You know it is. You're gonna get through this, and you'll be happy again. But you have to live through it to reach that point, right?" Her tears picked up, sprinkling from her eyes. "You want to live. You just don't want to live like this. And you won't have to because this will end. It's gonna hurt a little while longer, but then you can do whatever you want. You want to stab Max and your dad? You can, I'll hold 'em down for you." Her shaking lips pulled up a bit, struggling back a laugh. I smiled too. "Do you want me to? 'Cause I will. I'll do that for you, kid. Might get my ass handed to me for it, but I'll do it."

She smiled slightly. "You promise?"

I smiled back. "Promise. But you've gotta bear with us a little longer."

"But it hurts so b-bad," she whispered.

I frowned. "Yeah, I know it does. But let's not think about the pain. Let's think about something else. What's your favorite band?"

"I don't know."

"Sure you do," I said. "What're the kids listening to these days? Is *All Time Low* still a big thing?"

Laila chuckled.

"I guess that's a no. What about that other boy band? What is it— Something direction?"

"I don't like boy bands." Her nose crunched up.

I smiled. "Me neither."

"I—I like Dua Lipa," she muttered.

"Dua Lipa." I looked at Laila. "Do I know any Dua Lipa?"

"Probably not," Laila said.

"I like Halsey, too," Lydia made out.

"Halsey, I can jam to some Halsey." I smiled. "What's your favorite song?"

"Colors," she murmured. "I like Colors."

"Ooh, I know that one." I smiled wider. "Let's sing it."

"I can't sing."

"Everyone can sing. You don't have to be good at it to do it. C'mon, sing with me." I started into the opening verse. When she didn't join in, I paused, "You can't have me singing girly music without chiming in. Come on. Sing it with me."

She fought the smile creeping up her pale cheeks and shook her head.

"You wanna sing with me, Lai?" I glanced her way and picked back up into the opening verse. Laila peeked at me with a smile. She chimed in. Then Brody did too, smiling up at Lydia. Soon enough, she joined in, too. Poorly, I'll admit. But it served as a good distraction.

We sang our way through the next three hours. Lydia still cried, but she wasn't begging us to let her die. And somehow, she didn't. She pulled through.

When we were done though, Lydia was still panicked. Laila took her to the bathroom and helped her get cleaned up. She brought her in some of Jenna's clean clothes and spent a while talking to her in there.

Chris, Brody, and I cleaned up the blood. Thankfully, it was all on the hardwoods which made things easier. But all of our hands were shaking as we did.

Honestly, I was amazed. What we'd just pulled off was amazing.

But I kept thinking about what it'd be like to be Ray after what he'd done. We were all pretty torn up over the whole situation, but I couldn't imagine what was going through his head. He'd killed his own daughter and eaten parts of her insides.

He hadn't shown since we'd arrived, but I worried for what the following day would be like for the two of them. The rest of us would be gone fighting the next wave of the apocalypse. And they'd be stuck in the house together.

Even worse than I felt for Ray was how badly I felt for Lydia. Both of her parents had tried to kill her. The best of her childhood years were spent imprisoned by a madman from the future. Her mother shot her in the chest when she was eleven and her dad ate her stomach at fifteen. If those weren't the building blocks for psychosis, I didn't know what was.

CHAPTER SIXTY-FIVE

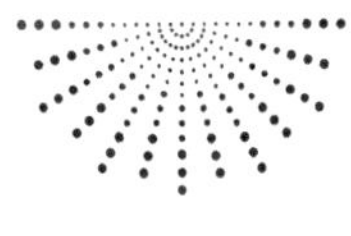

LAILA

Lydia was calmer than I expected her to be once she was healed. I guessed the poor kid had lived through so much trauma, she'd become practically desensitized to it. The two of us would always have that in common.

When I began to say something about how I was sure her dad hated himself for what happened, she cut me off with, "I don't want that."

After Amy had shot her in 2019, she held onto plenty of resentment toward her. Even after figuring that she'd probably done it to get her out of that prison, she still didn't forgive her. But that woman had destroyed her childhood. She bowed to the man that tortured and held captive almost a thousand of our people. She allowed, perhaps even forced, Lydia to watch as he ripped our people apart for his demented plan.

But Ray had spent every moment of the last five years since he had her back struggling to give her everything she needed. He was overprotective at times, but she had no doubt that he loved her with every fiber of his being. He worked his ass off to give her the normal, ordinary life she deserved.

Hell, he agreed to be turned into a beast so she could enjoy the rest of her adolescence. He didn't want it, he did it *for* her. And she recognized that. She knew what happened was a mistake, one that wasn't uncommon in our world.

<hr>

Jeremy collapsed to the bed beside me. "What a day."

"Another day in the life." I huffed, hand-drying my hair with a towel.

"How was she?" he asked. "Was she mad at her dad?"

"No, not at all really. She understands how the wolf thing works. He was literally just turned. And before I went to check on Jen, he said something about how no one was going to feed off her because he didn't trust any of them enough for that. Max kept talking about how I smelled so good. I should have thought about that. He was probably craving her blood and ashamed to admit it."

"Yeah, probably," he muttered. "That's good though. I'm sure he's gonna beat himself up bad enough for it. It isn't easy getting turned, adjusting to all those differences. That was a bad move on our part though. You can protect yourself, but Lydia's powers aren't defensive. We should have had her stay back here."

"I just figured with all of us there it'd be alright. Wyatt and Celena know what they're doing, but it just happened so quick." I teleported my towel to the hamper and pulled the blankets up over my chest. "I should have been out there. It happened when I went in to check on Jen."

"Can't be everywhere at once." He rolled to meet my gaze. "But how about that shit with Wyatt? Did you see the look he gave you?"

Nearly a scoff escaped me. "Yeah, threw me for a bit of a loop."

"Yeah, me too. I always thought he had that alpha gene in him, but after he told Brendon he didn't want the Eastern Atlantic Pack, I thought he'd decided he didn't want to be a leader," Jeremy said. "He definitely wants to put Ray and Max in their place though."

"A lot of bad blood there. He killed their last leader. He wasn't even a part of the pack. I wouldn't want to take over in Damon's place either. You need the allegiance of your people in one way or the other, and he'd never have that with them. He'd always be the outsider," I said. "Maybe he just didn't want to be the leader of *that* pack."

"Now he's got his own," Jeremy said. "Imagine that power struggle between him and Celena though." I laughed, and he smiled. "She's never gonna bow to him."

"No, but she does belly-up," I said. "The dog world's different though. Wyatt might end up making some calls, but he's still going to defer to his bitch."

Jeremy laughed. "Well, I guess the fact that they're soulmates helps. I know it's pretty hard to say no to you."

"I know the feeling." I smiled, twining my fingers between his against the pillow between us. With the question that came next, I let my smile fall. "So what happened where you were yesterday?"

His smile receded too. "Nothing good. And you?"

"Could have been worse. But could've been better," I muttered. "It just killed me how all of the people who did die wouldn't have if they would have gone through the portal to begin with."

He chewed his lower lip. "I get it though. When you were human, if a news report like that got broadcasted, would you believe it? Even if the government *was* urging you to?"

"No. Probably would have gone off on some conspiracy theorist tangent if I were them too," I muttered. "'Til I saw the evidence, anyway."

"If you didn't become part of the evidence first." His gaze was distant, hand tight around mine. "Tomorrow's gonna get bad, huh?"

I ran my thumb against the back of his. "Yeah, I think so. Lila and Nick said tomorrow is when the meteors start hitting the major cities."

"It's gonna be worse than nine eleven was. One building got destroyed then. But if tons of asteroids start falling on New York City at once…"

"Millions are gonna die," I murmured. He nodded slowly, gaze turning to our hands against the pillow. His eyes reddened as he blinked fast to keep them from watering. The color drained from his cheeks. I felt his hand start to tremble in mine.

This was hard on all of us. But I knew it was harder for him. He was connected to death on a more profound level than I could imagine. And judging by that dazed look in his usually vibrant eyes, it was eating him alive.

I had to try and keep him steady. So I changed the subject

Summoning a smile, I cleared. "You did great with Lydia though."

He forced a smile. "She was just scared. In that kind of pain, I'd probably want to die too."

"Can't say I blame her either," I muttered. "But still. You're great with that sort of thing. Calming people down, talking to kids. When we go back, maybe you should go to school to be a guidance counselor or something. Maybe even a teacher."

He laughed and met my gaze. "Well, you know what they say. Psychiatrists go into that field 'cause they're crazy too."

A chuckle left me. "You're not crazy."

"I'm feeling a little crazy this week," he muttered.

"I think we all are," I said quietly. "But I think this is the best way it could happen. We get a quarter of a century to prepare for this. So we can have a level head on our shoulders when we have to be the leaders."

"Mm," he said. "We should probably try and get some sleep though. Got another long day ahead of us in the morning."

"Yeah, we probably should. I love you."

"Love you too." He closed his eyes. "Sleep tight."

CHAPTER SIXTY-SIX

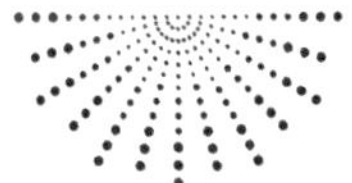

JANUARY 8 - JEREMY

Laila and I sat on the stoop outside of the diner waiting for Nick and Lila. Celena and Wyatt stood a few feet to the left sharing a cigarette. Chris, Leah, Adam, Brody, and Kai meandered along the outskirts of the building. Some of us talked quietly amongst ourselves while others remained silent. Laila and I were the latter.

There wasn't much to be said. Today would be death day. Millions, maybe even billions, of people were about to cross into the abyss. I tried not to think about it, but it was all that I could think.

It'd be worse than the pyroclastic flow of the volcano in California. It'd be worse than the tsunami in Washington. It'd be the worst day any of us had ever lived.

Knowing how shitty something is about to be should make it easier. But it doesn't. It almost makes it harder.

"I wonder how many people already went to the Fae Realm." Laila broke the silence quietly. "A few thousand at least, right?"

I licked my lips. "Probably a few thousand."

"So a piece of straw in a hay bale." Chris lowered himself to the concrete beside me. He lifted a cigarette to his lips and sparked it with a lighter in his other hand.

Laila craned past me to meet his gaze. "Since when do you smoke?"

"Since I don't have to worry about cancer." He took a puff. "And ya know. Since the world's ending, and I don't like weed."

"Bum me one?" I extended my hand out to his.

He fished in his coat pocket, pulled out a pack, and dropped it to my palm. As I lifted it to my lips and lit it with my finger, Laila extended her palm out to his. "I'll buy you a pack."

He laughed and handed her one.

I inhaled deeply and curled my lips down as I exhaled. "Ew, full flavor?"

"I like full flavor," Chris muttered.

"Then you're disgusting," I said.

"*You're* disgusting," he said.

"Menthol's where it's at." Laila took in a long drag. "When I smoked, it was always those Camel Crushes."

"Yeah, with the little flavor ball in the filter," I said. "Loved those things."

"Menthol is awful," Chris said. "It hurts my throat."

"Really?" Laila asked. "I actually smoked them when I had a sore throat. Still do sometimes. Menthol inhaled is herbal medicine that's been used for centuries."

"Yeah, used medicinally. In moderation. But daily, it causes irritation," Chris said.

"Eh, fair enough," Laila said.

I took in another drag and leaned back on my palms. My gaze shifted to the dark sky. As I exhaled, I watched the pale gray smoke, once so visible in the atmosphere, practically disappear on the dark backdrop.

I lifted the cigarette back to my lips.

"Look at that." I heard in front of me. "All on time."

"Except for you," Laila said as she stood.

"Got a little held up," Lila said.

I sat forward and looked ahead. Nick and Lila stood side by side. Older Brody was beside Lila. To Nick's left was a short woman I'd seen back at the tsunami but didn't know personally. Her hair was as white as a cloud, not much different than the color of her skin. It was too dark to make out the color of her angled eyes, but something about them was familiar.

In that instant, I knew that she and I had known each other for eons. I didn't recall her from any of my memories as Nix, yet I *knew* her. I had the notion that it was some type of hereditary familiarity though, because although she was easily one of the most beautiful women I'd met, I wasn't attracted to her in any way, shape, or form. I looked at her the same way I looked at Hannah and Leah.

"Brought a friend?" Chris gesturing to the woman.

She smiled as she met his gaze. "Don't remember me, love?" she said in a thick, dainty English accent.

"Can't say that I do."

Her smile widened, and she shrugged.

"This is Elira," Nick said. "As I know you guessed, Jeremy, one of us. The par animarum."

Chris arched a brow, and she laughed, shaking her head. "And no, not yours. I don't have that kind of equipment."

"Elira." Laila's hands went to her hips. "That's an Elvan name if I've ever heard one."

Elira smiled and pushed hair behind her ear to reveal a high point. "It is, in fact."

"We're splitting up again," Lila said. "But Jeremy, Nick, and Elira are taking New York City. You'll need all the hands you can get."

New York City was massive—the biggest city in the biggest country in the world. It was densely populated. How could three of us be enough to make anything more than a dent in what was to come?

"And that's all we get?" I asked. "Three people?"

"There are a lot of large cities, Jeremy," Lila said. "New York's getting three of our strongest. The rest are getting one or two."

"But that's it," I said. "You think the three of us can stop this."

"No, I know you can't," she said. "None of us can *stop* this."

"But we're going to do what we can," Elira said.

"And we have back up." Nick's eyes met mine. "Not as strong as us. But we have more teleporters lined up and ready."

"Teleporters," I muttered. "That's it, just teleporters?"

"This isn't a battle. It's an attack. There's no one to fight," Lila said.

"Our job is to slow the meteors that we can, heal the people that are injured, and move who we can out of immediate danger," Elira said.

A lump solidified in my throat, and my hands wettened with sweat. They were right. I knew that even then. The reality had been evident all week. There were only so many of us, and there were over seven trillion people on earth.

A slow breath left my nostrils.

"Where do you want me?" Laila asked.

"You're going to be sticking close to home too," Lila said. "Los Angeles."

Laila rubbed her jaw. "Gotcha. Back up there too?"

"Some," Nick said. "Not as much as you really need, but as much as we could get."

She took another hit off the cigarette and blew it out of her nostrils. "Guess I'll do what I can then."

"All you really can do," Nick murmured. "Micah will be there. L.A.'s his favorite city in the world. He'll help you save as many people as he can."

She rubbed her eye. "That's reassuring."

"It gets hit pretty hard," Lila said. "So be prepared."

As if that wasn't obvious. Everywhere was about to get hit pretty hard. The entire world was about to be rained on by hunks of space junk. It was going to be hell.

And that made my stomach spin.

"And the rest of us?" Chris asked.

"We're getting there," Nick said.

"But first," older Brody began, looking around. "You all have your cell phones?"

We all muttered a yes or a yeah. Then a thick, black, metal box appeared in his hands. It sunk downward upon impact. He clunked and spun some buttons on the top, It lifted open. He turned it to face us.

"Turn 'em off and drop 'em in," he said.

"What?" Laila asked. "Why?"

"Just trust me. You'll regret it if you don't."

"But how are we going to get in contact with each other?" Leah asked. "I don't have a soulmate, I can't just—"

"By nightfall, there isn't going to be a cellular network for your phone to tap into." He looked at the younger version of himself. "I know you don't want to lose what's on that phone. Drop it in."

Brody stared at him hard for a moment. It was the first time he met his older self. After a few long seconds, he reached into his pocket. As he turned it up to face him, I caught a glimpse of his lock screen photo. Gwen. "Turn it off first, you said?"

He nodded.

"What do you mean there won't be a cellular network to tap into?" Leah's eyes widened, being the techy that she was.

"You'll see," Nick muttered.

The box told me everything I needed to know. A Faraday cage. It was a box lined with many layers of aluminum and foil.

"No, what does that mean?" Leah asked. "What are we talking about here, a cyber attack too?"

"A massive EMP," Lila said. "More than just *a*, actually."

"Hence the lead, aluminum lined box," Nick said.

Damn. They weren't fucking around. Lead *and* aluminum.

"I need to get to my computer then," Leah said quickly. "All of my file—"

"I'll take you back real quick. You can bring it to our safe room," Nick said. "But come on, guys. Phones in the box."

Laila glanced up at me as she reached into her pocket. I did the same. Our phones had everything. Thousands of pictures of each other. Thousands of pictures of the kids. Videos of Micah and Milly kicking in Laila's stomach, then of Milly's first steps. Videos of Micah learning to play the guitar and ukulele. Their birthday parties, their first Christmas, their first rollercoaster rides.

Not to mention the thousands before they came along. Laila and I in Hawaii five years ago. Videos she'd taken of me performing at the diner. Record of every song we'd ever written together. And our journal entries from the last six years that would eventually become these books.

One day, those photos, videos, and documents would be all we had left from this life. Losing all of that would one day be like losing a piece of history.

I dropped my phone into the box on top of hers.

The older version of Brody walked between the crowd. Lila frowned as she looked between us. Her gaze moved over me carefully for a moment. Grief touched her eyes, and I made a puzzled face. She cleared her throat.

"Alright, so before we go, let's discuss the basics," she began.

"Today's gonna be the worst so far," Nick said.

"And long," Brody said.

"Today is gonna turn into tomorrow, Into Wednesday, Into Thursday," Lila said. "They'll all roll together."

"If you think Saturday was bad, just wait," Nick said. My stomach churned. The warmth of Laila's fingertips twined tighter between mine. "It's gonna be worse."

"And you're not going to want to stop," Lila said. "It won't be like Saturday. On Saturday, there was an end. You cleared an area, and that was that. But those were much smaller scales than what we're dealing with now. It was thousands and hundreds of thousands of lives we were trying to help."

"The next three days will be millions," Brody said.

"When you're surrounded by all of that, your instinct is going to tell you to keep going," Nick said.

"But you are not immortal. Not yet," Elira said. "You can't forget that."

"Even us." Lila gestured between the four of them. "We run on water and carbs. We'll have to take breaks."

"You have to stop to hydrate." Nick pulled his backpack off of his shoulders. He reached inside and began passing out metal water bottles with protein bars taped to their sides. "You have to eat. You have to piss, you have to shit, and you have to stop to breathe."

"You're no good to anyone unconscious," Elira said. "Hate to sound so new agey. But self-care is important, even now. You must stop. When you feel lightheaded, when your stomach hurts, when you can't catch your breath; stop."

"Even when you hear people screaming in the distance," Lila said.

"Even when you feel people dying." Nick eyes locked with mine as he handed me a bottle. "You have to stop. You still have to take breaks. You still have to breathe."

"Just like the memes say, you can't pour from an empty cup," Lila said.

"You will have to stop to sleep," Elira said. "It's unfortunate that we don't have limitless stamina, but none of us do."

"So here's how this is going to go," Nick said.

"If you don't stop to take a break when you need it, one of us will force you to," Lila said. "I hope that you use your common sense in this regard because it's just going to slow us down if you don't."

"Our point is that you can't feel guilty for being a person," Nick said. "We may be super-human, but that doesn't make us limitless."

"So when you start having a hard time standing, let your back-up know," Elira said. "Tell them you're tapping out for the night. Then go home and sleep. Set an alarm for six hours. Get the rest, eat a bowl of oatmeal, down a few bottles of water, then go back to your assigned location."

"Regardless, we all meet back at the house Thursday at eleven P.M.," Lila said. "I don't care what you're doing. I don't care if you're in the middle of healing an old friend. I don't care if you're holding a building in place with your bare hands. You get back to the house by eleven."

"Then you get your bags," Nick said. "We open the portal at midnight on January 12th, 2024. And you go through it."

"You'll have the hour between eleven and twelve to pack anything you forgot," Lila said. "But don't send us on a wild goose chase trying to track you down. None of us have time for that. Nick and I have things to tell you before you go."

"Your older selves all have a message for you, too." Older Brody glanced at our Brody.

"We have paperwork we need to hand out," Nick said. "Your new identities and everything else you're going to need to get started."

"And a few miscellaneous details," Lila said.

"So we all on the same page?" Nick asked, glancing around.

Not really. They just told me that I was going to have to ignore the cries of people begging for help. That I'd have to walk away from people pleading that I wouldn't let them die.

No. I was not on the same page. I had no fucking clue how I would be okay with that. But I supposed it had to be done.

We all nodded or muttered a yes. Nick said, "Alright then. Tell 'em where they're going, baby."

I turned to Laila and wrapped my arms around her shoulders. "I love you," I whispered.

"I love you more." Her arms tightened at my ribs.

We stayed like that for a moment. I didn't pay much mind to what Lila told the rest of the group.

I just closed my eyes and took in the smell of her hair and the comfort the warmth of her skin brought me. Eventually, she pulled back and touched her lips to mine. I kissed her back. She craned up until our foreheads rested against each other's. My hand found her cheek as my eyes moved between hers.

She forced a smile. "I'll see you Thursday."

"Thursday."

"And you better come back to me in one piece." Her smile widened.

A quiet chuckle left my lips. "I will. And you, too."

She kissed me once more. Her hand rested against my chest as mine tightened at her waist. After a moment, she stepped back. "Thursday."

Her hand dropped back to her side as she turned. "Where am I meeting Micah?"

"The Hollywood sign," Nick said.

She blew out a heavy breath and disappeared.

CHAPTER SIXTY-SEVEN

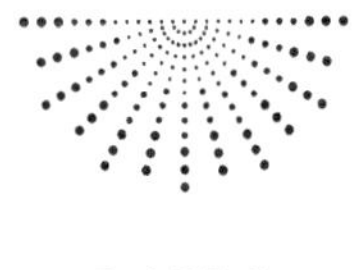

LAILA

Warm wind brushed stray hairs from my ponytail against my cheeks. I watched people jog along the suburb before me and tried to make out the city behind them, but it was masked by the dark cloud of smog lingering above. The muggy scent of hot asphalt and jasmine drifted into my nostrils. I thought about how ironic it was that even up there on the mountaintop, miles from the city, the pretentious smell still lingered.

Los Angeles. The city everyone loved to hate. Yours truly included.

It wasn't that I genuinely hated L.A. Overall, it was one of the less disgusting cities I'd visited. But the hypocrisy behind it was what appalled me.

The overpriced cost of living. The fact that the people who kept the city running couldn't afford to live within its confines without roommates or working two or three jobs. The preaching of equal rights and bettering the planet but remaining omnipresently oppressing.

Thousands of people lived in tents along the streets while those on the outskirts had fifteen bathrooms for two people—yet lived most of their lives on private jets. Everyone ranted about human connection while staring at their smartphones. So many went through ten-thousand-dollar after ten-thousand-dollar surgeries for nothing more than vanity while millions struggled to figure out how to put a meal on their table. They preached about the environment, but had more cars on their horrible roads than any other city I'd travelled through.

Everything vegan. Everything environmentally friendly. Yoga this, mental health that, meditation and essential oils are the cure to everything.

Don't get me wrong, I understood the importance of healthy living, and there were many things about L.A. I wished we had more of in my little town. I loved that I wasn't looked at like a quack for meditating while I was there. It was great to go to a restaurant with my son and find a meal that fit his dietary preferences that filled him up. I loved that I could do yoga on my hotel balcony with my kids without neighbors thinking I was trying to brainwash them into some occultist bullshit like the hicks back home. And I liked sage and patchouli as much as the next hippy.

The ideas the city held onto so deeply were great. But the half-assed execution disgusted me. If it weren't for the fact that so many people were about to die, the asteroids heading toward it wouldn't bother me in the slightest.

"Mom," a voice called from the ground beneath my seat on the H. "That's you up there, right?"

It sounded so strange. I was so accustomed to Mommy or Mama. But Mom, directed at me, coming from the mouth of a man who was three years older than me... A strange feeling.

I teleported to the ground beside him. "Yeah, it's me."

He smiled and he lowered himself to the ground. I sat beside him and pulled my knees to my chest. "I think we have a little time," Micah said. "Ten minutes or so."

"Should we start moving people now then?" I asked. "I mean, if we get people to the portal before it starts, then we'll be saving ourselves some time and more lives."

Micah pulled a protein bar from his pocket and tore it open. "If we knew where they were about to hit, sure. But if we start teleporting people from their houses right now, they might not be the people who are going to get hit. And they'll come to the portals willingly once they see the damage." He took a bite and offered it to me. I shook my head, and he inched it closer with a smile. "Mom told me to remind you to eat."

I laughed and took a bite. My face screwed up as I chewed the chalky substance in my mouth. "That's disgusting."

He laughed. "It is not."

"What the hell is that?" I spat it to the ground on my right. "Shit in a wrapper?"

Micah laughed again. "It's cookies and cream flavored. I think it's dates and almond milk with cacao powder."

"In what world is a date a cookie?" I wiped slobber from the corner of my mouth with my sleeve.

"It's delicious. You're crazy." He smiled and took another bite. "And it's good for you. Better than all that hydrogenated oil and corn syrup in that thing." He gesturing to the granola bar taped to my water bottle. "Just fillers in there. It doesn't have anything to actually keep your body moving. That stuff gunks up in your intestines. A bunch of wasted carbs and sugar. We need carbs, and we need sugar but not that over processed crap."

I glanced over him and smiled. Not much had changed. Older and wiser, but not much different than the little boy who insisted we add tofu to the menu at our little diner. And it was cute how he said crap instead of shit. My kid, but so much more PG-rated than me.

He noticed my staring and smiled. "But if you won't eat the healthy stuff, at least get some carbs in you."

"I'm saving it for later. I had oatmeal this morning." I smiled. "With you, actually."

His smiled widened a bit. He took another bite of his protein bar.

"This must be weird for you," I said. "A younger version of you existing out there. A younger mom and dad. Literally meeting us and everything."

He smiled. "Kind of. I don't know. I've adjusted. This isn't as new to me as it is to you."

I grew quiet, thinking of what to say next. "How long have you known about all this?"

"Uh." He thought for a moment as he chewed, aching a brow. "Almost eight years? I was twenty-one when you guys told me."

It did give me an ounce of solace to know that he didn't remember all of this. That he'd grow up normal, without the weight of the world on his shoulders. But it sucked too. That wasn't the life I'd built for him. I supposed, though, that in most regards, it was best.

"I met you once, you know," he said. "You said I could. That I could go to the diner and see the proof for myself."

"Oh yeah?" I cocked my head to the side. "Are you sure? I think I'd remember you."

"Yeah, I'm sure. I had lunch at Moe's. You waited on me. All I had was salad but." He smiled. "I don't know. It was cool. Seeing you like that. All young and innocent. Before the scars and the tattoos. I always wondered what you'd look like without them."

I exhaled slowly and turned my gaze back to the suburb.

"Not that they look bad," he said quickly. "It was just kind of weird, you know. You were like a whole other person."

I thought back to who I was eight years prior. Eighteen years old. In love for the first time. My whole life ahead of me. Trying to figure out who I was after learning *what* I was. "I *was* a different person then."

"Yeah. I guess you were. Practically human, really," he murmured. "I like this you better though."

I glanced his way with a smile, shaking my head a bit as I turned back to the distance.

That was doubtful. My sweet, compassionate little hippy liking me. *This* me? The one who'd killed so many, the one who had done so many awful things.

"No, really," he said. "I do. Don't take this the wrong way, but you were kinda weak." I laughed, and he smiled. "You weren't as powerful. You were nice and all, but you were... I don't know, you were naïve."

"Yeah, I was," I muttered. "But a big part of me wishes I could still be her. If I were, none of this would be happening. You and your sister could have normal lives. You wouldn't have the weight of the world on your shoulders."

I felt his gaze on me and turned. His disappointed eyes shifted over me. "I'm glad you aren't her."

I raised a brow. "Why's that?"

"Because then none of us would exist," he said. "You becoming who you are is what broke the curse. I might have lived, but my siblings wouldn't have been born. I wouldn't have my parents. I wouldn't have my family. The par animarum wouldn't be here, and I'd be fighting this on my own."

"Not if you hadn't been sacrificed," I muttered. "The apocalypse wouldn't have started if we hadn't let that happen."

"You think I wouldn't have been sacrificed if the two of you didn't become who you are?" he asked. "This was going to happen no matter what. Don't you remember what Peterson said? That it was always supposed to happen in this time?"

"What do you mean?" I asked.

He frowned. "Guess you haven't gotten to that part yet. But just… Look, Peterson was right. This was the best way for things to go. I know that's still hard to believe, but the world would be a lot worse off if you and Dad weren't here. Let's leave it at that."

"But what do you—"

A loud roar cut me off.

His head shot toward the dark sky. He jammed his wrapper into his jeans and teleported to his feet. "Here we go. Are you ready?"

Bright reddish orange light began to cut through the black sky. My heart picked up in my chest. I teleported beside Micah. As I nodded, he pointed to the light breaking through the cloud of smog. "Think we can break it before it hits the ground?" he asked.

"Worth a shot."

CHAPTER SIXTY-EIGHT

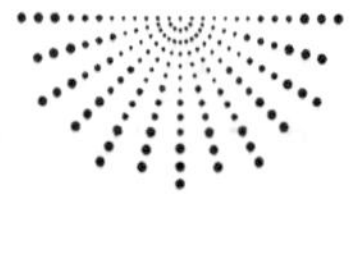

JEREMY

A bright yellow taxi raced past me, and the smell of exhaust wafted into my nose. I zipped up my jacket and pulled my beanie tighter over my ears. I noted all the people wearing masks, probably out of fear of the thick black cloud hanging above. A grungy dressed, middle aged man bumped past me, yelling to watch where I was going as if I wasn't standing still.

"I hate New York," I muttered.

"You and me both," Nick said.

"Not saying much now, is it?" Elira's gaze shifted between us. "I knew this day would come and all, but I've got to say, it's still incredibly surreal."

"You're telling me." I glanced at Nick and then back at her. "So where's this back-up you were talking about?"

Nick's gaze shifted up to the dark sky. "Waiting on the word."

"They aren't here?" I asked. "What good are they going to be then?"

"No good to us dead at all." Elira clicked the button for the cross-walk. "They're to help us clean up."

My stomach sunk. They weren't coming as back-up to the attack. They'd help us put out the fire once it started, but we were the ones on ground-zero.

"Where do we start then?" I asked.

"The schools." Nick gesturing to an inner-city elementary across the street. "Let's get as many kids as we can through the portals."

As the pedestrian light turned green, he stepped off the sidewalk. But I caught his arm and shot him a look. "We're just gonna kidnap a bunch of children in broad day light."

"We aren't kidnapping them. We're saving them." Nick's eyes met mine over his shoulder. "And it isn't exactly daylight."

"But we're just snatching them out of their classrooms and dropping them into a swirling vortex. What about their parents? What about when they—"

"Their parents had time to take them to the Fae Realm themselves and chose not to." He pulled his arm back. "Let's go, Jeremy."

"But—"

He turned quickly, eyes shifting between mine. "Twenty-four years ago to the day, I watched a meteor hit that building. I wasted fourteen hours digging through five-hundred dead children. I kept thinking one of them was alive. I kept telling myself at least *one* of them must have survived. But no. Not one. Not fucking *one*." His eyes shifted rapidly between mine. "You want to repeat history? 'Cause I don't. Let's go. Now."

I felt my hands tremble at my sides. I tightened them to fists.

He continued onto the crosswalk.

"I'm heading to Times Square," Elira said. "I'll catch up with you two soon."

Nick gesturing to her then continued across the busy street.

I wasn't ready for what I was about to do. Those kids were never going to see what we saved them from. They wouldn't understand what was about to happen. They'd always see my face in their mind and remember the man who ripped them from their busy human life on earth. I'd always be a villain in their minds. Or at least in some of their minds.

But I did it anyway, because I'd rather be hated for saving them than hate myself for failing to. Nick lived it. When he looked at me a moment prior, I saw that self-hatred. And I knew I'd have plenty of that regardless. But maybe I'd have a little less if we saved those kids.

As we approached the iron gate, I said, "How do we get in?"

He glanced around the busy New York City street. He shrugged and disappeared. A woman passing by gasped, hand flying to her chest. "Help!" she screamed. "It's one of those *things*!"

I sighed and followed his trail. I landed in a busy classroom. The teacher standing by the whiteboard gasped, and his jaw fell agape. Nick put his hand on two kids' shoulders and disappeared.

I thought about telling the teacher it was going to be okay. I thought about telling him we were there to help. But that'd just waste precious time.

So I grabbed the shoulders of two second graders and hopped onto Nick's trail. The children tried to scream between their vomit as he pushed them into the swirling vortex. I grimaced as I watched their arms flail in every direction before the swirling colors enveloped their bodies.

I wanted to tell them we weren't there to hurt them. I wanted them to know that it was their rescue mission, because if the roles were reversed and someone was saving my kid from an asteroid, I wished they'd give them that superhero moment.

The one where Superman tells them, 'You're alright now.' Or the one where Spiderman stops to pause for a photo. A moment to humanize the person who'd just saved their lives.

But we weren't superheroes. We were gods. We were brunt and forceful. We did what we had to do.

It took about forty-five minutes to clear the elementary school. Had to knock out a few security guards and throw a few teachers into the breach, but we got it done. We cleared the school.

Then we moved to another. We grabbed kids and dropped them in a spinning vat of colors into another dimension. And I didn't waste time asking questions.

It felt wrong. I won't deny that. We weren't giving them a choice to reunite with their families and pass into the other dimension in a reasonable manner. But as much as the kids deserved a choice, they didn't deserve a choice at the expense of their lives. When your child refuses a vaccine, you hold them down for the doctor to jam that needle in their arm because it is in their best interest whether they realize it is or not. You don't like it. It hurts you more to do it than it hurts them. But that's why you do it. Because their safety is more important than your feelings.

I prayed that the parents separated from their children would agree once they were reunited. *If* they reunited, anyway.

Some remnant in the back of my mind questioned it from the moment we began. But after the guilt I felt from Shasta and Dunsmuir, I didn't see the point in arguing.

Nick knew what he was doing. Better than I did, that was for sure. He'd gone through it already, and I wasn't about to tell him he was wrong because I knew he wasn't. I knew me. If he was snatching kids up from their classrooms, he was doing it because it was the right thing to do.

And once we finished, I wouldn't question a second of it. Because we did it. We saved those kids. Whether they resented us for it later or not, we saved their lives.

Nick dropped to the ground before the vortex, lifted his water bottle to his lips, and chugged for a long moment. When he noticed my eyes on him, he gestured to the bottle clipped to my belt loop. "Drink. And eat that granola bar. We won't have time for a break after this for a while."

I unclipped my water bottle from my pants. Elira lowered herself beside him and tapped the grass with a smile my way. "Come on, then. Rest your legs."

I eased myself to the ground as I twisted the lid off my water and took a long gulp. My eyes moved over the dancing colors in the grass before me. Those breaches weren't little person sized holes. They were massive, spanning at least fifty feet in each direction. You could drive an eighteen-wheeler straight into it. I guess they had to be to accommodate the line of people waiting their turn to jump through.

A few hundred must have been lined up. But considering it was the closest one to the most populated city in the world, I'd expected there to be more. At least a thousand. But no. Just a few hundred. The equivalent of people rushing into a suburban Walmart on Black Friday.

"Frustrating, isn't it?" Nick glanced to the line. "They saw. They saw the news from Washington. They saw what happened to Mount Fuji. They saw us teleporting injured people to a field outside of each location. They saw it all and just look at them."

"Not even a thousand people," I murmured. "It's like they want to die."

"Nah. They just don't believe it. They probably won't until they land. By then, it'll be too late."

"Why didn't we just make them?" I asked. "We could have. We could have forced them into the portals."

"Sure," Nick muttered. "Sure, if we wanted our allies in the Fae Realm to have to detain thousands of people. We have to think about them, too. They're putting themselves out taking in all these refugees. It's not really fair to make them a part in kidnapping. That's basically what we'd be doing. It's one thing with the kids, but the adults? We can't just force-rescue them. That isn't a rescue, it's a captive situation."

"We can't take their free-will." Elira's pale eyes washed over the crowd. "None of this would matter if they didn't believe they were in danger. Even if they are about to land in a beautiful, peaceful world. They wouldn't believe it. They'd claim it as some strange concentration camp, and they'd fight. Then our brothers and sisters back home would have to kill them all anyway."

"The power of disbelief." Nick wiped water from his lip. "It's a powerful thing."

"Nick," a familiar voice called, pushing through the busy crowd. I squinted to make her out through the bright lights. "Nick, I need to talk to you for a minute."

Her short black curls were wisped back into a neat puff. She wore a bullet proof F.B.I vest over her black long-sleeved shirt and dark blue slacks. Her gun sat securely on her hip.

"What's up, Tina?" Nick yelled.

"Get over here," she said.

Nick clasped his water bottle to his hip. "Duty calls."

She sent me a warm smile and gentle wave.

"How are you doing?" Elira nudged her shoulder into mine. "Doubt well after tossing hundreds of children through this thing."

"Hanging in there."

She smiled. "Just have to hang on a little while longer. Things will be better for you soon, you know."

I took in her minty green eyes and squinted a bit. "I know I know you from back then. But I... I can't place it. Who were you to me?"

Her smile lifted higher. "It's fascinating, you know. Getting to be the happier sibling for once."

"My sister," I murmured.

"Half-sister," she said. "The legitimate first child of our mother. No offense, of course."

It didn't come as a shock. When I'd seen her and felt her energy, I'd equated it to Hannah and Leah. My sisters.

"None taken," I said. My eyes narrowed a bit. "So who's your soul-mate then?"

She laughed. "Can't tell you that."

I frowned. "Why not?"

"Because then you'd know too soon, and things meant to happen wouldn't have their chance to," she said. "It's unfortunate. I wish I could have met him sooner. But things must happen as they're meant to."

I huffed and took another gulp of my water. "I hate this. The whole being a part of this giant picture but being stuck in a timeline where I'm not allowed to know shit."

She laughed. "Opposite for me."

My head tilted to the side a bit. "How's that?"

"I've known who and what I am for as long as I've lived in this body," she said. "When I was a wee one, I used to tell my mum, 'You're not my mother. And Xander is not my brother.' And she'd say 'No? Who is your mum then?' and I'd say, 'The Queen of the Elvan Nation.'" She laughed, head shaking a bit. "And I told her that my brother was the night, and that we called him Nix. She believed that I did, in fact, live a past life. Not uncommon where we're from, you know. But she didn't believe that I was the sister to the god of the dead."

"Can't say I blame her," I muttered. "What'd she do?"

"Took me to Temple. I made jokes to the friar of how useless that place was. That the gods weren't looking down on us any longer. They'd been gone for thousands of years because of the light." She chuckled again. "And his face dropped. Religion operates there not much differently than it does here, you know. A bit more wholesome, I'll admit but the principal remains. Tithes are taken, people pay the friars for their salaries and to help the poor. And I suppose he knew what I knew, that the gods had been gone for centuries. He asked to see my mind, and I showed him. I let him access to my memories. And he fell over after only a fraction of my thoughts. Not many have room in their minds for hundreds of thousands of years of memory." She shrugged a bit. "Nevertheless, he believed me once he came to. He told my mother to do as I asked. Help me get here so that I could find you. And well." She laughed. "As they say, the rest is history."

I looked over her for a moment. "You remembered everything. Even as a child."

"I do. Heavy burden to carry, I'll admit. But I'm grateful for the weight. And I'm grateful to have this chance with you now. Because when I arrive, you'll know just who I am."

I smiled. "Yeah, I guess so." She smiled back. She took a bite of her granola bar. "So you remember our mother."

"Clearly."

"What was she like?" I asked.

"Eh." She grimaced a bit as she shifted her legs into a lotus position. "A bitch, really." I laughed, and she smiled. "But she had to be. She was a queen. And not like queens here on earth, a *true* queen. A leader of armies. She had to do what she had to for her children and for our people."

"Mm," I murmured. "And me. How did I fit into that picture? If I was the illegitimate child and everything."

"Well." She took a sip from her bottle. "You didn't have rights to the kingdom. Men didn't rule on our world. That was mine upon Mum's death, and I was already Second Queen. But she loved you all the same. As did your father, but the same rule applied. You were not all their blood, so you could not become king. He was a decent man, truly. Either way, they worked out an agreement. In this day and age, we'd call it shared custody. But you had more pull in your father's world than ours. That's why you stayed there. At least, that's what you told me. But then Véa entered the picture." She smiled, letting out a quiet laugh. "Well, that's when things got messy. But you'll see all that one day. No need for me to go on."

I huffed and leaned back onto my hands. "Weird fucking life."

"Isn't that the truth," she murmured.

"Jeremy!" Nick yelled. "Elira! We have to go!"

I squinted to see him on the other side of the breach. He pointed up.

A flash of bright orange light pierced through the dark sky. This loud, roaring sound whooshed suddenly into my ears. Almost the way it sounds when you're speeding on the highway with the windows down. A *wah-wah-wah* sound.

My stomach sunk as Nick landed in front of us. "You know what to do?"

Elira nodded as she stood. "A rough idea. Guess we'll see if it works."

He grasped either of our shoulders, and we landed inside that thick black cloud above.

CHAPTER SIXTY-NINE

LAILA

Micah and I landed in the smog above the city. The massive black rock lit up with vibrant red and orange flames. By massive, I mean *massive*. It had to have been at least the size of a school bus, maybe even a bit bigger. My mom's entire house could have fit inside of that meteor. Part of me wanted to marvel at it, because admittedly, it was pretty cool looking. A giant hunk of space junk plummeting into the atmosphere. Not a sight you see every day, and a sight only few could survive seeing so close up.

I fought my curious urge and ripped the wind from behind me into it, hoping that maybe I could blast it back into space where it came from. But no amount of air was strong enough. Air worked to counteract air and to fuel fire, but it wasn't strong. All that it did was brighten the flames.

We can teleport it. Micah's voice said in my mind. *You can get one side, and I'll take the other. Let's drop it into the middle of the Pacific.*

That could leave us with another tsunami. There has to be a better way, I thought.

The wave wouldn't hit for a few hours, and it might dissipate before it makes it to the shore.

Might. It might *dissipate. No, I don't think that's a good idea. Chances are, we'll end up having two messes we need to clean up.*

What should we do then? Air isn't enough, and if we put it out with water, it'll just reignite before it hits the ground.

It was getting closer and closer to the earth, and my heart picked up speed in my chest. We were only a few hundred feet from the ground now. My mind raced. There had to be a way. I had a million powers, one of them had to be enough.

It occurred to me.

How hot's your fire? I asked.

At least as hot as yours.

Let's burn it up then. The smaller it is, the less of an impact it'll make.

That might work.

Grab ahold of your side, and I'll get mine. I teleported myself onto the hot asteroid. My fingers reached for something to grasp ahold of, some crater or divot for my fingertips, but it was smoother than porcelain.

I used the wind to hold my body in place and ejected hot fire from my fingertips.

But nothing changed. Nothing.

It didn't char where my fingertips touched it. It didn't fall apart in ash. It stayed just as it'd been, surface burning from the kinetic energy it incurred travelling through the atmosphere. But it didn't burn.

It didn't melt.

We made no impact on it whatsoever. We burned up our clothes, but nothing more.

The two of us cradled the meteor as it drew closer and closer to the city of Los Angeles.

What do we do, Mom? Micah said into my mind.

I wished I knew.

But it was just as Nick and Lila had said. There was nothing to fight. It wasn't a battle. It was a rescue mission.

We save who we can, I answered.

But this is about to hit the middle of the city. We have to do something.

I'm open to suggestions, but I don't see an option. Do you?
Silence.
Me neither. Let it go.

I released my hold and watched it plummet closer to the city. On the opposite side in a blur of violet light, I saw Micah gripping it still. But I wasn't going to force him off of it. He was immortal; he'd survive the impact. And if he could think of a way to destroy it that I hadn't I'd be happy he did.

My stomach dropped as I watched it get closer and closer. I can still see it in slow motion. That vibrant orb of red and orange light billowing into the bright city flooded with busy cars and people jogging mindlessly to their nine-to-fives. The violet fire emitting from the left side. Then that violet light appearing beside me as the asteroid made impact.

The cloud of black smoke billowing from the crater it'd created in the middle of Hollywood boulevard.

The loudest boom I'd ever heard. One that would echo between my ears for the rest of my life.

Then Micah's quiet cry beside me as his violet flames absorbed into his skin.

<hr>

The two of us landed naked in the center of the wreckage. I looked around for a remnant of life, but I couldn't make anything out through the smog. All I could see was black dust and the sound of a car alarm somewhere in the distance. But that was good. A car alarm meant that everything hadn't been wiped out, something I couldn't tell from my bird's eye view in the sky.

A boom rang through my ears just as Micah gripped my shoulders.

The world spun around me, and we stumbled to the grass. My ears rang, and my stomach hurt as if it were the first time I'd teleported. I couldn't see at first, my vision was a cloud of white.

Cool water slapped every inch of my skin. The world spun once more. Micah shook my shoulders, eyes wide, now standing before me.

I blinked hard a few times, trying to come to grips with the world around me. His petrified face began to manifest in my vision as the world adjusted.

He had teleported us into the ocean, and then a hillside.

The ringing in my ears subsided a bit as I heard him say, "Are you okay?"

"Yeah, are you okay?"

His eyes widened. "I'm okay. I think... I think the meteor exploded."

"Jesus Christ." I struggled to my feet. Micah drew in slow, deep breaths. His gaze shifted back to the sky. My eyes followed.

It wasn't just one. Not even two. But a whole fleet.

Like shooting stars of death. Dozens, maybe somewhere close to a hundred. All plummeting toward the earth.

"Mom," he whispered, shaking hand raising to his lips.

"I see it," I murmured.

As they eased closer to the city, my stomach sunk. I wanted to close my eyes, and in hindsight, I wish that I had. But it was one of those instincts no one managed to break after centuries of no longer needing that fight or flight response.

Like driving past an accident on your way to work. You know you should keep your eyes on the road. You know that no good will come of you looking at that kind of turmoil. But you look anyway. You watch the officers standing around talking amongst themselves. You take in the damage done to the vehicle. And you watch as they roll that black tarped person into their ambulance.

That's what Micah and I did that day on that warm California mountain. We watched as hundreds of bombs disguised as asteroids flew from the atmosphere into one of the most well-known cities in the world. We watched as each one made impact like a sonic boom, sending mushroom clouds into the already dense sky above. We watched a city get blown off the map.

"Mom," Micah whispered with watery eyes, gaze turning to mine. His lips curved, and his brows pulled together. Tears erupted down his smog-colored cheeks.

He looked just like my four-year-old in that moment. Just as my baby did when he watched an episode of something he shouldn't have or when he learned that eggs were, in fact, unborn chickens. He didn't look like a nearly thirty-year-old, cool musician. He didn't look like a man. He looked like a little boy that needed his mommy.

So I kept it together. I wanted to cry and break into a million pieces. Had he not been there, I'm sure that I would have. But I couldn't. Because he needed me.

I teleported a couple blankets from the linen closet back home into my arms. I tightened one around his shoulders and the other around my own. As I fastened it around my chest like a towel at the beach, he practically fell forward. His arms went around my shoulders as quiet, grief and guilt filled cries escaped his lips.

The wet tears poured to my shoulders as I laid my head against his chest and reached up to stroke his hair. With each boom that cracked to the earth, I felt his body jolt, and I squeezed him tighter. I murmured a "shh," sound as he cried harder and harder with each impact in the distance.

I hated myself in that moment. Despite what he'd told me just moments prior, that all of this would have happened regardless of whether Jeremy and I lived to tell the tale, I hated myself. My baby was hurting. He'd already hurt so much because of things I'd done, and now he was hurting again.

Maybe it would have happened no matter what. Maybe the world was always set to be returned to the people who created it.

But the longer I thought about it, the less that I hated myself and the more that I hated Lux.

He did this. He forced us into it.

Had we had the centuries to prepare that he'd had, we could have protected millions more. We could have saved billions more lives. We could have saved the world before it even began to end.

It was his fault. It would always be *his* fault.

CHAPTER SEVENTY

JEREMY

That whooshing sound was even louder from our place in the clouds. Nick held Elira beneath her shoulders as I flew a few yards away. I looked at her, mouth moving fast, thin arms outstretched before her. Her squinted gaze locked on the projectile headed toward us I hadn't had the balls to look at.

Luminous blue and white energy shot from her palms straight ahead. I wasn't sure what it was. It wasn't quite like the energy I produced. It almost danced from her palms, like some type of beautiful laser show.

After staring at it for a moment, I followed its stream to what she directed it to. My gaze shifted higher up. An orange ball of fire ripping through thick black dust.

It was the largest sphere of flames I'd ever seen. Bigger than the skyscrapers on the ground. Maybe the size of a football field, but perhaps even larger. There was nothing proportionately to compare it to, but a football field seemed like the best estimate.

In those fractions of a second, my mind replayed a documentary I'd watched with the kids a year or so prior. It was about the extinction of the dinosaurs. In layman's terms, they explained how a seven-and-a-half-mile wide meteor hit the water in Mexico and caused an explosion so large that wiped out almost everything on our little blue rock.

How the sky turned black from the explosion. How the lack of light for a year meant lack of food. So whatever didn't die in the impact died off in the coming year before the smoke dissipated.

They talked about what would happen if a large asteroid so large hit the earth now as it had then. That NASA would warn us. That we'd surely survive it, because humans were oh-so-much smarter than dinosaurs.

That one headed toward us wasn't seven and a half miles. But it was big enough to flatten everything in a five-mile radius the moment it touched the surface. When it hit the ground, New York would be decimated.

Another thought dawned on me then. Those people knew exactly what they were doing because they'd done it before. Humans to them were the equivalent of dinosaurs to us. Beasts. Vile creatures they couldn't possibly share the land with.

It was like tenting your house for fleas or roaches. It wouldn't kill them all, but it'd get rid of the brunt of them. And it'd make picking off the rest a hell of a lot easier.

I felt like I did in the clouds above Mount Shasta. Not paralyzed, but realizing the inevitable doom.

Elira was trying. Nick was trying. But I didn't know what difference it'd make.

We couldn't stop that thing. I wasn't sure what Elira was doing, but I knew Nick and I didn't have a power strong enough to stop something even half that size.

We're running out of time, I said to Nick's mind.

Just wait, his thoughts echoed into mine.

We're running out of time, we have to—

Just fucking wait. His gaze shot to me above Elira's shoulder. *Watch and wait.*

I clenched my jaw and looked back to the massive flaming rock.

We were fucked. No other way to say it. We were completely, utterly *fucked.*

My heart picked up speed in my chest as I watched it get closer and closer. I didn't look at Elira and Nick, just the blue light slamming toward it.

It was only a few hundred feet from us then. I was sure it was going to slam into us, and we'd all get squashed beneath it like ants on a playground.

Then the unthinkable happened.

The orange flames dulled and the rock vibrated blue. It slowed to a dead stop as the blue light engulfed it. The giant black sphere pulsated, vibrating as bright as the sun behind the black cloud.

It exploded.

Black chunks flew in a million directions. One the size of a golf ball slammed to my forearm, and I felt a snap. I fought the urge to scream out in pain as I watched the pieces fall to the ground.

Some the size of cantaloupes, some the size of beach balls, some as big as pick-up trucks.

I heard Nick yell out before joyously tossing Elira into the air. She laughed as he caught her a few feet below, arms tightening around her waist as his fist pumped to the sky.

But my stomach fell.

She stopped the enormous rock. But millions of smaller ones rained down onto the city, and there was no way to stop them all.

It wasn't a win.

I looked down. I watched again. I watched as thousands of car sized boulders fell onto the densely populated city. My stomach hurt, and I grew lightheaded as I felt it all over again.

I couldn't hear it. I couldn't smell it. But my entire body ached for them.

Souls lifting from their bodies. Death. So much death. So fast. In just the blink of an eye, hundreds, maybe thousands, of people were dead.

"What are you laughing about?!" I yelled, rushing toward them. "This isn't something to be happy about, this is—"

"A small victory." Nick pulled back from Elira. "You think this is bad? How bad would it have been if she didn't stop that?"

"She didn't stop it, she just—"

"It would have wiped out *everything*." Nick's gaze shot between mine. "You knew what this was, Jeremy. We couldn't stop it. All that we could do was slow the impact."

"We just watched!" I screamed. "We just let it—"

"We did what we could," he said. "Do you know a way that we could have stopped that thing that I don't? Because that bitch breaking apart and hitting the ground in chunks was better than the whole thing hitting and killing everyone in one fail swoop." I panted out deep angry breaths as my eyes moved rapidly between his. His did the same with mine. He huffed. "There's no point in arguing about it now. More are coming. Let's get down there."

I angrily teleported to the destruction.

***

It was worse than I thought it'd be. When I first landed, I just stood still for a moment. It was worse than Washington and Shasta combined. And I hadn't gotten any better at knowing where to start.

I could hardly see a thing, let alone breathe, through the thick dust. The smell of smoke wafted into my nostrils, and the warmth of fire touched my skin. Although I couldn't see the buildings above toppling over, my body shivered with each quake as they hit the ground.

Screams and clunks and crashes and bangs all soared into my ears at once. Car alarms, yells, pleas, groans.

"Go, Jeremy," Elira yelled somewhere close, though I couldn't see her through the smoke. "Look for life."

CHAPTER SEVENTY-ONE

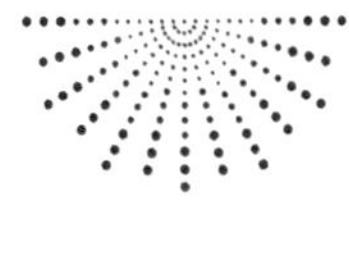

LAILA

I clamped my chattering, anxious teeth together as Micah and I landed in the city. So fun and exciting an hour before. Fruity and flowery, the city every budding artist strived to be featured in. Whether it be a struggling musician or a dancer fresh out of Julliard or an actress ready for her big break, L.A. was *the* place to achieve their dreams.

Such a cool city. Even if I did hate it personally.

But it'd quickly turned to a cemetery.

It was like something from a third world country. Something every American would see on TV and say, "Oh, that's so sad. It'd never happen here though."

Yet it did. It happened everywhere. Strategic, astrological bombs dispatched to the largest, most well-known cities in the world.

The buildings that once reached for the sky collapsed down into themselves. Portions laid in the center of the once busy roads, now littered with dozens of dead bodies. Cars were crashed into walls, bloodied figures slammed through broken windshields.

Glass coated the cracked pavement like a layer of snow. Dust and still burning ash, like that from fireworks on the Fourth of July, danced together in the thick, smoky air. Blood seeped into the rubble filled gutters along the roadsides.

With the fall of each piece of cement from a building or overpass, I could hear the sound of each impact that caused it. I smelled the now familiar scent of burned flesh, mixing with an array of chemical scents. Burning plastic, burning oil, burning wood. The scents touched my tongue, and I felt sick.

The banging of a car horn slammed into my eardrums. Screams from every direction billowed into my ears.

"Hello!"

"Help!"

"Somebody help! Please! Please *help me!*"

A nightmare. A terrible, hideous dream we wouldn't awake from. One I'd get a break from for twenty-four years, but one my son was experiencing for the second time, yet only able to recall for the first.

I looked around for a place to begin. But everywhere I looked, there was someone I could check for a pulse. I couldn't walk five steps in any direction without tripping over a body.

I turned to Micah. "I think we should call for that back-up."

He stared ahead for a moment, gaze locked on a dead woman against the cement holding a leash. But whatever was on the other end was smashed into a layer of blood and mush, seeping out from beneath a ten-foot-wide piece of cement.

I tapped his shoulder. "Micah."

He turned to me with wide, shocked eyes.

"We need back-up."

"Oh," he murmured. "Right."

His eyes closed, and his head lowered to his chest.

Never in my life had I seen such atrocities. Never in my life had I been surrounded by so much death and misery. Never in my life had I felt so much sorrow.

And that means a lot coming from a torture victim who'd saved a thousand people from captivity.

As I teleported between those carcasses checking for a pulse, though I hate to admit it, I began to understand why Peterson had done what he had.

He showed me what I was capable of. He forced me to overcome levels of anxiety I wouldn't be able to bear that day. He taught me that I could try with all of my might, but no matter how hard I fought, I'd never be able to save them all.

It was genius, really. Force me into becoming a warrior. Kindle a fire within me to hate him more than I hated anything. Take my child. Set me out on a wretched journey to bring my baby home, save hundreds of my people, and kill the man responsible for it all. Only to build me my own army of followers forever faithful to my cause after witnessing how much I'd sacrificed to save theirs, mine, and my child's life.

Yet, what I'd done for those survivors was child's play next to January 8th, 2024.

I hated him for hardening me the way he had. But I was grateful for it in the same breath.

The hours passed like seconds. Once the slew of our people arrived, things picked up even faster.

At least thirty wolves helped us smell out life. Half a dozen Witches helped us break into nooks and crannies, smoothing salves and ointments into burns and wrapping broken bones. Somewhere near twenty Guardians used their pocketbook full of powers to help in any way they could. At least fifty Demons, some I'd never dream of working beside but proved to be strong and reliable soldiers.

About six hours into the rescue, I noted the fact that none of us, victims included, were showing signs of radiation poisoning. The whole area had been bombed two times over, yet no nausea or vomiting. No diarrhea. No fevers, hair loss, headaches, dizziness, or disorientation. Micah and I may have been a bit shell-shocked. But we weren't ill.

When America dropped the bombs on Hiroshima and Nagasaki in the 40's, radiation only lingered at dangerous levels for a few hours because they exploded in the air. Yet, these exploded on the ground. And none of us had any traces of radiation. Even the wolves didn't smell it.

It was brilliant of them, really. Utilizing weapons that would have as much effect on the human race as a nuclear bomb without making the cities uninhabitable for any length of time. Yet using nukes in the atmosphere to black out the electrical grid.

They were so much smarter than us. They knew exactly how to destroy our people and our culture while keeping the planet in a perfectly livable position for themselves. It was our first rodeo, but it had to have been their millionth. That's what scared me the most.

I couldn't say what time it was because everything was dark from the moment we arrived. My Fitbit burned off when Micah and I were in the sky, although it'd make no difference anyway because the power grid was down. But it had to have been close to sixteen hours later when Micah found me in the wreckage of a car accident. He helped me fish out and heal the survivors, he pulled me aside.

"I think we both need to get some rest," he said.

"Yeah, I'll turn in soon. But you go ahead and get some sleep. I'll see you back here in a few hours."

"It's five in the morning. We've been at this for almost a day straight. We *both* need to sleep," he said. "And I don't see your water bottle, you need to eat and get hydrated."

I smiled and put my hands to my hips. "Who's the mom and who's the kid here?"

He managed out a quiet laugh. "You may technically be my mom, but I'm older. And my older mom told me to make sure you get some rest."

"Micah—"

"And she said if you won't listen to me, to go get her. And we both know she'll be a lot more forceful than I am." He smiled. "C'mon. You need to rest. I know I do, and I'm immortal."

I huffed. "Alright, fine."

"Before you do," a familiar voice said behind me. "How about that chat?"

I turned over my shoulder and smiled. Roland. His salt and pepper hair was combed back into a neat ponytail at the back of his head. He wore a pair of black denim jeans cut into shorts and nothing else. Not a shirt, not even a pair of shoes. His face was nearly black with dust and ash, but his amber eyes glistened in the luminosity from the makeshift fires lit for light throughout the streets.

"Listen to the boy, Laila," he said. "You do need to rest. My men and women will handle this for the night. But to my knowledge, you have little time left here, no? Do you still want to have that conversation?"

"Yeah, if you have a minute."

"I don't think any of us have a minute." He sighed. "But I could use a break. And you look tired."

"You know just what to say to a lady," I muttered, hands going to my hips.

"Mom," Micah said. "You need to sleep."

"This won't take long," I said. "Go ahead. I'll meet you back here in what—five hours?"

He turned to Roland and glared a bit. "Don't try to sleep with my mom."

Roland laughed. "Oh, I'll never stop trying. Doubt I'll ever succeed though."

Micah rolled his eyes and disappeared.

I turned to Roland and cocked my head to the side. "You know him?"

"We met yesterday." He smiled. "Your husband's filled him with all sorts of lies about me, you know."

"Oh yeah?" I asked. "Like what?"

"That I'm desperate for your affection." He grinned. "But you know that's not true."

"No, of course not." I smiled back. "You're just desperate to eat me."

His smile widened. "I guess the two go hand in hand, don't they?"

I rolled my eyes and fought the grin that pushed higher up my cheeks. "Let's go talk. I do need to get to sleep."

"Sure. Sure, my place then?"

"Mine's a little full." I reached my hand out for his.

CHAPTER SEVENTY-TWO

JEREMY

Wreckage doesn't come close to describing what New York City became that day. Warzone is closer, I guess. But as Nick had said, there was no battle. It was just total, complete decimation.

The city was destroyed. Skyscrapers laid on their sides. Busses were flipped over, full of dead and dying passengers. Smoke billowed into the sky every direction I looked. Fires burned everywhere. The ground shook again and again with impact after impact.

Everything was gone or falling apart.

My stomach sunk when I heard a loud collision in the sky above. I fought the urge to cry when I watched Times Square go dark from the EMP attack they'd warned us of earlier.

When the Empire State Building got hit, and I was about to teleport inside, Nick grabbed my wrist and shook his head. I asked why, and he just shook his head again. Then an explosion sounded from within. Smoke puffed from the broken glass, and it fell down as quick as the videos I'd seen of the Twin Towers.

I felt more souls slam from their bodies.

I had to teleport to the outskirts because as it went down, it destroyed everything a hundred yards in each direction.

It was overwhelming. So much was happening so fast, I didn't even get the chance to process it. I just kept grabbing shoulders and teleporting to the grass outside the vortex a few miles from the city. Teleport into an apartment complex, get the family as close together as I could, then drop them next to the swirling pit of colors.

When Elira forced me to stop for my first break ten hours in, it all dawned on me for the first time.

A knot the size of a basketball formed in the pit of my stomach. Every smell was amplified by a thousand. The burning buildings, the smoldering skin, the ash in the air.

My hands trembled as I looked at what remained of the city. I struggled to see straight, pondering if I was dreaming for a moment. Because it looked too scary to be real. It looked like an American hell.

The city that represented our country. The city known historically for welcoming immigrants from all over the world. The Big Apple burning like a pie left in the oven too long on Thanksgiving.

I thought back to the first time I'd visited New York. Dad took us shortly after Mom died. I remembered hating it. I remembered saying how much it stunk and how the people were so mean. He laughed and said we'd leave soon, but he wanted to show us somewhere first.

The Statue of Liberty. He told us the story of how it came to the United States. How it was a piece of both his side of the family's history and our mom's. How the French gave it to the Americans as an offering of peace.

I thought back to taking my own son to visit it a year before. How I told him the same story, how it was a piece of his history as much as it was mine. How his mother was American, and though I was too, since I was born in France, I considered myself French. So his heritage laid in that beautifully sculpted piece of copper too.

And I watched from the ground as a small asteroid, probably the size of a Fiat, slammed into the statue's gut. My favorite monument in the United States. Just blown to bits in less time than it took to chug a bottle of water.

I thought back to how it looked that day. The day Laila and I took the kids to see the sights. Celena gave us the best tour that only a local could. I thought about her too. And I was glad it was me that was here and not her, because she loved that city more than she loved air.

As much as I hated that city, seeing it destroyed the way that it was still shook me to my core. If they could wipe New York off the map so fast, what else could they do? What they did here was only a fraction of what they were capable of. How bad would it get when they touched down?

My head was all over the place. My thoughts were a mess of barely coherent rambles, faster than they'd ever been in my life. But as I sat there trying to catch my breath and rehydrate, I had to think about something. I had to think about anything other than what I was witnessing. I had to think about something other than the over-whelmed abyss, rapidly filling with vibrant hues of a million colors. I had to think about something other than the blood pouring into the streets like water after a hurricane.

But at some point, I couldn't distract myself any longer. The weight of reality fell quick and fast to my chest, like the meteors that rained down moments prior. It was too much. It was all just too much.

My breaths were too fast. My heart was pounding too hard. My hands were shaking more than an inmate on death row.

I just… lost it.

I erupted in violent sobs. My lips quivered, and my stomach ached. My extremities were completely numb, but they wouldn't stop shaking. I kept telling my body to relax, but it was like I had no control. My entire body was convulsing. Nothing felt real, yet everything seemed so terrifying in the same instant.

"Oh no," Elira whispered, arms moving around my shoulders. "Breathe, love. Breathe."

Hyperventilating gasps heaved into my chest.

I'd seen Laila have countless panic attacks. I knew what worked to stop hers, but I didn't know how to stop my own. I didn't even know that I could have them.

In hindsight, I do know what would have stopped it, or at least made me feel less terrified. If she were here, she could have calmed me down. But she was in midst of saving someone from a burning building herself. Even with the bond, I doubt she felt it. I never even mentioned it to her, actually.

I wasn't exactly a proud moment for me. Not that I viewed panic as a bad thing. But some part of me had been brainwashed by society to believe that men weren't supposed to have break downs. We were supposed to hold it together every second of every day, no matter what.

But I was watching the world end. I was trying to save lives, and only making a dent in the total loss.

Millions dead. Millions were dead, and millions more were dying while I sat in some dewy grass and *watched*. Yet again, I watched. I didn't act, I just *watched*.

"You're alright, love," Elira said softly. "You're alright, just breathe."

"I'm not," I whispered through trembling lips. "I'm not alright."

"You will be." Her hand rubbed my back. "Just breathe with me, alright? Close your eyes and breathe when I tell you to. Could you do that?"

"I don't know. I don't know. I-I—"

"You can," she said.

"So many people," I made out between gasps. "They're gone. They're just—"

"I know. I know, but don't think about that, okay?" she said gently. "Right now, just think about your breath. Close your eyes and listen to me. Do as I say, alright?"

I clenched my jaw tight with my eyelids.

"Breathe in until I tell you to stop," she said. "One, two, three, four. Now hold, hold that breath. One, two, three, four. And exhale. One, two, three, four. And again. One, two..."

***

I'd come to use that breathing exercise a lot in the coming days. Four-four-four, they call it. Tried, tested, and approved. Within three to four rounds, my heart rate practically cut in half. I didn't feel one hundred percent like myself. But I was a little better. I could flex and tighten my hands with ease. I wasn't struggling to catch my breath.

"There you are," Elira murmured, gingerly rubbing my upper arm. "It's alright. You're alright."

"I know I am. That's why I'm scared. Because I know I come out on the other end of this. But them." I looked at the demolished city, and my lip quivered again. I wiped snot from my nose. "They won't."

"Not if we can help it," she said softly.

"But we can't." I turned and met her gaze. "We can't save them. We —they're dying. They're all dying. Millions of people, they're all dying."

"Billions of our people died once. Your reaction then wasn't much different than it is today," she said softly. "But we bounced back. I told you we would, and we did. We came here and started anew. And we'll do that again, we'll rebuild—"

"But *them*," I said quickly, looking back to the city. "They're gone. And even if they weren't, we don't have a place to take them. We don't have a planet ready to be terraformed, we—"

"They aren't gone," she said. "Nothing is ever *gone.*"

"But they're going to take them. They're going to take their souls. That was the deal."

A half smile. "They're going to try."

"What do you mean?"

She smiled a bit wider and handed me a granola bar. "Eat, love. We'll cross that bridge when we get to it. For now, catch your breath. Drink some more water. Then we get back to work."

"But—"

"No, we focus on this moment. And we worry about the future when we get there. For now, we make it through the day. Alright?"

I looked over her firm gaze for a long moment. That me, Jeremy, didn't know her, not really. But the older part of me trusted her in a way I trusted all of my brothers and sisters. Nix knew her as Jeremy knew Hannah and Kai, and Celena and Wyatt.

So I took the granola bar, pulled back the packaging, ate it in a few bites, and chugged my bottle of water. Then Elira helped me to my feet. I took a quick piss. And we went back to ground zero.

We kept doing as we had since the asteroid first hit for the next ten hours. More of us arrived but I didn't pause to take names. None of us had the opportunity to get to know one another.

Nick and Elira were leading, technically. But there was no structure or organization to our rescues. There was no way *to* organize a situation like that. There may have been two hundred of us, and there were millions of people that needed help.

We all fanned in different directions and did whatever we could. We healed the people with bad injuries, but we left the minor ones to heal on their own. It wasn't worth wasting thirty minutes of healing time to hold someone down for a broken ankle or sprained wrist.

At some point, Nick pulled me aside and said it was time to rest. I told him that I was fine, that I could keep going. But he insisted. He said that if I didn't listen, he was going to get Lila, and she'd *make* me listen.

I reluctantly agreed to turn in for the night then.

CHAPTER SEVENTY-THREE

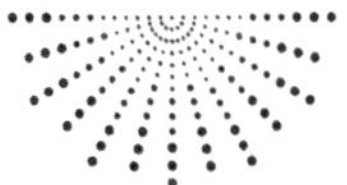

JANUARY 9 - JEREMY

When I made it home, it was early morning. I heard Rachel talking quietly to Milly and Micah in the living room and considered going out to give them a hug. But I knew that if I did, I'd fall apart all over again.

I couldn't look them in the eyes after the day I'd had. I couldn't even look at myself. The world was ending, and I watched it happen. I tried to stop it, yes, but I failed. And I couldn't let them see me like that.

I still remember instinctively reaching for the light switch. But no amount of flicking would turn it on. I walked to the bathroom and got undressed. I turned on the faucet, but it only spat and sputtered, sending small specks of water to the shower floor.

Well water relies on an electric pump. No electricity, no water. No water, no shower.

I huffed and tossed on a pair of clean sweatpants and plopped to the bed. I reached for my phone to set an alarm where I normally kept it on my side table and huffed again. I clunked backward and groaned.

No electricity, no clock.

I teleported the kitchen timer to my hand and set it for five hours.

CHAPTER SEVENTY-FOUR

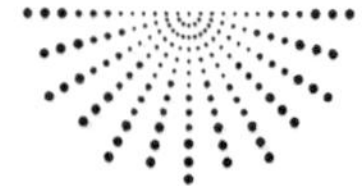

EARLY MORNING JANUARY 9 - LAILA

Roland struggled with a matchbox as I leaned against the side of his desk. He grumbled to himself, sliding the stick over the red strip again and again. I leaned forward and lit the pillar candle on the edge of the old wooden stand with my fingertip.

He sent me a gentle smile. "Thank you," I said. He walked to the bar cart beneath the large bay window. He lifted two glasses from the shelf beneath and glanced my way. "Can I get you a drink?"

"Just water, thanks," I said.

He poured some scotch into one glass and a bottle of water into another. His gaze shifted to the metal bucket in the corner. "No ice, I'm afraid."

I walked to the cart. "I like it warm anyway."

He sent me a smile as he handed me my glass. He turned to the window. I took a sip of the lukewarm liquid and followed his eyes to the thick black cloud.

"Usually has a beautiful view of the sunrise, you know," he murmured. "One of my favorites in the world. The trees over there, they cast this shadow on the ground that almost looks like a wolf. If you squint a bit." He paused. "Suppose it's a bit like looking to the clouds as a child and making pictures of them. You see what you want to."

I glanced over the trees. "No shadows anymore."

He took a long gulp from his glass. "Always hoped I wouldn't live to see the day." I turned to him and raised a brow. "The end, I mean. I suppose in a way, I hoped I would. The Monarch who ruled this region prior to myself probably wouldn't have handled it as I have. He was a bit mad."

I turned back to the black morning sky.

"I probably won't live to see the true end," he murmured. "I hope I live through the worst of it though. I'd like to guide my men and women for as long as I can."

"You don't know that," I said.

He smiled, chuckling. "I know I don't look it, but I am very old, mon ange. My days are numbered."

I raised a brow. "Are you sick?"

He laughed again, shaking his head. "No. No, I'm in good health. But I've lived for longer than any man is meant to. My time's approaching. Maybe a hundred years, maybe two. But the way things look now, maybe less so. I won't live to see the world that rises from these ashes." I felt his gaze heavy on me and turned back to him. His thick, chapped lips pulled up in a smile. "But you will."

I huffed and turned back to the field. "So I will."

He was quiet for a moment. "Perhaps in my next, I'll be fit enough as you. To attain eternal life, that is."

"Flattery will get you nowhere." I smiled. A quiet laugh eased from his lips. "I wouldn't say I'm exactly deserving of eternal life either, you know. But I can't give it to the world if I don't take it for myself. So I guess it isn't entirely egotistical."

"Yes, well, from what I know of you, you never seem to give yourself the credit you're due," he said.

I crossed my arms tighter against my chest. "I told you already. Flattery won't get you anywhere."

"Perhaps not, but I enjoy flattering you." His flirty grin stretched higher as he leaned onto the edge of the windowsill. "Fun little game we play. I run these circles around you and you try to hide your red cheeks."

I laughed and shook my head a bit.

His smile softened, and he took another gulp from his glass. "I don't usually have an affinity for women so young, you know. I thought it was the power you hold and the fury in your eyes that made you so intriguing to me. Now I see that's hardly it at all." He laughed quietly. "It does contribute in part. But genetics are the primary role at play."

I cocked my head to the side a bit. "What do you mean?"

"Your sister," he said.

"Celena?"

"The little blond pup?" He shook his head. "No. No, your eldest sister. Naomi."

My brows knitted. "Naomi? Naomi's not my sister."

He laughed a bit. "Well, your elder self said otherwise. As did she."

I huffed and leaned onto the other side of the window. "No shit." He chuckled. "She isn't in my book though."

Huh. I supposed it made sense. There was a correlation with DNA and the par animarum.

And nothing surprised me with Mary anymore. I knew she'd probably had many children over the years, as Moe had said, but he only listed the ones he knew of.

"Your book?"

"A journal from an old friend. The one who left me my diner. When he was murdered, he left a journal to me. In the back, he had a list of my siblings. Kai Callidy, Celena Jones, and one more. Adeline. No last name for her though, so I never tracked her down. But Naomi wasn't in there."

"Well, was your friend human?"

"Fae," I said.

"Short life span then," he said. "Naomi isn't exactly green, either. She was probably born decades before your friend."

"Mm," I murmured. "How do you know Naomi, anyway?"

He smiled and turned back to the field. "Old friends, you could say." I raised a brow, and he caught my gaze. He chuckled. "Naomi is the only woman I've ever loved. But she met Connor and, well." He took a gulp from his glass. "No one could compare. Didn't know why then, but I accepted it with grace. You know what they say. If you love someone, let them go."

"Noble of you."

He took another drink, gaze turning back to the grassy pasture against the black sky. "But what is it that you wanted this meeting for? You weren't specific in your message. I'm not in trouble, am I?"

I smiled. "No. No, the opposite actually. I wanted to get your advice on something."

"Oh?" He cocked his head to the side. "And what's that?"

"Your leadership." I sat my glass on the sill and crossed one leg over the other. "You're a damn good Monarch. Your people respect you. They look to you with love, but they also understand the risks of crossing you. You've laid down a set of laws, and they follow it. They fear you, but they're loyal to you."

He took another sip of his scotch. "And you want to know how I've done it?"

"Or just some helpful hints," I said. "I'll take any wisdom you can pass down. You've been at this for a long while, and you know what you're doing. I'm just getting my toes wet."

Roland filled his glass and took a sip. "Well, I'm no parent. But I imagine governing all these people is somewhat equivalent to being a father to a lot of children. Certainly feels that way some days. And you do that very well. I'm sure you'll make a good leader."

"Eh. Well, I'm glad you think so. But you haven't seen me with my kids often. You can't really be the judge there," I said. "Regardless, I need specifics. What did you do to become the leader you are? How do you manage all of these wolves like it's second nature?"

"I'm a born alpha," he said. "Just as you are a born leader. It's instinctive. You do what your intuition tells you is best."

I huffed. "My intuition wasn't so great the other day. Forced a bunch of bigots to their knees and caused quite a raucous for my older self."

"Oh, that video all over the internet?" He grinned. "I thought that was inspiring."

"You would." I rolled my eyes. "But it really pissed her off. And in hindsight, I agree. It was a bad move."

"I completely disagree," he said. "You didn't hurt anyone. You showed them who they were messing with. The media played it up to make you look like a dictator. But they're good at scare tactics. In the end, that scenario strengthened your role with *your* people. My people. The humans are fearful of all, but it was important for your reputation to make it clear where your loyalty lies."

I turned my head to the side, squinting. "My loyalty is with all the people. *All* people, not just ours. I care for the humans too."

"Of course. But again, you didn't hurt those people. You made a point. Maybe they did piss themselves in fear, but only fear as a whole of what you *are*, not of what you did." I made a face, waiting for him to go on. He brushed his fingertips along his scruff. "The world isn't going to be what we're accustomed to, any of us. What you did was teach them a lesson they needed to learn. Stomping their feet and crying to the sky is not going to solve anything. Perhaps you were painted as a villain, but how much would you like to bet that those same men loaded their families into their pick-up trucks and drove to the closest breach?"

"Maybe they did, maybe they didn't. Regardless, I would have handled it differently if I had another chance," I said. "Look, are there...Do you have a list of rules you follow? Some code of conduct to being a leader? Something you tell your alphas when they take on a pack?"

He thought for a moment as he sipped his drink. "The first thing I tell them is to be consistent. Whatever rules you do lay out for your people, stick to them, and abide by them yourself. No one wants to be governed by a hypocrite. Despite whoever you are, your statutes cannot be any more to expect of your people than you would expect for yourself if someone else was setting them."

"Consistency. Got it. That one definitely aligns with parenthood."

He tapped his finger against his glass and thought for another moment. "I always tell a new alpha to choose their trials carefully. There is no use in causing a war over a small indiscretion. But again, that goes hand in hand with consistency. If someone breaks a law you set forth more than once, or if it is one of most importance to you, you *must* make an example of them. That is important. But again, choose your trials carefully."

"Pick your battles," I murmured. "So the opposite of what I did the other night."

"Perhaps. But not necessarily. Had you done or said nothing to those men, you'd be making an example then too. You'd be showing that they were stronger than your people, stronger than your soldiers. The people they should be putting their trust in," he said. "That was a battle worth fighting if you ask me. But some are not."

"Such as?" I asked.

Again, he was quiet for a long moment. "We as leaders, as honest, *transparent* leaders cannot be hypocrites. But my people, we are animals. You don't toss a coyote into a field of chickens and expect them not to eat. That will be different now, obviously. Food is scarcer than it's ever been; my wolves will have to survive on what they can scrounge. But the fact remains. We must drink blood to survive, so I don't penalize anyone for killing so long as it's done to eat and not for the purpose of sadism."

Obviously, I couldn't tolerate cold blooded murder. But I did understand what he was saying.

I glanced out the window. "I only kill when it's justified. But I see your point. Nutrition is a justifiable reason. Still, options are limited now. Your packs can't be snacking on hikers anymore."

"That will be a trial I have to choose to fight," he murmured. "But if I can survive without my preferred meat, as can they."

I was quiet for a moment, wondering what else there was to ask. "Is that all?"

"One more important rule."

"And what's that?" I asked.

"You are their leader as much as they are yours. You may not have been elected to your position, mon ange, but you should always act as if you were. You should always act as if you could be voted out." His eyes moved gingerly between mine. "No true ruler wants blind followers. At least, they shouldn't. Blind following can quickly lead to blind hate. Make your stance clear. But listen when you've done something to hurt your people. And apologize when it's necessary. Admitting to imperfection is not a sign of weakness. It is a sign of strength and growth."

I thought long and hard for a moment. So far, I had followed that one already. When I told all the survivors what I thought of Peterson's plan, when we told the Chambers the truth.

"I like that rule."

"The best for last." He sent a gentle smile. "But as I'm sure you are, I'm a bit depleted. I think it's about time I turn in."

"Sure. Sure, thank you for your time." I set my glass on the drink cart. "I appreciate it."

He stood and extended his hand out to mine. I reached forward to shake it, but he pulled it to his lips and kissed my knuckles. As he released it, he lowered his upper half in a bow.

"The pleasure was all mine." He smiled and straightened back up. "Until we meet again, mon ange."

I smiled. "Goodbye, Roland."

I teleported home.

Jeremy lay outstretched on the bed, not even covering his filthy body with a blanket. He never went to bed without a shower. I noted the lack of light from the clock on the dresser and the dark ceiling, usually blinking red from the smoke detector.

No electricity. The electromagnetic pulse hadn't passed our home. Meaning there was no way for me to shower either.

I grunted and dropped to the bed beside him.

CHAPTER SEVENTY-FIVE

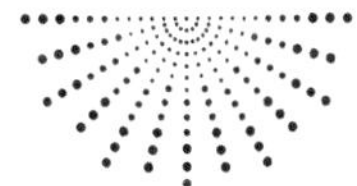

MID-AFTERNOON JANUARY 9 - JEREMY

When the kitchen timer buzzed, it took everything in me to sit up. I wasn't ready for another day of hell, but I knew I had to face it. Laila was beside me battling her way to the edge of the bed a moment later.

She said good morning and asked if I wanted anything for breakfast, though I think it was technically lunchtime. I reluctantly said sure. I stammered to the dresser and stepped into some jeans and pulled a T-shirt over my head.

When she made it back to the bedroom and handed me a tomato sandwich, she asked if I was okay. I'm pretty sure she knew that I wasn't. But I struggled a smile.

She asked if I wanted to talk. I did, but I couldn't. If I started to talk, I'd break down. If I broke down, I wouldn't be able to get back to New York and help.

So I held that forced smile a moment longer. She touched her lips to my forehead. She sat beside me, and we ate our sandwiches together quietly.

She tried to start a conversation a few times. She asked if there was anything in particular I wanted her to pack for me, but I just shook my head again. She told me she'd spoken with Roland. I said that was good, barely hearing the story as she told it.

But that quick remark was all that I could make out. A knot the size of a fist formed in the back of my throat the night prior and hadn't left since. When I did manage out a word or two, my voice cracked, and I had to disguise it with a cough.

Once we were done eating, she wrapped her arms around my chest. That embrace was the first shred of relief I'd had since it started. But as good as it felt, I started to feel guilty for it.

Wasting time. I was wasting time. Every moment I wasn't in that city, I was wasting time. Every second that I held her and she held me, another person died.

So I pulled away and kissed her forehead. I told her I'd see her later and disappeared.

Back to the rubble. Back to ground zero. Back to a dying city.

It all started to blur together on day two. I didn't even think about it anymore. I just teleported back into fallen buildings and dragged people from beneath pillars of fallen cement and ceilings.

Everything felt numb and unreal, yet terrifying and pained in the same instant. That description sounds like an oxymoron, and maybe it is. But it's one anyone who's suffered from anxiety or PTSD can understand perfectly.

I tried not to look at the people's faces that I saved and struggled even harder not to look at the people that I couldn't, because when I looked at them, my eyes became the source of waterfalls. That lump in my throat got thicker, and my chest got tighter.

Not thinking about it hurt just as much as thinking about it. No matter what I did, it hurt. Everything hurt.

Every moment that passed, I felt the abyss getting fuller and brighter. That made it even worse. An ability that constantly reminded me of our failure.

But I pushed on. Because there was no other option.

I took breaks when Nick or Elira told me to. I drank the water. I ate the granola bars. I got back to work.

CHAPTER SEVENTY-SIX

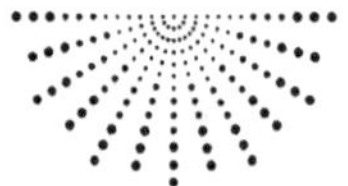

MID-DAY JANUARY 10TH - JEREMY

Some twenty hours later, Nick told me it was time to turn in. I finished healing the man I'd been working on, brushed off my jeans, and was about to teleport when he grabbed my shoulder.

"Are you alright, man?" he asked.

"You know I'm not," I said. "I'm falling apart. But I'd be even worse if I weren't here helping so that's what I'm gonna do. I'll get some rest and be back in a few hours."

He looked carefully between my eyes. "Sure. Sure, but why don't you and Lai finish packing your bags tonight? You only have the rest of today and tomorrow left, you're leaving—"

"I'll do that a few hours before we leave," I said.

"Jeremy—"

"If I do it now, I'm going to have a break down. That's just another thing that's going to make me panic. I'm taking this one battle at a time."

"Alright. I understand. I did the same thing when I was you. But maybe you should go get a bath. I know you don't have water, but you could go take a dip in the creek down the trail—"

"I'm good. Just gonna get some sleep and I'll be back."

"Jeremy—"

"Dude, you know what I'm gonna sas, and you know what I'm gonna do," I snapped. "Is it worth arguing with yourself? We both know you won't convince me to practice some self-care right now."

He cleared his throat. "I was just gonna tell you that you have a gash on your head. Want me to heal it?"

I rubbed my forehead and winced at the laceration above my right eyebrow. "Fuck. Didn't realize that was my blood."

"Here, let me." He lifted his hand, but I pulled back.

"I'm fine. Go save someone. I'll be back."

He opened his mouth to speak again, but I was already falling onto the pillows of my bed. I set the kitchen timer for five hours, closed my eyes, and fell fast into a deep sleep.

I heard what they said the other day. I listened when they said you couldn't pour from an empty cup. But my glass was drier than the dust covered cities worldwide, and I was still spilling into other's.

CHAPTER SEVENTY-SEVEN

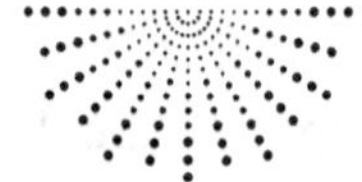

MID-DAY JANUARY 9 - LAILA

When I landed back in the destroyed city once known as Los Angeles, I struggled to grip reality for a moment. I knew what I was walking into, I'd witnessed the disparity as it happened. But somehow, it was still a shock.

It didn't look like a city any longer. Only a few buildings out of the thousands there still stood. Mounds of rubble littered with sprays of red were all that remained.

Fires lit the streets, although dulled by a layer of thick, gray haze. The terrifying sounds of screams and groans floated through it, echoing in every direction. I could hear my people, yelling things like, *"Over here!"* and *"I found another one!"*

Although warm, I felt cold. Fires burned in every direction, yet a chill eased up my spine and rose against my dry arms in a layer of tiny bumps.

I could literally smell the death now. Decay muddled with burned flesh wafted into my nose. The bodies of those we couldn't save had begun to fester. Rats scurried the ground, feasting on the corpses all over the debris coated road.

The smell was so strong, I could almost taste it. My stomach spun, and I continually swallowed down bile that rose to my esophagus. Physically, I knew that I was fine, but I felt sick.

Nonetheless, I got to work. I followed the sound of muffled pleas and cries for help to a building that collapsed in upon itself. As I teleported into the rubble, I realized I'd been within the same building the day before.

The young man crying for help had been trapped there for more than a day. I couldn't tell you how we missed him. Perhaps the wolves couldn't pick up on a good scent because of the smoke. Maybe he was unconscious when we were there, and we mistook him for dead. Regardless, I followed the sound of his screams.

"Help me!" his desperate cry cracked. "Somebody help me! Please, somebody!"

"Where are you?" I called, looking frantically through the dark building.

"Hey! Hey, over here!" Joy touched his voice. "I'm over here, I'm over here!"

"I'm coming." I guided myself through the pile of debris with a ball of violet light. "I'm coming, but I don't see you. Can you describe whatever's around you for me?"

"It's dark," he said. "It's-it's dark, and my phone won't turn on."

I looked down at the mound of rubble beneath my feet, surely full of caverns large enough to hold a person.

"Are you there?" he yelled. "God, please don't leave me. Don't leave me. I don't want to die. Fuck, I don't want to die. I don't want to die—"

"I'm not leaving you," I said. "I'm gonna find you, just calm down, alright?"

"I don't want to die," he said again. "I don't want to die. I'm too young to die. I—"

"How old are you?" I asked, trying to distract him from the inevitable fear coursing through his voice.

"I-I'm twenty-six," he said. "I just moved here last month. My-my mom told me not to. She said to find a job closer to home, but I-I... I should have listened."

"Hey, I'm twenty-six too." I climbed over a large steel beam. "Well, I will be in a few weeks."

"My mom was right." He started to cry again. "She-she's always right. Moms are always right, and we-we never listen. I should have listened. Now I'm gonna die. I'm gonna die. Just like Grace died." His cries got louder. "Grace's dead. She's dead, and now I'm gonna die with her."

"You aren't gonna die." I followed the sound of his voice, approaching a large pile of cement. "I just have to get to you, and I'll get you out of here. Are you hurt?"

"Yeah," he said. "Yeah, my leg's crushed, I can't move. Is there—is there a way to lift it? Is there—is there, like, a tool for this?"

"Something like that." I teleported to the other side of the pile. "Keep talking for me, hon."

"I'm over here," he said. "Over here."

"Is it just your legs?" I asked. "Is that the only place you're hurt?"

"I-I have some cuts and stuff but yeah, just my legs mainly," he said.

"Good, that's good." I looked around with my violet flames. Still no sign of life aside from his voice. I was close, I could tell by the sound, but if he was pinned and couldn't see, he must have been at least somewhat barricaded. "Alright, I need you to do something for me. I need you to close your eyes and think the world 'Laila' over and over. Can you do that?"

"What? What—why?" he asked. "How is that—"

"Just do it, alright?" I asked. "Just close your eyes and think the word 'Laila.'"

"How is that going to—"

"Do you want me to get you out of here or not?" I asked. "Don't argue with me, just do as I say."

"Don't leave. I'll do it. I'll-I'll do it."

I closed my eyes and focused. There was so much chatter in the minds of the countless other people still trapped. Focusing on any one person's thoughts was close to impossible. Unless I was searching for a keyword.

Laila, I heard. *Laila, Laila, Laila.*

The door to his mind opened to me. I stepped through and focused on his energy. I teleported to him.

My hand ignited in the small cavern between layers of cement. I couldn't make out his features in the dim light, nor did I care to in the moment. "See? That easy." I smiled.

His eyes shot open, and he jumped. He looked at the ball of light in my hand and shifted back, screaming in pain when he writhed against the cement that held him in place.

"Sh-sh-sh," I murmured as I shined the light toward his legs. There was no saving them. His foot was crushed far beneath a large barricade of cement. Yet, that cement was the only thing keeping him from bleeding out. My gaze shifted back up to his.

"What are you?" he barely whispered, eyes frozen in fear.

"Long story," I muttered.

"That girl," he said. "That girl in the video. That was you, wasn't it?"

I ignored him and eyed his legs a moment longer. "I'm gonna get you out from under here, but your foot's gone. Your leg might be too. I can't tell how much damage is done from here."

"Are you an Angel?" he asked. "Or are you-are you a Demon?"

I sighed and turned my eyes up to his. "I'm actually a god."

He blinked hard. "No shit."

"No shit."

"I'm catholic," he said. "My parents are, anyway."

"Yeah, well that god's a dick," I muttered. "But listen to me, alright? I'm gonna get you out of here, but when I do, you're gonna be in tremendous pain. I can heal you; it'll stop the bleeding. But it's gonna hurt like a son of a bitch. Are you ready for that?"

"It's gonna hurt more than this?"

"Way more."

His lips quivered, and he started to cry. "And my foot's gone?"

I pressed my lips together.

"And you can't heal that?" he whispered.

"I'm sorry. But no, I can't. I can save your life though."

Tears poured from his eyes, and his forehead wrinkled. He nodded.

I touched his bloody hand and teleported to the dust covered road outside. He screamed the loudest, ear-piercing scream as I climbed on top of his legs and started healing.

I was about eight hours in when I took my first break with Micah on the side of the road. I looked over the city a moment longer. My eyes steadied on a palm tree standing high and proud along the destroyed street. Everything around it was crumbled to rubble and ash, yet that palm tree still stood. I wondered how it survived. I thought about the boy trapped beneath the cement, and a woman and child I'd pulled from a burning car, and I wondered the same.

I thought about how the city looked when we first arrived. All the glitz, all the glamour, all the beauty. How none of that mattered. How it all was destroyed in such little time, and how that palm tree still stood.

Some things will always outlive their supposed stronger counterparts. Those cement, earthquake resistant buildings deteriorated. But not everything would. Life will always rise from the ashes of death. And that thought gave me hope.

I didn't know how. I didn't know when. But that palm tree reminded me that one day, all of this would end. We'd pull through and we would rebuild the world we loved.

CHAPTER SEVENTY-EIGHT

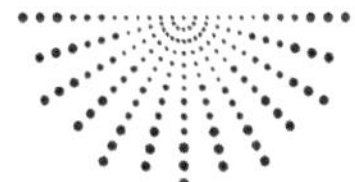

EVENING JANUARY 9TH - LAILA

I caught fire pulling two men from a burning car a few hours after my first break. My clothes burned with it. I didn't mind working in the nude, but it seemed a bit distracting to the men and women working beside me.

Nonetheless, it was approaching time for me to take another break anyway. So I teleported to my bedroom to change my clothes. As I landed, a quiet gasp echoed to my ears.

"Mommy," Micah whispered.

My stomach sunk as I turned to meet his gaze. Micah, Milly, and Mom sat on the floor beside a few open suitcases. Their eyes were as wide as the sky, light from my thousand candles glistening against them.

Mom's mouth fell and shut as she struggled to make words.

But my children's wide eyes sent a shiver down my spine.

Somehow, of all the horrible things I'd seen since it all began, this hurt the worst. My babies—my tiny, innocent babies—looking up at me in this state.

I hadn't looked in a mirror in well more than a day. But I felt soot all over my naked body. There was blood, and ash, and decay, and I knew I must have been a scary sight to see to anyone, but especially to such young children. I couldn't begin to image what was going through their little minds.

"Mommy," Micah whispered. He erupted in cries.

"Oh, baby." I dropped to the ground.

"We were packing," Mom made out. "I-I didn't think you'd be back, we were just—"

"It's okay," I said. "It's okay, Mom."

"What's happening?" Micah whispered as his lips curved down, and his teeth chattered. "Is you okay? Is you hurt?"

I pushed hair behind his ears and thumbed his tears away. "No, I'm okay. I'm okay, baby, I'm okay."

"You don't look okay."

"I am." I forced a smile. "I know I look kinda scary right now, but I'm okay. I'm not hurt."

"Where's Daddy?" he said. "I haven't seen him in so long. The lights went out yesterday, and they-they won't come back. It's scary, I'm scared."

"Oh, sweetie," I whispered. "It's okay, this is all gonna be over soon. It's okay, you're okay. We're all gonna be okay."

"Where's Daddy?" Water rained down his cheeks. "I need Daddy."

My eyes softened. "He's helping people. He'll be home later, I promise. Not tomorrow but the next day, this is gonna be over and things will calm down again."

His lip quivered as he reached forward to hug me. His little arms wrapped around my neck, and he squeezed. I rubbed the back of his hair and met Milly's gaze in the low light. Her eyes were wide and scared, but she didn't cry. She just stared at me.

I gestured for her to come closer. She stood and toddled to us. Her arms twisted around her brother's torso as her head fell to my other shoulder.

Mom met my gaze and teared up. "I'm sorry," she mouthed.

"It's okay," I mouthed back.

Ironic, I suppose. How I managed pulling dying people from the wreckage in a demolished city with a slow, steady heartbeat and still hands. But seeing my little boy so petrified made my stomach hurt and my eyes fill with water.

I held the kids for a few long moments. Once Micah stopped crying, I inched back and kissed his forehead with a reassuring smile. I told him everything was gonna be okay. But I had to get back and help more people. He wasn't exactly happy about it, but he toughened up and said he'd keep watching Milly and Gam for me.

I kissed Milly and tickled her sides. She giggled, bashfully lowered her chin to her chest, and kissed my cheek. I smiled wide and told her that me and Daddy would be home soon.

I stood and started to the closet. Mom told the kids to stay put for a moment and followed.

"I'm so sorry, Lai," Mom whispered. "I didn't know you'd be back. I was just making a game of packing. Micah's not doing so good, I was just trying to distract him."

Heart dropping, I lifted my shirt over my head. "What do you mean he's not doing so good?"

Her lips pressed together, gaze falling to the floor. She rubbed the side of her temple. "He just keeps crying. Out of nowhere, he just... cries. I don't know how else to say it. He's really worried about Jeremy though. He keeps saying that he needs to see his dad."

I frowned. It was a relief to hear that it was about Jeremy and not something else, but it was still far from ideal. "I'm pretty worried about Jeremy, too. He's...he's not handling this well at all. I barely got a word out of him when we left this afternoon. It's like he's not even here. Micah's telepathic and empathetic. He's probably feeding off of that."

"Maybe," she murmured. "I've been telling them that this is all gonna be over soon. It helped at first, but I don't think it is anymore."

"Probably not," I muttered. "Have you told them goodbye yet?"

Her gaze fell again. "No. No, I'm gonna do that tomorrow before I put them to bed. They don't need to worry about that too just yet."

"Good call," I said.

"That's what I figured too."

I struggled my jeans up my hips and sucked in to button the clasp. "If you hear Jeremy come in and you're still up, can you try to get him to eat something? I know pickings are thin without the fridge but even some dry cereal or something."

"Sure, hon."

As I situated my shirt around my hips, I felt her gaze on me and looked up. A smile pulled at my lips. "What?"

Mom smiled back. "Just you. Doing all of this. Fighting so hard and staying so strong through it." She wiped the corner of her eye. "I'm just so proud of you."

I smiled. "Thanks, Mom."

Her nostrils flared as she pressed her lips to a tight line. Water poured from her eyes, and I frowned. "C'mon, Mom, no sappy goodbyes. If you cry, I'm gonna cry, and I can't cry right now."

"I'm just so sorry," she whispered. "I just—I want you to know that I'm sorry I'm not coming with you. I'm sorry for how much I'm going to miss, and I'm sorry I won't be there to help you with your babies. I'm sorry I won't get to watch my grandbabies grow. I'm sorry I won't be there to hold your hand when the next one comes, and I'm sorry—"

"Mom." I leaned forward and took her hands. "No sappy goodbyes."

She tried to smile through the tears. "No sappy goodbyes."

I smiled wider and leaned forward. "I love you."

"I love you too," she whispered. "I love you so much."

I hugged her for a few seconds. Finally, I pulled back, still holding my smile. My thumb rubbed against the back of hers, and I let go.

I walked back into the bedroom and squatted between Micah and Milly. "I'll be home later, but you'll probably be asleep. But can you do me *huge* favor while I'm gone?" Micah nodded. "Can you find some tiny stuff laying around the house that your daddy *really* loves and pack it up for me? Nothing too big so we still have room for his clothes and stuff but some stuff that you know he really likes."

Micah thought for a moment. "Yeah, I can do that."

I smiled. "Thank you, buddy." I touched my lips to his forehead and then to Milly's. As I started to my feet, Micah spoke.

"But, Mommy?" he said.

"Yeah, baby?" I asked.

"Daddy doesn't like to be alone when he's sad, okay?" His eyes moved back and forth between mine. "I know you do but Daddy doesn't. He told me."

My heart grew three times its size, and I had to fight back tears of adoration. "I know, kiddo."

"So you have to find him when you can because he needs you," he said. "He needs you, Mommy."

My eyes glistened with tears. "I know. And I will. Don't worry about Daddy, alright? I'll take care of him."

He nodded softly.

"I love you guys. And I'll see you real soon. Be good for Gam," I said.

"I will. I'll take care of them, you'll see." Micah wrapped his arm around his sister's shoulder. Milly glared at him, pulling out from beneath his arm.

I smiled. "I know you will."

January 9th quickly turned to January 10th. I continued taking regular breaks between rescues, but Micah didn't force me to leave. His concept of time seemed to dissipate as well.

It was almost busier than the day of initial rescues. I'm not sure why. Maybe because we'd developed a decent groove and had adjusted to the fast-pace. Neither of us were as emotionally drained as we'd been when it began, and maybe that played a part too.

After long enough, situations like those just become a matter of rinse and repeat. I couldn't count how many scenarios I faced like the one with the man whose foot got smashed beneath the cement in those following days.

It hurt. Despite my composed, bubbly demeanor, it did hurt. But I was good with stressful situations. My anxiety around strenuous times always came after the fact, never during. I could handle it in the moment when I was needed.

Although, as much as it pains me to admit, all of that death, all of those bleeding souls, every moment of it was easier than what happened five years prior. Losing my son was ten times as hard as saving those lives. Maybe that was because I was selfish and loved my children more than I loved anything. Or maybe it was because at that point, I'd trained myself to deal with such atrocities.

CHAPTER SEVENTY-NINE

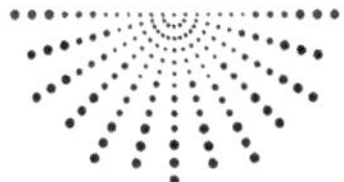

LATE NIGHT JANUARY 10TH - LAILA

"Mom," Micah said as I lowered a woman to the ground beside the spinning vortex. "Mom, I think I have to turn in."

I straightened up and took a few steps away, ushering him with a hand on his shoulder. "Are you alright?"

He rubbed his droopy eyes. "Yeah, I'm good. Just burnt out. I've been at this for too long. We should have stopped hours ago. It's been more than a day straight now."

I rolled my head to either side to crack my neck. "Yeah, I'm beat. My back's killing me, and I'm starting to get a little dizzy. I agree. We should get some rest."

"Yeah. I told my friend to cover for us while we're gone. He'll handle things until we get back. But before we go, I wanna talk to you for a minute."

"Oh yeah?" I turned my head to the side. "What about?"

His gaze shifted between mine for a moment. I could see his thoughts twisting behind his electric eyes, struggling to make the words he wanted to. "We're gonna be busy tomorrow. Like we were today and everything."

"Sure." I waited for him to go on. He ran his hand against the back of his neck. "Is something wrong?"

"No," he said. "I mean, not more than anything else that's going on here."

"What's the matter then?" I asked. "I know that face, what is it?"

He turned his gaze to the ground. He cleared his throat and gave an intense, blunt expression. "I just have to tell you this before you go back."

"Alright," I said. Silence continued, and I laughed. "Ready when you are."

His face was still serious. Not angry, not harsh, just not so bubbly. "When I meet Avery and Asher, don't tell me."

I tilted my head to the side. "Don't tell you what?"

He drew in a deep breath and shook his head. "Just don't tell me."

"But what do you mean?"

"You'll know." He pressed his lips together. "Just...things happen the way they're meant to. So don't tell me."

My head cocked further to the side. "But, sweetie, I—"

"You heard what I said, right?" he asked, eyes moving gently between mine.

I stared at him for a moment, hoping he would explain more but realizing that he wouldn't. "Yeah. I heard you."

A smile came to his lips. "Okay. I'll see you back here tomorrow then."

"Micah—"

"Love you." He smiled wider and disappeared.

A huff left me. I placed my hands at my hips and shook my head. I teleported home.

CHAPTER EIGHTY

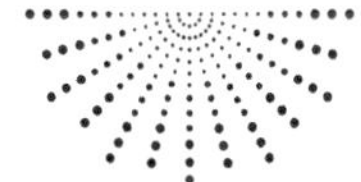

EARLY JANUARY 11 - JEREMY

Just as the kitchen timer sounded, Laila collapsed to the bed beside me. She lifted a ball of violet fire to the air for a light source. I sat forward. The flames dissipated when I touched my lips to hers. She barely had the energy to lean up and kiss me back, but she did. When I started to pull away, her forehead bumped mine, and a stabbing pain throbbed through my head. She murmured an "ow" as I leaned up to get dressed.

But she grabbed my wrist and yanked me closer.

"Baby, I have to go," I said.

Her palm went up in flames. "No, you have to let me look at that." Her brows furrowed far over her bloodshot eyes in the dim light. They moved quickly over the gash above my eye. "That looks bad, why didn't you get it healed?"

"A lot of people need more healing than this." I pushed her hand away. "It's nothing. You can heal it tonight when we get the rest of our shit together."

"It isn't nothing." She sat forward, squinted, and cupped my cheek in her hand. "It's yellow and pussing. Jesus, why didn't I feel it?"

"I don't know, probably because I don't," I muttered. "Lot of adrenaline pumping these past few days. But I'm fine, really. You can—"

"You can sit your ass down and let me clean this." Her bright eyes turned to mine. "I know that you want to get back there but this needs—"

"It won't kill me by this time tomorrow when we're going to be safe in another time," I said quickly.

"I'm fixing this. The longer you argue with me, the longer until you can get back out there."

"Laila—"

"Don't argue with me, Jeremy." Laila's pitch sharpened. "I've had a long ass day, too. And you aren't going to die from an infection that spread to your brain before I get the chance to make you immortal. Sit your ass down and hold a flame up for me. Now."

"Lai, I'm—"

"Going to listen to your wife? Great, thank you. I'd appreciate that." She used the same tone she took with Micah and Milly when they wouldn't cooperate.

I sat on the bed in front of her. My hand lit with vibrant, spinning shades of blue electricity. "Happy?"

"Ecstatic." She sat up and teleported a few rags and a bottle of rubbing alcohol from the bathroom to her lap. "I don't want to blind you with this. Lay your head down."

"Babe—"

"Stop making this more complicated than it has to be, Jeremy," she said.

I knew better than to argue.

I huffed and lifted my legs back to the bed. They hung off the end as I rested my head into her lap. She pushed hair from my face and tucked it behind my ear.

"Hold the light a little closer, please."

I lifted my hand to my chest and angled it near my face. My eyes met her focused gaze in the soft blue light as she twisted the lid off the plastic bottle. "That better?" I asked.

"Yeah, that's perfect. Close your eyes for me."

I shut them and kept the light firm against my chest. The feel of her skin against mine brought me more comfort than anything had since the volcano. It didn't make any of the heartache go away, but it made it feel bearable for a moment. Peaceful, and relaxed. I wished I could stay there with my head in her lap, but neither of us could, and it almost made it easier to not feel her touch at all.

"I'm not trying to be a dick, I'm just—"

"Scared for the people out there. I know. I'm going through it too," she murmured. "But we're not immortal yet. Our wounds can still kill us."

I nodded slightly.

"Alright, keep them closed," she said.

The cold liquid touched my forehead and burned like fire as it seeped into the open flesh. I winced and pushed my eyes closer together. Deep breaths panted out of my nose as she doused it again. She lathered the rough cloth into the wound, and I groaned.

"Fuck, why do you have to rub so hard?" I spit as the alcohol ran into my mouth.

"Because you should have had it healed before infection set in. God only knows what kind of bacteria's in this thing."

I clamped my teeth tight together and pushed out deep breaths. "Since when do you need to clean a wound before you heal it anyway?"

"Again, shit head. Since you let infection set it," she said, battling the pain in her own head as she poured more alcohol to the wound.

"God damn," I murmured. "Fuck, I forgot how much this hurts."

"You're telling me," she said. "I haven't felt anything burn in years."

I grimaced as she rubbed some more. "I'm sorry. I didn't realize it was bad. I didn't feel it when it happened, and I just crashed when I got home."

"It's alright. Pretty sure I have some floating around too." The rag dug deeper into the gash for a moment before she lifted it away. "I think I got all the puss out. Let me heal it real quick."

Her fingertips touched my forehead. That white hot, radiating pain vibrated into my skin. I shuddered at the agony and panted out deep breaths. Another rag slid along my eyes as she spoke again.

"Alright, you're done. Just keep your eyes closed long enough for that alcohol to evaporate."

I nodded.

"While I have you here, I know they said to be back by eleven. But try and get here by ten. We have to get cleaned up before the kids see us or they'll be more terrified than they already are."

I opened my eyes and instantly regretted it when the burn soared through them.

"Jesus fuck, I told you to keep them closed, damn it," she said.

"Sorry." I rubbed my eyes "But the kids, they're scared?"

"Yeah, to put it mildly. I stopped by earlier to get changed. I'd caught fire, and it's kind of hard to navigate a war zone naked. They were in here with Mom, and they saw me. I was covered in blood and dust and..." She paused. "Anyway, I told them it was okay, but yeah, they're kind of a mess. They started freaking out when the power grid went down, Mom said. Micah's been just...I guess he's been just breaking out in tears a lot. I don't know what he's seeing, but Mom tells him it's just a bad dream."

That hurt. It hurt a lot. But I still had to get through this last day, and I couldn't think about that right now. Because if I did, I wouldn't be able to leave to do what needed done.

I rubbed a hand down my face. "I wish we could be there for them right now. I haven't been away from Milly this long since she was born, and Micah since we got him back. But I can't be around them during this. I want to, ya know, but I just..."

"No, I know," she murmured. "We just have to make it through today. Or tomorrow, I guess. Whatever day it is."

"Kinda hard to keep track of time with no clocks and no sun." My eyes slowly peeled open, and I met her gaze in the low light of my hand. "But I'll tell Nick to let me know when it hits ten, and I'll be back here. I'm sure he'll be pushing me out of there well before ten anyway, but I'll make sure to tell him."

Her eyes flicked over me for a moment. "Alright. I'll see you tonight then. Be careful out there."

I sat forward. "I will. And you too. Sleep tight."

She reached forward and caught my face between her palms. Her lips leaned into mine. I touched her jaw. After a short moment, she pulled back and touched our foreheads together. "I love you," she murmured.

"I love you, too," I whispered.

"Now go save lives."

I forced a smile.

Then back to ground zero.

The worst of my anxiety seemed to taper off throughout that day. The first three were filled with shock and terror. Though the terror lingered, the shock of it seemed to dissipate.

It became almost routine. Teleport into a building, fish out the survivors I sensed, heal their wounds, and teleport to the portal. Acknowledging each of them would have been more inspiring and may have made for a better story, but times of war are grittier than we romanticize them to be.

Despite how ashamed I am to admit it, I stopped looking at those I saved as people. Not thinking about them as individuals with unique, beautiful lives made it easier. Realizing they each had brothers and sisters, children and parents, friends and lives that had just been bull-dozed in the blink of an eye felt like a dagger to the chest.

So I ignored that harsh reality. I focused on the mission itself, not the people. At least, I did until late that night when I couldn't anymore.

It was approaching eight o'clock. I know that because Nick had just told me not to start any major healings that I couldn't take care of quickly because it was almost time for me to go. I told him "okay," and to give me a twenty-minute warning when my time was approaching. I teleported to the closest human soul in my vicinity.

The fallen in apartment complex was in the dead center of Hunts Point. I remembered Celena laughing as she told us to lock our doors when we drove through that part of the city and to make sure we carry a gun if we planned on walking. And to *never* walk through there at night, especially not with the kids.

But that didn't matter now. I wasn't worried about myself. I was worried about accomplishing my goal. Saving anyone I could. Regardless of who they once were, or where they were from, or if they sold drugs or their bodies to make ends meet. I didn't care who they were. I just wanted to save them.

When I landed in that building, the first thing I remember noticing was the smell. Like smoke and curry. I must have landed near the remnants of someone's apartment making what smelled like a bomb ass dinner before shit hit the fan.

I can still recall how thick the dust filled air felt as I drew it into my lungs. I can still remember how silent it was. That memory stuck out the most because every other building I landed in was full of sobs or screams.

"Hello?" I called. "Is anyone in here?"

Then a cheerful yell. "Over here! We're over here!"

I teleported to the sound of the woman's voice. When I landed, it felt like every other rescue thus far. Then the skinny young redhead turned up to me with a smile beneath her bloodied cheeks. Though bleeding and clearly injured, she wasn't pinned. She was entirely capable of standing and walking out on her own. But I cracked it up to trauma at first. She certainly wasn't the first one to freeze in fear.

"I knew someone would come." She nodded fast. "I knew it. I saw the videos; I know what you all are. You're angels. I've been praying since it started. I knew God would send someone. I knew he would. God loves his children."

Any addict would have recognized the delirious look in her glazed eyes. The sadness behind them. The touch of madness if you looked close enough.

I forced a smile. "Come on then."

"I can't. My son."

I furrowed my brows, looking around. "Where is he?"

Her gaze turned to the rocks at her feet. "Right here. He's right here. He can't move."

My eyes followed hers.

At her knee in the rubble, a hand jutted from beneath a large chunk of cement. Nothing else. Just a hand. A small, bloodied hand nearly purple in color.

And my stomach hit the floor.

I lowered myself to my knees. "Is he alive?"

"He just squeezed my hand."

My fingertips moved to the child's wrist. A faint, but fast pulse throbbed against my fingertips.

I turned to the woman. "What's your name?"

"Cleo," she said.

"Nice to meet you, Cleo, I'm Jeremy." I forced a calm smile. "What's your son's name?"

"Oliver." She smiled, moving her hand around her son's. "This is my Olly."

My head lifted gently, and I held my smile. "Nice to meet you, Cleo, I'm Jeremy. I can get Oliver out from under here. And I can heal him. But this boulder is really big. I don't know what he's going to look like when I get him out, so I want you to close your eyes for me, okay?" She nodded. "I'm gonna get you out of here too. And it's not gonna feel so great at first. You'll probably puke. So when you do, make sure you're facing the other way because vomit and wounds don't mix." She nodded once more. "And when I heal him, it won't be like it is in the movies. He's going to be in a lot of pain. He's gonna scream, and he'll probably fight me, and I'm gonna have to hold him down. But don't look. Okay? Can you do that for me?"

She nodded.

"Alright, give me your hand." I extended my palm to hers. She cupped her hand around mine, and I squeezed the boy's. "This is gonna hurt, Oliver, but I'm gonna help you."

His little hand tightened as far as it could around mine, and I fought the water that burned my eyes.

"Thank you, Jeremy." Her head bowed to kiss my knuckles. "Thank you. And thank you, lord."

I gave a sad smile. I teleported to the street outside. Cleo bent over vomiting to the pavement, and I got my first look at Oliver.

He looked about Micah's size, maybe a few inches taller. His blond hair was cropped close to his bloodied skull beneath the layer of thick dust.

But his face was so swollen that I couldn't make out anything else. Not the shape of his jaw. Not the color of his blackened eyes. Not the structure of his cheekbones, not even the true color of his purple skin. It ballooned to twice its size since I'd removed him from the cement crushing his body.

His chest and abdomen weren't much different. Distended and growing by the second. His legs were smashed to a red mush of blood and tendons from the thigh down, as was his right arm from the elbow. The only workable appendage he had left was his left arm but even it was purple and engorging.

He screamed in agony for all of two seconds before crimson vomit spewed from his lips. The amount of internal damage was so severe, I'm still amazed he managed out a scream at all.

My heart hammered, and my stomach spun as I struggled with where to start. I only had two hands, and his entire body needed healed just as badly. No matter where I began, he could bleed out from another wound just as quickly.

But his brain. His brain mattered the most. I started at the head and focused on Nick.

Nick, I said into his mind. *I need help. Like now.*

As soon as I'd thought the words, I heard him drop to the ground on the other side of Oliver. His gaze met mine for a brief moment as he ripped his belt from his jeans and teleported a rope to the ground. "I'll tie off the bleeding. You focus on his head."

I soared bright light into his face. It worried me that he was out cold, but I felt his soul. It was still in his body. He wanted to live. His soul was hanging on to his body like a hamster to the edge of its cage. So long as he was trying, I'd try too.

Nick and I went on healing Oliver for what felt like a moment, but I'd soon realize was closer to an hour and a half. I heard Cleo behind me reciting the Lord's Prayer over and over.

"Our father who art in heaven, hallowed be thy name. Your kingdom come. Your will be done on Earth as it is in heaven. Give us this day our daily bread, and forgive us our trespasses, as we forgive those who trespass against us. Lead us not into temptation but deliver us from evil. For thine is the kingdom, the power, and the glory... Our father who..."

The same prayer my dad forced me and my siblings into reciting each night before bed. The words that brought me comfort as a child but chilled me to my core after what I'd learned in the last few years. I thought about turning around and telling her to shut the fuck up because those words appalled me.

His kingdom come? We were standing in the midst of his kingdom's dawn and it was the reason that little boy was holding onto the edge of his life.

His will be done? Fuck his will. If this was his will, then fuck his god damned will.

Give us this day? What day? It wasn't a day, we were in the middle of endless night. A night*mare*, at that.

Forgive us our trespasses? What about *his* trespasses? What about when he told Abraham to climb to the top of a mountain and sacrifice his child to him? Or when Abraham's son Jephthah had to burn his daughter alive or deal with his wrath? What about when he gave Samson the power to murder thirty men? What about when he turned Lot's wife to salt? What about when he helped the Israelites murder countless people in Jericho and Bashan? What about when he killed all of the first born sons in Egypt?

What about when he killed his own damn kid?

What about when he killed mine?

What about when he killed twenty-four of his closest allies, including the one who gave him the eternal life he'd brag for centuries about disponing to the same people he tortured endlessly in his holy book?

What about when he killed the whole world? Not the first time, but the second.

His kingdom? *His* power? *His* glory?

He didn't deserve a kingdom. My wife and I were far more powerful. And he didn't deserve an ounce of glory after the shit he'd done to us and every other living thing on earth.

But I wasn't the type of god that he was. I was actually out there. Helping. Fighting for the people we brought to the planet. I didn't want glory.

No one truly powerful does.

If they wanted to worship him, if they wanted to find comfort in his bullshit, I wouldn't condemn them for it. If those convoluted and complete insane fairytales gave them comfort, I was glad something did.

It was like letting my children believe Santa was a nice old man who left presents under the tree instead of addressing the fact that he supposedly broke into our home while we were sleeping, stalked around for a while, and got comfortable with our plate of Christmas cookies. It made them happy, so we emphasized the parts that weren't crazy fucking bullshit.

So I bit my tongue and kept healing the woman's son as she prayed for help from the man who destroyed my life a million times over and caused the boy's injuries in the first place.

But after those short ninety minutes, I felt what I feared from the moment we began healing him. Those claws of his soul digging into the edges of his body slipped away and plummeted into the abyss.

Nick felt it too. His gaze met mine and the bright light of his palms burned out. He fell to his bottom.

"What are you doing?" I asked. "You heal him, I'll hold his soul in his body."

His head shook slightly. "He's gone, man."

"And I can bring him back," I said. "Just keep healing him so I can get him."

"This body is too weak to return to. Life in the Fae Realm won't be like life is here for disabled people. A paraplegic child with injuries like this that are sure to cause long-term damage and has no clue how to navigate the world in his new body won't survive. And if he does, it'll be a life of hell or a slow and painful death. People there will have to work to survive, all of them and he—"

"That's the most ableist bullshit I've ever heard." I glared. "We can't j—"

"It isn't ableist. It's the truth. And we've been healing for an hour. He let go. He's tired of fighting, Jeremy." Both Nick's tone and expression were gentle. "We have to let him go."

"No." I kept my white palms aglow above his chest. "No, I won't. I told him I'd help him; I'm going to help him."

"Every minute we waste on him is a minute someone else dies. You realize that's what you're doing, right? We're wasting time having this conversation. He's gone—"

"Just keep healing him," I said with tears in my eyes. "Please. Just keep healing him."

His eyes moved slowly between mine. He drew a slow breath into his nose and exhaled it through his downturned lips. "Fine. I'll keep healing. But I want you to realize the call you're making right now. That the time we're spending trying to save his life could cost someone else theirs. Understand that."

"Fine, I understand. I understand, just help me," I said again.

Nick released another slow breath. His hands lit up and replaced mine above his abdomen.

I closed my eyes and disappeared into the abyss.

But the moment I appeared there, a gasp left my lips, and my body soared with pain.

It was brighter than staring straight into the sun. I reflexively tried to close my eyes, but since my metaphysical existence didn't *have* eyes, that proved entirely useless.

Calling it the abyss now was arbitrary. There was no abyss to it. Every atom of blackness was taken up by the iridescent hues of souls. If it were a can, it'd surely implode from the pressure.

But I told him I'd help him.

I called to him. The name Oliver. It echoed through my mind. And then the lambency of that place intensified.

Many people named Oliver were surely there. Maybe some from this life, maybe some recognized it from a former.

Regardless, thousands of souls grew more luminant.

If I brought one of those brilliant lights back to that body, I'd never know if it was the right Oliver. I didn't know the boy; his soul wouldn't stand out from familiarity amongst the others.

And if I brought the wrong one back, I'd be bringing them back to a dying body. I'd torture them for who knows how long before his body entirely healed—if it would heal at all. If by some shotty chance we could heal the body, the fact still remained. The child would be cursed to a hellish life in the Fae Realm.

In that moment, my mindset shattered.

Nick was right. I had to let the boy go.

I dropped back into my body. My lip quivered as I looked down at the swollen, dead child on the ground. Tears flowed from my eyes, and Nick caught my gaze. His expression was as heartbroken as my own as the light in his palms dimmed to darkness.

"I'm sorry," he murmured.

I chewed my lower lip to keep it in place. "Me too."

"You should get back to Lai," he said gently. "It's almost time anyway."

"Already?" I asked.

He glanced at his watch. "Quarter to ten."

I swallowed hard and gave a nod.

But I heard Cleo behind me praying still. My stomach sunk.

I turned to face her. She rocked back and forth on her knees, hands folded in the center of her chest.

I looked at Nick. "Let me…"

He nodded.

My legs swiveled until I kneeled just before her. As she prayed and prayed, I brought a slow glow to my hand and raised it to the cut above her temple. It was a small scrape and a low light, so the pain it brought on was no worse than the wound was already causing. Still, I expected her to wince or grimace. Yet, she smiled and opened her eyes.

"Is he better?" she asked. "Is Olly okay?"

I struggled to keep her gaze. "I'm sorry, Cleo. I couldn't save him."

Her praying hands fell apart and drooped to her sides. "What?"

"I'm so sorry," I whispered. "I tried as hard as I could, but he just... He was tired of fighting. He was in a lot of pain, and he wanted it to end."

"No," she said. "No, you're an angel. God sent you to save us. I know he did. He did, he sent you to save my baby."

My wan eyes trickled tears from the corners. "Maybe he sent me to save you."

"No!" she almost yelled. Her lip began to quiver. "No. I wasn't supposed to live. I don't deserve it; my baby does. He's innocent. I'm not. I'm not supposed to live if he's dead. I'm not. Take me. Take me instead. Please, just save my son. Save my baby, take me instead."

I blinked fast to keep the tears from falling. "It doesn't worth like that, Cleo."

"Yes it does," she said. "Yes it does, take me. Take me. I'll die so he can live. Just bring him back. Bring him back. He deserves to live. He's only five. He needs to live."

In her shoes, I'd have done no different. Even when we lost Micah. I'd have offered myself in his place, and that's what made this so much more painful. That there was no equal sacrifice to be paid in a scenario like this.

Water from my eyes ran down my esophagus. My throat grew so tight. "I'm so sorry for your loss."

"No."

Before I could stop her, she turned back to her son for the first time since I teleported him out from beneath that cement. She screamed out a long, pained sob.

"My baby," Cleo cried. "My baby."

I stayed quiet as she pulled her dead, amputated child to her chest. My eyes filled with tears. Nick's did too. I stayed put for a moment. I knew I had to get back to Laila, but I couldn't leave her yet. She just watched her baby die the worst, most excruciating death I could imagine.

I knew how it felt to watch your child die. I knew that pain. But mine was momentary and hers was permanent.

She needed someone beside her.

"My baby." Her whole body quaked with sobs.

She repeated it over and over as she had with the prayer, passionately rocking him back and forth as if it'd resurrect him.

Nick glanced at me and mouthed for me to go. But I shook my head.

My eyes were full of tears, and it felt like a hole had just been punched through my gut. Guilt was overflowing within me like a tea kettle on a hot stove. I would never wish that pain on anyone because it's a kind of agony that never goes away. It aches for the rest of your life.

Before I even had time to think, Cleo ripped a piece of glass from the cracked pavement and slammed it into her chest.

My mouth fell open.

That hole in my stomach expanded over my entire body.

She pulled the glass out and slammed it into her chest again, and then a third time.

I grasped her shoulders and looked to Nick. His sorrowful eyes turned to the ground.

"Take me," she made out as the two of them fell to my chest. Her pale blue eyes shifted between mine. She smiled, tears still sliding from her eyes. "Bring him back and take me."

"What did you do," I whispered.

"Take me." Her eyelids slowly fell.

My eyes overflowed with tears. I couldn't find her in the abyss, and her heart stopped beating. I couldn't bring her back.

Cleo was gone too.

I'd just spent the last hour and forty-five minutes on two people that I couldn't save. At least a dozen other people could have been helped in that time. And I made the conscious decision to focus on the two of them alone.

I may as well have just watched.

"She thinks you brought him back," Nick murmured. "She died with the comfort of thinking she sacrificed her life for her son. I hope that can comfort you, too."

My head shook, lips trembling. I pulled the two of them into my chest and hugged them as tight as I could.

I didn't even know Cleo and Oliver.

But their deaths impacted me in a way nothing else ever had.

When it hit ten o'clock, Nick told me it was time to go. He promised he'd give the two of them a decent burial. I was reluctant to leave, but I had to reconcile myself before I went home, and time was running out. So I gingerly moved their bodies to the pavement.

"I'll see you at the house at eleven," Nick murmured.

I wiped snot from my nose. I teleported to the creek half a mile from the house. The icy water felt like a million needles piercing my skin, but the air was so much better in my lungs than what I'd breathed in New York City.

As I washed Oliver and Cleo's blood from my body and watched it float down the creek, I struggled with everything in me to contain my composure. I tried to stop crying. I tried to keep a normal breathing rhythm. I tried to slow my shaking hands.

I did as Elira had taught me. The four-four-four breathing technique. I tried with every fiber of my being to relax.

But nothing worked.

I just wanted to calm down, but I couldn't. I'd never felt like that in my life, and I didn't know how to make it stop.

I had to look my wife in the eyes. I had to finish packing my bags. I had to carry my children from their beds to another time, and I couldn't calm myself down.

But I knew what could.

Funny, because even just the thought made the panic stop.

Yet, I teleported a set of clothes on and flashed there anyway.

The pharmacy in town.

I brought a flame to my hand and walked to the locked cabinet in the corner. Of course that's where what I was looking for would be. They wouldn't have locked up the Advil.

My hot hand melted the lock on the mechanism, and I pulled the drawer open with the other. I held my flaming hand as a light and searched for my drug of choice. Just about anything with 'odine' at the end would do the trick.

Even better. Opana. Ten milligrams.

I twisted off the lid to the massive bottle and contemplated popping one and pocketing the rest. But the world was ending. Injured people would need it. At least I was courteous enough to think of them. The only reason I did, though, was because I was still sober.

Instead, I lifted four from the bottle and tossed them into my pocket.

I thumbed through the benzos. Mixing them could be dangerous, but I'd be immortal in two hours so that didn't really matter to me.

Ativan. Two milligrams.

I fished out five of those too. I dropped them to my pocket, closed the bottle, plopped it back to the drawer, and slammed it shut.

I teleported to the diner. I sat down at the office desk and lit the vanilla scented candle Laila kept beside the photo of us with our two kids.

As I crushed them up on the dusty wooden table, I couldn't stop thinking about Cleo. That prayer, again and again, to a god who didn't give a flying fuck about her. Then to Oliver.

His little body torn to shreds. That tiny hand barely squeezing mine. The sound of his scream, the only sound I'd ever hear leave his lips.

I thought about the end of their story. Cleo shoving that rugged glass into her heart. Her smile as she said to take her instead.

I thought about Lux.

He built an entire religion based upon the murder of a child. The murder of *his* child. And if that wasn't enough for people to see how awful of a creature he was, I didn't know what was.

Sacrificing your child is not what a loving parent does. If he'd done that to one of his children, what would stop him from doing it to the rest?

Nothing. Infallibly *nothing*.

He let them die. He let all of our children *die*. Slow, agonizing, and painful deaths.

No.

Sacrificing yourself for your child is the most noble death imaginable. There is absolutely no nobility in killing your baby.

CHAPTER EIGHTY-ONE

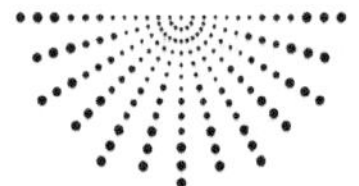

JANUARY 11 - LAILA

January 11th moved as rapidly as the days that preceded it. The emotional impact of the apocalypse had settled with the dust over Los Angeles. Truthfully, all the stories of rescues that day blurred together.

They all stung but not one hurt more than another. Not one was easier than another. They were all tragic, and they were all incredibly similar.

I teleported someone from a crashed car, healed their major wounds, I dropped them beside the portal. I teleported into a building, healed the major wounds of any survivor I found, and I dropped them beside the portal.

No story stands out more than any of their congruent counterparts.

I saved people. I stopped to catch my breath, drink some water, and eat a granola bar. I pissed a few times. I shat a time or two. It was identical to the three days I'd just lived.

The only major difference was that my head was nowhere near L.A. My mind was on my husband.

He was struggling worse than I'd ever seen him struggle with anything. Even Micah's 'death' and following disappearance was easier on him than those four days. We lived without our son for two and a half years—not to mention my three months in captivity before his birth—and I thought that he could never hurt more than he did then.

But I was wrong. I could see it in his expression the night before when I healed the gash on his forehead. The light had dulled in those electric eyes.

Peterson broke me. And Lux broke him.

In some ways, I'd always still be the girl that climbed into that van. But it started an evolution in me. An evolution not much different than my ancient soul's first life.

Similarly, Jeremy would always be the man who carried me out of that burning building four and a half years before. But something changed in him during those three days as well. Ultimately, he'd always be that same person I fell in love with. But his evolution had begun. And it'd take a long while before I saw a glimpse of the positive parts of the man I married again.

***

"Mom." Micah caught my elbow as I stumbled to stand after healing a man.

"Nine o'clock already?" I asked as I caught my balance.

"Five 'til, to be exact."

Deeply, I inhaled as I looked over the demolished city. Taking it all in for one last time. Reminding myself what my future had in store for me.

I turned to him. "Time to pack then."

He frowned. "Guess it is."

I glanced at his tattered watch. "How's that still working? Even the batteries in my fire detectors went out."

"It's old," he said. "An old mechanical one. There's no microchips in it, just kinetic energy from turning the knob. Since it isn't connected to the power grid—"

"It'll still work after an electromagnetic pulse," I murmured. "Good to know. Old wind-up watches are the way to go."

He gave a smile. "See? Healthy, off-grid living isn't so bad."

I grinned. "I never said it was. But that gluten free, dairy free protein bar was literal horse shit."

He laughed. "It was nice to meet you, Mom. This you. You haven't changed much, but still. It was nice."

I smiled back. "You haven't changed much either. But it was nice to meet you too."

"Well, that's because of you." He held his smile. "Wouldn't be who I am if you didn't give me the freedom to."

All throughout that day, I hadn't shed a tear. Seeing bodies become rat and crow food in the streets didn't force me to tears. Healing amputated wounds didn't bring a drizzle. But hearing my grown son tell me that I always gave him the freedom to be his self instantly choked me up.

I pressed my lips together to keep from ugly crying.

He laughed. "Are you crying?"

"No." I shook my head as my lips pulled up. "No, I'm not crying."

"You and your happy tears." He grinned.

I laughed, wiping the corners of my eyes. "I love you, Micah Christopher Skoulda."

"I know." He smiled. "I love you too, Mom. I'll handle this for a few hours, and I'll meet you guys back at the house at midnight. Go take care of little me. He misses you."

"Wait, do you remember this? Being him right now?"

He raised his shoulders. "Vaguely. I remember being scared. I remember being sad when Gam told me I wouldn't see her for a long time. I remember being really happy when you and Dad got me out of my bed."

"Then we better go get you out of your bed."

"I guess you better."

***

After that brief conversation with Micah, I teleported home. First, I turned over the decorative—yet incredibly functional—hourglass on my dresser. I walked to the closet and lit my hand with flames for light. I didn't exactly have any Y2K styled clothes. Were high waisted jeans a thing then? Or was it the low riding hipsters? You wouldn't catch me dead in a pair of those, but I had high waisted jeans for days.

I hoped they were in because that's what I grabbed. I leafed through my shirts. Even after the revival of crop tops in the 2010's, that still wasn't my taste. Maybe for a concert or something of the likes, but not for day to day. Blouses were always in though, right? I had plenty of baby-doll tops. So I grabbed one of those too and tossed the rest into a pile on the floor.

Sundresses never went out of style, I did know that. I pulled some of those from the hangers and tossed them to the ground. I grabbed a few pairs of Jeremy's sweatpants, some of his band tees, and a few pairs of his faded blue jeans. Thankfully, he didn't stay up on what was in and usually wore what was comfortable, so most of his shit was perfectly acceptable in any time. Lord knew his Converse would fit in from the 70's on. I had a pair of those too, so I grabbed them to put on after my bath in the creek.

I turned to the drawer and got a set of my pajamas out. I figured it didn't matter if those were in; no one would see me wearing them but my family. A pair of South Park pants and a bleach-stained T-shirt. I rummaged for a pair of socks and underwear too, and completely forgot to toss a handful into the pile.

I lifted a towel and a washcloth from the top shelf and I teleported to the creek. Goosebumps rose over my skin as I set the pajamas and towel on the frozen grass. I shivered as I stepped out of my jeans and T-shirt. I lit my body aflame and stepped into the water. I'd never tried to warm frozen water with my body, but it worked pretty well surprisingly. Which made sense because water wasn't enough to extinguish my flames.

As I dunked my body into the water, I kicked myself for forgetting soap and shampoo. But we'd be at a hotel in a few hours. I could take a real shower then.

Part of me was intimidated by the lack of light and black haze in the air. But I kept reminding myself it'd all be over soon. At least, temporarily. That we'd be prepared for this time when it came back around.

Unless we could prevent it altogether.

I heard Lila when she said they'd tried, and I didn't doubt that they had. But we'd try too. Maybe we could change the whole story. Maybe Jeremy and I could find some way to live happily ever after with our children and brothers and sisters without destroying the world.

Maybe there was a way for everyone to have a happily ever after.

I hurried my way through the makeshift bath, dried myself with my towel, then teleported back to my bedroom. My flaming fingertip touched each candle around the room. I put my hands to my hips and took a long look around.

My eyes moved from the French doors that led to my darling little garden to the chairs beside it. Jeremy and I found them at a flea market when I was pregnant with Milly. I gasped when I saw them. The low back, the ugly green velvet seats, the intricately carved spiraling legs nicked up with a million scratches and dents. I said they must have been so beautiful once, and Jeremy grabbed them. I laughed and said they were hideous now; I didn't want them in my brand new home.

But he said, "Just because they're a little bent up doesn't mean they can't be beautiful again."

He worked on them in the garage back at the main house for weeks. I told him I wanted to help, but all he'd let me do was the upholstery because he didn't want me breathing in all those chemicals while I had a baby in my belly. So he showed me how to do that too. How to rip out each old staple and line the old foam with new batting. He showed me to reposition the cushions on the newly refurbished frame and helped me nail them back into place.

My eyes moved back to the blackness outside, and I remembered that phrase. "Just because they're bent up now doesn't mean they can't be beautiful again."

He taught me that. He taught me to find a diamond in the rough and shine its luster back to new. And we'd do that again.

One way or another, we'd get the world back to its former glory.

Whether it be by preventing the apocalypse entirely or fighting those bastards that tore it apart like hell. We would rebuild our world.

"Knock-knock," Mom said quietly in the door's threshold.

I turned with a smile. "Hey."

"Hey." She smiled back beneath her sad eyes.

"How'd the kids take the news?" I asked.

"Milly didn't really understand. Micah cried. But the older him seems to understand so... That's what matters, I guess."

"Doesn't make it any easier," I murmured.

"No." She sat on the foot of my bed. "No, it doesn't."

I walked across the dimly lit room and sat beside her. My arms raised and wrapped around her shoulders and hers did the same. I laid my head against her shoulder. My eyes closed as I breathed in the way she smelled for the last time I would in twenty-four years.

She hadn't bathed in at least two days. Yet, she smelled no differently than I remembered as a child. That comforting scent of laundry detergent mixing with the hint of tobacco she tried to hide with Chanel No. 9.

"I'm gonna miss you," I whispered.

She kissed my forehead and pulled me a little tighter. "I'm sorry I won't have the chance to miss you."

I fell quiet.

"But you know what?"

"What?" I asked.

"I'm so proud of you. I know your dad is too. Everything you've accomplished, all the people you've helped." She squeezed me and kissed my head. "That tattoo on your neck should have been a monarch, because that's what you are. My miracle baby grew up to be quite a leader."

I smiled. "I'm more of a purple kind of gal."

"You always have been." She laughed. "Purple and green since you could tell us what your favorite color was. Blue was up there too. Always had a thing for those cool colors. I used to think it was because they were calming, but I guess I can see some poetry in that now. The purple in your flames, the green in you and your daughter's eyes, and the blue in your husband's and your son's."

Maybe. But maybe it had something to do with that beautiful green and purple orb that gave me the power to grant people with eternity.

"More of an instinct than poetic, I think," I murmured.

"Maybe," she said. "Maybe so."

I leaned back and met her mint-colored eyes in the flickering light. "Since I won't be able to ask you when I need to, what advice would you give me as a parent? 'Cause you did a damn good job. And I want to do as well with my kids as you have done with me."

"Just keep doing what you're doing. You're a great Mom, sweetie. I wouldn't tell you to do anything different."

"Sure, with kids. But they're gonna grow up. And I don't know shit about raising a teenager."

"You do good with Lydia." She smiled. "You'll be fine, baby, I know you will."

"Yeah, but what do you wish someone would have told you before you had me and Jen?" I asked.

She looked around the room and thought for a moment. "Well, I wish I would have known not to take it to heart when you guys started wanting to do stuff without me. When you'd rather hang out with your friends than hang out with me. It kind of hurt my feelings then, especially after your dad was gone. But it wasn't because you didn't love me anymore, it was just because you weren't an extension of me. You were your own people. And you had to get to know that person on your own."

A sad smile pulled at my lips. "Really regretting those days I spent with my friends that I could have spent with you now."

Her smile widened. "No, it's okay. You needed those experiences. And it was a beautiful thing to watch you become this person, with or without my influence. I'm sure you'll feel the same way about your babies one day." I smiled back and waited for her to go on. "And I wish someone would have told me that I was doing the right thing when I let you be who you were. I wish I wouldn't have felt so guilty for not watching you like a hawk. Because all the books said I was doing it wrong. I knew you were out there getting high and making bad choices, and I let you, because I thought you'd learn from your mistakes. And I was right, you did. But I wish I knew that I was making the right call then."

"So that's your advice." I grinned. "Let my kids party in their teenage years?"

She laughed, shaking her head. "No. I don't know, maybe. It worked out alright for you. But your parents weren't addicts. So maybe that isn't the best advice. I guess a better way to put it is to let them make their mistakes. Don't force them to learn from books, let them learn from their own experiences. That's what I'm really trying to say."

"That's pretty good advice," a quiet voice said in the doorway. "A far better route than I travelled."

I looked up and met her gaze. My real mother. Mary.

"I thought so," Mom said.

Mary smiled slightly. "Rachel, would you mind if I had a moment with Laila?"

Mom squeezed my hand and stood. "Yeah, sure. I'm gonna go over your bags and make sure there's nothing major you're forgetting."

"Thanks, Mom." I brought myself to my feet and stared at her as Mom brushed past. A slow breath left my nostrils. "Hey, Mary."

"Hello, Laila." She smiled gently. "How are you doing with everything that's happening?"

"Seen better days. But I'm alright. What about you? I'm sure this was a bitter pill for you to swallow too."

"It was. But one I took down many years ago now. I've come to terms with it."

"Many years, huh?" I asked. "How many is that again?"

"About eight," she said. "Since I heard about the apocalypse, anyway. All the details didn't come until later."

"What details do you mean?" I asked.

"Lila said that I can't tell you exactly how and when I learned what I did."

As much as I wanted to, I couldn't argue with myself. Elder me knew better. She'd lived it. I'd let her be the judge.

I huffed. "Fair enough then."

"I'm sorry," she blurted. "I want you to know that I'm sorry for what I've done. I've already apologized to Jeremy, and I'm still apologizing to Nick. I don't think I'll ever stop. But I want you to know that. Truly, from the depths of my soul, I'm sorry, Laila."

My eyes shifted between hers for a moment. "I know you are."

She cleared her throat. "I just wanted you to have a good life. I didn't want you to carry the burden you have now. When I heard what would happen, when I... I only wanted you to have a good life. But I shouldn't have done what I did. I shouldn't have killed Moses. I shouldn't have commissioned that siren. I shouldn't have interfered. I should have let things happen as they were meant to, and if I could reset it and do things differently, I would. And I... I just want you to know that."

"We've had this conversation before," I said. "You shouldn't have done the things you did, but I do understand *why* you did. And like I said before, I'd have done worse to protect my children. I *have* done worse to protect my children. And I'd do it again."

Her eyes moved carefully over mine, waiting for the but.

"But I wish you would have told me when. You didn't have to tell me everything. But I wish you would have told me to treasure the last year," I said. "It would have been nice to know the date."

A quiet laugh left her.

"What are you laughing at?" I asked.

"The way you phrased that. When Lila told me *not* to tell you, her exact words were 'She may not realize it, but she'll treasure that time with her family more than she would if she were counting it down on a clock.'"

I stifled a yawn. "Well. I guess if you got the advice from yours truly, it'd be a bit hypocritical to blame you then, huh?"

She smiled. "You've always been a bit fickle that way. We all are, I suppose. New experiences show us new perspectives. Perhaps you'll feel differently for yourself. Perhaps you'll tell the younger version of me to relay the message. Or perhaps, you'll do exactly as she did. I suppose you'll come to that conclusion on your own."

"I suppose so," I murmured. "I was bombarded the other day. It was a lot of information to take in at once. But I'm not angry with you, Mary. You don't have to look at me like that."

"Like what?" she asked.

"Like I hate you," I said. "I don't, you know. You may not be my favorite person in the world, but I kind of love you."

Her lips lifted slowly, hazel eyes glossing over.

And I did. I hated what she'd done. I hated how much she'd hurt my husband. But I did love her. She was there for me through so many things when I first found out about this world. I would always care for her.

I laughed quietly. "How about I cut the kind of and just say it flat out? I love you, Mary. You've pissed me off to no end at times, but I do. I love you. And I especially love the person you've become. You weren't always someone I admired, but you are now."

"You admire me?" A huff of a laugh escaped her lips. "Why?"

"Because you learned," I said. "You saw the bigger picture, and you learned from your mistakes. You became a better person. You wiped away centuries of brainwashing. For a thousand years, you bowed to a man because that's what you'd been taught. But once you learned who he truly was, and the plans he had in store for his people, you didn't continue to blindly follow him. You started fighting for the right cause, even though it was against everything you'd ever been taught. And that's something worth looking up to."

She smiled, then pressed her lips together to keep them from trembling. Her dewy eyes leaked at the edges.

I smiled back. "Come here."

She took a few steps forward into my outstretched arms. I tightened them around her back as hers knotted at my waist. They grew so forceful that I could hardly breathe, but I stayed put and tightened just as hard.

That was the first time I hugged my mother. Things had always been rocky between us. But in the last few days, an inevitable realization dawned on me.

I was the only person capable of granting eternal life. Meaning that

I was the ultimate judge. And a judge must be fair. A judge must see every perspective before they make a ruling.

As Roland had said, I had to choose my trials.

Mary's indiscretions were nothing compared to some. Next to her father, they were barely even wrongdoings. After all, she'd made the mistakes she had from a place of love. Maybe the path to hell is paved with good intentions after all, but the intent is what matters most when making a ruling about one's fate.

That isn't to say she was ready for eternal life.

Only that I had come to realize no one is perfect. Not even parents.

As the hour stretched on, Mom helped me gather up the rest of my things. I'd barely made a dent in Jeremy's, but I said we'd take care of that when he got home. Mom agreed, and the two of us started leafing through Micah and Milly's bags. We loaded only a few diapers for Milly, deciding not to take up space on something I could get when we made it back. But we made sure to pack their favorite toys. Micah's lamb. Milly's stuffed, singing, wind-up rocking horse. The necklace Heylel had given us from our first life and the hand-carved wooden figurine came back as well.

For myself, I just needed the basics. The clothes on my back, my wedding ring, and my father's anklet. Pants, shirts, underwear, socks, and a jacket. And my photos. Those were the only frivolous things I brought back. Everything else could be replaced, but those memories couldn't.

There was one other thing I packed that I didn't necessarily need to. But I couldn't leave it, and it didn't take up much space in my suitcase anyway. The Elvan ore flask Heylel gave me at Micah and Milly's first birthday party. It was the only physical remnant I possessed from that life. Touching it carried me back to the first time I fell in love. And I refused to leave it behind.

When the sand in the hourglass went out, I flipped it over once more. Ten o'clock, and Jeremy hadn't returned. I assumed he was still held up on a rescue and gave him a few minutes longer. But once a quarter of the granules passed from one side of the glass to the other, I got a little nervous.

Do you need help? I asked into his mind. *It's after ten. I need help packing your bags.*

I'm at the diner, his thought echoed into mine.

Why? Did you need to grab something there?

Silence.

"I'll be right back. I'm gonna go check on Jeremy," I told Mom. "Could you grab his White Stripes T-shirt from the closet for me? I know he'd want to take that."

"Sure, hon," she said.

"Thanks," I said.

I teleported to the front of the diner.

A silence louder than the bombs fell into my ears. The air colder than ice brushed against my bare arms as I took in the smell of old grease in the fryer. I lit my hand to see, gaze traveling over the empty room.

"Babe?" I pushed open that swinging steel door for the last time. "Baby, are you here?"

"In here," he said quietly from the office.

I took a few steps down the hall. My flame went out, following the dim light from the candle. As I stepped into the doorway, my gaze steadied on Jeremy at the other side of the desk.

"Hey, it's almost time to go. I'm not sure what else you wanted to bring so I was waiting on you to..." My train of thought dropped off when I got a good look at him.

Jeremy's elbow leaned against the arm of the old spinning chair. His hand gripped a clump of damp hair on the side of his head. The usual creamy color of his cheeks had turned to a soft shade of red. Thin lines of water on his face twinkled against the throbbing light of the candle. His bloodshot, unblinking eyes were distant and vacant, locked with the desktop.

My eyes followed his to the old wooden table, and my heart picked up speed in my chest faster than it had all week.

A rolled-up dollar bill. An ivory powder littered with specks of peach.

"Baby," I whispered.

"I didn't take it." His gaze was still locked on the powder. The race of my heart slowed, and I let out a breath of relief. "I wanted to. I still want to. I *really* want to. But that picture of you and our kids is just staring at me." He paused. "I flipped it over once. But that made me feel like shit too, so I put it back."

I stayed quiet as I cut away at the distance between us. "What happened?"

His eyes filled with tears. His lip quivered, his nostrils flared, and his brows knitted close together.

"Jeremy, talk to me." I crouched down beside him. I laid my hand over his and tried to meet his gaze, but it stayed steady on the table. "Talk to me, baby, tell me what's going on."

"You know what's going on." The tears bubbled from his eyes. His lips pressed firmly together, falling to the saddest expression I'd ever seen on his face. "Millions of people are watching their children die, and we aren't strong enough to save them. We're gods, and we can't stop this. And their god isn't coming to help either. We're at this alone, and we can't win."

I stayed quiet and twined my fingers between his.

"It isn't fair," he whispered. "This is all happening because of decisions that we made. We didn't act fast enough, and he got to us first. We all died. Our babies died. He fucked us over again and again and a-fucking-gain, and now he's fucking them too. And children shouldn't have to pay for the sins of their parents. That's a fucked principle, and I fucking hate that it's true. I hate it. I hate all of this. We should have done better. We were just as powerful as he was; we shouldn't have let this happen. None of this should have happened. The world should have been a different place for the last five thousand years, and it isn't because we weren't strong enough. We weren't strong enough then, and we aren't strong enough now." His head shook again. "My brain just won't shut off. Everything's moving at a mile a minute, and I just want it to stop." His water filled eyes turned from the desk to mine. "I just want it to stop."

"We will be," I said. "We'll be strong enough. We'll make this right."

"We *can't*, Lai," he whispered. "They're gone. And they'll be gone again when we make it back to this time. I saw them out there. They were doing everything they could, and it wasn't enough. There's no darkness in the abyss now. I can't bring anyone back because they're all pushed so close together. I can't tell anyone apart. That's how bad it is. That's how many people are dead. That's how many souls don't have a body. And it hurts." His lip quivered, and the tears overflowed from his eyes. "It hurts so much."

"We can," I said. "We can and we will." His gaze fell. But I cupped his face and forced his eyes to mine. "How many times have we had to rebuild from the ashes, Jeremy? How many times have we had to start over and rebuild? We've done it before, and we'll do it again. We will, baby, we'll beat this."

"How?" His hand moved to my wrist against his face. "How can we rebuild from *this*?"

"I don't know yet, but I know that we will," I said. "We will. *You* taught me that anything broken can be fixed. Anything can be rebuilt. And we're *going* to rebuild from this. Just like we rebuilt ourselves, just like we rebuilt each other, just like we rebuilt our marriage. It's going to be okay one day. I know it is."

"That doesn't make it hurt any less right now." The tears kept sliding down his cheeks, and his lip shook. "I just want it to stop hurting. I want to feel good again."

I thought for a moment as my eyes shifted between those dull, watery spheres.

There was nothing I could do to make this better. It was out of my hands. He was right about how much this sucked, and how fucked it was, and how much it hurt, and there was nothing I could do to change that. But I would do anything to make him feel just the slightest bit better.

I leaned forward and pushed my lips to his. My fingers slid to the back of his neck and rubbed the golf ball sized knots.

He curved into me slightly, shaking lips molding into mine and steadying. His hands moved to my hips and pulled them closer to him. My back arched until our chests touched.

Still rubbing the back of his neck, I veered away and touched my forehead to his. I whispered, "I can't make this go away. But I can make you feel good for a few minutes."

He looked into my eyes for a moment. he grabbed my waist with one hand and my neck with the other. He pulled my face into his and kissed me fast and hard.

I leaned closer as he stood and reached for the drawstring of my pants. My hands slid from his neck down his torso. I ripped open the zipper and shimmied his jeans off. He tore my pajamas down my legs and grabbed my hips.

Usually, our sex was a bit more intimate and not so fast-paced. But this time was about relief, not about making love. He needed a rush of dopamine and endorphins, and I wanted to give him that. I wanted him to get those happy chemicals from my body and not a substance.

He backed me onto the desk as my legs locked around his waist. My lips still on his, a moan crept from my mouth as he pushed himself inside me. His hand slid up my shirt and cupped my breast. As his mouth traveled from mine down my neck and onto my chest, I bent my head back.

My eyes fixed on that powder and dollar bill a few inches from my bare ass. I lowered my hands from his neck to the desk to hold me up. I brushed it to the floor and moaned again as he pushed himself deeper inside of me.

Sometimes, sex is the only healthy release we have.

About a minute and a half later, Jeremy let out a quiet groan at my ear. His head fell to my shoulder. "Damn it."

Warmth filled me, and I laughed softly. "Did you come?"

He inched out of me. Pulling back to meet my gaze, his fingertips slid from my waist between my thighs. "Lean back," he whispered.

"It's okay." I smiled. "We have to get going anyway. We can—"

"We have a few more minutes." His lips brushed against mine. "Just a couple more minutes."

"I don't have to—"

"The last time I fuck you on this desk for twenty-four years can't be a quickie where you didn't even climax." He kissed me again, thumb brushing against my clit.

"Baby—"

He pushed our lips firmly together. One hand grabbed ahold of my hair as the other pushed deeper inside me. A sigh broke through our kiss as his thumb moved in circles on my clit. "Lean back," he whispered.

Well. I couldn't argue with that.

I laughed. I moved my hands from around his shoulders and propped myself up on the tabletop. "Well, if you insist."

He smiled. His lips touched mine once more as he pushed his fingers deeper. The hand at my hair coursed to my waist, then to my thigh. His mouth moved to my cheek, then my jaw. They inched down my neck and onto my collar bone. A gasp left my mouth as they moved to my breast. His tongue traced circles around my nipple in perfect sync with his thumb on my clit.

I closed my eyes as his lips trailed down my bare stomach to my pelvis. When they found my thigh, a low sigh coursed from my parted mouth. My head tilted back, stomach flipping with joy and anticipation for the first time in so long. His tongue moved in a slow circle, and he sucked my skin into his lips, a teasing precursor of what he was about to do a little north.

His hand at my thigh gripped firmly before gingerly yanking it to the side. I opened my eyes and met his gaze as his lips moved to mine. The red cascade to them had faded to a relaxed—yet taunting—seductive stare. He kissed them gently for a second, eyes still locked with mine. Then his tongue parted through.

Perhaps he wasn't the only one that needed the release, because as I looked into those eyes as he licked my clit and massaged my G-spot, euphoria flooded through me too.

This was us. This was what the gods of fertility turned to when everything else was shit. We buried ourselves in one another, because nothing, absolutely *nothing*, could give us so much peace, pleasure, and joy all at once.

His tongue lifted and fell in a circle around my clit. His fingers pulled toward him. My mouth dropped open, moan falling from its cavern. Butterflies flapped in my stomach, sending pleasant shivers to where his tongue flicked back and forth.

My hand propping me up lifted to the hair in his face. My fingers dug through the loose curls into his scalp and his tongue flicked faster.

I gasped and watched light flicker in his eyes. If his mouth wasn't so deep between my labial, I'm sure I'd have seen a grin.

Happy. He looked happy. I'd do anything to keep that expression on his face, and if getting my pussy licked did it, I didn't have an ounce of objection.

His tongue moved in fast circles, lips pushing closer into me. My head rolled back, and I moaned again. He picked up the pace even faster.

It never took long when he went down on me. I guess when you've been fucking the same person for a few hundred-thousand years, you start to know their body as well as you know your own, maybe even better.

As my sighs and moans got closer together, just when he knew I was about to climax, he lifted his head back to mine and pushed his dick back inside of me. I gasped against his mouth. His thumb slid in circles on my clit, and his hand swiveled around my bare waist. He pulled me closer into him. My trembling legs tightened at his waist, and I moaned again.

"Say my name," he murmured at my mouth, eyes moving between mine.

"What?" I whispered between gasps.

"This is the last time I'm fucking you as Jeremy," he said quietly, pushing himself as far in as he could. I groaned at his hips swiveling in a circle. "Say my name."

I tried to ignore the sadness that fell over me at that realization. I kissed him. My hands twined around his back, and my legs tightened at his hips. I touched my forehead to his.

"Jeremy," I murmured in ecstasy.

I felt his shoulders straighten at the word. He pushed harder, arm around my waist cradling me closer. His hand on my clit moved up to hold my face as my eyes moved between his. His pelvis grinded into my clit and again, I moaned, "Jeremy."

With each time the name eased from my lips, I watched that light in his eyes grow. The more turned on he became, the more the moisture dripped between my legs.

I didn't care what name he wore. He could be Jeremy, or Nick, or Nix, or any other call he'd answered to over the eons we spent together. But it mattered to him. It made him feel like the man he'd worked so hard to become. He'd faced so many trials as Jeremy, and that name dying in 2024 hurt him almost as much as what we'd witnessed in the last few days.

So I said it. Again and again, until I was screaming. Not like we had to be quiet with all things considered. And each time I did, we drew closer and closer until my body shook. I yelled it out once more as my muscles tightened around him. Just as they did, warmth flooded within me, and his mouth fell open against mine. Deep breaths panted from his lips as his hips grinded harder against my clit.

He smiled when my head fell to his chest.

His arms tightened around my waist, warm hands soothing my goosebump covered spine. My hands cradled his shoulders. I felt his lips on my hair, and a quiet laugh left his lips. Still inside me, yet both finished, he nodded softly. "That's a better way to go out."

I laughed and closed my eyes, holding him intimately one last time before we left our life behind to start over and build a new one a quarter of a century in the past.

CHAPTER EIGHTY-TWO

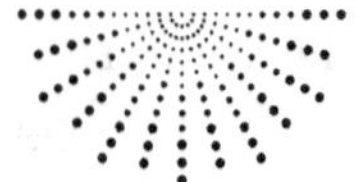

JANUARY 11, 10:45 P.M - JEREMY

"We should go," Laila whispered against my chest.

My fingertips slid over her warm skin. It was the first time in four days that I felt like I could breathe. I wasn't ready to go. I wasn't ready to leave this moment. I wasn't ready to pack my bags and move to another life.

I wanted to stay here forever. The comfort of the place we'd called home for our first year of marriage. Though cold now, it still felt warm. Warmer than outside where death lurked at the edge of every street. Warmer than the life I was destined to jump into. Warmer than any place in any time. It felt like home.

She felt like home.

My eyes shifted around the office space one last time. "I'm just gonna miss this place."

She pulled back to look around. Her eyes moved around the small, cold room. "Yeah. Me too. But we'll be back for it one day."

A slow breath left my nostrils. I turned to the ground and passed Laila the shirt and pants I'd ripped off her body. "One day."

"It's ironic, isn't it?" She lifted the shirt over her arms. "How that fucker used to tell us 'one day, you'll understand. One day, one day, one day.'" She huffed. "Now it's our catchphrase too."

I huffed, pulled my jeans to my hips, and buttoned them. "Starting to see a lot of irony these past few days."

"Yeah. Me too," she murmured.

As I grabbed my shirt from the ground, my eyes caught on the rolled-up dollar bill. And the white and pink dust beside it. They stayed there for a moment. A lump formed in my throat.

I met her eyes and straightened back up. "I'm sorry."

She hopped from the desk and pulled her pants up, cocking her head to the side. "For what?"

I gesturing to the bill on the floor. "I shouldn't have—"

"Don't." She caught my hand and twined her fingers between mine. Her lips curved into a hopeful smile. "Don't apologize. The amount of willpower it must have taken for you to stare at that and not take it is amazing. Don't apologize, you did nothing wrong."

"I almost did." The lump in my throat got thicker, and I swallowed it back down. "I probably would have—"

"But you didn't." Her other hand cupped my jaw, and she smiled. "You didn't."

I forced a smile back. "I'm glad that's how you see it."

Her smile slowly fell. Her eyes moved between mine. She lifted our knuckles to her lips. "Let's go."

I took one last look around.

She leaned down to blow out the candle, and it all turned to darkness.

"Do you want to bring these, baby?" Laila said from the closet.

I heard her, but it went through my eardrum and vibrated right back out. All I kept thinking about was the bowed doorframe that I'd told myself I was going to fix since we moved in but never got around to. We'd replaced the door after Adam tore it down, but I missed that damn piece of trim where the door clicked into place. Every night for almost two years when I had to yank it into place, I told myself I'd fix it one day the following week. But I never did. I wondered if I ever would. Would I remember it in twenty-four years? Would I care? I cared now, but would I always?

"Jeremy," Laila said, peeking her head out of the closet.

"Huh?"

"Do you want to bring these?" She held up a pair of dress pants.

"Should I want to bring those?"

Her gaze narrowed above her smile. "Well, you did marry me in them."

"Oh." My face flushed, and I smiled. "I don't know, probably won't be marrying you again in the next twenty-four years. So no, I guess. I won't need them."

"Fair enough." She stepped back into the closet. "What about your Five Finger Death Punch T-shirt? You wear that all the time."

"They won't exist for five years so probably not the best idea," I muttered.

"Right," she called. "You know, this is close to impossible. All that you wear are band tees, and most of these bands won't exist in the time we're going to."

"I've got some Pink Floyd and Lynyrd Skynyrd in there," I said. "Think there's a Bob Marley one tucked in the back somewhere too."

"I already packed those, and your Beatles shirt, but that's a total of five. You need more than five shirts," she said. "Jeans and sweatpants for days. But no damn shirts."

"Five's plenty," I said. "It's not like department stores didn't exist in 2000."

"Fine. You're right."

As she continued mumbling to herself about my lack of items, I thought about the finances. Laila and I had almost a million apart from the kid's money. Leah had less than ten grand. Brody had enough for a decent car, and Chris had somewhere near fifty thousand.

It sounded like a lot after adding it up the first time. But I considered the logistics. We were starting over entirely. We needed a house big enough for fifteen people, new wardrobes for fifteen people, beds and furniture for fifteen people, appliances, Hannah's tuition to finish up law school, and transportation for at least half of us. And let's not forget about money to start a new business.

That's when it dawned on me.

Our cushy lives were over. We'd quickly go from being comfortably wealthy to poor. Not living in a box on the side of the road poor, but date night at Denny's poor. Being unable to travel the world and buy our kids everything they wanted poor. Not broke. But close enough to it.

I instinctively felt my hand fall to my pants pocket.

I only crushed up one of those opanas. I knew it'd been year's, and I had no tolerance. I wasn't trying to kill myself. I just wanted to take the pain away.

And I had. Or she had, I guess.

But it crept back up like the sun in the morning. And with it came the craving for the dark.

"Jeremy." Laila's hand wafted in front of my face. "Anybody in there?"

I forced a smile. "Sorry, what'd you say?"

She outstretched a small golden ring in her palm. My dad's wedding band. "Do you want to bring this?"

My stomach spun, and I sucked my teeth. "I guess. One of the guys might want it so... Yeah, bring it, I guess."

"Will do," she said. "Packing for you isn't easy, you know. I don't know what matters to you."

I stood from the bed. I followed her to the closet and wrapped my hands around her waist from behind. "You," I murmured at her ear. "I don't really care what I bring. I just need you and the kids."

She chuckled and craned up to meet my gaze. Her hands touched mine at her stomach. "That's it? Just me and the kids?"

"You three are all I need." I smiled. "Wish we could bring the house too, but you guys are a good consolation."

She laughed and smacked me away. I chuckled as she spun to meet toward me. "Why don't you go wish it farewell then? I'll finish the packing."

"Are you sure?" I asked.

"You're just sitting there anyway." She swatted me away. "Go on. Say goodbye to your pride and joy."

I smiled and kissed her hair.

———

The living room was empty for the first time all week. A mess from everyone's shit, but still. My favorite room in the world, and I was glad to be alone with it for a moment.

I lifted myself to the kitchen counter and looked at the front door. A smile lifted my lips as I remembered the first time I showed it to Laila. My parade of siblings kept walking in on us just as things were about to get heavy back at the main house, so I took her hand and ran with her down the tree canopied driveway. I can still hear her laugh as she begged me to tell her where we were going.

I remembered the expression on her face when I started down the narrow path to the cabin from the road. She stopped dead in her tracks and put her hands at her hips. "This isn't gonna end like it does in the movies, right?" she'd asked. "You aren't taking me to the lair you lure girls to before you chop them up into a million itty bitty pieces?"

I laughed. "I guess you'll have to follow me and find out."

"Uh-uh. Not until you promise you aren't gonna chop me up into a million itty bitty pieces."

"Fine, I promise I won't chop you up into a million itty bitty pieces."

"That wasn't very convincing," she said.

"C'mon." I laughed and took her hand.

"Fine, but if you kill me, I'm haunting you until you die. So keep that in mind, mister." She grinned. I pulled back the overgrown shrubs. She muttered rhetoric like that the rest of the way. When we made it to the cabin, she stopped again.

I laughed. "I know it looks creepy from here, but it's actually pretty homey inside."

"No." She shook her head.

"I'm not fucking with you. It's actually really nice. I think there's some wood by the fireplace. I can light it. And don't worry, there's a toilet with running water and it's—"

"No." She laughed. "No as in no, I'm not scared."

I grinned. "So you're not worried I'm gonna chop you up into a million itty bitty pieces?"

"Jury's still out on that one." She smiled, eyes still shifting over the cabin. "But I don't think you will here."

"No?" I turned my head to the side. "Why's that?"

"Because this is a good place." She smiled. "I can feel things like that, you know."

I laughed. "Oh yeah?"

"Mhm," she said. "And this is a good place. It's not creepy at all. It's a little cottage in the woods. I have a thing for little cottages in the woods."

I smiled and reached my hand out for hers. "Come on then."

She grinned, twining her fingers between mine.

I remembered pushing open that old door with my hip and flicking on the lights. I remembered her grin as she plopped to the couch. "A little rustic but it has potential," she'd said. Her gaze turned up to mine. "You know what?"

"What?" I walked to the fireplace.

"You made a big mistake bringing me here," she said.

"Oh?" I glanced at her over my shoulder and loaded some wood into the pit. "Why's that?"

"Because it's perfect. No wi-fi, no TV, no noise pollution. I could get a lot of writing done at that desk with the view of the trees out that window over there." She smiled, leaned back into the old sofa, and propped her legs onto the coffee table. "Now that I've been here, you'll never get me to leave. It's over for you now, Jeremy Skoulda. You're stuck with me."

My eyes glistened with tears. Both from my moment of reminiscence, and the fact that she was right. I was stuck with her for the rest of my eternal life. And I wouldn't have it any other way.

But I wanted to be stuck with her *here*.

In our home. In the place that made me Jeremy and that made her

Laila. In the place where we were one for the first time. In the place where she became her. In the place we built from a cabin to a house with our bare hands and a few hundred grand.

I'd worked so hard. I'd done everything I could to become the man I was *finally* proud to be. After years of fucking up. After losing our child. After losing one another. We built this place together to grow past the mistakes that led us here.

And I knew we had to, but I didn't want to leave. I didn't want to leave behind the life I'd busted my ass for. I didn't want to leave the life I loved more than I loved anything.

Most of all, I didn't want to leave the man I'd become behind.

"Hey, hon," Rachel's voice said from the steps.

I stepped to the ground and sat at the bar. "Hey. How were the kids? They give you a hard time?"

Rachel turned to the kitchen She laughed and sat on the stool beside me. "They were good. They're always good. I had a hard time, but…" She frowned. "They're alright."

"Good," I muttered. "That's good. I'm sure they'll be happy once we settle in back there. It's gonna be a little rough at first, but… but they'll be okay."

"They will," she said. "That, they will."

"Thank you, by the way," I said. "For watching them all week. I don't know where we would have been without you the past few days. Or these past few years, for that matter. You've always been here. Around, ya know. I think we kind of took that for granted. Now that we won't have you." I stopped.

I wanted to tell her how much I was going to miss her. How much she meant to me. How grateful I'd been these past few years to have a mother in-law that accepted me and loved me the way that she did. But I couldn't put it into words.

"Well, we're gonna miss you."

She smiled, but it looked sad. "I'm gonna miss not being around. But…but it is what it is, I guess. Everything happens for a reason. I truly believe that."

I forced a smile. "Yeah, it does."

She turned and met my gaze. "And thank you, Jeremy."

"What for?" I asked.

She smiled. "Being a good husband to my daughter. And for being a good father to my grandbabies. Providing for them. Helping them. Loving them. And not just for doing it, but for doing it the right way. You worked really hard at Moe's, even before the kids. You took care of my daughter when she needed you—every single *time* she needed you. Without fail, you were always there for her. And when the kids need your help with something, you get down to their level and help them in a way that they understand. And you love them the way a man's supposed to love his wife and children. You're gentle, and you're loving, and you're kind. Your heart's bigger than you give yourself credit for. And I'm so happy that my baby found you. Because if I could have designed the perfect man for my Laila, it'd be you. I'm proud to call you my son in-law."

My eyes burned with tears, and my lip involuntarily quivered.

It meant so much to hear her say that. Fuck, I loved that woman. She was so sweet, and so kind, and I was so grateful I'd gotten to be a part of her life for the past few years. I just wished she'd be around for the rest of ours.

I didn't know what we were going to do without her. When Milly got a bad cold at four months old, and her pediatrician was closed, and we didn't know what to do, we'd called her. When Micah got a rash in the summer last year and Laila just about had a panic attack, we called her. When I didn't know how to make Laila's favorite chicken recipe, I called her. When I forgot what the rule was for which cleaning chemicals not to mix when scrubbing the bathroom, I called her.

I didn't know who I was gonna call now.

But to hear her say she was proud of me, my heart grew three times its size and lit me up with warmth.

I fought the knot forming in my throat as I smiled. "I just try and do the right thing."

"And nine times out of ten, you do."

When those words left her lips, the pills in the bottom of my jeans pocket practically caught fire and burned me with guilt. They were the ten percent when I didn't do the right thing. Sober me knew that. Sober me knew that my shortcomings almost always came as a result of my addiction.

Her eyes glistened with tears as she smiled. "You take care of them for me, okay? You keep being the great husband and dad that you are because they need you. I know Laila acts like she needs no one, but she does need you. And those babies need you even more. So you take care of them for me. Alright?"

I turned my gaze away. My steady hands started to shake.

"Jeremy?" Rachel said.

I reached up to stroke my beard. I cleared my throat. And it took everything in me, but I reached into my pocket. My lustful fingertips stroked those eight tiny pills. I dropped them back to the fabric, I shook my head and lifted them to my palm again.

As I raised my shaking hand out to hers, I felt my heart pick up speed in my chest. I met her gaze with watery eyes. "I'll take care of them, but can you do me a favor first?"

She looked at my outstretched hand. She lifted hers. I dumped them to her palm. "Can you get rid of these?"

Rachel stared at the pills in her palm.

"I didn't take any," I whispered. "I just... I want to, but I... I don't want to. If that makes any sense."

She tightened her hand to a fist around them. She lifted her head to face me. Tears filled her eyes. She wrapped her arms around my shoulders.

I relaxed into her embrace a bit and blinked back tears. She squeezed tight and reached onto her tiptoes to kiss my cheek. "That's exactly what I mean, Jeremy. You're a good man."

I didn't believe that. Yeah, I handed her the pills, but I didn't want to take them any less. I felt guilty for it, but that didn't change how *badly* I wanted them. It didn't change that I thought about snatching them back from her palm the moment I'd set them into it.

"Thank you, Rachel."

She pulled back and wagged her finger. "Mom, damn it. I've been telling you this for five years. Stop calling me Rachel. You married my daughter. You are my *son.*"

I smiled. "Maybe I'll catch onto it in twenty-four years."

She laughed, eyes glistening with tears. "Maybe."

My eyes moved over the trees in the distance as I stared off the balcony. I pulled my hoodie tighter over my shoulders and breathed in that cool Pennsylvania air. Rain drizzled from the clouds above and smacked me in the cheeks.

I turned and looked into the bedroom behind me. I couldn't make out much in the total darkness, but I saw Tink's white fur against the lump in Micah's bed. He was safe. Dreaming peacefully. Meanwhile, in every other city worldwide, there was a little boy like Oliver, pinned beneath a boulder, bleeding out internally and dying a slow, painful death.

It wasn't fair. I didn't deserve my kid any more than any of them. And I felt so guilty for it, but I wouldn't change it.

"Hey," Laila said a few feet away.

I turned and forced a smile. "Hey. Did you finish packing?"

She laughed and sat on the patio chair. Her head shook.

I noted her hair at her shoulders and the dust over her face. "Oh. You are not my wife."

She smiled. "Not for twenty-four years."

She did look a lot like her in that moment though. Gentler. Kind. The same look Laila had given me at the diner.

I swallowed hard.

"Time's approaching, you know. About half an hour now." She pushed hair behind her ear. "I just wanted to talk to you for a minute."

"What about?" I asked.

She raised her shoulder. "I don't know. Anything. Everything. There's just... Well, a lot's happened. And it's kind of refreshing to see you like this. So young. Before you remember everything. Before you become him."

I turned my gaze downward.

"It's not a bad thing." Her voice was still soft and gentle. "You becoming Nick. Or more like Nix, I guess. He's still you. It's just... It's nostalgic. I mean, if you could go back ten years and see who you were then, wouldn't you want to? For no reason aside from taking a trip down memory lane?"

I huffed a bit and leaned against the railing. "I would not want to hang out with eighteen-year-old me again."

She laughed. "Kinda cringey, right? When you think about the things you said and did when you were so young?" I nodded slightly, and she smiled. "One day, you'll think that about this day too. You're still a baby."

I smiled and narrowed my gaze. "I'm not a baby."

"To me you are." She grinned. "I've raised children older than you. You're a baby."

"Micah's my age. He isn't older."

"Eh, close enough. You're a baby." She held her grin, stood, and took a few steps closer. She leaned against the railing and looked out over the yard. "You've only lived a few years where you had it all together. My husband has had it together for a few decades now."

I looked down at her. "Really?"

Her eyes turned up to mine, and she smiled.

A wave of relief flooded over me.

She put her fingers over mine and twined them together. Reflexively, I wanted to pull them back. It wasn't common for me to hold another woman's hand. But she was technically my wife. It was a confusing moment. But I kept it there as our eyes locked.

"I know how hard it's been. I know how hard you've fought to be the man you are. I know, Jeremy, I do." Her eyes shifted between mine. "But going back doesn't take that away. Your name changes, but you're still you. I know how hard it is for you to see right now. But Nick fought just as hard to become the man he is. The only difference is age, really. You two are the same. He's still you. Just an older, wiser you."

My eyes moved between hers for a moment. I nodded.

She laughed quietly. "I know you don't believe that. But it's true.

And one day, you'll see that too. It might take you twenty-four years, but you will."

I pulled my hand away and put it into my hoodie pocket.

She laughed.

"What?" I smiled.

She grinned. "I'm her, and you still feel guilty for holding my hand. You're him, that's for sure."

CHAPTER EIGHTY-THREE

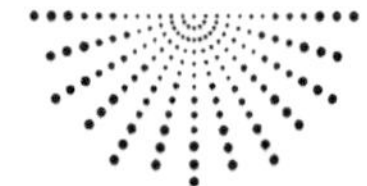

JANUARY 11, 11:12 P.M - LAILA

Once I'd finished packing mine and Jeremy's bag, I heard Milly cry in her crib. Just in the nick of time, I'd just closed the zipper on mine. So I teleported to her room.

I brought a flame to my hand when I landed beside her bed. Her watery eyes lit with warmth. "Mommy, Mommy." She reached up for me, hands clenching and releasing.

"Hey, baby." The light went out in my hands. I put them into her armpits and lifted her to my chest. My arms tightened around her little shoulders. The warmth from her body radiated into mine. I breathed in her soft baby scent. "I missed you. I missed you so much."

"I miss you mowe," she said. Her head pushed tighter into my chest.

I stood there with her for a long moment. My hips swayed from side to side in a gentle rock. I embraced that moment as if it were my last. Me and my little girl in her cozy bedroom. Just the two of us and nothing else.

"Knock-knock," a quiet voice said in the doorway.

I squinted, noting his short hair in the candlelight from downstairs. My husband. But not my husband.

I smiled. "How long have you been standing there?"

"Long enough." Nick smiled back. "Just nice. Seeing you two like this. I miss it."

I turned to Milly. "I think we need to get you dressed for the trip, kiddo."

"Whewe we going?" she asked.

Another long sigh. I touched my lips to her forehead and sat her on the changing table. Nick appeared beside me with a pink onesie from her basket on the dresser. I glanced up at him and smiled. "Thanks."

He smiled back, took a step back, and leaned against the crib.

As I unzipped her sleeper, I met his gaze in the low light. "So what's the story with the hair?"

He laughed. "That's what you're wondering. I know what your life looks like for the next twenty-four years, and you're wondering about my hair?"

Well, I could ask questions for days. But he wouldn't answer most of them. And truthfully, I wanted a glimpse into the husband I'd have in two decades.

"It's kind of a signature look."

"What, you don't like it?" He smirked.

"No, I do." I smiled. "It's mature. Kinda sexy."

His grin stretched higher. "Watch it, lady, I'm a happily married man." I laughed, and his smile widened. "I don't know. Guess I got tired of babies pulling on it."

I huffed. "Good reason." I lifted Milly's shirt above her shoulders and tossed it to the hamper in the corner. I changed her diaper and pulled her arms through the new onesie.

"I thought so," he said. After a moment, Nick cleared his throat. "You haven't told him yet, have you?"

I raised a brow and met his gaze. "Told him what?"

"You know."

"I know what?" I asked.

He cocked his head to the side. "That you're pregnant."

My brow raised higher. "That I'm what?"

He smiled beneath his raised brow and released a laugh. "You didn't know yet." My heart dropped, and my face must've shown it.

""You guys were trying, right? I know we were. Right before all this happened. But I guess I don't know the conception date. It could've been tonight at the diner."

I felt my cheeks redden and lifted Milly back to my chest. "You remember that?"

He grinned, glancing me over. "Kinda hard to forget."

My mind began to course back through the last month. I didn't remember my last period off the top of my head, but it wasn't too long ago. I kept it all in my phone. I didn't know the exact date.

"Are you sure?" I asked. "That I'm pregnant, I mean."

"I really hope so." He laughed. "My kids didn't disappear so I think I'm sure."

I blinked hard a few times. "Well, I guess I could be."

"Pretty sure you are." He smiled. It slowly fell. "But check before you tell him. She didn't tell me until she was a little bit in. There was a lot happening at the time. Trying to start a new life and everything. I was happy when she did though."

I grew quiet as he looked over Milly in my arms. He smiled and met my gaze. "Can I hold her?"

I turned to Milly. "Can he?"

She looked over him. I watched her think hard for a moment. She outstretched her arms to him. He smiled wide and lifted her from my arms to his. He tossed her in the air and smiled the biggest grin I'd ever seen. She giggled.

He laughed, holding her tight against him. "I forget how sweet she used to be sometimes."

"She does seem like quite the pistol," I murmured.

He huffed, still holding his smile as he looked down at the toddler in his arms. "That's one way to put it."

I stayed quiet, watching him toss her in the air a few more times. My ovaries practically screamed. If he were right and I was pregnant, that'd be the best news I'd heard all week. It'd definitely serve as a good distraction when we got back there. I'd get to redo all my favorite things. Buying baby clothes, picking out cribs and rockers, finding cool new baby trinkets.

As he'd said, Jeremy and I had been trying. That thought had completely faded from my mind throughout the last eleven, hellish days. But no part of me would ever be disappointed over another child. I loved babies. I loved motherhood. There was nothing I loved more, not even him. Being a mom was what I was made for. I supposed that was how I got the title of great mother.

And seeing him a quarter of a century older playing with our daughter with the same loving gaze my husband had just assured me more. He was the best father in the world. I couldn't wait to have more children with him.

Well, my him. Not this him.

After a long moment, Nick turned back to me. "I didn't just want to say hello. I did want to talk to you about something."

"Which is?" I asked.

His eyes moved between mine, and he cleared his throat. "I know this was hard on everyone. I know this hurt you too even though you act like it didn't. I know you're good at handling stress. But he's not. He doesn't handle this well, Lai. Not the first time around, anyway."

Not exactly news to me by this point.

"That's why I tried to get him to reconcile with Heylel. I didn't either when I was him, but I hoped he would. Because when you guys get back there, he feels like he has no one that he can really talk to. He knows he has you. But it's not like he can just go talk to a therapist about the trauma that these past few days did to him. I figured if he'd talk to him, he'd have someone outside of the family to put his burdens on. But he won't because he's mad and he's hurting." I turned my gaze downward. "He's really hurting."

"I know he is," I murmured.

"But he does get through it," he said. "He comes back. But...he's not...he won't be the Jeremy you know for a while again."

I swallowed hard and nodded. I wasn't sure how else to respond. No, I didn't want it to be true, but I knew my husband.

He got quiet for a moment. "I probably don't have the right to tell you this, but I'm going to anyway." My gaze lifted to his. His big blue eyes were nearly begging. "Be patient with him. He's not...He just can't handle it all at first. But he still loves you. He loves you and these kids more than he loves anything. He really does. So just…just try to be patient with him."

I felt my eyes sting as I looked to Milly in his arms. We both knew what he meant. We both hoped that we were wrong, but we knew.

"But when enough is enough, you tell him." His gaze hardened. "He doesn't get to be a dick just because he's hurting. Everyone's hurting. And it isn't any more their fault than it is his. So you tell him when you're not gonna put up with his shit anymore. He won't like it, but he'll thank you for it later."

A lump grew in the back of my throat. Fuck. What did that mean? How bad was it going to get? Even when Jeremy had used in the past, I'd never thought of him as an asshole. So what was coming? What was he going to do?

My gaze fell back to the floor. "What's your clean date, Nick?" I whispered.

He grew silent for a moment. "Not August 2020."

My eyes filled with water, and I felt my lip tremble. I bit it to keep it steady and nodded hard. I clamped my jaw tight together.

"I'm sorry," he whispered. "He will be too. Even as he does it. I know that doesn't make it any easier but… I just think you should know that."

I nodded once more.

"I should probably get going though. We all have to go over some things before you go." He passed me Milly.

As I took her in my arms, he lowered his lips to her forehead. Then to mine. I fought my trembling teeth as I felt his guilt radiate toward me.

"It will be okay eventually." His voice lowered, soft and gentle. "We can rebuild anything."

Jeremy hadn't believed me when I said that earlier. And it meant so much to hear that one day, he'd come to that same conclusion.

I felt my eyes sting with tears. I forced a smile. "I know we can."

He smiled back. He started to the door. I pulled Milly closer into my chest and struggled to keep it together.

It was ironic how watching millions of people die hurt my heart less than realizing that my husband was going to relapse yet again. I wished that he wouldn't. But I saw his face when I landed in the diner. Complete and utter despair, more heartbroken than I'd ever seen him. Like there was nothing left to fight for.

"And Lai?" Nick said in the doorway.

I met his gaze. "Yeah?"

"Bring my dad's guitar. I know he said he didn't want it, but he's gonna need it. He'll be too concerned about money to buy another one and he... He needs that guitar."

CHAPTER EIGHTY-FOUR

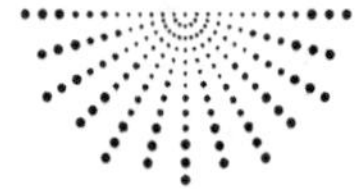

JANUARY 11, 11:50 P.M - LAILA

"Okay, who's carrying the least number of bags?" Lila said with a look around, outstretching a small canvas bag to the twelve of us.

"I can take it." Leah reached forward and lifted the bag over her shoulder. "What is it?"

"Those are all of your IDs, social security cards, and birth certificates," Lila said.

"Faker than a Barbie doll but more believable than God to the Catholic church," Nick said.

Jeremy huffed, and Nick smiled.

"Regardless." Lila's eyes grew serious against Leah's. "Don't drop it. For the love of god, do not drop it. We were given that same bag twenty-four years ago, and I don't have a clue how to remake those documents."

"Well, I do," Leah muttered. "But I got it. Don't worry."

"I know you do," Lila said. She turned to me. "Did you pack Moe's journal?"

"Yeah, I have it."

"Good," she murmured. "And Thompson. That's Addy's last name."

494

"Who?" I arched a brow.

She smiled. "Adeline. Our last sister. Once you get settled in, start looking for her. She's not going anywhere, so no rush. But she needs you. So make sure you find her."

I let that register for a moment. "Adeline Thompson."

Her lips rose in a smile. "Spelled exactly how it sounds."

"Got it."

"And the rest of us will come to you," Lila said. "One way or another, they'll find you. Just make sure you find Addy. We need her."

"Well. Someone does." Nick smiled. I creased my brows a bit, and his smile widened. "Just find her, alright?"

My brows dipped, but I gave a nod.

"Wait," Jeremy said. "You said we introduced Connor and Naomi. If they come to us, how did we introduce them?"

"Timelines are complicated." Nick held his smile. "You'll see."

"But otherwise," Lila said, "Just keep a low profile. Don't draw attention to yourselves. Don't investigate every scary story and missing persons that shows up in the news. You may still be Guardians, but ghosts and rogue Demons are small fish now. For the next twenty-four years, they aren't your concern. Your business now is preparing for 2024."

"By any and all means necessary. But not at the expense of your cover. The only people you tell where you're really from is the family and the rest of the par animarum," Nick said. "And Heylel. You can obviously tell him."

"Obviously," Jeremy muttered under his breath.

"If anyone else finds out, take care of them," Lila said.

"Are you telling us to just go busting caps?"

"If you have to," Nick said. "But you can incinerate people. There's no use in leaving a body behind." I made a face, and he smiled. "You can also fuck with people's heads. Give them memories they didn't live and take memories you don't want them to have. So you won't have to bust many caps."

"Not *many*, huh?" I asked.

"Maybe none." Lila gave Nick a narrowed gaze. "Regardless, do what you have to do. Just keep the family secret a family secret."

"But that just about covers it." Nick said. "We'll get your bags. You guys go get the kids and meet us in the garden back at the main house."

CHAPTER EIGHTY-FIVE

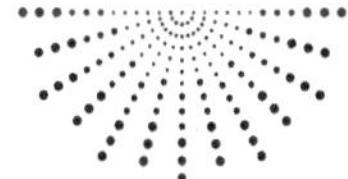

JANUARY 11, 11:59 P.M. - LAILA

"Hey, buddy," Jeremy said softly, shaking Micah's shoulder. "Wake up, bud."

Micah's eyes flickered open in the soft glow of my violet hand. When his eyes met his dad's, they shot open. He jumped forward in the bed and tightened his arms around his shoulder. "Daddy, you're back! You're back. I missed you so much."

Jeremy laughed and locked his arms around Micah's chest. "I missed you, too."

He held him long and hard a moment longer. He tilted his head up to meet his gaze. "Are the storms over?"

Jeremy struggled to form his frown to a smile. "Yeah, they are for now."

Micah's mouth raised into a smile. "So you're not leaving again?"

"Not for a really long time," Jeremy said gently. "But we've got to go, okay? We've got to get to that safe place before the storms start again."

"Okay, I'm ready. I left Tink's harness on so we was ready to go. Her leash is right there."

He laughed. "Good job, buddy." I grabbed it from the dresser with

497

the hand beneath Milly's bottom and passed it to Jeremy. He clipped it into place. "You got your shoes?"

Micah spun his feet off the bed. He reached underneath. "And Gam was helping me learn to tie them earlier. I can *almost* do the bunny ears now."

"Almost, huh?" Jeremy smiled, leaned down, and helped his feet into the tennis shoes. "We'll work on teaching you the rest of the way later."

Micah stood. "Okay. Let's go."

I smiled. "You all set? You're not forgetting anything important?"

"Well, I'm leaving tons of stuff," Micah said. "But Daddy said we'd be back for it one day."

The sweet curve of my lips pulled down slightly. "Yeah. One day."

Mom stood outside the bedroom door waiting for us to finish getting the kids packed up. Once Micah got his jacket on and grasped ahold of Tink's leash, we walked into the hallway. She bent down and hugged him tight. He cried and asked if she was sure she couldn't come. She said that she was. That she'd miss him like crazy, but that she loved him, and she'd see him again. One day.

She turned to me and wrapped her arms around my waist. Tears poured from my eyes as she held me tight. I pulled back and wiped them fast. "No sappy goodbyes."

"No sappy goodbyes." She smiled beneath watery eyes.

I smiled back. I lifted Milly higher against my hip, took Micah's hand in the other, and Jeremy's hand cupped around his.

Then we spun to the grass just outside back at the main house.

CHAPTER EIGHTY-SIX

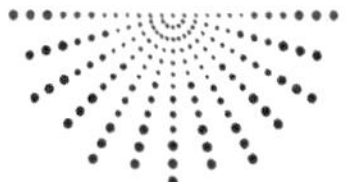

JANUARY 12, 12:06 P.M. - LAILA

As we landed, the first people I squinted at were the heads with pink hair and the messy black waves. Micah and Milly. They stood facing one another. Milly's arms were crossed against her chest with a narrowed gaze. Micah wore a half smile and shrugged. When Milly noticed the four of us, she turned with a smile.

"Look who's early," she said.

"Really? I thought we were late," I said.

"Well, first ones here. Mom and Dad aren't even back yet," she said.

"Where'd they go?" Jeremy asked.

Milly huffed. "They'll be back soon. Just get your bags on your backs."

"But make sure your hands are empty," Micah said. "Put whatever carry-ons you have on the ground in front of you."

Younger Micah stared up at him. He looked at me and Jeremy with a quizzical gaze. Older Micah laughed and took a few steps toward us. He lowered himself to his knee and smiled. "Hey, buddy. What's your name?"

Micah looked up at Jeremy. He smiled. "Go ahead, he's a friend."

"Micah," he murmured.

"That's a really cool name." Older Micah grinned.

"Who are you?" he asked.

"Like your dad said." He smiled, glancing up at Jeremy. "An old friend."

"Are you another of Daddy's brothers?" He turned his head to the side. "You look a lot like Daddy."

Older Micah smiled. "Something like that."

Micah stared up at him a moment longer, pulling that damn stuffed lamb tighter to his chest. I gazed at them in awe for a second. There was a time I never thought I'd see my son at all. In fact, I'd thought that for the first two and a half years of his life. And suddenly, I was looking at two of him at the same time.

Older Micah leaned down and ran his fingers through Tink's fur. Younger Micah smiled. "She likes you. She doesn't like most people."

"She's a good judge of character." Older Micah smiled. "But hey, can I tell you something?" Little Micah nodded. "In a couple minutes, you're gonna go through something pretty weird. Kind of like that thing you went through in the ground when you went to the Fae Realm last year, do you remember that?" Little Micah nodded again. "Yeah, well this is gonna be kinda like that. But this time, your dad isn't going to hold you. He'll be in right after you, and Uncle Chris is gonna go before you, but you're going to walk through this one, alright?" Young Micah blinked a few times. "Because, you know how your dad kept you safe last time?" Micah nodded again. "This time, it's your job to keep Tink safe."

"How do I do that?"

"Well, you hold onto her really tight. Not by her leash, but right here." He leaned forward and hooked his hand around the part of her harness at her shoulders. "You hold onto her as tight as you can, and you don't let go until Uncle Chris tells you to. Okay? Can you do that for me? Can you keep Tink safe?"

Micah looked up at Jeremy. He smiled down at him. Micah turned back to his older self. "Awesome. You're gonna do great, kid."

He scratched Tink's head and brought himself back to his feet. As he turned to walk back to Milly, young Micah said, "Wait. What's you name?"

Older Micah smiled. "My name's Micah."

"But that's my name."

"Huh. I guess it is." Micah grinned. "What a coincidence."

I couldn't help the quiet laugh that left my nostrils as everyone began to appear through the grass nearby. Celena and Wyatt. Kai and Hannah. Jenna and Adam. Brody and Chris with Leah, Max, Lydia, and Ray. Then Moriah.

I sighed as I looked over the group. It was a strange feeling. I can't quite describe it. Joy that we'd survive, yet grief and anxiety for the lives we were about to lose. We'd get them back one day. But that didn't make leaving it behind any easier.

I heard Lila. "Alright, get your bags on. We've got to open this thing up."

And I turned.

Lila and Nick stood a few feet apart wearing the same tattered, dust-colored clothes they'd worn a few minutes prior.

But between, held in place by either of their hands, stood another man.

Taller than me but shorter than Jeremy. Broad but weak shoulders. Neat white button-up and clean black slacks. Short, sandy blond hair. And captivating brown eyes.

Eyes I hadn't looked into for five thousand years but recognized as well as I recognized myself in the mirror.

"What the fuck is he doing here?" Jeremy's voice deepened to an octave I didn't realize it could reach.

"Nice to see you too, esiasch." Lux smiled.

"Jeremy—" Lila began.

But Jeremy had already dropped Micah's hand and teleported in front of him. He raised his fist and smacked it into his jaw. The ache vibrated through mine, but I embraced it. Fuck that piece of shit. He deserved a good sucker punch.

Micah grasped my leg, and I pulled him closer. "Close your eyes."

"Mommy—"

"Close your eyes, Micah," I said again, firmer that time. "And cover your ears."

"Jeremy, stop," Nick said.

"What the fuck is wrong with you?" Jeremy screamed. Older Micah gripped his shoulder and pulled him back. "Why the fuck—" He flailed angrily from Micah's grip, not even realizing who he just punched in the face. As he did, his mouth dropped. "I didn't—I thought you were—"

"It's fine." Micah rubbed his jaw. "It's fine, don't apologize."

"Why is he here?" Jeremy said again, eyes locked on Lux.

"Aww, come on now," Lux said. "No need for the hostility. I'm trying to help you."

"*Help* me?" Jeremy took a step forward. Micah grabbed his arm and held him in place. He glanced at him before he looked back to Lux. "After everything you've done? After what you did to us? After what you did to your own people? To the people who begged and prayed to your sorry—"

"I gave you everything," Lux barked in a deep, roaring voice. "You got it all. You got the girl. You got your kids. You got the family you always wanted so much more than you wanted your own—"

"You gave me nothing!" Jeremy screamed, stepping toward him again, bright blue eyes pulsing with rage. Micah yanked him back further as he yelled again. "This life isn't a gift; this was a way to break a curse you should have never put us under in the first place!"

"He's a means to an end, Jeremy." Lila stepped between them. She put his hand to his chest to edge him back. "That's all that he is. A means to an end."

"He should be *at* his fucking end," Jeremy barked.

"He will," she said. "He will. But we need him. We can't send this many of you back without him."

"Love when she talks all sweet about me like that." Lux grinned.

Nick jabbed him in the gut with his elbow. Lux grimaced, glaring up at him. "Shut your mouth."

A smile lifted at the edge of my cheeks. Not to say that I enjoyed seeing other people get hurt... But, well. I did enjoy seeing *that* fucker get hurt.

Lux huffed and straightened back up.

"A means to an end." Milly took Jeremy's hand. "That's all he is, Dad."

Jeremy panted out deep breaths, still glaring at Lux. His hands trembled at his sides and his jaw snapped shut.

Milly squeezed his hand. "That's it. Nothing more. Come on. We're running out of time."

Jeremy looked down at her. His stiff gaze softened a bit. She walked him back to me. He defensively placed his hand on Micah's shoulder but kept his gaze hard against Lux.

"Laila, we need you over here," Lila said. "Pass Milly to someone else."

I looked at Celena. "You have the hands?"

"I'll make room," she said.

"Hold her tight," I said. "Drop my baby and—"

"I'm not dropping no baby." She gingerly lifted her from my arms and hoisted her to her hip. "Aunt Cece got ya, huh?"

Milly glanced at me and then dropped her head to her aunt's chest.

I leaned forward and kissed her forehead. I turned to Micah. "Listen to Daddy, okay?"

He nodded slow with confused, teary eyes.

I started toward them. But I couldn't lift my gaze to Lux. I was filled with a thousand emotions over that man, but more than the rest was hatred. I hated him like I hated nothing else. But if they needed him, if *we* needed him, then we'd use him. I couldn't waste that hatred now. It'd have to boil for a while yet.

"You can hold my hand if you'd like." He gave a cunning smile.

"You can go fuck yourself." I smiled back.

He huffed but held his grin.

"Here, Mom." Micah extended his hand out for mine.

I clasped it tight and drew in a deep breath.

"Alright," Lila called. "We open the portal with joined hands. It stays open for about a minute and a half once we break the circle. So get your bags ready now. Then form a line and get ready to jump. Go in whatever order you see fit, but Laila goes through last. She'll be helping me hold the tree of life in the vortex."

Milly took my other hand. I glanced her way, and she smiled.

Lila took her other hand. Nick held hers in one and Lux's in the other. And Lux held Micah's. I almost asked him to switch me spots. The thought of him being within a million miles of my baby made my stomach ache. But I'd have probably killed him if Micah weren't standing between us. Or at least, tried to kill him. He couldn't die. I couldn't actually kill him. But *fuck*, did I want to.

"Why don't we need Jeremy?" I asked Lila.

"Because it isn't our bond that's helping to create this," Nick said. His nose crunched up as his jaw clenched. He glanced at Lux. "It's ours."

I made a confused expression. "I don't understand."

"I need his power to move more than myself and one other through time," Lux said.

"Like I told you before," Lila said. "I can move through time as I please. Nick can too. So can Lux. But to move more than a couple, we need a group."

"And since Jeremy doesn't know how to do this yet, he couldn't help," Nick said.

"But does that mean if he did know, we could have brought back more people?" I asked. "Why didn't you teach him?"

"He's a slow learner," Lux said.

"Shut the fuck up," I snapped in unison with Lila.

Nick smiled at that. "It wouldn't have mattered. The only way he was willing to help was if Jeremy didn't. Only twelve. Twelve and the kids."

"There's six of us, and we can each travel two people through time," Milly said. "If it were Dad instead of dickhead, it'd still be twelve."

I huffed and glared his way. And he just smiled. This smug, 'ha-ha, fuck you' kind of smile.

"But we're running out of time," Lila said. "So let's do this before it's too late. You know what to do, right, Laila?"

I nodded.

"Alright then."

Lila and Nick closed their eyes. Then Milly and Micah. But not me and Lux. Our eyes locked. I'd never close my eyes in his presence again. Even if he was allegedly helping us.

The violet light with lines of green coasted from my skin. Then from Milly and Lila's. But Micah's and Nick's were different. Rather than purple, it was blue, like the brilliant shade of their eyes. Nick's was closer to a dark, electric shade of blue, while Micah's was more of a soft, sky blue.

And Lux's was white. Bright, nearly blinding white. Yet, my eyes stayed wide open.

The vibrant lights rose up in a dome above us. They twisted and swirled together, illuminating all of the yard more than the sun had in days. All the while, Lux's gaze stayed locked with mine.

In hindsight, I wonder what Jeremy thought of our little stare down from his place in the crowd behind me. I wonder if it made him feel inferior or threatened in some way. But I wished I would have sent a thought into his mind. Something about how much I hated that piece of shit, or something about how I couldn't wait to do to that bastard what he'd done to us.

But there was nothing to that gaze. I should make that clear. No aged sexual tension brewing. No possibility of a future. He may have hoped there was. But for me, the only emotion I possessed for that man was hatred. Nothing but furious, vengeance crazed hatred. Especially after what he'd done in the past few days. Or rather, the lack of what he'd done.

The vivid lights above us dropped to the ground. It almost looked as though the earth had split open.

Lila opened her eyes and looked at the cluster of people lined up behind me. "Now, Mills. Let go."

Milly dropped my hand and took a step closer to Lila. "Go," she yelled to Wyatt and Celena at the front of the line. "Go now."

Wyatt jogged forward with a large duffle and Jeremy's guitar case. He smiled and jumped into the vortex. Celena held Milly tight with both arms beneath her bum and a hand on the back of her head. She jumped.

Kai brushed past me, hand tight in Hannah's as the two of them rushed into the swirling pit. Max and Moriah followed. Adam and Jenna were close together, her arms wrapped tightly around little Luka. I watched the terror on her face and the hesitation of her steps as she drew closer to the swirling colors. Adam grasped her hip and yanked her in.

Brody was next, a slow breath falling from his lips as he dropped face first in a belly flop like the vortex was a pool on a hot summer day. Ray and Lydia followed, hands tightly wound with each other's. Chris was next, hand sliding over my shoulder. He jumped in with Leah close at his tail.

Then Micah. He looked up at me with Tink close by his hip.

"It's okay, baby." I smiled down at him. "It's okay, you're alright. Me and Daddy are right behind you."

"You promise?"

"I promise." I smiled.

"Go on, boy," Lux yelled.

My head snapped to him, and my eyes glowed. "Don't talk to my son."

He squinted slightly. He smiled and lifted older Micah's hand to the air.

"Just shut up," older Micah muttered.

"It's okay, bud," Jeremy said with a hand on his shoulder. "It's okay. I'm right here. I'm right here. Go ahead."

Micah took a few steps forward. Tink's paws sunk in to the dirt but he grabbed her tight. "It's okay, Tink. I got you."

He teleported with her above the pit. I watched the two of them fall in slow motion, and my breath caught.

Jeremy squeezed my hip and kissed my hair. "I'll see you on the other side," he whispered at my ear.

Goosebumps rose over my skin, and I smiled. That was almost verbatim what he'd said the first time I granted us with eternity.

He took a step forward and jumped into the portal.

"Go, Lai," Nick said on the other side of the pit. "Go before it closes."

I grabbed my bag from the ground and grasped the straps of my backpack. I stood just before the portal and met Lux's gaze.

"One day, you're gonna pay for what you did," I said. "You'll wish you never met me."

"Old news, darling." He glared. "And maybe one day. But not today."

My eyes snapped between his. He dropped Nick's palm and made a shooing motion. "Run along now."

My teeth clamped to a hard line. I took a step forward.

———

It was not like traveling to the Fae Realm. It was *nothing* like traveling to the Fae Realm. It was absolute fucking agony.

Every cell in my body felt like it was on fire. Not just the surface of my skin, but within. I'd never felt an organ before, but I certainly did when it was enduring a process that made it automatically regenerate.

My stomach. My intestines. My heart. My brain. My eyes. My muscles and tendons.

Every fiber of my body felt like it'd been doused in gasoline, lit a flame, then thrown into a blender at the same time. I couldn't process what I was seeing if I tried because all that I could do was scream.

I thought about my babies and gasped.

My poor babies.

That's what Micah meant when he said he remembered the shift.

He remembered me telling him, "It's okay, baby. Everything's gonna be okay," then forcing him into the worst agony we'd ever felt.

No wonder a human couldn't survive the transformation because it felt worse than any pain I'd ever experienced. I'd been tied to a table and had my back torn to shreds. I'd been viciously raped by a serial killer. I'd been stabbed and punched and bludgeoned, but *nothing* hurt like the shift.

Yet, the moment I shot back into the earth's atmosphere, soaring toward the bright moon in the sky, starting at a bright white moon, the pain was over. I felt sick to my stomach and dizzier than a kid on a merry-go-round, but the agony ended as quick as it'd started.

And unlike any of the other physical pain I'd experienced, there was no emotional pain tied to that misery.

Only joy.

Odd how it made me so miserable for those few moments, or more like seconds, then left me with a happiness I'd never felt.

It wasn't a joy I'd mustered up on my own. And it wasn't like being high. It was close to the euphoria of an MDMA high, but crisper. Cleaner.

Like taking in a breath of fresh spring air after a long, cold winter.

For a second anyway.

Until I forgot to catch myself before slamming to the cold snow.

"Fuck," I moaned out as my arm snapped on the impact. But It radiated with warmth. And within the time it took for Jeremy to find me on the frozen grass, the pain was gone.

"Are you okay?" He lifted my face to meet his frightened gaze.

I nodded. "Are the kids?"

He nodded. "Micah's comforting Tink. She's puking. But yeah, we're okay."

A slow sigh of relief left my lips. He did the same. He helped me to my feet.

"Jesus Christ," Leah yelled out. "Holy fuck, that was awful."

"Nothing like the trip to my realm," Kai muttered as he helped Hannah stand.

"Who is that?" a woman's voice called in the distance. "Who's out there?"

Jeremy stopped dead in his tracks. He turned to the house.

"Jéan, did you hear that?" the woman said. "There's someone out there. Maybe a few someones. I can feel them. Do you feel them?"

My gaze moved to the woman on the porch. Her white nightgown hung just below her knees. Her long dark hair flowed in the cold, icy wind. I couldn't make out much else, but she looked familiar.

"Get the bags," Chris said fast, teleporting between the suitcases and collecting them into a pile.

"Who is that?" I asked.

"That's..." Jeremy whispered, voice cracking. "That's..."

Suddenly beside me, gaze fixed on the woman on the back porch, Adam murmured, "Our mom."

The story continues in *Lost to Time*. Turn the page for a sneak peek, or click the link below to download now:
https://www.amazon.com/dp/B0995CYPVN/

Sign up for Charlie's newsletter and receive a free copy of the Eluding Destiny prequel, *Blood Bar*:
https://liquidmind.media/eluding-destiny-prequel/

If you enjoyed this story, please consider leaving a rating or review on Amazon:
https://www.amazon.com/gp/product/B0973L2BKF/

Join Charlie's private reader group on Facebook and discuss all things Eluding Destiny and Charlie Nottingham:
https://www.facebook.com/groups/661440911724435/

LOST TO TIME CHAPTER ONE

JEREMY

Why hadn't I thought of this?

We'd just travelled twenty-four years into the past. The portal we opened was in the back yard of my family home. Common sense should've told me it'd open in the same place twenty-four years in the past. I should have realized.

Yet, I hadn't.

I hadn't thought about the fact that twenty-four years ago, my mom wasn't dead.

I hadn't thought about the fact that we appeared in her back yard out of nowhere, that she would feel the power of our energy signatures, and that she would come running outside in fear that a Demon or some other monster was here to attack.

Chris grabbed my forearm. "We have to go, Jeremy."

I heard him, but my eyes were stuck to her.

Between the naked tree branches, I saw her standing on the back patio. Her fingers curled around the recently stained wooden railing, eyes squinting toward us in the moonlit forest. A long, flowing white nightgown billowed around her in the wind. Snow danced from the clouds above to her curtain of black hair.

Chris was right. We needed to move. We had to leave before she ran down those steps and saw the twenty-eight-year-old version of her four-year-old standing in the woods outside her home, staring at her like a lunatic.

But the last time I saw her, she was lain out on silk line casket, body decaying, and I'd never been able to get that image out of my mind. I wanted this one instead. I wanted this to be how I envisioned her for the rest of my life.

"Jèan, get out here," she yelled. "Someone's in the yard!"

"Baby," Laila said, grasping my hand. "Your dad's going to come out here any second. Chris is right. We have to go."

"That's my mom," I barely whispered.

"I know." She took my face in her hands, wide green eyes shifting between mine. "I know, but we need to go."

"You heard them, Jeremy," Chris said. "No one can know."

"Daddy," Micah whispered, tugging my pant leg. His voice snapped me from my trance. I turned to meet his gaze. "Tink's sick. She won't get up."

That one image of her would have to do.

I turned back to my wife. "Get him. I'll get Tink."

"Come here, buddy." Laila bent down and lifted our four-year-old to her chest.

I teleported to the big white husky lying on her side. My fingers kneaded her thick scruff as I struggled to catch my breath. "Hey, girl," I whispered. "You're alright. You're alright. You just need some water."

"You know where to go, Lai?" Celena asked, lifting my traumatized daughter further up her hip.

Laila nodded. "Follow my trail, everyone." She disappeared.

I tightened my backpack straps at my chest, fastened the diaper bag around my shoulders, glanced at the porch where Mom walked into the house still yelling for Dad, then looked back to Tink. "I'm sorry, girl."

I closed my eyes, jumped onto Laila's trail, and teleported our dog to the new town we'd call home.

Tink struggled forward, body lurching as she vomited more foam to the ice-covered ground. I stroked my hand along her fur, murmuring a "shh," sound. "You're okay. You're alright."

"Where the hell are we?" Leah asked as Micah joined me on the ground beside Tink.

"Minnesota," Laila said. She lifted our daughter from her sister's grasp and brought herself to the ground beside me and Micah.

"Minnesota." Leah huffed. "Of all places. Couldn't be Santorini or Bora Bora. Oh, no. That'd just be too much fun. Had to be damn Minnesota."

I wrapped an arm around Laila's shoulders and the other around Micah's. A calming breath eased from my mouth as my eyes closed. My heart rate gradually slowed in my chest, and I pulled them in closer.

I'd never been so happy in my life to be in Minnesota.

"Is she gonna be okay?" Micah asked quietly. "You said we'd keep her safe, why's she sick?"

"You know Tink doesn't do well with teleporting," Laila said. "She'll be alright. Trust me."

"She's gonna be fine." I opened my eyes and gave him a smile. "She's gonna live forever."

His eyes widened as he turned up to me. "Really?"

I laughed. "Really, really."

"You promise?"

I smiled. "I promise." I turned to Laila and Milly. Laila petted Tink in the snow as Milly focused hard on her surroundings. "How is she?"

"She's okay," Laila said.

"Here." I outstretched my arms toward her. Milly's little hands stretched open as Laila passed her to me. I held her close to my chest and kissed the brown hair of her crown. Her little body quivered in my arms, but she didn't cry. She just stared around in confusion. "You're okay, huh, kiddo?"

Milly's big green eyes shifted up to mine. "I scawed."

Of course she was scared.

The world just ended, and we travelled back in time to avoid it.

I was pretty damn scared too.

But I was the parent, and it was my job to pretend like I was fearless.

"It's okay." I gave her a smile and pressed my lips to her messy brown braid. "It's alright. I've got you. Everything's okay."

"We're all here, right?" Adam asked with a look around.

Well, I hope because it'd be really shitty if we left someone behind to fend for themselves at the end of the world.

I turned and began counting all of my brothers and sisters.

Leah was a few strides behind me, messy purple hair more visible than everyone else's in the light of the moon. The contrast of her pink hoodie against her sepia skin was easy to spot as well.

Brody—my youngest brother—was holding his stomach, reclined against a tree, dark waves of brown plastered to his clammy white skin with sweat. My little sister, Hannah, was holding her husband Kai's shoulder for stability. And he was holding a tree.

Supposed the three of them were not taking well to time travel.

Adam—one of my older brothers—was beside him with his girlfriend, Jenna, and their son, Luka. The three of them seemed better than the rest of us. A bit pale, a little sweaty, but not fighting the urge to vomit. Although, they had their kid with them too. Maybe those of us who were parents were doing our best not to look our worst right now.

Celena, my sister-in-law, and Wyatt, her boyfriend were both crouched on the snow, patting some on their face to dull the sweat we'd all gotten from the ride. Wyatt's always warm brown skin was redder than usual, and Celena wasn't much different, as though she was about to catch aflame.

Chris seemed the best of us all. He was on two feet, scanning the perimeter, as if to check if any humans had seen us all teleport to this wooded path off the busy highway beside the hotel.

Max—an old family friend—looked the worst. Bent over on all fours, heaving in deep breaths, mousy mop of brown partially shielding his pasty white cheeks.

Moriah, despite her usual elegance, had a hand over her lips, like she was fighting the urge to hurl. She always had a peaches and cream complexion to her, but now, she reminded me a bit of a Vampire. Pale, sickly, and drained.

But sixteen of us had come back in time. Twelve adults and four children.

I counted eleven adults, and three children.

We were missing our oldest family friend, and his teenaged daughter.

"Where're Ray and Lydia?" I called over the crowd.

"Back here," Lydia called. "We're right back here."

The worry in my heart settled.

"We did it." A smile slid all the way into Laila's big green eyes as they met mine. "Everyone's okay. We made it."

I laid my head against hers, taking only a moment or two to exhale with relief.

We had. We made it.

But in twenty-four years, we'd have to do it all over again.

"I know everyone's relieved to breathe for a second and all," Brody said, bringing himself upright and stumbling back into the tree, "but maybe we could all take a deep breath in an hour? Once we check into a hotel and get changed into some dry clothes?"

"Yeah, and I'm starving," Max said.

"I's hungwy too," Milly said in my lap.

"Well, I think we're shit out of luck," Leah said. "We're in Minnesota at midnight. No where's open."

"It's eleven actually," Celena said. "Time zones and all."

Getting into a hotel sounded nice. Vending machine food would do. Central heating, and a hot shower, and clean clothes…

Fucking Christ, I never realized how much I took those little things for granted.

I pulled away from Laila. "Where's the bag with the money?"

"I have it," Wyatt called.

I passed Milly to Laila and stood. "And you have the IDs, Leah?"

She dug in the messenger bag hanging over her shoulder. "Yeah, someone shine me a light."

I walked across the wooded cluster and raised a ball of fire to my palm. She dug for a moment. "Lena Salesky." She scoffed. "What the hell kind of name is that?"

"Not mine so..." I made a rolling motion with my hand.

"Salesky," she mumbled, still sifting through the bag. "I don't know why they gave me the same last name anyway. It's not like we're actually related. We don't even look alike. I mean—"

"Leah." I agreed that the name thing was stupid considering we were adopted siblings, but I didn't have the energy right now. "I'm tired. And I'm wet, and my feet are frozen. Can we bullshit once we get settled into a room?"

"Fair enough." She plopped a plastic card to my palm. "Ah-ha. Nick Salesky. Here we go."

"How much do you think it'll be?" Wyatt asked, unzipping the duffle bag full of cash. "And how many rooms are we getting?"

My thought was that we should all bunk as much as we could. We had a bag of money right now, but it'd be gone in no time considering we had over a dozen people to clothe and home.

After some bickering over who was bunking with who, who snored too loudly, and whatever else irritated some of us about each other, we decided on seven. Since many of us were still sick to our stomachs, it was decided that I'd be the one to book it.

I looked down at my wife, still cuddling both of our kids close and petting the husky mutt at her feet. "You gonna stay here with the kids, Lai?"

"Yeah. We'll be here," Laila said.

As I walked into the warm Holiday Inn lobby, I stared down at the fake driver's license in my hand. Nick Salesky. Still Pennsylvania though.

I supposed I'd have to get that changed. Which made sense since I didn't have an address yet.

It was me. The same photo on my real license. I wondered how they pulled that off for a second. But a phony ID was less crazy than what the past two weeks had been. It wasn't even worth the thought, honestly.

"Can I help you, sir?" the man at the reception desk asked with a wide, friendly grin. Way too friendly for this hour and the day I'd had.

"Oh, yeah." I forced a smile back as I approached the counter. "You guys aren't booked up, are you?"

"We've got some vacancies." He clicked onto the dinosaur of a desktop. "How many rooms ya looking for? One or two?"

"Seven, actually."

"Oh my, I didn't see a bus pull in. How'd ya fit that many in a car?"

"Uh, we didn't." I wasn't a bad liar, but I didn't have a good one immediately on hand. "It's kind of a long story. Family road trips, car troubles, issues with the U-Haul. Anyway, my wife's in the parking lot a few places down. Her and the kids are freezing. She told me to make it quick."

"Goodness gracious, better hurry then." His smile coasted back up his cheeks. He fiddled with the mouse for a moment. "Well, I've got an adjoining room. A king bed in one and five with two queens. But that actually fills the place up. I'm sorry, we only have the six rooms available, sir."

"Fuck," I muttered.

His eyes widened again. As though that word was the devil himself.

Jesus Christ, I was being a dick. It wasn't my usual. I was typically a friendly enough person. It'd just been one hell of a day. But it wasn't this guy's fault, and I was in another time. One where cussing was viewed a lot differently.

"Sorry, it's been a rough day."

"Oh, sure. I can imagine. My in-laws just left from the holiday. I've never been happier. Bet you're ready to get back home. Where ya coming from, anyhow?"

"Home, actually." I passed him my ID. "Pittsburgh. We're moving here."

"Ya don't say. That's a long drive." I shrugged, and he continued, "Well, welcome to Minnesoota, pal. Friendliest state in the country, you know."

"I see that," I said. "So just the six rooms, huh?"

"Unfortunately. Sorry about that, sir," he said. "We've got a couple checking out in the morning. We can get the last room ready for you then if you're staying more than a night."

"Sure. Sure, that'll work. Thank you," I said.

"Oh, you betchya." He grinned. "Give me just a minute here, and I'll find those keys."

"No problem. By the way do you guys allow dogs?"

He looked up from the desk and frowned. "Sorry, sir. We don't."

I bit back my *fuck my life.* "Might have to hold off then. Any hotels nearby that do?"

"There's a motel a little while down the ways, but I wouldn't go there if you're traveling with kids."

I closed my eyes and rubbed them. No way in hell did we just turn our dog immortal to tie her up in woods while we slept in a hotel.

The man glanced around and leaned forward. "I tell ya what. What kinda dog is it?"

"She's a mutt, but mostly husky," I said.

He thought for a moment. "I can tell you need someone to cut you a break tonight, huh?"

"I could really use one."

"Personally, I love dogs. But the day shift manager... Well, she's kind of a stickler for the rules. So I'd say to keep the dog as quiet as you can, and have her stay in the room on the first floor. There's a side door there, and as long as you're careful, you might just be able to sneak her in and out without being noticed. If she does find out though, I didn't know about any dog." He smiled as he extended his hand across the counter. "Deal?"

I smiled. "Yeah, of course. Thank you so much."

"Oh, you betchya." He firmly shook my palm in his. He pulled away and started sliding keycards through a reader behind the counter.

As he sifted through them, I watched him for a long moment.

I wondered where he'd be in twenty-four years. I wondered what a good, decent guy like him would be doing when the natural disasters began. I wondered if he'd cross over to the other realm, or if he'd stay wherever he was until the meteors fell.

I wondered if he'd survive. I wondered if I or one of the others had stepped over his lifeless body on the bloodied streets we'd just traveled from.

I wondered if I should warn him.

"Alright, here we are." He smiled as he passed me the handful of cards. "Now, you all let me know if you need anything. I'll be here all night. Breakfast starts at seven and ends at nine."

Maybe we all deserved a little peace for the next twenty-four years.

I forced a smile. "Sure. Thanks again."

LOST TO TIME CHAPTER TWO

LAILA

"Micah, take your sister out to the car please." My eyes were heavy on Jeremy as his jaw clenched. He sucked his teeth and shook his head.

"But we was supposed to play a song." Micah's brows pulled together. "Right, Daddy?"

"We'll play a song tonight, bud." Jeremy rubbed his hand over his mouth and forced a smile. "I promise. Please, just take Milly out to the car with you."

Micah sighed. He took Milly's hand. They started down the hall toward the back door, and I stepped closer to Jeremy. I lowered my voice. "What do you mean they think you killed that woman?"

He closed his eyes and let out a slow, calming breath. "I took Brody's truck yesterday. I told him I was going to lunch with you, but I teleported out and... you know."

"Got drugs?" I asked.

His expression grew uncomfortable as he cleared his throat. "I came back here, and you told me to call off the rest of the day. I completely forgot about Brody's truck."

"Okay, but what does that have to do with the hiker?"

He raked a hand through his long black waves. "It was a ten-minute walk from the pile of blood. They thought it might have been

Brody. That he got out of the truck to piss, and an animal took him down. But before they told me that, I said that I was the one driving his truck. I thought they were gonna write me a ticket or something. I didn't realize I told them the truck I was driving was parked next to a fucking murder site."

My stomach sunk. "Jesus Christ."

"I told them we were all fine and accounted for, and Dylan asked where Brody was. He came out, saw him, then gave me one of those accusative cop glares. And he asked where you were, and I stumbled because I wasn't sure if you still looked like you were fifteen."

I hadn't looked like I was fifteen; I'd looked like I was around seventeen. Maybe sixteen. But point taken.

I put my hand on my head for a moment. "Why didn't Ray's dumb ass tell me he left a puddle of blood?"

"I don't know, but I'm gonna fucking kill him." Jeremy's jaw tightened. "I swear to god, if I get called into the police station for—"

"Just relax for a second." I rubbed my forehead and thought hard. "There's no way you could have transported a body if the truck's still parked there, right? So this wouldn't stand up in court. Dylan's just looking for something to use against you. He doesn't have a leg to stand on."

"Plus, if I were gonna kill a woman, why would I lead them to me? I wouldn't have told them I was driving the truck if I knew that it was parked by a body. And even an idiot would know not to leave their truck ten minutes from the place they just murdered someone."

That was it then. No harm, no foul. Plus, I knew how these things worked. No body, no murder. They may have suspects, but without a body, they'd never get a conviction. Especially not on a story this feeble.

"They don't have anything on you. We're fine. But we'll need an alibi for you. Other than just having lunch with your wife."

"We were with Ray." He shrugged. "He's a cop. His word counts to them. And he's the one who actually did it, so he better know how to lie."

Rubbing my tense temples, I said, "I'll see him at lunch and go over the details. But for now, our story's we were supposed to meet up at the café, but your car broke down. You came back here because it's closer, you called me, and I came here for lunch. Ray was here when you were walking up the drive. That's our story."

"That should work," he said. "We just have to lie low once they figure out who that woman was. We didn't know her, we aren't connected to her, they have no reason to look at us. My DNA's on the truck, but it's not at the scene."

"This will work." I wasn't sure if I was trying to convince him or myself. "We just have to do what we've always done. We know nothing. As long as we don't incriminate ourselves, they have nothing to use against us."

Brody rode with us to his truck. There were half a dozen cops parked about a quarter mile down the quiet back road. But we acted natural. They knew why we were there, no big deal. The boys loaded in, and I got the kids to school.

I went to the café. Again, the morning was busier than an amusement park on a hot summer day. I didn't have the chance to think about the stress building up in every area of my life, and I liked it that way.

But I did find myself mulling over the memory that shifted me to a fifteen-year-old girl. It fascinated me. Not the royalty aspect; I knew that already.

Although the memories had been fleeting from my first life, they'd given me a fair bit so far. The first memory that came to me was of my death when the Archangels killed me, my children, and the other gods that ruled alongside of Lux.

I'd yet to truly get to know Lux. I'd relived a dream where we had sex with his second wife, Stella, but I didn't know much about him aside from what Jeremy had gathered from his memories. Specifically, the fact that Jeremy had been my guard, the hand of the king, Lux, and that Lux had been my husband.

That we'd had an affair that somehow led to the two of us taking his throne.

In some sense, I could see Lux justifying killing the two of us in response to that. But it wasn't only us that he killed. He killed all of the par animarum, the gods, and took power over Earth.

Not only that, but he'd killed my children. Nix had been Lux's brother, meaning that man had killed his own niece and nephew. That was the ending, but even prior to that, he'd done awful things. He'd forced me into marriage because he wanted my power of eternity. When he learned of the affair while I was pregnant with Nix's child, he'd violently assaulted me, and I'd lost my baby as a result.

Knowing all of that, it was that final line from the memory I recalled this morning that meant so much. *"Any who receive eternity must first prove themselves worthy not by their words but by their actions time and time again."*

The child version of who I once was had a far greater understanding of becoming eternal than I did. That bared the question though. If Véa knew how important it was to use caution when gifting eternal life, why did she give it to Lux? Especially knowing that he, too, had power over the abyss and was of the few people that could take the gift I'd given?

That question had been in my head since the moment I learned I gave immortality to the god that would eventually kill my children and curse my friends and family for several thousand years. Now, I was even more confused. Why would I ever find him deserving? How did we make amends after he forced me into a marriage I didn't want?

I supposed the memories would show me soon enough.

But another thing kept running through my mind.

I knew how to shapeshift now. I'd always imagined it would be like the change the wolves experience, but it was nothing of the sorts. It felt fluid. In fact, I wondered why I hadn't mastered it sooner. Shifting back was seamless. I stared at myself in the mirror for a moment, closed my eyes, and focused on Laila. Just myself. My experiences, my scars, my stretchmarks, my hair, my skin. And then when my eyes opened, I was me once more.

It gave me some ideas for the future. The ability to shapeshift gave me opportunity. I could use it to see Moe and my parents at the diner. They wouldn't know it was me, but I'd get to see them in the flesh. I'd get to watch Mom and Dad laugh at one of those red leather booths while my sister and I sipped our milkshakes through paper straws on the other bench.

But I could use it for more important things. I could use it to cover our asses. I wasn't quite sure how yet, but I knew that I could. It opened up a world of possibilities.

When lunch came, my racing thoughts came to a halt as a flock of officers walked in the door.

I pasted on a fake smile as Ray and Dylan approached the counter. Dylan didn't look accusative as he had this morning. He wasn't flashing that flirty grin either. His expression was nearly blank.

I went on making the macchiato for the man at the register, gazing at Ray in my peripheral vision. His jaw was tight, as if trying to keep it from shaking. His hands at his sides trembled before he shoved them into his pockets. The pull in his brows made me think something was wrong, even more so than I already knew.

I passed the man his macchiato with a smile and looked at Ray and Dylan. "Hey, guys. What can I get for you?"

"Just a coffee with cream and sugar please." Dylan's eyes were on the counter as he tossed a ten down. "And one of those donuts, I guess."

"Black coffee." Ray forced a smile.

"Alright." My eyes caught Dylan, yet again, as I pressed the lever on the coffee machine. "Why the long face?"

His eyes stayed steady against the granite, clearing his throat. "My mom's missing."

Holy fucking shit.

A pit dropped through my stomach. I barely contained my internal gasp. My eyes met Ray's. His nostrils flared as he quickly blinked tears away.

That's where I recognized her from. The *"Vote Perry for County Judge"* signs posted over town.

"Oh, wow, I'm so sorry." I poured some cream and sugar into his cup, snapping a lid on as I spoke. "I'm sure she'll turn up."

"We found her necklace in the snow by that... um, that... that puddle of blood."

My chest tightened, and my stomach spun. Not only did Ray leave the blood, but he left a piece of her jewelry? I was ready to reach over that counter and bash his head on it. I didn't even have to fake the shock in my tone as I said, "Oh my god."

"Yeah. Yeah, we're gonna run some tests on the samples but... It's not normal for mom to be gone like this. My dad said he kissed her goodbye before her afternoon jog yesterday. He went up to Minneapolis for the night. When he came home this morning, the dinner she had in the crockpot yesterday was still going. Her car's still in the garage, her keys are in the house. We, uh..." I passed him the cup. As I reached into the pastry case, he cleared his throat once more. "I don't know."

Not only did Ray kill a woman. He killed one of the most important people in this town. The one who's nosy son had a thing for me, and I'd told off two days prior.

I was ready to incinerate Ray. Dylan was still in shock, but in a few days, I knew he'd be pointing fingers. And who better to point at than the guy who'd parked his truck ten minutes from the murder site?

"I'm so sorry to hear that." I passed him the donut. "Do you guys have any leads?"

"That's what's weird." He paused, deep in thought. "There were tracks in the snow. A couple sets actually. Mom's, an animal's that looks a lot like coyote's but bigger, and a man's. But the weirdest part is that the man's aren't a shoe. They're bare feet."

My heart was slamming against my ribcage now. Not just with anxiety, but fury.

He killed a woman and *left tracks*? Wolf tracks, victim tracks, *and* his own?

But I forced a look of sympathy. I couldn't show my angst. *Sympathy, nothing but sympathy, Laila.*

"Oh god, I'm so sorry, Dylan."

"Yeah. Yeah, thanks." He raised his cup and took a sip.

"Do you think it was an animal then?" I asked.

"I would if there was a body." He sipped his coffee once more, eyes uncertain. "But I don't know what the hell I think right now. Maybe she was abducted or something. Or maybe she fought the animal off and tried to get back to civilization for help. Maybe she did, maybe she's at a hospital right now. Maybe she turned up on the highway and someone loaded her up to the hospital."

"Maybe." I gave a hopeful, yet sympathetic gaze. "Maybe she'll turn up soon."

"We're looking into Jane Does in the city now. But I just..." He blew out a deep breath. "I just don't know." Dylan forced a smile. "But I'm gonna head out to the cruiser, Roy. Nice seeing you, Lila. Keep the change."

"Sure," Ray said.

I met Ray's gaze with darting eyes. He swallowed hard. I glanced at the line of five or six customers as Dylan walked outside.

"Max, can you take over up here?" I called to the back.

"Yeah, just give me a second," he said.

I clenched my jaw as I poured Ray's coffee.

Max huffed and took my place at the counter.

I passed Ray his coffee. "In the back. Now."

"You're a god damned cop." My eyes narrowed, speaking in a hushed yell. "You didn't think to cover the fucking tracks? Or clean up the puddle of blood? Or—oh, I don't know—*pick up the woman's necklace*?! Are you kidding me?"

"Laila—"

"He's going to try to get Jeremy for this, do you realize that?" I snapped.

"What?"

"He borrowed Brody's truck yesterday, pulled off to the shoulder, teleported out to get drugs, and then teleported back to the house. And ya know where he left the truck?" My piercing gaze darted between his. "Right beside the murder site."

"Shit." Ray blinked hard.

"*Shit.*" I huffed. "That's what you have to say for yourself. Shit."

"I was panicking. I—I figured without a body, they wouldn't have anything to go on. Blood or not—"

"Sure, maybe. If my husband didn't admit to being at the scene at the time of the murder."

He raised his hand to his mouth, rubbing hard. His eyes turned to the ground. "I'm so sorry."

"You're sorry?" He opened his mouth to speak again, but I took a step forward and let my eyes glow in their sockets. "When he starts pointing fingers at my family because of something *you* did, you better fucking fix it, Ray. Or I swear on my children that your ass will never see the light of day again. My husband's not going down for a murder *you* committed."

Judging by his shaking hands, my speech had made the needed impact. "I will."

"You better," I said.

He blinked hard a few times. He met my gaze. "He said he stopped by the house this morning. What did you tell him?"

"That Jeremy's car broke down, he walked home, and we met up there for lunch."

"Okay. Okay, I was there. I'm his alibi. I—me and him, we talked for a while before you made it home. Then when you did, I-I saw you guys go up to your room, and you stayed there for an hour or so. Then you came back here."

I thought over that for a moment. It might work. But if they looked harder, there were still plot holes. I wasn't sure how accurate forensics were in this time. Without a body though, they couldn't pinpoint an exact time of death. That left a lot of room in terms of an accusation. He didn't have a car, so he couldn't have moved the body, but that didn't mean it wasn't enough to at least issue a warrant for his arrest. Considering the fact that the dead woman was a judge, her husband was the sheriff, and their son was a cop, they'd be damned and determined to pin it on someone. Circumstantial evidence or not, they could make an arrest.

"Guess that's the best we've fucking got," I muttered. "But I swear to god, Ray—"

"I know, you'll give me a punishment worse than death. I know," he said quickly. "But this will work."

I wasn't so sure about that. But I didn't see another option. I didn't know who all Dylan and Bill had relayed the information to. There wasn't a way to wipe Jeremy and the placement of Brody's truck from all of their memories. Granted, I should have checked yesterday when Ray showed up with the body. But he was a cop. I didn't think I'd have to sweep the murder site. When he said that no one saw him, I assumed that meant the site was handled.

I should have known better.

Loving *Lost to Time*? Click the link below to download now!
https://www.amazon.com/dp/B0995CYPVN/

New Normal: Celena's Story Part 1

Reprisal: Celena's Story Part 2

Origins of the Gods

(Completed Trilogy—fantasy romance, more information on the origins of the Fae and Angels, how life began on earth, where Guardians came from, and— most importantly—a badass forbidden romance)

Origins

The Thrones of Ore and Ice

Creation

Stand Alone Novels

Curse of the Gods: The Bridge Between Origins of the Gods and the Eluding Destiny Series

Sign up for Charlie's newsletter and receive a free copy of the Eluding Destiny prequel, Blood Bar:

https://liquidmind.media/eluding-destiny-prequel/

ABOUT THE AUTHOR

Charlie is a... Okay, talking about myself in third person is weird.

Nice to meet you! My name's Charlie Nottingham, and my whole world revolves around fantasy. When I'm not writing a new book, I'm either hanging out with my dogs, talking with my fans online, or reading some amazing urban fantasy, paranormal romance, or fantasy romance series (always a series, never a stand-alone, because I hate to fall for a character and never see them again). Or re-watching some Buffy or Supernatural. (They never get old!)